Fyrentennimar, wings beating fiercely, pivoted in the air, whipping the smoke and dust about. The dragon dipped into a short stoop, reared again, and fell over the remaining group of monsters, tail thrashing, spiked foreclaws slashing, great hind legs kicking, and wings beating a hurricane of wind. A swoop of the dragon's tail sent four goblins soaring, splattering them against the valley wall with force enough to shatter most of the bones in their bodies, then the tail itself connected on the wall, opening a huge crack in the stone and leaving crimson marks where the goblins had been.

"Glad he's on our side," Ivan said, his voice barely a whisper.

Cadderly grimaced at the words, remembering again the tone Fyrentennimar had used when ordering him down, and studied the dragon's lusty, hungry movements as old Fyren reveled in the blood and carnage.

"Is he?" the young priest said under his breath.

Books by
R. A. Salvatore

THE ICEWIND DALE TRILOGY

Book One: The Crystal Shard
Book Two: Streams of Silver
Book Three: The Halfling's Gem

THE DARK ELF TRILOGY

Book One: Homeland
Book Two: Exile
Book Three: Sojourn

THE CLERIC QUINTET

Book One: Canticle
Book Two: In Sylvan Shadows
Book Three: Night Masks
Book Four: The Fallen Fortress

The Legacy

FANTASY ADVENTURE

The Fallen Fortress

R. A. Salvatore

TSR Inc.

THE FALLEN FORTRESS

Copyright ©1993 TSR, Inc.
All Rights Reserved.

Random House and its affiliate companies have worldwide distribution rights in the book trade for English language products of TSR, Inc.

Distributed to the book and hobby trade in the United Kingdom by TSR Ltd.

Distributed to the toy and hobby trade by regional distributors.

Cover art by Jeff Easley.

First Printing: June 1993.
Printed in the United States of America.
Library of Congress Catalog Card Number: 92-61090

9 8 7 6 5 4 3 2 1

ISBN: 1-56076-419-8

TSR, Inc.
P.O. Box 756
Lake Geneva, WI 53147
U.S.A.

TSR Ltd.
120 Church End, Cherry Hinton
Cambridge CB1 3LB
United Kingdom

To Nancy, for
showing true courage.

Prologue

Aballister walked along Lakeview Street in Carradoon, the wizard's black cloak wrapped tight against his skin-and-bones body to ward off the wintry blows whipping in from Impresk Lake. He had been in Carradoon less than a day, but had already learned of the wild events at the Dragon's Codpiece. Cadderly, his estranged son and nemesis, had apparently escaped the assassin band Aballister had sent to kill him.

Aballister chuckled at the thought, a wheezing sound from lips withered by decades of uttering frantic enchantments, channeling so many tingling energies into destructive purposes. Cadderly had escaped? Aballister mused, as though the thought was preposterous. Cadderly had done more than escape. With his friends, the young priest had obliterated the Night Mask contingent, more than twenty professional killers, and had also slain Bogo Rath, Aballister's second underling in the strict hierarchy of Castle Trinity.

1

All the common folk of Carradoon were talking about the exploits of the young priest from the Edificant Library. They were beginning to whisper that Cadderly might be their hope in these dark times.

Cadderly had become more than a minor problem for Aballister.

The wizard took no fatherly pride in his son's exploits. Aballister had designs on the region, intentions to conquer it given to him by the avatar of the evil goddess Talona. Just the previous spring, those intentions appeared easy to fulfill, with Castle Trinity's force swelling to over eight thousand warriors, wizards and Talonan priests included. But then Cadderly had unexpectedly stopped Barjin, the mighty priest who had gone after the heart of the region's goodly strength, the Edificant Library. The following season, Cadderly had led the elves of Shilmista Forest in the west to a stunning victory over the goblinoid and giantkin forces, chasing a sizable number of Castle Trinity's minions back to their mountain holes.

Even the Night Masks, possibly the most dreaded assassin band in the central Realms, had not been able to stop Cadderly. Now winter was fast approaching, the first snows had already descended over the region, and Castle Trinity's invasion of Carradoon would have to wait.

The afternoon light had grown dim when Aballister turned south on the Boulevard of the Bridge, passing through the low wooden buildings of the lakeside town. He crossed through the open gates of the city's cemetery and cast a simple spell to locate the unremarkable grave of Bogo Rath. He waited for the night to fully engulf the land, drew a few runes of protection in the snow and mud around the grave, and pulled his cloak up tighter against the deathly cold.

When the lights of the city went down and the streets grew quiet, the wizard began his incantation, his summons to the netherworld. It went on for several minutes, with Aballister attuning his mind to the shadowy region between the planes, attempting to meet the summoned spirit halfway. He ended the spell with a simple call: "Bogo Rath."

The wind seemed to focus around the withered wizard, collecting the nighttime mists in a swirling pattern, enshrouding the ground above the grave.

The mists parted suddenly, and the apparition stood before Aballister. Though less than corporeal, it appeared quite like Aballister remembered the young Bogo—straight and stringy hair flipped to one side, eyes darting inquisitively, suspiciously, one way and the other. There was one difference, though, something that made even hardy Aballister wince. A garish wound split the middle of Bogo's chest. Even in the near darkness, Aballister could see past the apparition's ribs and lungs to its spectral backbone.

"An axe," Bogo's mournful, drifting voice explained. He placed a less-than-tangible hand into the wound and flashed a gruesome smile. "Would you like to feel?"

Aballister had dealt with conjured spirits a hundred times and knew that he could not feel the wound even if he wanted to, knew that this was simply an apparition, the last physical image of Bogo's torn body. The spirit could not harm the wizard, could not even touch the wizard, and by the binding power of Aballister's magical summons, it would answer truthfully a certain number of Aballister's questions. Still, Aballister unconsciously winced again and took a cautious step backward, revolted by the thought of putting his hand in that wound.

"Cadderly and his friends killed you," Aballister began.

"Yes," Bogo answered, though Aballister's words had been a statement, not a question. The wizard silently berated himself for being so foolish. He would only be allowed a certain number of inquiries before the dweomer dissipated and the spirit was released. He reminded himself that he must take care to word his statements so that they could not be interpreted as questions.

"I know that Cadderly and his friends killed you, and I know that they eliminated the assassin band," he declared.

The apparition seemed to smile, and Aballister was not
certain whether the clever thing was baiting him to waste
another question or not. The wizard wanted to go on with
the intended leading conversation, but he couldn't resist
that bait.

"Are all . . . " he began slowly, trying to find the quickest
way to discern the fate of the entire assassin band. Aballister wisely paused, deciding to be as specific as possible and
end this part of the discussion efficiently. "Which of the
assassins still live?"

"Only one," Bogo answered obediently. "A traitorous firbolg named Vander."

Again, the inescapable bait. "Traitorous?" Aballister repeated. "Has this Vander joined with our enemies?"

"Yes—and yes."

Damn, Aballister mused. Complications. Always there
seemed to be complications where his troublesome son
was concerned.

"Have they gone for the library?" he asked.

"Yes."

"Will they come for Castle Trinity?"

The spirit, beginning to fade away, did not answer, and
Aballister realized that he had erred, for he had asked the
apparition a question which required supposition, a question which could not, at that time, be positively answered.

"You are not dismissed!" the wizard cried, trying desperately to hold onto the less than corporeal thing. He reached
out with hands that slipped right through Bogo's fading
image, reached out with thoughts that found nothing to
grasp.

Aballister stood alone in the graveyard. He understood
that Bogo's spirit would come back to him when it found
the definite answer to the question. But when would that
be? Aballister wondered. And what further mischief would
Cadderly and his friends cause before Aballister found the
information he needed to put an end to that troublesome
group?

"Hey, you there!" came a call from the boulevard, followed by the sounds of boots clapping against the cobblestone. "Who's in the cemetery after nightfall? Hold where you are!"

Aballister hardly took notice of the two city guardsmen who rushed through the cemetery gate, spotting him and making all haste toward him. The wizard was thinking of Bogo, of dead Barjin, once Castle Trinity's most powerful cleric, and of dead Ragnor, Castle Trinity's principle fighter. More than that, the wizard was thinking of Cadderly, the perpetrator of all his troubles.

The guardsmen were nearly upon Aballister when he began his chant. He threw his arms out high to the sides as they closed in and started to reach for him. A cry of the final, triggering rune sent the two men flying wide, hurled through the air by the released power of the spell, as Aballister, in the blink of an eye, sent his material body cascading back to his private room in Castle Trinity.

The dazed city soldiers pulled themselves from the wet ground, looked to each other in disbelief, and fled back through the cemetery gates, convinced that they would be better off if they pretended that nothing at all had happened in the eerie graveyard.

* * * * *

Cadderly sat upon the flat roof of a jutting two-story section of the Edificant Library, watching the sun spread its shining fingers across the plains east of the mountains. Other fingers stretched down from the tall peaks all about Cadderly's position to join those snaking up from the grass. Mountain streams came alive, glittering silver, and the autumn foliage, brown and yellow, red and brilliant orange, seemed to burst into flame.

Percival, the white squirrel, hopped along the roof's gutter when he caught sight of the young priest, and Cadderly nearly laughed aloud when he regarded the squirrel's

eagerness to join him—a desire emanating from Percival's
always grumbling belly, Cadderly knew. He dropped his
hand into a pouch on his belt and pulled out some cacasa
nuts, scattering them at Percival's feet.

It all seemed so normal to the young priest, the same as
it had always been. Percival skipped happily among his
favorite nuts, and the sun continued to climb, defeating the
chill of late autumn even this high up in the Snowflakes.

Cadderly saw through the facade, though. Things most
certainly were not normal, not for the young priest and not
for the Edificant Library. Cadderly had been on the road, in
the elven wood of Shilmista and in the town of Carradoon,
fighting battles, learning firsthand the realities of a harsh
world, and learning, too, that the priests of the library, men
and women he had looked up to for his entire life, were not
as wise or powerful as he had once believed.

The single notion that dominated young Cadderly's
thoughts as he sat up there on the sunny roof was that
something had gone terribly wrong within his order of
Deneir, and within the order of Oghman priests, the
brother hosts of the library. It seemed to Cadderly that procedure had become more important than necessity, that the
priests of the library had been paralyzed by mounds of useless parchments when decisive action was needed.

And those rotting roots had sunk even deeper, Cadderly
knew. He thought of Nameless, the pitiful leper he had met
on the road from Carradoon. Nameless had come to the
library for help and had found that the priests of Deneir and
Oghma were, for the most part, more concerned with their
own failure to heal him than with the consequences of his
grave affliction.

Yes, Cadderly decided, something was very wrong at his
precious library. He lay back on the gray, slightly pitched
roof and casually flipped another nut at the munching
squirrel.

One

No Time for Guilt

The spirit heard the call from a distance, floating across the empty grayness of this reeking and forlorn plane. The mournful notes said not a discernable word, and yet, to the spirit, they seemed to speak his name.

Ghost. Clearly it called to him, beckoned him from the muck and mire of his eternal hell. *Ghost*, its melody called again. The wretch looked at the growling, huddled shadows all about him, wicked souls, the remains of wicked people. He, too, was a growling shadow, a tormented thing, suffering punishments for a life villainously lived.

But now he was being called, being carried from his torment on the notes of a familiar melody.

Familiar?

The thin thread that remained of ghost's living consciousness strained to better recall, to better remember its life before this foul, empty existence. Ghost thought of sunlight, of shadows, of killing. . . .

7

The *Ghearufu!* Evil Ghost understood. The *Ghearufu*, the magical item he had carried in life for so many decades, was calling to him, was leading him back from the very hellfires!

* * * * *

"Cadderly! Cadderly!" wailed Vicero Belago, the Edificant Library's resident alchemist, when he saw the young priest and Danica at his door on the huge library's third floor. "My boy, it's so good that you have returned to us!" The wiry man virtually hopped across his shop, weaving in and out of tables covered with beakers and vials, dripping coils and stacks of thick books. He hit his target as Cadderly stepped into the room, throwing his arms about the sturdy young priest and slapping him hard on the back.

Cadderly looked over Belago's shoulder to Danica and gave her a helpless shrug, which she returned with a wink of an exotic brown eye and a wide, pearly smile.

"We heard that some killers came after you, my boy," Belago explained, putting Cadderly back to arm's length and studying him as though he expected to find an assassin's dagger protruding from Cadderly's chest. "I feared that you would never return." The alchemist also gave Cadderly's upper arms a squeeze, apparently amazed at how solid and strong the young priest had become in the short time he had been gone from the library. Like a concerned aunt, Belago ran a hand up over Cadderly's floppy brown hair, pushing the always unkempt locks back from the young man's face.

"I am all right," Cadderly replied calmly. "This is the house of Deneir, and I am a disciple of Deneir. Why would I not return?"

His understatement had a calming effect on the excitable alchemist, as did the serene look in Cadderly's gray eyes. Belago started to blurt out a reply, but stopped in midstutter and nodded instead.

"Ah, and lady Danica," the alchemist went on. He reached out and gently stroked Danica's thick tangle of strawberry-blond hair, his smile sincere.

Belago's grin disappeared almost immediately, though, and he dropped his arms to his sides and his gaze to the floor.

"We heard about Headmaster Avery," he said softly, nodding his head up and down, his expression clouded with sad resignation.

The mention of the portly Avery Schell, Cadderly's surrogate father, stung the young priest profoundly. He wanted to explain to poor Belago that Avery's spirit lived on with their god. But how could he begin? Belago would not understand; no one who had not passed into the spirit world and witnessed the divine and glorious sensation could understand. Against that ignorance, anything Cadderly might say would sound like a ridiculous cliché, typical comforting words usually spoken and heard without conviction.

"I received word that you wished to speak with me?" Cadderly said instead, raising his tone to make the statement a question and thus shift the conversation.

"Yes," Belago answered softly. His head finally stopped bouncing, and his eyes widened when he looked into the young priest's calming gray eyes. "Oh, yes!" he cried, as if he had just remembered that fact. "I did—of course I did!"

Obviously embarrassed, the wiry man hopped back across the shop to a small cabinet. He fumbled with an oversized ring of keys, muttering to himself all the while.

"You have become a hero," Danica remarked, noting the man's movements.

Cadderly couldn't disagree with Danica's observation. Vicero Belago had never been overjoyed to see the young priest before. Cadderly had always been a demanding customer, taxing Belago's talents often beyond their limits. Because of a risky project that Cadderly had given the alchemist, Belago's shop had once been blown apart.

That had been long ago, however, before the battle in Shilmista Forest, before Cadderly's exploits in Carradoon, the city to the east on the banks of Impresk Lake.

Before Cadderly had become a hero.

Hero.

What a ridiculous title, the young priest thought. He had done no more than Danica or either of the dwarven brothers, Ivan and Pikel, in Carradoon. And he, unlike his sturdy friends, had run away from the battle in Shilmista Forest, fled because he could not endure the horrors.

He looked down at Danica again, her brown-eyed gaze comforting him as only it could. How beautiful she was, Cadderly noted, her frame as delicate as that of a newborn fawn and her hair tousled and bouncing freely about her shoulders. Beautiful and untamed, he decided, and with an inner strength clearly shining through those exotic, almond-shaped eyes.

Belago was back in front of him then, seeming nervous and holding both his hands behind his back. "You left this here when you came back from the elven wood," he explained, drawing out his left hand. He held a leather belt with a wide and shallow holster on one side that sported a hand-crossbow.

"I had no idea that I would need it in peaceful Carradoon," Cadderly replied easily, taking the belt and strapping it around his hips.

Danica eyed the young priest curiously. The crossbow had become a symbol of violence to Cadderly, and a symbol of Cadderly's abhorrence of violence to those who knew him best. To see him strap it on so easily, with an almost cavalier attitude, twisted Danica's heart.

Cadderly sensed both the woman's gaze and her confusion. He forced himself to accept it, thinking that he would probably shatter many conceptions in the days ahead. For Cadderly had come to see the dangers facing the Edificant Library in ways that others could not.

"I saw that you had nearly exhausted your supply of the

darts," Belago stammered. "I mean . . . there's no charge
for this batch." He pulled his other hand around, producing
a bandolier filled with specially crafted bolts for the tiny
crossbow. "I figured I owed it to you—we all owe it to you,
Cadderly."

Cadderly nearly laughed aloud at the absurd proclamation, but he respectfully held his control and accepted the
very expensive gift from the alchemist with a grave and
approving nod. The darts were special indeed, hollowed out
in the center and fitted with a vial that Belago filled with
volatile *Oil of Impact*.

"My thanks for the gift," the young priest said. "Be
assured that you have aided the cause of the library in our
continuing struggle against the evil of Castle Trinity."

Belago seemed pleased by that remark. Head bobbing
once more, he accepted Cadderly's handshake eagerly. He
was still standing in the same place, smiling from ear to ear,
as Cadderly and Danica walked out into the hall.

Cadderly could still sense Danica's continuing unease
and could see the disappointment etched in her features.
The young priest's narrowing stare attacked that disappointment. "I have dismissed the guilt because it has no
place in me," was all the explanation he would offer. "Not
now, not with all that is left to be done. But I have not
forgotten Barjin or that fateful day in the catacombs."

Danica looked away down the hall, but hooked Cadderly's arm with her own, showing her trust in him.

Another form, shapely and obviously feminine, entered
the corridor as the pair moved toward Danica's room at the
southern end of the complex. Danica tightened her grip on
Cadderly's arm at the scent of an exotic and overpowering
perfume.

"My greetings, handsome Cadderly," purred the shapely
priestess in the crimson gown. "You cannot imagine how
pleased I am that you have returned."

Danica's grip nearly cut off Cadderly's blood flow; he felt
his fingers tingling. He knew that his face had blushed a

deep scarlet, as reddish as Priestess Histra's revealing gown. He realized, sensibly, that this was probably the most modest outfit he had ever seen the lusty priestess of Sune, the Goddess of Love, wearing, but that did not make it modest by anyone else's standards. The front was cut in a low V, so low that Cadderly felt he might glimpse Histra's navel if he got up on his toes, and though the gown was long, its front slit was incredibly high, displaying all of Histra's shapely leg when she brought one foot out in front of the other in her typically alluring stance.

Histra did not seem displeased by Cadderly's obvious discomfort or by Danica's growing scowl. She bent one leg at the knee, her thigh slipping completely free of the gown's meager folds.

Cadderly heard himself gulp, didn't realize that he was gawking at the brazen display until Danica's small fingernails dug deep lines into his upper arm.

"Do come and visit, dear young Cadderly," Histra purred. She looked disdainfully at the woman on Cadderly's arm. "When you are not so tightly leashed, of course." Histra slowly, teasingly moved into her room, the door's gentle click as she closed it lost beneath the sound of Cadderly's repeated swallowing.

"I—" he stammered, at last looking Danica in the eye.

Danica laughed and led him on down the hall. "Fear not," she said, her tone more than a little condescending. "I understand your relationship with the priestess of Sune. She is quite pitiful, actually."

Cadderly looked down at Danica, perplexed. If Danica was speaking the truth, then why had little lines of blood begun their descent on his muscled arm?

"I am not jealous of Histra, certainly," Danica went on. "I trust you, with all my heart." Just outside her room, she stopped and faced Cadderly squarely, one hand brushing the outline of his face, the other tight about his waist.

"I trust you," Danica said again.

"Besides," added the fiery young monk in very different,

stronger tones as she turned into her room, "if anything romantic ever happened between you and that single-minded, over-painted lump of too-too quivering flesh, I would put her nose somewhere in back of one of her ears."

Danica abruptly disappeared into her room to retrieve the book of notes she and Cadderly had prepared for their meeting with Dean Thobicus. The young priest remained in the hall, considering the threat and privately laughing at how true it could be. Danica was fully a foot shorter than he, and easily a hundred pounds lighter. She walked with the grace of a dancer—and fought with the tenacity of a bee-stung bear.

The young priest was far from worried, though. Histra had spent all of her life in the practice of being alluring, and she made no secret of her designs on Cadderly. But she hadn't a chance; not a woman in the world had a chance of breaking Cadderly's bond with his Danica.

* * * * *

A blackened, charred hand tore up through the newly turned earth, reaching desperately for the open air above. A second arm, similarly charred and broken at a gruesome angle halfway between the wrist and the elbow, followed, grasping at the mud, tearing at the natural prison that held the wretched body.

Finally the creature found enough of a hold to pull his hairless head from the shallow grave, to look again upon the world of the living.

The blackened head swiveled on a neck that was no more than skin shriveled tight to the bone, surveying the scene. For a fleeting instant, the wretch wondered what had happened. How had he been buried?

A short distance away, down a little hill, the creature saw the glow of the evening lamps of a small farmhouse. Beside it stood another structure, a barn.

A barn!

The thin sliver of the consciousness that had once belonged to a man known as Ghost remembered that barn. Ghost had seen this body, his body, charred by that wicked Cadderly in that very barn! The evil corpse drew in some air—the action could not be called breathing where this undead thing was concerned—and dragged his blackened and shriveled body the rest of the way out of the hole. The notes of that distant, yet strangely familiar, melody continued to thrum in the back of his feeble consciousness.

Unsteadily, Ghost loped more than walked toward the structure, the memories of that horrible, fateful day coming back more fully with each stride.

Ghost had used the *Ghearufu*, a powerful device with magical energies directed toward the spirit world, to steal the body of the firbolg Vander, an unwilling associate. Disguised as Vander, with the strength of a giant, Ghost had then crushed his own body and had thrown it across the barn.

And then Cadderly had burned it.

The malignant monster looked down to his bone-skinny arms and prominent ribs, the hollow shell that somehow lived.

Cadderly had burned his body, this body!

A single-minded hatred consumed the wretched creature. Ghost wanted to kill Cadderly, to kill anybody dear to the young priest, to kill anybody at all.

Ghost was at the barn then. Thoughts of Cadderly had flitted away into nothingness, replaced by an unfocused anger. The door was over to the side, but the creature understood that he did not need the door, that he had become something more than the simple material wooden planking now blocking his way. The shriveled form wavered, became insubstantial, and Ghost walked through the wall.

He heard the horse whinnying before he came fully back to the material plane, saw the poor beast standing wild-eyed, lathered in sweat. The sight pleased the undead thing; waves of a new sensation of joy washed over Ghost as he smelled the beast's terror. The undead monster ambled over to stand before the horse, let his tongue drop out of his mouth hungrily. With all the skin burned away from the sides of the tongue, its pointy tip hung far below Ghost's blackened chin. The horse made not a sound, was too frightened to move or even to draw breath.

With a wheeze of evil anticipation, Ghost put deathly cold hands against the sides of the beast's face.

The horse fell dead.

The undead creature hissed with delight, but while Ghost felt thrilled by the kill, he did not feel sated. His hunger demanded more, could not be defeated by the death of a simple animal. Ghost moved across the barn and again walked through the wall, coming into view of the lights within the farmhouse. A shadowy shape, a human shape, moved across one of the rooms.

Ghost was at the front door, undecided as to whether to walk through the wood, tear the door apart, or simply knock and let the sheep come to the wolf. The decision was taken from the creature, though, when he looked to the side of the door, to a small pane of glass, and saw, for the first time, his own reflection.

A red glow emanated from empty eye sockets. Ghost's nose was completely gone, replaced by a blacker hole edged by ragged flaps of charred skin.

That tiny part of Ghost's consciousness that remembered the vitality of life lost all control at the sight of that hideous reflection. The monster's unearthly wail sent the barnyard animals into a frenzy and shattered the stillness of the quiet autumn night more than any violent storm ever could. There came a shuffling from inside the house, just behind the door, but the outraged monster didn't even hear it. With strength far beyond that of any mortal, he drove his bony hands through the center of the door and pulled out to the sides, splintering and tearing the wood as though it were no more than a thin sheet of parchment.

A man stood there, wearing the uniform of a Carradoon city guardsman and an expression of sheer horror, his mouth frozen wide in a silent scream, his eyes bugged out so far that they seemed as if they would fall from his face.

Ghost burst through the broken door and fell over him. The man's skin transformed, aged, under the creature's ghostly touch; his hair turned from raven black to white and fell out in large clumps. Finally the guardsman's voice returned, and he screamed and wailed, flailing his arms helplessly.

Ghost ripped at him, tore at his throat until that revealing scream was no more than the gurgle of blood-filled lungs.

The creature heard a shuffle of feet, looked up from the kill to see a second man standing beyond the foyer, in a doorway at the other side of the house's small kitchen.

"By the gods," this man whispered, and he dove back into the far room and slammed the door.

With one hand, Ghost lifted the dead man and hurled him out the shattered portal, halfway across the barnyard. The undead creature floated across the floor, savoring the kill, yet hungry for more. His form wavered again, and he walked across the room and through another closed door.

The second man, also a city guardsman, stood before the wicked thing, swinging his sword frantically at the horrid monster. But the weapon never touched Ghost, slipped right through the insubstantial, ethereal mist the creature had become. The man tried to run away, but Ghost kept pace with him, walked past furniture that the man stumbled over, walked through walls to meet the terrified man on the other side of a door.

The torment went on for a long and agonizing time, the helpless man finally stumbling out into the night, losing his sword as he tumbled down the porch steps. He scrambled to his feet and ran into the dark night, ran with all speed for Carradoon, howling all the way.

Ghost could have, at any time, rematerialized and torn the man apart, but somehow the creature felt that he enjoyed this sensation, this smell of terror, even more than the actual killing. Ghost felt stronger for it, as though he had somehow fed off of the horrified man's emotions and screams.

But now it was over and the man was gone, and the other man was long dead and offered no more sport.

Ghost wailed again as the thin sliver of remaining consciousness considered what he had become, considered what wretched Cadderly had created. Ghost remembered little of his past life, only that he had been among the highest paid killers in the living realm, a professional assassin, an artist of murder.

Now the creature was an undead thing, a ghost, a hollow, animated shell of evil energies.

After more than a century of being in possession of the *Ghearufu*, Ghost had come to consider mortal forms in a much different way than others. Twice the evil man had utilized the powers of the magical device to change bodies, killing his previous form and taking the new one as his own. And now, somehow, Ghost's spirit, a piece of it at least, had come back to this plane. By some trick of fate, Ghost had risen from the dead.

But how? Ghost couldn't fully remember his place in the afterlife, but sensed that it was not pleasant, not at all. Images of growling shadows surrounded him; black claws raked the air before his mind's eye. What had brought him back from the grave, what compelled his spirit to walk the earth once more? The creature scanned his fingers, his toes, for some sign of the regenerative ring Ghost had once worn. But he distinctly remembered that the ring had been stolen by Cadderly.

Ghost felt a call on the wind, silent but compelling. And familiar. He turned glowing eyes up toward the distant mountains and heard the call again.

The *Ghearufu*.

The malignant spirit understood, remembered hearing the melody from his place of eternal punishment. The

Ghearufu had called him back. By the power of the *Ghearufu*, Ghost walked the earth once more. At that confused, overwhelming moment, the creature couldn't decide if that was a good thing or not. He looked again to his shriveled, gruesome arms and torso, wondered if he could withstand the light of day. What future awaited Ghost in such a state? What hopes could the undead thing hold?

The silent call came again.

The *Ghearufu!*

It wanted Ghost back—and by its power, the creature's spirit could surely steal a new form, a living form.

In Carradoon, not so far from the farmyard, the horrified guardsman stumbled to the closed gate, screaming of ghosts, crying for his slaughtered companion. If the soldiers manning the gate held any doubts about the man's sincerity, they needed only to look into his face, a face that appeared much older than the man's thirty years.

A large contingent of men, including a priest from the Temple of Ilmater, rode out from Carradoon's gate less than an hour later, hell-bent for the farmhouse, prepared to do battle with the malignant spirit. Ghost was far gone by then, sometimes walking, sometimes floating across the fields, following the call of the *Ghearufu*, his one chance for deliverance.

Only the cries of the nighttime animals, the terrified bleating of sheep, the frightened screech of a night owl, marked the ghost's passage.

Two

Step Over
A Dangerous Line

The dawn had long since passed, but the room Cadderly entered was darkened still, shades drawn tight to the windows. The young priest moved to the bed quietly and knelt, not wanting to disturb Headmistress Pertelope's sleep.

If Headmaster Avery had been Cadderly's surrogate father, then wise Pertelope had been his mother. Now, with his newfound insight into the harmonious song of Deneir, Cadderly felt that he needed Pertelope more than ever. For she, too, heard the mysterious notes of that unending song; she, too, transcended the normal boundaries of the clerical order. If Pertelope had been beside Cadderly in his discussion with Thobicus, then his reasoning would have been bolstered, and the withered dean would have been forced to accept the truth of Cadderly's insights.

But Pertelope could not be with him. She lay in her bed, deathly ill, caught in the throes of a magical enchantment gone wild. Her body had been trapped in a transformation somewhere between the smooth and soft skin of a human and the sharp-edged denticles of a shark, and now neither air nor water could satisfy the headmistress's physical needs.

Cadderly stroked her hair, more gray than he remembered it, as though Pertelope had aged. He was somewhat surprised when she opened her eyes, which still held their inquisitive luster, and managed a smile in his direction.

Cadderly strained to return that look.

"You must recover your strength," he whispered to her. "I need you."

Pertelope smiled again, and her eyes slowly closed.

Cadderly's sigh was one of helpless resignation. He started to turn away from the bed, not wanting to tax Pertelope's depleted strength, but the headmistress unexpectedly spoke to him.

"How went your meeting with Dean Thobicus?"

Cadderly turned back to her, surprised by the strength in that voice, and surprised also that Pertelope even knew he had met with the dean. She had not been out of her room in many days, and on the few occasions Cadderly had come to visit her, he had not mentioned his upcoming meeting.

He should have expected that she would know, though. As he considered the revelation, he reminded himself that she, too, heard the song of Deneir. She and Cadderly were intimately joined by forces far beyond what the other priests of the library could even understand, joined by a communal bathing in the river that was their god's song.

"It did not go well," Cadderly admitted.

"Dean Thobicus does not understand," Pertelope reasoned, and Cadderly suspected that the headmistress had suffered many similar meetings with Thobicus and other priests who could not comprehend her special relationship with Deneir.

"He questioned my authority in branding Kierkan Rufo," Cadderly explained. "And he ordered that I hand the *Ghearufu* . . ." Cadderly paused, wondering how he might quickly explain the dangerous device. Pertelope squeezed his hand, though, and smiled, and he knew that she understood.

"Dean Thobicus ordered me to turn it over to the library supervisor," Cadderly finished.

"You do not approve of that course?"

"I fear it," Cadderly admitted. "There is a will within the artifact, a sentient force almost, that may overcome any who handle it. I, myself, have had to struggle against the alluring calls of the *Ghearufu* since I took it from the assassin's burned body."

"You sound arrogant, young priest," Pertelope interrupted, her emphasis on the word "young."

Cadderly paused to consider the response. Perhaps his feelings could be considered arrogant, but he believed them nonetheless. He could control the force of the *Ghearufu*, had controlled it to this point, at least. Cadderly realized that he held a special insight now, a gift from Deneir, that others of his order, with the exception of Pertelope, seemed to lack.

"That is good," the headmistress said, answering her own accusation. Cadderly eyed her curiously, not quite understanding where her reasoning was leading.

"Deneir has called upon you," Pertelope explained. "You must trust in that call. When you first discovered your budding powers, you did not understand them and you feared them. It was only when you came to trust in them that you learned their uses and limitations. So it must be with your instincts and your emotions, feelings heightened by the song that ever plays in your mind. Do you believe that you know what is the best course concerning the *Ghearufu*?"

"I know," Cadderly replied firmly, not caring that he did indeed sound arrogant.

"And concerning Kierkan Rufo's brand?"

Cadderly spent a moment considering the question, for Rufo's case seemed to encompass many more edicts of proper procedure, procedures that Cadderly had obviously circumvented. "I did as the ethics of Deneir instructed me," he decided. "Still, Dean Thobicus doubts my authority with good cause."

"From his perspective," Pertelope replied. "Yours was a moral authority, while the dean's power over such situations comes from a different source."

"From a created hierarchy," Cadderly added. "A hierarchy that remains blind to the truth of Deneir." He gave a chuckle, unintentionally derisive. "A hierarchy that will hold us in check until the cost of a war with Castle Trinity multiplies tenfold, a hundredfold."

"Will it?"

It was a simple question, asked simply by a priestess who had not the strength to even rise from her bed. To Cadderly, though, the question's connotations became quite complex, implicating him and his future actions as the only possible answer. He knew in his heart that Pertelope was calling upon him to prevent what he had just predicted, was asking him to usurp the authority of his order's highest ranking priest and bring Castle Trinity's influence to a quick end.

Her coy smile confirmed his suspicions.

"Have *you* ever dared to overrule the Dean?" Cadderly asked bluntly.

"I have never been in such a desperate situation," the headmistress replied. Her voice sounded weak suddenly, as though her efforts to be strong had reached their end.

"I told you when you first discovered your gift," she went on, pausing often to collect her breath, "that many things would be required of you, that your courage would often be tested. Deneir demands intelligence, but he also demands courage of spirit so that intelligent decisions can be acted upon."

"Cadderly?" The quiet call came from the door, and Cadderly looked back over his shoulder to see Danica, her face grave. Behind her stood the beautiful Shayleigh, elven maiden, elven warrior, from Shilmista Forest, her golden hair lustrous and her violet eyes shining as the dawn. She made no greeting to Cadderly, though she had not seen him in many weeks, out of respect for the obviously solemn meeting.

"Dean Thobicus is looking for you," Danica explained quietly, her tone full of trepidation. "You did not give the *Ghearufu* . . ." Her voice trailed away as Cadderly looked back to the bed, to Pertelope, who appeared very old and very tired.

"Courage," Pertelope whispered, and then, as Cadderly looked on with full understanding, the headmistress peacefully died.

* * * * *

Cadderly did not knock and wait for permission to enter the office of Dean Thobicus. The withered man was sitting back in his chair, staring out the window. Cadderly knew that the dean had just received news of Headmistress Pertelope's death.

"Have you done as you were instructed?" Thobicus snapped as soon as he noticed that Cadderly had entered, and by that time, Cadderly was already up to the man's desk.

"I have," Cadderly replied.

"Good," Thobicus said, and his anger faded, replaced by his obvious sorrow for Pertelope's passing.

"I have bid Danica and Shayleigh to assemble the dwarven brothers and Vander by the front door, with provisions for the journey," Cadderly explained, popping on his blue, wide-brimmed hat as he spoke.

"To Shilmista Forest?" Thobicus asked tentatively, as though he was afraid of what Cadderly was about to say. One of the options Thobious had offered to Cadderly was to go out and serve as emissary to the elves and Prince Elbereth, but he didn't think that was what the young priest was now hinting at.

"No," came the even answer.

Thobicus sat up very straight in his chair, a perplexed expression on his hollow, weathered face. He noticed then that Cadderly wore his hand-crossbow and the bandolier of explosive darts. The spindle-disks, Cadderly's other unconventional weapon, were looped on the young priest's wide belt, next to a tube that Cadderly had designed to emit a concentrated beam of light.

Thobicus considered the clues for a long while. "You have turned the *Ghearufu* over to the library supervisor?" he asked directly.

"No."

Thobicus trembled with mounting rage. He started to speak several times, but wound up chewing his lips instead. "You just said that you had done as you were instructed!" he roared at last, in as furious an outburst as Cadderly had ever seen from the normally calm man.

"I have done as Deneir instructed," Cadderly explained.

"You arrogant . . . you . . . sacrilegious—" Thobicus stammered, his face shining bright red as he stood up behind the desk.

"Hardly," Cadderly corrected, his voice unshaking. "I have done as Deneir instructed, and now you, too, are to do Deneir's bidding. You will go down with me to the front hall and wish my friends and me good fortune on our all-important mission to Castle Trinity." The dean tried to interrupt but something that he did not yet understand, something intruding into his very thoughts, compelled him to silence.

"Then you will continue the preparations for a springtime assault," Cadderly explained, "a reserve plan in case my friends and I cannot accomplish what we set out to do."

"You are mad!" Thobicus growled.

Hardly.

Thobicus began to argue back—until he realized that Cadderly had not spoken the word. The dean's eyes narrowed and then popped wide as he came to realize that something was touching him—inside his mind!

"What are you about?" he demanded frantically.

You need not speak, Cadderly telepathically assured him.

"This is . . . " the Dean began.

" . . . preposterous, an insult to my position," Cadderly verbally finished for him, sensing and perfectly revealing the words before Thobicus ever spoke them.

The dean fell back in his chair. *Do you realize the consequences of your actions?* he mentally asked.

Do you realize that I could shatter your mind? Cadderly responded with all confidence. *Do you further realize that my powers are bestowed by Deneir?*

The dean's faced screwed up in confusion and disbelief. What was this young upstart hinting at?

Cadderly held no love for this ugly game, but he had little time to handle things the way the proper procedures of the Edificant Library demanded. He mentally commanded the dean to stand, then to stand on the desk. Before he knew what had happened, Thobicus found himself looking down at the young priest from a high perch.

Cadderly looked to the window, and Thobicus telepathically sensed the young priest privately musing that he could quite easily persuade the dean to jump out of it—and suddenly Thobicus believed that Cadderly could! Without warning, Cadderly released Thobicus from the mental grip, and the dean slumped down from the oaken desk and slid back into his chair.

"I take no pleasure in dominating you so," Cadderly explained sincerely, understanding that the best results might be gained by restoring the defeated man's pride. "I am allowed the power by the god that we both recognize. This is Deneir's way of explaining to you that I am correct in these matters. It is a signal to us both, nothing more. All that I ask—"

"I will have you branded!" Thobicus exploded. "I will see that you are escorted from the library in chains, tormented every step of the way as you leave this region!"

His words stung Cadderly profoundly as he continued

his tirade, promising every conceivable punishment allow-
able by the Deneirian sect. Cadderly had been raised under
those rules of order, under the precept that the dean's word
was absolute rule in the library, and it was truly terrifying
to the young priest to cast aside convention, even in light of
the greater truth playing within the notes of the Deneirian
song. Cadderly focused his thoughts on Pertelope at that
terrible moment, remembering her call for courage and
conviction.

He heard the harmony of the song playing in his mind,
entered its alluring flow and found again those channels of
energy that would allow him into the private realm of Dean
Thobicus's mind.

Cadderly and the dean exited the library a few minutes
later, to find Danica and Shayleigh; the giant Vander (who
was using his innate magical abilities to appear as a huge,
red-bearded man); and the two dwarves, stocky, yellow-
bearded Ivan, and round-shouldered Pikel, his beard dyed
green and pulled up over his ears, braided with his long
hair halfway down his back, waiting for them. The smiling
dean wished Cadderly and his five companions the best of
fortunes on their most important mission, and waved a fond
farewell as they walked off into the Snowflakes.

Three

Justifying the Means

Aballister leaned in close over Dorigen's shoulder, making the woman somewhat uncomfortable. Dorigen let her focus drift away from the images in the crystal ball and shook her head vigorously, purposely letting fly her long salt-and-pepper hair so that it smacked nosy Aballister in the face.

The older wizard backed up a step and pulled a strand of hair from his lips, glowering at Dorigen.

"I did not realize that you were so close," Dorigen weakly apologized.

"Of course," replied Aballister in similarly feigned tones. Dorigen clearly recognized his anger, but understood that he would accept her insult without too much complaint. Aballister had broken his own scrying device, a magical mirror, and the experience had left him fearful of any more attempts at clairvoyance. He needed Dorigen now, for she was quite skilled at the art. "I should have announced my presence and waited for you to complete your search," Aballister said, which was as close to an apology as Dorigen had ever heard from the man.

"That would have been the appropriate course," Dorigen agreed, her amber eyes flashing with . . .

With what? Aballister wondered. Open hatred? Their relationship had been on a steady decline since Dorigen had returned from her humiliating defeat in Shilmista Forest, a defeat she had suffered at the hands of Aballister's own estranged son.

The older wizard shrugged away the personal problems. "Have you found them?" he asked evenly. He and Dorigen could settle their score after the immediate threat was eliminated, but for now, they both had greater problems. The spirit of Bogo Rath had returned to Aballister the previous night, with the information that Cadderly was indeed on his way to Castle Trinity.

The report inspired both trepidation and exhilaration in the older wizard. Aballister was obsessed with conquering the region, a goal given to him by the avatar of Talona herself, and Cadderly certainly seemed to be among the foremost obstacles to those designs. The wizard could not deny the tingle of anticipation he felt at the thought of doing battle with his formidable son. By all reports, Cadderly did not even know his relationship to Aballister, and the thought of crushing the upstart youth, both in magical battle and emotionally with the secret truth, inevitably widened a grin across cruel Aballister's angular features.

The news of Cadderly's march inspired nothing but fear in Dorigen, however. She had no desire to tangle with the young priest and his brutal friends again, especially not now, with her hands still sore from the beating Cadderly had given them. Many of her spells required precise hand movements, and with her fingers bent crooked and joints smashed, more than one spell had backfired on her since her return from the elven forest.

"I have seen no sign of Cadderly," Dorigen replied after a

long pause to study again the blurry images in the crystal ball. "My guess is that he and his companions have just recently left the library, if they have left at all, and I dare not send my magical sight so near our enemy's stronghold."

"Two hours, and you have found nothing?" Aballister did not sound pleased. He paced the edge of the small room, running withered fingers across a curtain that separated this area from Dorigen's boudoir. A smile spread across the wizard's face, though, despite his trepidation, when he remembered the many games he and Dorigen had enjoyed behind this very curtain.

"I did not say that," Dorigen answered sharply, under-standing the conniving grin, and she turned back again to the crystal ball.

Aballister rushed back across the room to peer over his associate's shoulder. At first, only a gray mist swirled within the confines of the crystal ball, but gradually, with Dori-gen's coaxing, it began to shift and take on definite form. The two wizards viewed the foothills of the Snowflakes, obviously the southeastern mountain region, for the road to Carradoon was plainly in sight. Something moved along that road, something hideous.

"The assassin," Aballister breathed. Dorigen regarded the older wizard curiously.

"The spirit of Bogo was cryptic on this point," Aballister explained. "This thing you have discovered was one of the leaders of the Night Mask band, the one called, appropri-ately it would now seem, Ghost. Apparently our dear Cad-derly took from Ghost a magical device, and now the wretched creature has come back for it. Can you sense the spirit's power through your ball?"

"Of course not," Dorigen answered indignantly.

"Then go out to the mountains and watch over this one," Aballister growled at her. "We may have a powerful ally here, one that will eliminate our problems before they ever make their way to Castle Trinity."

"I will not."

Aballister straightened as though he had been slapped.

"I have not yet recovered," Dorigen explained. "My spells are not dependable. You would ask me to go near a malignant ghost, and near your dangerous son, without full use of my abilities?" Her reference to Cadderly as Aballister's son made the older wizard cringe, the obvious implication being that this entire trouble was somehow Aballister's fault.

"You have at your disposal one far more capable of estimating the strength of this undead monster," Dorigen went on, not backing down in the least. "One who can communicate with the creature if necessary and who can certainly learn more about its intentions than I."

Aballister's wrath melted away as he came to understand Dorigen's reasoning. "Druzil," he replied, referring to his familiar, a mischievous imp of the lower planes.

"Druzil," Dorigen echoed, her tone derisive.

Aballister put a crooked hand up to his sharp chin and mumbled. Still, he seemed unconvinced.

"Besides," Dorigen purred. "If I remain at Trinity, perhaps you and I . . . " She let the thought hang, her gaze directing Aballister's to the curtain across the small room.

Aballister's dark eyes widened in surprise, and his hand drooped back down by his side. "Continue your search for my s . . . for Cadderly," Aballister said to her. "Alert me at once if you discover his location. After all, I have ways of striking at the foolish boy before he ever gets near Castle Trinity."

The wizard took his abrupt leave then, seeming flustered, but with an obviously hopeful bounce in his step, and Dorigen turned back to her crystal ball. She didn't immediately return to her scrying, though, but instead considered the action she had just taken to prevent Aballister from sending her away. She held no love for the man anymore, no respect even, though he was certainly among the most powerful wizards she had ever seen. But Dorigen had made a decision—a decision forced by her will to ride this whole adventure out to a safe conclusion. She knew herself well enough to admit that Cadderly had truly unnerved her in the elven wood.

Her thoughts led her to contemplations of Aballister's intentions for his son. The wizard had allies, enchanted monsters kept in private cages in his extradimensional mansion. All that Aballister needed was for Dorigen to point the way.

Dorigen looked down at her still swollen and bruised hands, remembered the disaster in Shilmista, and remembered, too, that Cadderly could have killed her if he had desired.

* * * * *

They set their first camp on a high pass in the Snowflakes, sheltered from the biting, wintry wind by a small alcove in the rocky mountain wall. With Vander's gigantic bulk standing to further block the gusting breezes (the cold did not seem to bother the firbolg in the least), Ivan and Pikel soon had a fire roaring. Still, the wind inevitably found its way in to the companions, and even the dwarves were soon shivering and rubbing their hands briskly near the flames. Pikel's typical moan of "Oooo," came out more as "O—o—o—o," as his teeth chattered through the sound.

Cadderly, deep in thought, was oblivious to it all, oblivious even to the fact that his fingers were beginning to take on a delicate blue color. His head down and eyes half-closed, he sat farthest from the flames—except for Vander, who had moved out around the edge of the natural alcove to feel the full force of the refreshing wind against his ruddy cheeks.

"We're needing sleep," Ivan stuttered, aiming his comment at the distracted priest.

"O—o oi," Pikel readily agreed.

"It w—will be hard to sleep with the cold," Danica said

rather loudly, practically in Cadderly's ear. The four companions looked incredulously at each other, and then back at Cadderly. Danica shrugged and moved closer to the flames, rubbing her hands all the while, but Ivan, always a bit more blunt in his tactics, took Shayleigh's longbow, reached across the fire with it, and bopped Cadderly several times atop the head.

Cadderly looked up at the dwarf. "What?"

"We was saying that it's a mite chilly for sleeping," Ivan growled at him, his claims accentuated by the puff of frosty breath accompanying each chattered word. Cadderly looked around at his shivering companions, then seemed to realize his own tingling extremities for the first time.

"Deneir will protect us," he assured them, and he let his mind's eye slip back to the pages of the *Tome of Universal Harmony*, the most holy book of his god. He heard again the flowing, beautiful notes of the endless song, and pulled from them a relatively simple spell, repeating it until its enchantment had touched all of his friends.

"Oo!" Pikel exclaimed, and this time his teeth did not chatter. The cold was gone; there was no better way to explain the sensation that instantly came over each of them at Cadderly's blessed touch.

"Took ye long enough," was Ivan's last muttered sentiment before he dropped back against the comfortable (to a dwarf, at least) mountain rock, clasped his hands behind his head, and closed his eyes.

The dwarves were snoring in a matter of minutes, and soon after, Shayleigh, her head against arms that grasped her propped longbow, was also resting easily. Cadderly had resumed his previous contemplative posture, and Danica, guessing that something was bothering her love terribly, fought away the temptation of sleep and kept a protective watch over him.

She would have preferred that Cadderly willingly open up to her, initiate the discussion that he obviously needed. Danica knew the man better than to really expect that, knew that Cadderly could sit and mull something over for hours, even days.

"You have done something wrong?" she asked as much as stated to him. "Or is it Avery?"

Cadderly looked up at her, and his surprised expression told Danica much, though she did not immediately elaborate on her suspicions.

"I have done nothing wrong," Cadderly said at length, a bit too defensively, and the perceptive monk understood then which of her guesses had hit the mark.

"It seems amazing how completely Dean Thobicus changed his mind concerning our quest," Danica said slyly.

Cadderly shifted uncomfortably—more evidence for Danica's perceptive eye. "The dean is a cleric of Deneir," Cadderly replied, as though that explained everything. "He seeks knowledge and harmony, and if the truth becomes known to him, he will not let pride stand in the way of changing his mind."

Danica nodded, though her expression remained doubtful.

"Our course was the proper one," Cadderly added firmly.

"The dean did not think so."

"He learned the truth," Cadderly answered immediately.

"Did he?" Danica asked. "Or was the truth forced upon him?"

Cadderly looked away, saw Vander at the edge of the firelight, pacing in the blasting wind, continually sniffing at the mountain air as he walked his watch, though his eyes were more often turned toward the crystalline, star-dotted sky than to the rugged mountain landscape.

"What did you do to him?" Danica asked bluntly. Cadderly's glare fell over her in an instant, but she didn't back away in the least, trusting in her lover, trusting that the young priest could not lie to her.

"I convinced him." Cadderly spit out every word.

"Magically."

How well you know me! the priest thought, truly amazed.

"It had to be done," he said quietly.

Danica rolled up onto her knees, shaking her head, her almond-shaped brown eyes widening.

"Was I to allow Thobicus to lead us down a path of devastation?" Cadderly asked her. "He would—"

"Thobicus?"

Cadderly's face screwed up with confusion, not understanding the significance of Danica's interruption.

"Who has let pride temper his judgment now?" Danica asked accusingly. Still Cadderly did not understand. "Thobicus?" the monk reiterated. "Are you referring to *Dean* Thobicus?" Her emphasis on the title showed Cadderly the truth. Even the headmasters of the library would rarely refer to the highest ranking priest without the proper title.

Cadderly spent many moments considering his slip. Always before, he had taken care to refer to the respected dean in the proper fashion, always the name had come to him with the title unconsciously attached, and sounded discordant if he or someone else did not identify the man as the dean. Now though, for some reason, the simple reference to Thobicus seemed more harmonious.

"You used your magic against the leader of your order," Danica stated.

"I did what needed to be done," Cadderly decided. "Do not fear, for Thobicus,"—he had honestly meant to say "Dean Thobicus" this time—"does not even remember the incident. It was a simple thing to modify his memory, and he actually believes that he sent us out on a scouting mission. He expects that we will soon return to report on our enemy's activities, so that his foolish plans for a sweeping strike might be implemented."

There could be no doubt concerning the level of horror that Cadderly's admission had instilled in Danica. She actually backed away from the young priest, shaking her head, her mouth hanging open.

"How many thousands would perish in such a war?" the young priest cried loudly, getting Vander's attention, and causing Shayleigh, too, to open one sleepy eye. Predictably, the dwarven snoring went on uninterrupted.

"I could not let Thobicus do it," Cadderly continued against Danica's silent accusations. "I could not let the man's cowardice cause the deaths of perhaps thousands of innocent men, not when I saw a better way to end the threat."

"You act on presumption," Danica replied incredulously.

"On truth!" Cadderly shot back angrily, his tone leaving no doubt that he believed his claim with all of his heart.

"The dean is your superior," Danica reminded him, her tone somewhat more mellow.

"He is my superior in the eyes of a false hierarchy," Cadderly added, similarly softening his tones. He looked around at Shayleigh and Vander, both now keenly interested in what had been a private conversation. "Headmistress Pertelope was truly the highest ranking of the Deneirian priests," Cadderly asserted.

The statement caught Danica off guard—mainly because she had held Pertelope in the highest regard and had no doubt that Pertelope was among the wisest of the Edificant Library's hosts.

"It was Pertelope who guided me along this course," Cadderly went on. He seemed vulnerable suddenly, small and uncertain, an edge of doubt finding its way through his stubborn resolve.

"I need you beside me," he said to Danica, quietly so that Shayleigh and Vander would not hear. The elven maiden grinned, though, and respectfully closed her glistening violet eyes, and Cadderly knew that her keen ears had caught every syllable.

Danica stared into the starry sky for a long moment, then moved beside Cadderly, gently taking hold of his arm and shifting in close. She looked back to the fire and closed her eyes. Nothing more needed to be said.

Cadderly knew that Danica held some doubts, though, and he did, as well. He had taken a huge gamble in men-

tally attacking Thobicus, and had certainly shattered the
tenets of brotherhood and accepted hierarchy at the
library. Now he was on the course he knew in his heart to
be the proper one, but did the end justify the means?

With so many lives hanging on the decision, Cadderly
had to believe that, in this instance, it did.

* * * * *

At a campsite far down the mountain trails from Cadderly's company, four adventuring travelers slept soundly.
They did not notice their campfire take on a blue hue
momentarily, did not notice the dog face of Druzil the imp
peering out at them from within the flames.

Druzil muttered curses under his raspy breath, using the
crackle of flames to cover his undeniable anger. The imp
detested this scouting service, figured he would spend
many hours of sheer boredom listening to the snores of
inconsequential humans. He was Aballister's familiar,
though, in service (if not always in willing service) to the
wizard, and when Aballister had opened a planar gate in
Castle Trinity and ordered him away, Druzil had been compelled to obey.

The fiery tunnel had led here, warping through the
dimensions to the campfire Dorigen's scrying had targeted
in the eastern foothills of the Snowflakes. Using a bag of
magical blue powder, Druzil had turned the normal campfire into a gate similar to the one in Castle Trinity. Now the
imp clutched a pouch of red powder which could close the
gate behind him.

Druzil held back the red powder for a few moments,
wondering what fun he might find in allowing the planar
gate to remain open. What excitement might a host of
denizens from the lower planes cause?

The imp reconsidered immediately and poured the red
powder onto the flames. If he left the gate open and the
wrong creatures stepped through, then Castle Trinity's

plans for conquest of the region would be lost in a swirl of chaos and destruction.

He sat in the flames for more than an hour, watching the unremarkable men. "Aballister *bene tellemara*," he muttered many times, a phrase in the language of the lower planes which basically attributed the intelligence of a slug to Druzil's wizard master.

A movement to the side, beyond the campsite, caught Druzil's attention, and for a moment he thought—he hoped—that something exciting might happen. It proved to be just another of the men, however, walking a perimeter guard, apparently as bored as the imp. The man was gone from view in a few moments, back out into the darkness.

Another long hour slipped past, and the fire burned lower, forcing Druzil to crouch down to remain concealed by the flames. The imp shook his dog-faced head, his floppy ears waggling about the sides of his canine face. "Aballister *bene tellemara*," he hissed defiantly over and over, a litany against boredom.

The wizard had sent him out with the promise that he would find the mission enjoyable, but Druzil, used to the mundane activities most often associated with familiars, such as standing guard or gathering spell components, had heard that lie before. Even Dorigen's cryptic reference to "someone that the imp might find akin to his own heart," gave Druzil little hope. Cadderly was on his way to Castle Trinity—that was the place Druzil wanted to be, watching the magical explosions as Aballister finally blasted away his troublesome son.

The imp heard a noise again from the perimeter, a sort of gasping sound followed by some shuffling. Druzil lifted his dog face clear of the flames to get a better view, and saw the guard backpedaling, scrambling, his sword out in front of him and his mouth opened impossibly wide in a silent caricature of a scream.

It was the creature stubbornly pursuing the guard that sent shivers of warped delight up the imp's lizardlike spine.

It had once been human, Druzil guessed, but was now a
charred and blackened corpse, hideous and hunched, and
appeared as though all its bodily fluids had been sizzled
away. Druzil could actually smell the permeating evil that
had brought this wretched thing back to its undead state.

"Delicious," the imp rasped, his poison-tipped tail whipping about the embers behind him.

The guard continued to retreat, continued his futile
attempt at a scream. The creature slapped the horrified
man's sword to the side and grabbed him by the wrist, and
Druzil squeaked aloud with pleasure as the skin of the
doomed man's face took on a wrinkled, leathery appearance and his hair lost its youthful luster, lost all color, and
began to fall out in clumps.

The ghost's hand hit the man again, in the face, and his
eyes bulged and seemed as if they would pop free of their
sockets. From his opened mouth came gurgling, choking
sounds, and a wheeze of breath from lungs suddenly too
old and hardened to properly draw breath.

The dying man tumbled backward over a log and lay
very still on the ground, eyes and mouth still open impossibly wide.

A cry from the side of the camp showed that the commo-
tion had awakened one of the others. A sturdy man, a warrior judging from his well-muscled arms and chest, charged
across in front of the fire, boldly meeting the ghost. The
warrior's great sword sliced across, diving at the creature's
shoulder.

It seemed to connect, somewhat, but then passed right
through the undead thing, as though this creature was no
more than an insubstantial apparition. The ghost came on,
reaching with his one working arm, seeking another victim
for his insatiable hunger.

Druzil clapped his oversized hands together a hundred
times in glee, thoroughly enjoying the play. The other men
leaped up from their slumbers, one running off screaming
into the woods, but the other two coming to the aid of their

bold companion.

The creature caught one by the hair, seemingly oblivious to the frantic man's chopping axe as it turned the man's head aside and bit his throat. With hideous strength, the monster hurled the bloodied corpse away, to crash into the trees twenty feet beyond the edge of the campsite.

The remaining two men had seen enough, had seen too much. They turned and fled, one throwing his weapon aside in total, incomprehensible terror.

Ghost lunged for them once but missed, and then stood and watched their flight for just a moment before he began shuffling past the ruined campsite on his way once more, moving up into the Snowflakes as if this entire slaughter had been no more than a coincidental encounter. Druzil understood that the thing was savoring the screams of the fleeing men, though, taking perverse pleasure in their terror.

Druzil liked this creature.

The imp stepped out of the flames, looked down to the aged, dying man, laboring for breath, showing pain with every movement. Druzil heard the man's arm bone simply snap with age as he reached up for the air, heard a groan mixed in with the futile gasps.

The imp only laughed and looked away. Druzil had overheard part of Aballister's conversation with the spirit of Bogo Rath, and though that conversation had been cryptic, the imp now suspected that this horrid creature might hold a particular grudge against Cadderly. Certainly the monster seemed to be moving with purpose; it hadn't even taken the time or effort to pursue the fleeing men.

Druzil willed himself into a state of invisibility and flapped his leathery bat wings, rising up in pursuit of the ghost, thinking that perhaps he had been wrong to doubt Aballister's promises that this would be an enjoyable mission.

four

A Taste of What's to Come

Aballister walked through a large room filled with cages, admiring his private menagerie of exotic monsters. "Dorigen has spotted the young priest and his friends," the wizard said quietly, coming to a stop between two of the largest cages, each occupied by strange-looking beasts that seemed a mixture of two or more normal animals.

"Are you hungry?" Aballister asked one winged leonine monstrosity, its tail covered with a multitude of iron-hard spikes. The creature roared in reply and butted its massive, powerful chest against the bars of its cage.

"Then fly," the wizard cooed, opening the cage door and running his skinny hands through the monster's thick mane as it ambled past. "Dorigen will guide you to my wicked son. Do teach him a lesson." The old wizard cackled heartily. He had spent many private hours in this extra-dimensional region. He had actually created the place while studying in the Edificant Library. Aballister's biggest concerns at that time were the hovering priests always looking over his shoulder, making sure that his work was in accord with their strict rules. Little did they know that Aballister had circumvented their watchful gazes, had created this extra pocket of real space so that he could continue his most precious, if most dangerous, experiments.

That had been more than two decades before when Cadderly was a babe, and when, the wizard mused, the leonine monster and the three-headed beast behind it were also babes.

Aballister laughed aloud at the thought: he was sending two of his children out to kill the third.

The two powerful beasts followed Aballister out of the room and out of another door in the extradimensional mansion that led to the rocky ridge above Castle Trinity, where Dorigen, her crystal ball in hand, waited.

* * * * *

"We are too high up," Vander protested as the party trudged along a narrow mountain trail more than halfway up a twelve-thousand foot peak. A few scraggly branches, bare of leaves, dotted the trail, but mostly the place was wind-carved rock, ridged in some places, polished smooth in others. In this place, winter had already come in full. The snow lay deep, and the wind's bite, despite Cadderly's magical protection spells, forced the companions to continually rub their hands to keep their fingers from growing numb. The narrow trail was mostly bare to the stone, at least, perpetually windblown so that little snow had found a hold there.

"We must stay far from the lower trails," Cadderly replied, having to yell to be heard through the growling wind. "Many goblins and giantkin are about, fleeing Shilmista in search of their mountain holes."

"Better to face them than what we might find up here," Vander argued. The booming voice of the twelve-foot-tall giant, thick red beard crusted by blowing ice, had no trouble cutting through the din of the wind. "You do not know the creatures of the lands where the snow does not melt, young priest." The rugged firbolg was talking from some experience, it seemed, and the dwarves, Shayleigh, and Danica looked to Cadderly, hopeful that Vander's warning might carry some influence.

"Yeah, like that big bird I spotted, floating on the winds a mile away," Ivan put in.

"It was an eagle," Cadderly insisted, though only Ivan had actually seen the soaring creature. "Some of the eagles in the Snowflakes are quite large, and I doubt . . ."

"A mile away?" Ivan balked.

"I doubt that it was a mile," Cadderly finished, to which Ivan only shook his yellow-haired head, adjusted his helmet, which sported a pair of deer antlers, and cast a less-than-friendly glare Cadderly's way.

By that time, Cadderly had found a new person to argue with, as Danica came up behind him and put a hand on his shoulder. He looked at her grim expression and recognized at once that she was in agreement with the others.

"I fear no monsters," she explained defensively, for she alone understood the pains the young priest had endured to get this quest underway. "But the land here is treacherous, and the wind uncomfortable at best. A slip on the ice could send one of us tumbling down the mountainside." Danica looked up the slope to their right and continued ominously, "And the snow hangs thick above us."

Cadderly did not have to follow her upward gaze to understand that she was referring to the very real threat of an avalanche. They had passed the remnants of a dozen such disasters, though most were old, probably from last year's spring melt.

Cadderly took a deep breath and reminded himself of his secret purpose in being up this high, and he remained adamant. "The snow here is seasonal," he replied, calling ahead to Vander. "Except for the very tops of the mountains, where we shall not go."

Vander started to protest—Cadderly expected that the firbolg would argue that these fearful snow creatures might easily come down from the mountaintops when the snow lay so deep. He had barely uttered the first syllable of protest, though, when Cadderly interrupted him with a telepathic message, a magical plea that the firbolg lead on without further argument, that standing and talking only delayed the time when they could go back down to more hospitable climes.

Vander grunted and turned about, flipping his white bearskin cloak back over one shoulder to reveal to the others that his huge hand rested uneasily on the sculpted hilt of his giant-sized sword.

"As for the wind and the ice," Cadderly said to Danica, "we shall be careful with our steps and hold fast to our resolve."

"Unless we get plucked off by a passing bird," Ivan said dryly.

"It was only an eagle," Cadderly insisted again, turning on the dwarf, his anger flaring. Ivan shrugged and walked away. Pikel, seemingly oblivious to all the arguing and quite willing to go wherever the others led him, bobbed happily at his brother's side.

"Ye ever seen an eagle with four paws?" Ivan snarled over his shoulder when he and Pikel had moved away.

Pikel considered the question for a long moment before he stopped in his tracks, his smile melting away, and let out a profound, "Oooo."

Then the green-bearded dwarf skittered quickly to keep pace with the stomping Ivan. Together they walked right behind the firbolg and moved to Vander's sides when the trail was wide enough to accommodate them. The firbolg and the dwarves had become fast friends over the last days, continually trading tales of their respective homelands, places somewhat similar in rugged terrain and wicked beasts.

Cadderly came next in the procession, alone with his thoughts, still trying to reconcile his magical attack on Thobicus and contemplating the trials he knew that he would soon face, both at Castle Trinity and after Castle Trinity.

Danica allowed Cadderly to get some distance away before she resumed the march, her eyes revealing a mixture of contempt and pain at the way Cadderly had just rebuked her.

"He is scared," Shayleigh said to Danica, coming to her side.

"And stubborn," Danica added.

The elf maiden's sincere smile was too infectious for Danica to hold her grim thoughts. Danica was glad that Shayleigh was beside her once more, feeling an almost sisterly bond with the spirited elf. Given Cadderly's recent mood and recent secretive actions, Danica felt as though she desperately needed a sister.

For Shayleigh, the trip was both a debt repaid and an act of sincere friendship. Cadderly, Danica, and the dwarves had come to the fighting aid of Shilmista's elves, and during their time together, Shayleigh had come to like all of them. More than one of Shilmista's haughty elves had joked at Shayleigh's expense, at the thought that an elf could so befriend a dwarf, but Shayleigh took it all in without complaint.

Less than a half hour later, on an exposed section of trail where the mountain to their right sloped up at a gentle angle, though the drop to their left remained steep, Vander pulled up short and put his great hands out to the sides to halt the dwarves. It had begun to snow again, the wind whipping the icy flakes so that the companions all had to keep their traveling cloaks tight about their faces. In that poor visibility, Vander was unsure about the unusual shape he noticed on a wide section of trail up ahead.

The giant took a tentative step forward, drawing his massive sword halfway from its sheath. Ivan and Pikel leaned backward and looked to each other from behind the firbolg.

With simultaneous nods, they clutched their weapons, though they had no idea of what had put Vander on the alert.

Then Vander relaxed visibly, and the dwarves shared another shrug and tucked their hands back under their thick cloaks.

Two steps later, the shape, which Vander had identified as a snowbank, coiled up like some huge serpent and lashed out at the giant, brushing against his outstretched fingers.

Vander cried out and leaped back, grabbing at his suddenly bloody hand.

"The damn snow bit him!" Ivan yelled and rushed up, chopping with his double-headed axe. The blade passed right through the weird monster, clanging against the bare stone underneath, cutting nearly a quarter of the creature's bulk away.

But that quarter was just as alive, and just as vicious, as the main bulk, and now there were two monsters to fight.

Vander rushed in, chopping his sword with his one good hand.

Then there were three monsters.

Ivan felt an agonizing burn along one arm, but, blinded by the whipping wind and the battle frenzy, the dwarf did not realize the results of his actions. He brought his axe to bear repeatedly, unwittingly multiplying the monstrous ranks.

Cadderly had only just noticed the frenzied movements when Shayleigh's cry from behind turned him about. The young priest's eyes widened considerably when he saw the truth of Ivan's "eagle," a leonine beast taller than Cadderly and with a wingspan fully twenty-five feet across. The swooping creature did not come in close to Shayleigh and Danica, but instead abruptly broke the momentum of its dive, rearing in the air and whipping its tail over one muscled shoulder.

A volley of iron spikes shot out at the two. Danica pushed Shayleigh to the side, then contorted her own body somehow, miraculously avoiding any serious hits, though a line of blood, stark red against the white background, appeared immediately along the side of one arm.

Shayleigh was quick to ready her bow, but the leonine creature swooped away, and her shot was a long one, lost in the wind and the driving snow.

Up ahead, Vander got hit again and shrieked as Cadderly would never have believed the stoic and proud giant ever could. The young priest stumbled forward to discern the cause of the fighting, squinting and shaking his head, for he could not believe that his friends were fully surrounded by some sort of animated snow!

Their repeated blows had no effect—other than to create more monsters.

Cadderly fell into the song of Deneir, the logic that guided the harmony of his universe. He saw the spheres, not just the celestial spheres, but the magical spheres of elemental and energy-based powers. The simple and evident truths led Cadderly quickly to the conclusion that snow would best be battled with fire, and, hardly thinking about the movement, the young priest lifted his fist toward the largest section of creature between himself and his friends and uttered "*Fete!*" the Elvish word for fire.

A line of flames shot out from Cadderly's gold and onyx ring, engulfing several of the snow monsters in a sizzling blaze. Animated snow became insubstantial steam and gases, blowing away on the wind.

Then something struck hard against Cadderly's back, hurling him to the ground. Fear told him that the leonine monster must be back and he swung about, his clenched fist out in front.

He saw Danica standing protectively behind him and realized that it was she who had struck him. She now faced the newest beast that had entered the fray, a beast that had apparently been intent on the distracted young priest.

"Chimera?" Cadderly asked as much as stated when the winged, three-headed monster rushed in at Danica. Its central head and its torso were, like the other beast, those of a lion, but this one also had an orange scaled neck and head of a small dragon flanking it and a black goat's head behind.

The creature reared in midair; the dragon's head breathed forth a line of flame.

Danica jumped to the side away from Cadderly, then leaped up and caught a handhold on the stone above her, tucking her feet up high and somehow escaping the searing blast. She came back to the ledge after the fires had expired, but found no safe footing, for the flames had melted away the snow and weakened the integrity of that section of ledge. Ice reformed almost immediately in the freezing temperatures, and the young monk fell down hard onto her back. And then, dazed, Danica slipped out over the ledge.

Cadderly's world seemed to stop.

* * * * *

Farther down the trail, Shayleigh put her bow to deadly use, firing arrow after arrow at the leonine monster. Even with the powerful winds, many of her shots hit the mark, but the beast was resilient, and when its spike-throwing tail whipped about once more, Shayleigh had nowhere to run.

She grimaced at the dull thuds as several missiles blasted her to a half-sitting, half-leaning position on the mountain slope. She felt the sudden warmth of her own lifeblood flowing from several wounds. Stubbornly, the elf maiden put another arrow to her bowstring and let fly, scoring a solid hit in the monster's thick-muscled chest.

* * * * *

Cadderly dove flat to the stone, reached out desperately for Danica, who had gained a tentative handhold several feet below the ledge. She couldn't possibly climb up the ice in the driving wind and snow, and Cadderly, for all his straining, couldn't reach her.

The priest sang along with the song of Deneir, again seeking out an elemental sphere, this time searching for answers in the realm of air.

Danica heard his singing and looked up plaintively, knowing that her one hand would not keep her in place for very long.

Moments later, Cadderly ended the song, looked back at Danica, and commanded her in magically enhanced tones to jump up at him.

She did, trusting in her lover. Their hands brushed, just for a moment, but in that instant Danica heard Cadderly utter an arcane rune, a triggering word to a spell, and she felt a tingle as some power passed between them.

Then Danica plummeted away.

Cadderly had no time to watch her descent, had to trust fully in the revealed truths of his god. He looked all about and was relieved to see that the strong wind was working for them, forcing the two winged monsters to take long runs to get near the ledge.

Up ahead, Vander had used the break caused by Cadderly's fire to get out of the encircling monsters, and had taken Ivan with him, holding the dwarf in midair with a hand that seemed almost skinless.

Pikel had moved up a rock, but was again surrounded, beating the many vicious creatures back wildly with his tree-trunk club.

Cadderly lifted his onyx ring, but saw no clear angle. He fell into the song instead, entering the realm of fire.

"Me brother!" Ivan wailed, pulling free of Vander's grasp. The yellow-bearded dwarf expected Vander to rush in beside him, but when he glanced at the firbolg, he realized the awful truth. The snow creatures had hit Vander several times, on both hands and forearms and once, probably when the giant had stooped to hoist up Ivan, on the side of his face. In each of these places, Vander's skin had simply dissolved, leaving garish, brutal wounds.

Now the firbolg was beyond comprehension, swaying from side to side as he barely managed to stand.

"Oo, ow!" came a cry from ahead.

Pikel needed help.

Ivan took a running stride toward his brother, then fell back in absolute shock as a ring of flames erupted around Pikel and rolled down the rock.

"Me brother!" Ivan cried again, above the sudden roar. He wanted to go forward, was willing, in spirit at least, to throw himself through the unexplained fiery curtain and die beside his dear brother. But the heat was too intense as the flames continued outward, the curtain fully twenty feet high. Steam mixed with the fires as snow and ice and the creatures were fully consumed.

Above his despair, Ivan heard a cry of hope, heard Cadderly shout out for Pikel to "Stand fast!"

A goat head butted Ivan hard on the shoulder, and a lion's paw swatted the dwarf's head, launching him backward. He cracked into Vander's knee, his deer-antlered helmet tearing firbolg skin, and his momentum knocking the stunned giant's feet out from under him. Down came Vander, on top of Ivan.

* * * * *

Blood had filled one of Shayleigh's clear violet eyes. She saw Cadderly, though, lying on the ledge, saw the chimera strike the dwarf, then swoop away, caught by the mighty wind.

Cadderly drew out something small, fumbled with the heavy belt strapped diagonally across his chest, and began to sing. From the desperate look in the young priest's eyes, Shayleigh guessed that the leonine beast had returned.

It was barely visible, perhaps thirty feet out from the ledge. Shayleigh could see that its target this time was Cadderly, and possibly the fallen dwarf and giant not far from Cadderly's flank.

The monster darted in suddenly and reared, its deadly tail snapping forward.

"No!" the elf maiden cried, readying her bow. Looking back fearfully to the trail, she noticed a slight shimmer appear in the air before the priest. Shayleigh dismissed it as an optical trick of the snow and wind—until the mutant manticore's spikes entered that area and somehow reversed direction, shooting back out at the surprised beast!

Gouts of blood exploded against the leonine chest, driving the beast backward in the air. Shayleigh looked back to see Cadderly poised, hand-crossbow steadied across his free wrist. She quickly put an arrow into the monster's flank, thinking that Cadderly's tiny crossbow would be of little use.

The crossbow dart raced out at the monster. The lion roared—then roared louder as the quarrel stung its nose. For a moment, the bolt seemed a puny thing against the sheer bulk and strength of the beast, but then it collapsed on itself, crushing the vial of *Oil of Impact*. The resulting explosion sent bits of the monster's face and teeth scattering to the winds and drove the front end of the dart through the beast's thick skull.

Four paws flailing wildly, the dying monster dropped from sight.

Cadderly looked back to his ring of fire, confident that it had dispatched the snow creatures. All that remained was the chimera, floating somewhere out on the winds behind the blinding snow.

"Behind!" Shayleigh cried suddenly, spinning about and firing two quick arrows. The swooping chimera shrieked; its dragon head came in line with Cadderly, ready to loose its fiery breath once more.

Cadderly countered with a quick and simple magic, pulled from the element of water. A gusher erupted from his hands at the same time as the dragon head breathed, the fiery breath dissipating into a cloud of harmless steam.

The chimera burst through the gray veil right above the

young priest, foreclaws slashing at Cadderly and knocking him to the ground.

"Ye mixed up bag o' body parts!" Ivan hooted, finally extracting himself from under the fallen giant. Two running steps put the infuriated dwarf alongside the soaring monster, and he leaped up, grabbing a horn of the black goat's head and pulling himself astride the beast.

Shayleigh followed their swooping path, ready to let fly another arrow, but she pulled up suddenly, stunned.

Danica had come back up to their level. She was walking in midair!

The chimera, all three heads looking back at those it had left behind on the ledge or at the furious dwarf scrambling about on its back, never saw the monk. Danica's spinning kick cracked the leonine jaw and nearly sent the five hundred pound monster tumbling headlong, and then agile Danica was up beside Ivan before the chimera could begin to react.

She drew out a silver-hilted dagger from one boot, wrapped its sculpted dragon head with her free hand and went to vicious work on the central leonine head. Even more furious was Ivan Bouldershoulder, hands clasped about the goat horns, wrestling the thing back and forth.

The chimera banked in a steep roll, coming alongside the ledge so that Shayleigh managed another two shots before the snowstorm swallowed the beast and her friends.

The chimera came around again a moment later, and the elf prepared to fire. But Ivan suddenly popped up and regarded her incredulously, one of Shayleigh's arrows splintered and hanging from his deer-antlered helmet.

"Hey!" the dwarf bellowed, and she lowered the bow. Ivan's distraction cost him, though, for the goat's head broke free of his grasp momentarily and butted hard against his face and forehead. Ivan spit out a tooth, grabbed the horns in both hands and butted back, and it seemed to Shayleigh that the dwarf's attack had been by far the more effective.

Then they were gone again, behind the blinding sheets of snow. All was suddenly silent, save the howl of the wind. Vander stirred and propped himself up on his elbows; Cadderly's enchanted wall of fire came down, to reveal Pikel sitting comfortably on the stone, munching a leg of mutton he had opportunistically pulled from his pack and roasted in the magical flames.

"Oo," the green-bearded dwarf said, hiding the meat behind his back when he noticed Cadderly's amazed expression.

"Do you see them?" Shayleigh asked, limping to Cadderly's side and directing his gaze back to the empty air.

Cadderly peered through the snow and shook his head. When he looked back to Shayleigh, though, all thoughts of his monster-riding friends were replaced by the immediate needs of the wounded elf maiden. Several spikes had struck Shayleigh, one grazing the side of her head and opening a wicked gash, another deep into one thigh, a third driven into her wrist so that she could not close her hand, and a fourth sticking from her ribs. Cadderly could hardly believe that the elf was still standing, let alone firing her bow.

He listened for the song of Deneir immediately, bringing forth magics that would allow him to begin the mending of Shayleigh's wounds. Shayleigh said nothing, just grimaced stoically as Cadderly slowly drew out the spikes. All the while, the elf maiden held fast to her bow, kept her gaze out to the wide winds in search of her missing friends.

Minutes slipped past. Cadderly had the worst of the wounds closed, and Shayleigh signaled that to be enough for the time being. Cadderly didn't argue, turning his attention back to the search for Danica and Ivan.

"If the monster shakes free of them . . . " Shayleigh began ominously.

"Danica will not fall," Cadderly assured her. "Not with the enchantment I have put upon her. Nor will she allow Ivan to fall."

There was honest conviction in the priest's tone, but he sighed with some relief anyway when the chimera finally came back into view, speeding on a course that would take it directly above the ledge. Shayleigh lifted her bow, but her injured wrist would no longer allow her to pull the string back fast enough. Cadderly got a shot with his crossbow, but the chimera banked and the explosive quarrel flew harmlessly wide.

The monster roared in protest as it passed without any attacks, and the friends on the ledge could see that both its dragon and goat heads flopped lifelessly in the wind. Ivan, clutching the leonine mane, howled with enjoyment as he attempted to steer the beast by tugging one way or the other.

"Jump free!" Danica cried to the dwarf as the mountain loomed before them. The young woman stepped off the creature as it passed the ledge, skipped down across the empty air (to Pikel's amazed cry of "Oo oi!" and Vander's incredulous stare) to join Cadderly and Shayleigh.

"Jump free!" Danica yelled again, this time with Shayleigh and Cadderly joining in.

The yellow-bearded dwarf didn't seem to hear them, and Danica prudently rushed back out from the ledge in case the beast headed out into the empty air once more. The chimera did bank against Ivan's stubborn pull and start back out, but this time, both Cadderly and Shayleigh were presented with perfect shots. Shayleigh's arrow dove deep into the chimera's torso, and Cadderly's quarrel got the beast on the wing, its explosive force shattering bone and sending the beast into a repeated barrel roll.

Ivan tugged and yanked frantically, looking for some place to safely land as the creature flopped about, turning back toward the towering mountain.

"Jump!" the companions pleaded with the dwarf.

"Snowbank!" Ivan yelled in high hopes, twisting the monster's head in line with a white pile jutting above the smooth slope of the mountain, just a dozen or so feet above the ledge. "Snowbank!"

Not quite—the inch of snow covering the jutting boulder did not, by any definition, constitute a snowbank.

"Boom," remarked a grimacing Pikel as the chimera and Ivan crashed heavily, the dwarf bouncing back, skidding and slipping until he came to a stop, amazingly on his feet on the ledge.

The crushed chimera thrashed about near the rock until Shayleigh's next arrow sank into the leonine head, ending its agony.

Ivan turned to regard Cadderly and the others, his pupils rolling about their sockets independently of each other. Somehow, Ivan still wore his deer-antlered helmet, and somehow, Shayleigh's splintered arrow had not been dislodged.

"Who knowed?" Ivan asked innocently, giving a lame attempt at shrugging his shoulders as he fell facedown on the path.

Five

Test of Willpower

Cadderly and Shayleigh broke immediately for the stunned dwarf, but Danica rushed back to the ledge, grabbed Cadderly and spun him about, her lips crushing against his as she kissed him hard. She backed off suddenly, her features twisted with admiration and appreciation—and ecstacy.

Her breath came in excited gasps; her eyes darted wildly, from the open air beyond the ledge to her enchanted feet and to the man who had saved her life. "I want to do it again!" she blurted, fumbling over the words as though she couldn't help but say them.

Cadderly seemed perplexed, until he realized that his love had just walked on air. What an incredible experience that must have been! He stared at Danica for a long moment. Then, remembering Ivan's situation, he looked to Pikel, who was happily munching on his roasted mutton once more (apparently, Ivan was not too badly injured), and

looked to the rock where Ivan and the chimera had abruptly
ended their wild ride. All of this apparent insanity in the
midst of a desperate plan, the success of which could well
determine the very existence of the peoples of the region.

And Danica's sparkling brown eyes, so full of admiration,
told Cadderly something more. He was coming to the forefront of it all, inevitably taking up the lead in this crusade.
He had grabbed at this responsibility—fully when he had
bent Dean Thobicus's mind—but now, as the true weight of
that responsibility became clearer to him, he was worried.
Always before, Cadderly had depended on his powerful
friends. He pointed the way, and they, through stealth and
sword, facilitated the plans. Now, though, judging from the
look in Danica's eyes, Cadderly's burden had increased.
His mounting magical powers had become the group's pri-
mary weapon.

Cadderly would not shy away from his new role, would
fight on with all his heart and all his strength. But he wondered if he could live up to his friends' expectations, if he
could continue to keep Danica's eyes sparkling.

It was all too much for the burdened young priest. What
began as an embarrassed chuckle ended with Cadderly
sitting on the stone ledge, laughing at the very edge of hysteria.

The sight of Vander, up again and moving toward him,
sobered Cadderly. Although Vander's brutal wounds had
already somehow begun to mend, the giant's face showed
his pain, and showed that Vander did not see anything
humorous about their situation.

"I told you that we were too high up," the firbolg said in a
low, firm voice.

Cadderly thought for a moment, then began to explain to
the giant that, while the strange, animated snow creature
might have been natural to the region, both the chimera
and the other winged beast, the mutated manticore, were
magical in nature and not denizens of the cold and desolate
high peaks. Cadderly never finished the explanation,

though, suddenly realizing the implications of his own thoughts.

Magical creatures?

What a fool I've been! Cadderly thought, and to Vander and his friends he offered only a sudden, confused expression. The young priest closed his eyes and mentally probed the region, sought out the magical eye of the scrying wizard—for someone had certainly guided the two monsters! Almost immediately, he felt the connection, felt the directed line of magical energy that could only be the probing of a scrying wizard and promptly released a countering line to disperse it. Then Cadderly threw up magical defenses, put a veil around himself and his friends that would not be easily penetrated by distant, probing eyes.

"What is it?" Danica demanded when he had at last reopened his gray eyes.

Cadderly shook his head, then looked to Vander. "Find a sheltered area where we might set a camp and mend our wounds," he instructed the firbolg. Danica was still staring at him, waiting for an explanation, but the young priest only offered another shake of his head, feeling positively foolish for not warding them all against scrying wizards much earlier in the journey.

Again Cadderly wondered if he would disappoint those who had come to trust in him.

* * * * *

The chimera and the manticore were Aballister's creatures, his children, brought into existence and nurtured to mighty maturity by the magics of the powerful wizard. When they fell in the mountains, Aballister sensed the loss, as though a part of his own energy had been stripped from him. He left his private quarters so abruptly that he didn't even bother to close his spellbook, or to put up wards against intruders. The old wizard bounded down the hall to Dorigen's room and pounded on the door, disrupting the woman's studying.

"Find them," Aballister snarled as soon as Dorigen opened the door, pushing his way in.

"What do you know?" she asked.

"Find them!" Aballister commanded again. He spun about and grabbed Dorigen by the hand, pulling her to the seat before her crystal ball.

Dorigen tore her hand free of Aballister's grasp and eyed him dangerously.

"Find them!" the older wizard growled at her for the third time, not retreating an inch from her threatening glare.

Dorigen recognized the urgency in Aballister's wizened face, knew that he would not have come in here and treated her with such disrespect if he was not terribly afraid. She uncovered the crystal ball and stared into the item for a long while, concentrating on reestablishing the connection to Cadderly. Several moments passed with the ball showing nothing but its swirling gray mist. Dorigen pressed on, commanding the mist to form an image.

The ball went perfectly black.

Dorigen looked up to Aballister helplessly, and the older wizard pushed her aside and took her place. He went at the ball with all his magical strength, throwing his incredible willpower against the black barriers. Someone had warded against scrying. Aballister growled and threw more magical strength into the effort, almost punching through the black veil. The power of the defenses told him unmistakably who the defender might be.

"No!" Aballister growled, and he went at the barrier again, determined to force his way through those wards.

The ball remained inactive.

"Damn him!" Aballister cried, slapping the crystal from its stand. Dorigen caught the solid ball as it rolled off the table's edge. She saw Aballister wince, though the wizard stubbornly did not grab at his already swelling hand.

"Your son is more formidable . . . " Dorigen began, but

Aballister cut her short with an animal-like growl. He leaped up from his seat and sent the stool bouncing away.

"My son is a troublesome insect," Aballister sneered, thinking of many ways that he might make Cadderly and his friends pay for the loss of the chimera and the manticore. "The next surprise that I will send to him will be a measure of my own powers."

A shudder coursed along Dorigen's spine. She had never heard Aballister more determined. She was Aballister's student, had witnessed many powerful displays of magic from the older man—and had known that those were just a fraction of what he was capable of launching.

"Find them!" Aballister growled again between sharp, hissing breaths, and, on as close an edge of uncontrollable rage as Dorigen had ever seen him, he swept from the room, slamming the door behind him.

Dorigen nodded as though she meant to try, but as soon as she was convinced that Aballister would not immediately return, she replaced the ball in its support and draped a cloth over it. Cadderly had countered the magic, and the scrying device would not function for at least a day, Dorigen knew. In truth, she didn't expect to find any more success the next day, either, for Cadderly was apparently on to her secret prying now and would not likely let his guard slip again.

Dorigen looked to the closed door and thought again that Aballister did not understand the power of his son. Nor the compassion, she realized as she clenched her still-mending hands and considered that, by Cadderly's mercy alone, she was still very much alive.

But neither did Cadderly understand the power of his father. Dorigen was glad that Druzil, and not she, had been sent out near the young priest, for when Aballister struck out at Cadderly the next time, it seemed to Dorigen that mountains would be leveled.

* * * * *

When Danica awakened, the glow of the fire was low, barely illuminating the nearest features of the wide cave the party had found. She heard the comforting snores of the dwarves, Ivan's grumbles complementing Pikel's whistles, and could feel that Shayleigh was soundly resting near the wall behind her.

Vander, too, was asleep, propped against a stone on the other side of the low fire. The night was dark and calm, and the snow had ceased, though the lessened wind continued a quiet, steady moan at the wide cave door. By all appearances, the campsite seemed quite serene, but the monk's keen instincts told her that something was not as it should be.

She propped herself up on her elbows and looked about. A second glow showed in the cave, far to the side and partially blocked by Cadderly's sitting form. Cadderly? Danica looked to the wide cave entrance, to where the young priest should have been standing a watch.

She heard a slight rattle, and then some soft chanting. Silently, Danica slipped out of her bedroll and eased her way across the stone floor.

Cadderly sat cross-legged before a lit candle, a parchment spread on the floor beside him, its ends anchored by small stones. Next to that was the young priest's writing kit and the *Tome of Universal Harmony*, the holy book of Deneir, both opened. Danica crept closer, heard Cadderly's low chanting, and saw the young priest drop some ivory counters to the floor in front of him.

He marked something on the parchment, then tossed a fresh quill into the air before him, watching as it spun to the stone, then making a note of its direction. Danica had been around priests long enough to understand that her love was engaged in some sort of divination spell.

Danica nearly jumped and cried aloud when she felt a hand on her back, but she kept her wits enough to take the moment to recognize Shayleigh moving up beside her. The elf looked curiously to Cadderly, then back to Danica, who only shook her head and held her hands up wide.

Cadderly read something from the book, then fumbled with his pack and produced a small, gold-edged mirror and a pair of mismatched gloves, one black and one white.

Danica's mouth dropped open. Cadderly had brought the *Ghearufu*, the evil three-piece artifact that the assassin had carried, the same powerful item that Dean Thobicus had insisted be turned over for inspection!

The significance of the *Ghearufu* sent a myriad of questions hurtling through Danica's thoughts. From what she had seen, and from what Cadderly had told her, this was an item of possession—might Cadderly's strange behavior, his hysterical laughter on the ledge, and his insistence that the group remain dangerously high in the mountains, be somehow linked to the *Ghearufu*? Was Cadderly himself fighting against some sort of possession, some evil entity that clouded his judgment while leading them all astray?

Shayleigh again put a hand on Danica's back and looked to the monk with concern, but a movement to the side distracted them both.

Vander crossed the floor in three easy strides, grabbed Cadderly by the back of his tunic, and lifted the young priest from the floor.

"What are you about?" the firbolg demanded loudly. "Do you stand your watch from inside . . . ?" The words caught in Vander's throat; the blood drained from his ruddy face. There before him lay the *Ghearufu*, the evil device that had held him as a slave for many tragic years.

Danica and Shayleigh rushed over to them, Danica fearing that Vander, in his surprise and horror, might hurl Cadderly across the cave.

"What *are* you about?" Danica agreed with Vander, but as she spoke, she crossed in front of the firbolg and strategically placed her thumb against a pressure point in Vander's forearm, quietly forcing the giant to release his grip.

Cadderly scowled and straightened his tunic, then went to gather his possessions. At first, he seemed embarrassed, but then, when he looked back to Danica's resolute stare, he steeled his gray eyes resolutely.

"You should not have brought that," Danica said to him.

Cadderly did not immediately respond, though his thoughts were screaming that the *Ghearufu* was the main reason that they were there.

The other three exchanged worried glances.

"We have come for Castle Trinity," Danica argued.

"That is but one reason," Cadderly replied cryptically. He wasn't sure whether he should tell them the truth or not, wasn't sure that he wanted to compel them to accompany him to the terrible place where the *Ghearufu* could be destroyed.

Danica felt Vander's muscles tighten, and she leaned back more firmly against the firbolg to prevent him from leaping out and throttling the young priest.

"Do you always keep such important secrets from those who travel beside you?" Shayleigh asked. "Or do you believe that trust is not an essential element of any adventuring party?"

"I would have told you!" Cadderly snapped at her.

"When?" Danica growled at him from the other side. He looked back between the two, and to Vander's outraged expression, and seemed to be losing his nerve.

"Has the *Ghearufu* found a hold on you?" Danica asked bluntly.

"No!" Cadderly shot back at once. "Though it has tried. You cannot imagine the depth of evil within this artifact."

Vander cleared his throat, a pointed reminder that the firbolg had felt the *Ghearufu*'s sting long before Cadderly even knew that the item existed.

"Then what use might it be?" Shayleigh snarled.

Cadderly bit his lower lip, glancing one way and the other. He suspected that his companions would not agree with his priorities, would still consider Castle Trinity the most important of their missions. Again doubts about being in the forefront assaulted the young priest. He told himself that he owed his friends an explanation at least.

But that was just a rationalization, Cadderly knew. He wanted to tell his friends, wanted them to line up beside him on this most dangerous of duties.

"We have come out in search of Castle Trinity," he explained, his conscience gnawing over every word. "But that is only one purpose. I have done much searching and have discerned that there are few—very few—ways in which the *Ghearufu* might be truly destroyed."

"This could not have waited?" Danica asked.

"No!" Cadderly retorted angrily. At his suddenly explosive tone, the three doubters again exchanged concerned glances, and Danica virtually snarled as she regarded the *Ghearufu*.

"If I had left the *Ghearufu* at the library, we cannot even guess the extent of the disaster we would have found upon our return," Cadderly explained, his voice even once more. "And if we take it with us all the way to Castle Trinity, our enemies might find a way to use it against us." He, too, looked down at the item, his face flushed with fear.

"But it will not get to that dangerous point," the young priest insisted. "There is a way to end the threat of the *Ghearufu* forever. That is why we took the high trails," he explained, eyeing Vander directly. "There is a peak near here, somewhat legendary in the region."

"Fyrentennimar?" Danica balked, and Shayleigh, recognizing the dreaded name, gave an unintentional wheeze.

"The peak is called Nightglow," Cadderly continued, undaunted. "In decades past, it was said to burn with inner fires in the dark of night, a glow that could be seen from Carradoon and all across the Shining Plains."

"A volcano," Vander reasoned, remembering his own rugged home, tucked among many lava-spewing peaks.

"A dragon," Danica corrected. "An old red, according to the legend."

"Older still since the tales date back two centuries or more," Shayleigh added gravely. "And not just a legend," she assured them. "Galladel, who was King of Shilmista Forest, remembered the time of the dragon, remembered the devastation old Fyren brought to Carradoon and to the forest."

"The damned fool boy is thinking o' waking a dragon?" Ivan bellowed, storming up to join the circle about Cadderly. In the intrigue, no one had noticed that the rhythmic dwarven snoring had ceased.

"Uh-uhhh," Pikel said to Cadderly, waggling one finger back and forth in front of his face.

"Do you wish the *Ghearufu* destroyed?" Cadderly asked simply, aiming the thought at Vander, whom he considered his best prospect for an ally against the rising tide of protest.

The firbolg seemed truly torn.

"At what cost?" Danica demanded before Vander could sort out his thoughts. "The dragon has slept for centuries— centuries of peace. How many lives will it need to satisfy its hunger upon awakening?"

"Let a sleeping wyrm lie, me Pappy always said," Ivan piped in.

"Yup," added Pikel, nodding eagerly.

Cadderly gave a resigned sigh, scooped the *Ghearufu* into his pack, and hoisted it over one shoulder. "I have been directed to destroy the *Ghearufu*," he said, his voice full of resignation. "There is only one way."

"Then it must wait," Danica replied. "The threat to all the region . . . "

"Is a temporary danger in a temporary society," Cadderly finished philosophically. "The *Ghearufu* is not temporary. It has pained the world since its creation in the lower planes many millennia ago.

"I'll not force this upon you," Cadderly went on calmly. "I have been directed by the precepts of a god that you do not worship. Go and speak among yourselves, come to a decision together or individually. This quest is mine, and yours only by your own choice. And you are right," he said to

Shayleigh, seeming sincerely apologetic. "I erred in not revealing this to you all when first we left the library. The situation was . . . difficult." He looked at Danica as he ended, knowing that she alone understood what he had gone through to "convince" Dean Thobicus.

The others moved across the cavern floor slowly, each of them glancing back at Cadderly many times.

"The boy's daft," Ivan insisted, loudly enough so that Cadderly could hear.

"He follows his heart," Danica replied quietly.

"I, too, do not doubt Cadderly's sincerity," Shayleigh added. "It is his wisdom that I question."

Pikel continued to nod his eager agreement.

"To wake a dragon," Vander said grimly, shaking his head.

"A red," Danica pointedly added, for red dragons were the wickedest and most powerful of all the evil dragons. "Perhaps an ancient red by now."

Still Pikel nodded, and Ivan slapped him on the back of his head.

"Oo," the green-bearded dwarf said, glaring at his brother.

"Ye don't go waking wyrms," Ivan put in, again loud enough for Cadderly to hear.

"There is something else I fear," Danica said. "Is Cadderly being correctly guided by his god, or is the *Ghearufu* wrongly leading him to where it might find a powerful ally?"

The thought made the others rock back on their heels, brought profound sighs from Shayleigh and Vander and a drawn-out "Ooooooo" from Pikel and Ivan, who then, apparently realizing that he was mimicking Pikel, snapped his head about to regard his brother suspiciously.

"What do we do?" Shayleigh asked.

They stood quietly for many moments before Danica dared a decision. "The threat now is Castle Trinity," she declared.

"But the *Ghearufu* does not come along with us," Vander insisted, barely able to keep his giant voice quiet. "We can bury it here, in the mountains, and return for it when the other business is completed."

"Cadderly will not agree," Shayleigh reasoned, looking at the resolute young priest.

"Then we won't ask him," Ivan replied with a sly wink. He looked Danica's way and nodded, and Danica, after a plaintive look at the man she loved, returned the nod. Alone, she moved toward Cadderly, and Ivan figured the young man would be in the bag in a moment.

"You will not go along to Nightglow," Cadderly stated, not asked, as Danica approached.

Danica said nothing. Unconsciously, she clenched and unclenched a fist at her side—a movement that Cadderly did not miss.

"The *Ghearufu* is paramount," the young priest said.

Danica still did not reply. Cadderly read her thoughts, though, saw that she was struggling with her decided course and understood that course to be one hinting at treachery. He began to sing under his breath as Danica moved in at him. Suddenly her manner became urgent; she tried to grab him, but found that he had become something insubstantial.

"Help me!" Danica called to her friends, and they rushed over, Ivan and Pikel diving for Cadderly's legs. The dwarves knocked their heads together, locked in a wrestling tumble, and it took them a few seconds to understand that they had grabbed on to nothing more than each other.

For Cadderly's corporeal form was fast fading, scattering to the wind.

On the Path

Druzil sat on a broken stump, clawed fingers tapping anxiously against his skinny legs. The imp knew the way to the Edificant Library from this point, and knew that the malignant spirit had veered off in the wrong direction and was now headed into the open and wild mountains.

Druzil was not overly disappointed—he really didn't want to go near the awful library again, and doubted that even this powerful spirit would last very long against the combined strength of the many goodly priests living there. The imp was confuscd, though. Was this spirit guided by any real purpose, as Druzil had initially believed, as Aballister had led him to believe? Or would the wretched thing wander aimlessly through the mountains, destroying whatever creatures it accidentally happened upon?

The thought did not sit well with the impatient imp. Logically, Druzil realized that there must be some important connection with this monster, probably a connection

concerning Cadderly. If not, then why would Aballister
have dispatched him to keep a watch over the uncontrollable thing?

Too many questions assaulted the imp, too many possibilities for Druzil to consider. He looked at the monster,
tearing and slashing its way along a northern trail, frightening animals and ripping plants with seemingly endless savagery. Then Druzil looked inward, brought his focus into
that magical area common to extraplanar creatures, and
sent his thoughts careening across the mountain passes,
seeking a telepathic link with his wizard master. For all the
urgency of his call, he was nevertheless surprised when
Aballister eagerly responded to his mental intrusions.

Where is Cadderly? the wizard's thoughts came to him.
Has the ghost caught up to him?

Many of Druzil's questions had just been answered.
Aballister's mental interrogation rolled on; the wizard prodded Druzil's thoughts with a series of questions so quickly
that Druzil didn't even have time to respond. The conniving
imp understood immediately that he held the upper hand in
this communication, that Aballister was desperate for
answers.

Druzil rubbed his clawed hands together, enjoying the
superiority, confident that he could get all the information
he needed by bargaining answer for answer.

Druzil opened his eyes many minutes later, having a new
perspective on the situation. Aballister had been nervous—
Druzil could sense that, both from the intensity of the wizard's telepathic responses and from the fact that Aballister
had apparently left little unanswered this time. The wizard
was a cryptic sort, always withholding information that he
did not believe his lessers needed to know. Not this time,
though. This time, the wizard had flooded Druzil with information about the ghost and Cadderly.

Given the imp's understanding about his master's
demeanor, there could be no doubt that Aballister was tee-
tering on a very dangerous edge. Ever since the wizard had

called Druzil to his side, the imp had longed to see Aballister's power revealed in full. He had seen Aballister strike down a rival with a lightning bolt, literally frying the man; he had seen the wizard engulf a cave of upstart goblins with a ball of fire that had scored the stones and killed every one of the beasts; he had traveled to the far northland with the wizard, and had watched Aballister wipe out an entire community of taers, shaggy white beasts.

But those were just hints, Druzil knew, tantalizing tastes of what was yet to come. Even though he had never truly respected the wizard (Druzil had never respected any being from the Material Plane), he had always sensed the man's inner power. Aballister, nervous and edgy, outraged that his own son would be the one to threaten his designs on the region, was boiling like a pot about to blow.

And Druzil, malicious and chaotic in the extreme, thought the whole thing perfectly delicious.

He gave a flap of his wings and set off in pursuit of the now-distant ghost. Following the creature's trail—a wide swath of near-total destruction—was not difficult, and Druzil had the creature in sight in less than an hour.

He decided to try to contact the creature, to solidify his alliance with the ghost before it caught up to Cadderly, and before Aballister could lay claim to its destructive powers. Still invisible, the imp flew around in front of the marching ghost and perched on a low branch in a pine tree farther up its intended path.

The ghost sniffed the air as Druzil passed, even took a lazy swing that was far behind the fast-flying imp. As soon as Druzil had moved beyond its reach, it seemed to pay the unseen disturbance no more heed.

Druzil materialized as the ghost approached. "I am a friend," he announced, both in the common tongue and telepathically.

The creature snarled and came on more quickly, a blackened arm leading the way.

"Friend," Druzil reiterated, this time in the growling and

hissing language common to the lower planes.

Still the advancing creature, focused on Druzil as though the imp was simply one more thing to be destroyed, did not respond. Druzil hit the ghost with a telepathic barrage, every thought signifying friendship or alliance, but the monster remained unresponsive.

"Friend, you stupid thing!" Druzil shouted, hopping to his feet and snapping his knuckles against his hips in a defiant stance. The creature was only a few yards away.

A snarl and a leap brought the monster right up to Druzil, the one unbroken arm coming about. The imp squeaked, suddenly realizing the danger, and gave a frantic flap of his wings to lift away.

Ghost ripped the branch right from the tree, hurled it aside, and smashed on viciously, and Druzil, caught within the canopy of thick evergreen boughs, scrambled for his very life, wings beating and claws tearing, trying to force some opening where he could slip through to the open air. He willed himself invisible again, but the monster seemed to sense him anyway, for the pursuit remained focused and relentless.

The creature was right behind him.

Druzil's whiplike tail, dripping lethal venom, snapped into the creature's face, blowing a wide hole in its hollowed cheek.

The creature didn't even flinch. The powerful arm came about again, tearing away a large branch, opening up the tangle enough so that the next attack would not be deflected.

Druzil clawed and kicked, fighting against the canopy wildly. And then he was through, bursting into the air where a few wingbeats brought him far from the snarling monster's reach.

The undead monster emerged from the battered tree a few moments later, stalking along the path, apparently giving no more concern to the latest creature that had fled from its terrifying power.

"Bene tellemara," the thoroughly shaken imp muttered, finding a perch on a jutting stone overlooking the trail and watching the uncontrollable monster's steady and undeniable progress.

"Bene tellemara."

* * * * *

Waist-deep in snow, Cadderly looked up the high, steep slope to the fog-enshrouded peak of Nightglow. Even using his magical spells to ward off the cold, the young priest felt the bite of the blasting wind and a general numbness creeping into his legs. He considered calling upon his most powerful magics then, as he had done to escape his misinformed friends, so he could walk along the wind up the mountainside.

Cadderly quickly reconsidered, though, realizing that he could not afford to expend any more magical energy—not with an old red dragon waiting for him. He shook his head determinedly and trudged on, step after step, hoisting one leg out of the deep, bogging snow and setting it firmly ahead of him.

One step at a time, higher and higher.

The sun had risen, the day bright and clear, and Cadderly had to squint constantly against the stinging glare of the rays reflecting off the virgin snow. Every now and then a section would shift under his weight and groan, and Cadderly would hold very still, expecting an avalanche to tumble down about him.

He thought he heard a call on the wind, Danica perhaps, shouting out his name. It was not an impossibility; he had left his friends not so far from here, and he had told them where he was headed.

That thought made Cadderly realize again how vulnerable he must now seem, a black dot on an exposed sheet of whiteness, climbing slowly, barely moving. Were any more chimeras or other winged beasts circling the area, hungry

for his blood? he wondered. Right before he had begun the
climb of this last slope, he had mentally searched for any
signs of scrying wizards. None were apparent, but Cadderly had put up a few wards anyway.

Still, standing in the open on that slope, the young priest
was not comforted. He pulled his cloak up tighter about his
neck and considered again what magics he might call upon
to facilitate this brutal climb.

In the end, though, he used only sheer determination.
His legs ached, and he found his breathing hard to come by
because of the thinner air and the exertion. He found a
region of bare stone again higher up, under the foggy veil,
and was somewhat surprised until he realized the reason
that this area seemed much warmer. Using the warmth as a
guiding beacon, Cadderly worked his way around a jutting
hunk of stone and found a cave opening of good size,
though certainly not large enough for the likes of an adult
dragon.

The young priest understood that he had found Fyrentennimar, though, for the lair of only one type of creature
could emanate enough warmth to melt the snow atop wintry Nightglow.

Cadderly unwrapped some of his outer clothing and
plopped down to catch his breath and rest his weary limbs.
He considered again the mighty foe he would soon face and
the repertoire of spells he would need if he was to have any
chance at all in this desperate quest.

"Desperate?" Cadderly whispered, pondering the sound
of the grim word. Even the determined young priest had
begun to wonder if "foolhardy" might be a better descrip-
tion.

Seven

Awe

Cadderly could not believe how warm the air grew as soon as he moved through the opening on the mountainside. He was in more of a tunnel than a cave, its walls running tight and uneven, gradually making its wormhole way down toward the heart of the mountain.

The young priest removed his traveling cloak, bundled it tight, and put it in his pack, carefully wrapping it about the *Tome of Universal Harmony*. He considered leaving the great book, and some of his other most prized possessions by the entrance, fearing that even if he somehow survived his encounter with Fyrentennimar, some of his items might be burned away.

With a defiant shake of the head, Cadderly replaced the pack over his shoulder. Now was not the time for negative thinking, he decided. He took out a cylindrical metal tube and popped off the end cap, loosing a concentrated beam of light (from a magical enchantment placed on a disk inside the tube) ahead of him. Then he set off, recalling the song of Deneir as he went, knowing that he might have to call on his magical energy in an instant's notice if he was to have any chance at all against the great dragon.

Twenty minutes later he was still walking, creeping down a loose-packed slide of rocks. The heat was more intense now; even after Cadderly dispelled his cold-protecting magic, the sweat beaded on his forehead and stung his gray eyes.

He passed through several larger chambers as he moved down the tunnels, and he felt vulnerable indeed with only a small area illuminated in front of him and thick darkness looming to both sides. A twist of the outer metal shell of his device retracted the tube, somewhat widening the light beam, but still, Cadderly had to fight the nervous urge to call upon his magic and brighten the entire area.

He breathed easier when he went back into a narrow tunnel, too narrow, certainly, for any dragon to squeeze through. The floor sloped downward at an easy, gradual angle for more than a hundred feet, but then suddenly turned vertical, a crawl hole dropping away into the darkness.

Sitting on the lip, Cadderly secured his gear and strapped his light tube under the bandolier so that it aimed down below him. Then he eased himself over, picking his way carefully.

The air was stifling, the rocks pressed in on him, but Cadderly continued the descent, moving until he found the hole suddenly opening wide below him. For an instant, his feet kicked free in empty air, and he nearly fell through. Somehow he managed to secure his position, hooking one elbow over a jag, and getting his feet back up so that he could press them against the solid wall. With his free hand, the young priest tentatively reached for his light tube, angled it down and out from him to find that he had come to the ceiling of a wide cavern.

A wide and high cavern, Cadderly feared, for the light

did not reveal any floor below him. For the first time since he had entered the tunnels, he wondered if his path would actually get him anywhere near the dragon. Obviously, the small cave opening in the side of the mountain was not the huge dragon's doorway; Cadderly had not considered that perhaps the cave networks within the mound were intricate and possibly impassible.

Stubbornly, the young priest tightened the beam's focus, the sliver of light reaching far below. He then made out the subtle hue shift, the darker stone of the floor, twenty or so feet beneath him. He considered dropping—for the moment it took him to remember that he was wearing a bandolier full of vials of volatile *Oil of Impact*!

Cadderly cursed his luck; if he had any intention of continuing along this course, he would have to call upon his magic—magic that he knew he would need in full against the likes of old Fyren. With a resigned sigh, he focused on the song of Deneir, remembering that part he had sung to Danica when she had tumbled from the mountain trail. Then he was walking down toward the cavern floor, walking in the empty air.

Cadderly understood Danica's ecstacy, understood the almost speechless excitement the young woman had felt when similarly enchanted. All logic told Cadderly that he should fall, and yet he did not. Using magic, he had completely defied the rules of nature, and, he had to admit, the sensation of air walking was incredible, better than stepping into the spirit world, better than lessening his corporeal form so that he might drift with the wind.

He could have stepped down to the stone a moment later, but he did not. He continued along through the wide chamber and into the tunnels, marching a foot off the ground, justifying his enjoyment by telling himself that he was moving more silently this way. In spite of the ever-present eeriness, in spite of the fact that he had run away from his friends and gone off into such danger alone, by the time the enchantment wore away, the young priest was smiling.

But the heat had intensified, tenfold it seemed, and what
sounded like a distant growl soon reminded Cadderly that
his path neared its end. He stood very still on the edge of
yet another wide chamber for a few moments and listened
intently, but couldn't be sure if the rhythmic breathing he
thought he heard was his imagination or the sounds of the
dragon.

"Only one way to find out," the brave priest muttered
grimly, forcing one foot ahead of the other. He started
across the floor in a crouch, light tube and crossbow held
out in front of him.

He saw that the chamber was rock-filled and was curious
about the fact that all of the stones seemed approximately
the same size and were similarly reddish in hue. Cadderly
wondered if these might be something created by the
dragon, some remnant of the beast's fiery breath, perhaps.
He had seen cats expel hair balls; might a dragon cough up
rocks? The notion brought a nervous chuckle to Cadderly's
lips, but he bit it back immediately, eyes wide with surprise.

One of the stones blinked at him!

Cadderly froze in his tracks, trying to keep the beam of
light steady on the creature. To the side, another "rock"
shifted, forcing Cadderly's attention. As soon as he brought
the light around, he realized that these were not stones all
about him, but giant toads, red-colored, with their uplifted
heads higher than Cadderly's waist.

Just as Cadderly decided that he must not make any sudden moves, must try to ease his way beyond these weird
creatures, a toad shuffled somewhere behind him. Despite
his determination, Cadderly spun about, bringing the light
to bear and startling several other monsters.

* * * * *

"I ain't going up there to fight any damned wyrm!" Ivan
protested, crossing his burly arms over his chest, which
put them about three inches above the level of the deep

snow. The dwarf pointedly looked away from the rising slope of Nightglow.

"Uh-oh," Pikel muttered.

"Cadderly is up there," Danica reminded the stubborn, yellow-bearded dwarf.

"Then Cadderly's stupid," Ivan grumbled without missing a beat. A giant arm wrapped about him suddenly, and he was hoisted into the air, tucked in close to Vander's side.

"Hee hee hee." Pikel's mirth did little to brighten Ivan's mood.

"Why, ye thieving, dwarf-stealing son of a red-haired dragon!" Ivan roared, kicking viciously but futilely against the firbolg's powerful hold.

"We should scale straight to the opening," Danica reasoned.

"Right along Cadderly's trail," Shayleigh agreed.

"Might we hurry?" Vander asked of them. "Ivan is biting my arm."

Danica was away in a moment, scrambling with all speed up the slope, following Cadderly's obvious footprints. Shayleigh came right behind, the nimble, light-footed elf having little trouble managing the deep snow. She kept her bow out and ready, playing a watchful role while Danica tracked.

Vander plodded along behind her, trying to resist the urge to cave in the vicious Ivan's thick skull, and Pikel came last, bobbing easily in the cleared wake of the giant firbolg.

They stood in the melted region before the cave entrance a few minutes later. Shayleigh peered in, using her elven heat-sensing vision, but she poked her head back out in a moment and shrugged helplessly, explaining that the air was too warm inside for her to make out anything distinct.

"Cadderly went in," Danica said, as much to firm her own resolve as to the others. "And so must we."

"Nope," came Ivan's predictable reply.

"The enchantment that Cadderly put over you last night will not hold for long," Shayleigh reminded him. "The air is too cold this high up for even one of a dwarf's toughness."

"Better freezed than toasted," Ivan grumbled.

Danica ignored the remark and slipped into the cave. Shayleigh shook her head and followed.

Vander set Ivan on the ground, drawing curious looks from both the dwarves.

"I'll not force you into a dragon's cave," the firbolg explained, and he walked by without waiting for a reply, squeezing in through the narrow entrance.

"Oo," Pikel moaned, not so filled with humor now that they had come to a critical moment.

Ivan stood resolute, his burly arms crossed over his chest and one foot tap-tapping on the wet stone. Pikel looked from his brother, to the cave, back to his brother, and back to the cave, not sure of what he should do.

"Aw, go on," Ivan growled at him a few seconds later. "I'm not for leaving the thick-headed fool to fight the dragon alone!"

Pikel's cherubic face brightened considerably as Ivan grabbed him and led the way in. When the green-bearded dwarf remembered that they were marching on their merry way to face a red dragon, that impish smile disappeared.

* * * * *

Far down the trail from the face of Nightglow, Druzil watched the black forms disappear under the high, enshrouding veil of fog. The imp had no idea of where the giant had come from—why would a giant be marching beside Cadderly?—but he was fairly confident that the other distant forms, particularly the two bobbing, short, and stout creatures, belonged to Cadderly's friends.

The undead monster seemed certain enough. Whether the creature could actually "see" the distant party, Druzil could not tell, but the monster's chosen path was straight and furious. Some beacon was guiding this otherworldly

spirit, leading it on without hesitation through the dark of
night and under the light of day. The creature hadn't
slowed, hadn't rested (weary Druzil was beginning to wish
it would!), and it and Druzil had covered a tremendous
amount of ground in a very short time.

Now, with the goal apparently in sight, the creature
moved even more furiously to the base of Nightglow's tree-
less high slope, ripping through the snow angrily, as if the
white powder's hindering depth was some deliberate conspiracy to keep the ghoulish thing away from Cadderly.

As a creature of the fiery lower planes, Druzil was not
fond of the chilling snow. But as a creature of the chaotic
lower planes, the imp eagerly moved along behind the
undead monster, rubbing his clawed hands at the thought
of the savagery that was soon to come.

* * * * *

Cadderly gently slid one foot in front of the other, inching his way toward the chamber's far exit. The giant red
toads had settled again, but the young priest felt many eyes
upon him, watching him with more than a passing interest.

Another few feet put him right in line with the exit; ten
running strides would have gotten him through it. He
stopped where he was, trying to muster the courage to
break into a run, trying to discern if that would be the wisest course.

He started to lean forward anxiously, was mentally
counting down to the moment when he would spring away.

A toad hopped across to block the exit.

Cadderly's eyes widened with fear and darted from side
to side, looking for some other path. Behind him, toads had
quietly gathered in a group, cutting off any retreat.

Was this a deliberate herding tactic? the young priest
wondered with complete astonishment. Whatever it was,
Cadderly knew that he had to act quickly. He considered
his magic, wondered what aid he might find from the song

of Deneir. He decided immediately to act more directly and began flicking his light beam at the blocking toad up ahead, trying to startle the thing out of his path.

The toad seemed to settle down more fully, grinding its considerable belly against the stone. It jerked upward suddenly—Cadderly feared for an instant that it was leaping at him—but only its head came forward, its mouth popping open and a gout of flame bursting forth.

Cadderly fell back a step as the small fireball erupted just short of him, reddening his face. He let out a cry of surprise and heard the toads shuffling rapidly behind him. Instinctively, the young priest brought his hand-crossbow up. He didn't look back, but kept his focus on the escape ahead and launched the quarrel. He ran off at once, following the dart's wake, fearing that a dozen small fireballs would incinerate him from behind before he ever got near the exit.

The toad's mouth flicked at the small missile, sticky tongue catching it in midflight and drawing it in.

The quarrel had not exploded! The tongue had apparently caught it without crushing the vial. And Cadderly, in full flight toward the toad and with nowhere else to run, had no readied alternatives, didn't even have his enchanted walking stick or spindle-disks in hand. He flicked the light tube frantically again, hoping against all reason to startle the formidable toad away. The thing just sat there, waiting.

Then the creature made a strange belching sound, its throat puffing and then retracting, and a moment later it blew apart, toad guts flying in all directions.

Cadderly threw his arms up in front of his face as he crossed through the spray and prudently ducked his head to avoid cracking it against the top rim of the low tunnel. He was many running strides out of the cavern before he dared to look back and confirm that no toads had come in pursuit. Still the frightened young priest ran, careening down the winding way, skidding to a stop and looking back, though he sensed that the tunnel had widened suddenly around him.

Cadderly stopped, frozen in place, no longer thinking about the toads but more concerned with the sound of rhythmic breathing, breathing that sounded like a tempest wind in a narrowing tunnel. Slowly, Cadderly turned his head about, and, even more slowly, he brought the light tube to bear.

"Oh, my dear Deneir," the young priest mouthed silently as the light ran along the scaly hide of the impossibly long, impossibly huge wyrm. "Oh, my dear Deneir."

The light passed the dragon's spearlike horns, crossed down the awesome beast's ridged skull, past the closed eye to the maw that could snap giant Vander in half with hardly an effort.

"Oh, my dear Deneir," the young priest muttered, and then he was kneeling, not even conscious of the fact that his knees had buckled under him.

Eight

Old Fyren

The beast was a hundred feet long, its curled tail a hundred feet again, and armored, every inch, with large, overlapping scales that gleamed like metal—and Cadderly did not doubt for a moment that those smooth red scales were every bit as strong as tempered plates. The dragon's great leathery wings were folded now, wrapping the beast like a blanket on a babe.

But that illusion could not hold against the reality of Fyrentennimar. Had an unsettling dream inspired those six-inch deep claw marks in the very stone near the dragon's forelegs? Cadderly wondered. And how many humans had been part of the meal that had so sated the beast's hunger that it could sleep for centuries?

In the next few moments, Cadderly thanked the gods a thousand times that he had stumbled upon Fyrentennimar while the dragon was asleep. If he had come running in here blindly and old Fyren had been awake, Cadderly would have never known what happened. His luck continued, for none of the toads were following him—the little creatures were smarter than Cadderly had expected. Still, Cadderly knew that dragon slumber was an unpredictable thing at best. He had to work fast, get his magical defenses up, and prepare himself mentally to battle the awe-inspiring beast.

He summoned the song of Deneir into his thoughts, but for many moments—interminable moments to the terrified Cadderly—could not hold the notes in any logical sequence, could not fully appreciate the harmony of the music and find his devotional *focus* within its mystical notes. It was that very harmony, the understanding of universal truths, that lent Cadderly his magical strength.

Finally Cadderly managed to enact a magical shielding sphere, an elemental inversion of the material air about him that would, he hoped, protect him from the fires of dragon breath.

The young priest took out the *Tome of Universal Harmony*, flipping to a page he had marked before leaving the Edificant Library. The origin of dragons was not known, but it was obvious to scholars that these creatures did not follow the natural and expected laws. Large as they were, there was no logical way that a dragon's wings should have been able to keep the creature aloft, and yet dragons were among the fastest fliers in all the world. Typically druidic magic, powerful against the mightiest of animals, had little power over dragons, so special protective wards had been devised to guard against these mighty beasts, by wizards and priests trying to survive in the wilder world millennia before. The page in the *Tome of Universal Harmony* showed Cadderly these wards, guided his thoughts to the song of Deneir in a slightly different manner, altering some of the notes. Soon he had erected a barrier, called dragonbane, from wall to wall a few feet in front of him that, according to the writings, the mighty wyrm could not physically pass through.

Fyrentennimar shifted uneasily; Cadderly figured that the wyrm probably sensed the magical energies being enacted in the room. The young priest took a deep breath and told himself over and over that he had to go through with this most important quest, had to trust in his magic and trust in himself. He took the evil *Ghearufu* out of his pack, tucked his feeble weapons away (even his potent hand-crossbow would do little damage against the likes of this beast), and wiped his sweaty palms on his tunic.

He uttered a simple spell so that the clap of his hands sounded as a thunderstrike. Great wings hummed as they beat the air, uplifting the front portion of the wyrm. Old Fyren's head shot up from the ground in the span of a heartbeat, hovering a dozen feet in front of Cadderly, and the young priest had to fight the urge to fall on the stone and grovel before this magnificent creature. How could Cadderly dare to presume that anything he might do would even affect the awesome Fyrentennimar?

And those eyes! Twin beacons that scrutinized every detail, that held the young priest on trial before a word had been spoken. Surely they emanated a light of their own as intense as that coming from Cadderly's enchanted tube.

The weakness in Cadderly's legs multiplied tenfold when the dragon, tired and cranky and not at all in the mood for a parley, loosed its searing breath.

A line of flames came at Cadderly but parted as they hit his magical globe, encircling him in a fiery blaze. His translucent globe took on a greenish hue under the assault, the protective bubble seeming thick at first but fast thinning as the dragon continued to spew forth its fire.

Sweat poured from Cadderly, his tongue went dry in his mouth, and his back itched as though all the moisture in his body was being evaporated. Wafts of smoke came up from the edges of his tunic; he had a hand on the adamantite spindle-disks, but had to let go as the metal heated, and similarly had to flip his metallic light tube gingerly from hand to hand.

Still came the fires as the great dragon lungs expelled their load. Would old Fyren never end?

And then it was over. "Oh, my dear Deneir," the young priest mouthed when the green hue of his magical bubble faded and he looked at the floor just outside of his protected area. He needed no light tube to witness this spectacle. Molten stone glowed and bubbled and fast-cooled, hardening in a wavelike formation from the force of the flames.

Cadderly looked up to see the dragon's slitted lizard eyes widen with disbelief that anything could survive its searing breath. Those evil eyes went narrow again quickly, the dragon issuing a low, threatening growl that shook the floor under Cadderly's feet.

What have I gotten myself into? Cadderly asked himself, but he forced the fearful notion away immediately, thought of the evil the *Ghearufu* had spread on the land and would continue to spread if he did not destroy it.

"Mighty Fyrentennimar," he began bravely, "I am but a poor and humble priest, come to call upon you in good faith."

The sharp intake of Fyren's breath drew Cadderly's cloak around him, nearly pulled him forward beyond the line of magical dragonbane.

Cadderly knew what was coming and desperately fell back into the song, chanting at the top of his voice to reinforce his thinned fire shield. The breath came in a wicked blast, mightier than the last, if that was possible. Cadderly saw the thin green bubble diminish to nothingness, felt a blast of warmth and thought that he would sizzle where he stood.

But a blue globe replaced the green, again driving the fires harmlessly aside. Cadderly's entire body ached as though he had fallen asleep under a high summer sun; he had to stamp out small flames on the laces of his boots.

"I have come in good faith!" he cried loudly when the blast ended, old Fyren's eyes wider still with disbelief. "I need but a simple favor and then you may return to your slumber!"

Amazement turned to an unbridled rage beyond anything Cadderly would ever have believed possible. The dragon opened its mouth wide, rows of ten-inch fangs gleaming horribly, and then its head shot forward, neck snapping like a snake's coiled body.

Cadderly groaned and nearly fell over, for a moment sure that he was losing consciousness and soon his life.

But the young priest nearly laughed aloud, in spite of his terror, when he peeked out to regard Fyrentennimar, the dragon's face pressed and distorted weirdly against the line of magical dragonbane. Cadderly could only think of the mischievous young boys at the Edificant Library, who would press their faces against the glass of the windows in the study chambers, startling the disciples within, then run off laughing down the solemn halls.

His unintentional lightheartedness actually aided the fortunate young priest, for the dragon backed away and looked all about, seeming unsure of itself for the first time.

"*Thief!*" Fyrentennimar bellowed, the power of the dragon voice blowing Cadderly back a step.

"No thief," Cadderly wisely assured the wyrm. "Just a humble priest . . . "

"*Thief and liar!*" Fyrentennimar roared. "Humble priests do not survive the breath of Fyrentennimar the Great! What treasures have you taken?"

"I come not for treasure," Cadderly declared firmly. "Nor to disturb the slumbers of a most magnificent wyrm."

Fyrentennimar started to retort, but seemed to reconsider, as though Cadderly's "most magnificent" compliment had given him pause.

"A simple task, as I have said," Cadderly went on, going with the momentum. "Simple for Fyrentennimar the Great, but quite beyond the abilities of any other in all the land. If you will perform . . . "

"*Perform?*" the dragon roared, and Cadderly, his hair

blown back by the sheer force of the dragon's hot breath, wondered if his hearing would be permanently damaged. "Fyrentennimar does not perform! I am not interested in your simple task, foolish priest." The dragon surveyed the area right in front of Cadderly, as if trying to discern what barrier had been enacted to keep it at bay.

Cadderly considered the few options that seemed open to him. He felt that his best chance was to continue to flatter the beast. He had read many tales of heroic adventurers successfully playing to the ego of dragons, particularly of red dragons, which were reputably the most vain of all dragonkind.

"Would that I might better see you!" he said dramatically. He snapped his fingers, as though a thought had just come to him, then whipped out his slender wand and uttered *"Domin illu."* Instantly the wide chamber was bathed in a magical light, and all of Fyrentennimar's magnificence was revealed to him. Silently congratulating himself, Cadderly replaced the wand under his cloak and continued his survey, noting for the first time the mound of treasure across the way, beyond the bulk of the blocking dragon.

"Would that you might better see *me,*" Fyrentennimar began suspiciously, "or see my *treasure,* humble thief?"

Cadderly blinked at the words and at his possible mistake. The murderous expression on Fyrentennimar's face was not hard to decipher. Then Cadderly felt his light tube growing warm, uncomfortably so, and he had to drop it to the ground. His forearm brushed against his belt buckle, and he winced in pain as bare skin contacted the fast-heating metal. It took Cadderly just a moment to understand, a moment to remember that many dragons, too, could access the realm of magical energies.

Cadderly had to act fast, had to humble the wyrm and make old Fyren desire parley. He chanted immediately, pointedly ignoring the wisps of smoke rising from his leather belt near the buckle.

A whirling ring of magical blades appeared in the air

above Fyrentennimar's head.

"They will cut!" Cadderly promised, and he willed the blades lower, dangerously close to the dragon's head. He hoped to drive old Fyren down so that the beast would not be in such a position of physical superiority, hoped that his display of power would make the wyrm consider that continuing this fight might not be so wise a choice.

"Let them!" old Fyren bellowed, and his wings beat on, lifting his huge head higher, meeting the spell full force. Sparks flew as the blades chipped off of dragon armor. Tiny pieces of scales flecked away, and, to Cadderly's ultimate dismay, Fyrentennimar's roar seemed one of glee.

The dragon's tail whipped about, slamming Cadderly's magical barrier viciously, the waves of the concussion shaking the chamber and knocking Cadderly from his feet. The line of dragonbane held, though Cadderly feared that the chamber's ceiling would not. He realized then how vulnerable he truly was, how pitiful he must seem to this wyrm that had lived for centuries and had feasted on the bones of hundreds of men more powerful than he.

He had enacted protection from the fiery breath, had enacted a barrier that the beast could not physically pass through (though neither, he feared, would hold out for long), but what defense could Cadderly offer against Fyrentennimar's no-doubt potent array of spells? He realized then that his defeat could be as simple a thing as Fyrentennimar tearing a hunk of stone from the wall and hurling it into him!

The dragon whipped its armored head to and fro, challenging Cadderly's enchanted blades, mocking Cadderly's spell. Foreclaws dug great ridges into the chamber's stone floor and the great tail whipped about, shattering rock and cracking apart the walls.

Cadderly could not hold out for long, was certain that he had nothing in all his arsenal that could begin to wound this monster.

He had only one alternative, and he feared it almost as

much as he feared Fyrentennimar. The song of Deneir had taught him that the magical energies of the universe could be accessed from many different angles, and the way that one accessed those energies determined the grouping, the magical sphere, of the spells found within. Cadderly, for instance, had approached the universal energies differently for enacting his line of magical dragonbane than he had when entering the sphere of elemental fire to create the protective barrier against Fyrentennimar's flames.

Deneir was a deity of art, of poetry and soaring spirits, praising and accepting of a myriad of thoughtful accomplishments. Deneir's song rang out across the heavens, thrumming with the powers of many such energies, and thus a priest attuned to this god's song could find access, could find many various angles, to bend the universal energies in countless directions.

There was one particular bent of those energies, though, that ran contrary to the harmony of Deneirian thinking, where no notes rang clear and no harmony could be maintained. This was the sphere of chaos, a place of discord and illogic, and this was where young Cadderly had to go.

* * * * *

"It's a five-dwarf drop!" Ivan protested, holding fast to Danica's wrist. Danica could not even see the floor beneath the vertical chute and had to trust in the estimate of Ivan's heat-sensing vision. That estimate, "five-dwarf drop," twenty feet, was not so promising. But Danica had heard the thunderstrike of Cadderly's dragon-awakening clap, knew in her heart that her love was in dire need. She pulled free of Ivan's grasp, scrambled the rest of the way down the narrow chute and without hesitation dropped into the darkness.

She prayed that she could react quickly enough when at last she reached the end of the drop, hoped that the dim light of the torch Shayleigh held up in the chute would show her the floor before she slammed against it.

She saw the gray and turned her ankles to the side as she hit, launching herself into a sidelong roll, half twisting as she went. Her roll took her over backward, so that she came squarely back to her feet. Never slowing, having not absorbed enough of the fall's energy, Danica sprang into the air, turning a backward somersault. She landed on her feet and jumped again, spinning forward this time. She came up in a roll and hit the ground running, the rest of her momentum played out in long, swift strides.

"Well, I'll be a wine-drinking faerie," Ivan muttered in disbelief, watching the spectacle from above. For all his complaints, the dwarf could not let his friends endure any danger without him, and he knew that any hesitation now would force Danica to face the coming trials alone.

"Don't ye try to catch me, girl!" he warned as he let go. Ivan's landing technique was not so different than Danica's. But while Danica rolled and leaped, somersaulting gracefully and changing direction with subtle, stressless twists, Ivan just bounced.

He was up quickly, though. He adjusted his deer-antlered helmet and caught Danica by her flowing cloak as she ran back the other way, following the continuing sounds to the east.

Vander dropped down next, the tight chute posing more trouble for the firbolg than the not-so-high (for a giant) drop. Shayleigh dropped into his waiting arms, virtually springing from him in quick flight after Ivan and Danica.

Pikel came last, and Vander caught him, as well. The firbolg eyed the nestled dwarf curiously for a moment, noting that something seemed to be missing. "Your club?" Vander started to ask, and he understood a split second later, when Pikel's club, tumbling down behind the dwarf, bounced off his skull.

"Oops," the green-bearded dwarf apologized, and in looking at Vander's scowl, he was glad that they had no time to stand around and discuss the matter.

Danica would have outdistanced Ivan in no time—except that the dwarf had a firm grip on her trailing cloak and would not let go. They heard the rumble of Fyrentennimar's distant voice by this point, and though they couldn't make out any words, it guided them easily. Ivan was glad when he noted that Shayleigh, still holding her torch, was gaining on them.

They passed through a few chambers, down several narrow corridors, and one wide passage. The mounting heat alone told them that they were nearing the dragon's chamber and made them both fear that Fyrentennimar had already loosed its killing breath.

Shayleigh passed Ivan, seeming as desperate as Danica, and the dwarf promptly reached out and grabbed a hold on her cloak, too. He understood their urgency, understood that both of them were fostering images of a deep-fried Cadderly, but Ivan remained pragmatic. If the dwarf had anything to say about it, they would not run helter-skelter into old Fyren's waiting maw.

Shayleigh's torch showed that they were nearing yet another wide chamber. They saw light up ahead, a residual glow, it seemed, and that led them to one inescapable conclusion.

For all of his earlier protests and stubbornness, Ivan Bouldershoulder showed his true loyalties at that point. Thinking that the dreadful Fyrentennimar waited just ahead, the tough dwarf yanked back on both cloaks, springing past Danica and Shayleigh and leading the way into the chamber before he had even had time to draw out his double-bladed battle-axe.

A flicking tongue hit him two steps inside the door—hit him, wrapped him, and pulled him sideways. Danica and Shayleigh skidded in behind, to find the chamber filled with very anxious, giant red toads. They spotted Ivan, spotted his boots at least, sticking out from the mouth of a contented-looking toad to the right. Danica started for it but was intercepted by a mini-fireball, and then another, as two more toads took up the attack.

Shayleigh hurled her torch out in front of her, had her bow up in an instant, and put it to deadly work.

Ivan didn't know what had hit him, but he understood that he was quite uncomfortable, and that he could not get his arms around to retrieve the axe strapped to his back. Never the one to listen to his own many complaints, Ivan followed the only course open to him and began thrashing about, trying to bite, trying to find something to grasp and twist. The deer rack atop his helmet snagged on something up above and again Ivan did not question his misfortune, just snapped his head up as forcefully as he could.

A toad leaped long and high at her, but Shayleigh's three arrows, fired in rapid succession, broke the thing's momentum in midflight and dropped it dead to the ground. Two more toads came flying at the elf simultaneously, and though she hit them both with perfect shots, she could not deflect their flight. One clipped her shoulder, the other crashed against her shins, and back she flew.

She would have hit the cavern floor hard, but Vander, coming in from the corridor, caught her gently in one giant hand and kept her on her feet. The firbolg was beyond her in an instant, his great sword slashing back and forth, slicing the two attacking toads in half.

A third monster came flying in from the side, but Pikel skidded in between it and Shayleigh, holding his tree-trunklike club tight over one shoulder, both his hands grasping the weapon's narrow end. With a whoop of delight, the green-bearded dwarf batted the flying toad aside. It dropped, stunned, and Pikel stood over it, squishing it with repeated strikes.

Danica fell to her back and rolled about frantically to avoid the fiery blasts. She tucked her feet in close, hoping to roll back to a standing position, and grabbed at her boots, drawing two daggers, one golden-hilted and sculpted into the image of a tiger, the other a silvery dragon.

She came up throwing, scoring two hits on the nearest

toad. It closed its eyes and squatted down low to the floor, and Danica couldn't tell if she had killed it or not.

Nor could she pause to find out. Another toad was near her, flicking its sticky tongue.

Danica leaped straight up, a mongoose against a striking snake, and tucked her legs tight. She leaped again as soon as her feet touched stone, forward and high, before the toad could flick its tongue again. This time, Danica came down hard on the creature's head. One foot planted firmly, she spun fiercely, her face passing close to her ankle, her other foot flying high, straight above her. As she completed the circuit, her momentum cresting, she tightened the muscles in her sailing foot and drove it right through the toad's bulbous eye.

The weight of the blow forced Danica down from the dead thing, and she spun about, searching out the next target.

At first she thought the toad she saw to the side to be among the most curious of crossbred creatures. But then Danica realized that its antlers were not its own, but rather belonged to the indigestible dwarf it had foolishly pulled in.

The antlers jerked, this way and that, and Ivan's slime-covered head popped through. The dwarf grunted and contorted weirdly, twisting all the way about so that he was looking at his own heels, protruding from the toad's mouth, and at Danica, staring in disbelief.

"Ye think ye might be helping me outa here?" the dwarf asked, and Danica saw the now-dead toad's eyes hump up and then go back to normal as Ivan shrugged.

* * * * *

The familiar song played in Cadderly's mind, but he did not fall into its harmonic flow. He sang it backward instead, sang it sideways, randomly, forcing out whatever notes seemed to be the most discordant. Shivers ran through the marrow of his bones; he felt as if he would break apart

under the magical assault. He was exactly where a priest of
Deneir should not be, mocking the harmony of the universe, perverting the notes of the timeless song so that
they twanged painfully in his mind, slamming doors in the
pathways of the revelations the song had shown to him.

Cadderly's voice sounded guttural, croaking, and his
throat was filled with phlegm. His head ached; the intensity
of the shivering waves along his spine stung him repeatedly.

He thought he would go insane, had gone insane, had
gone to a place where every logical course seemed to
meander aimlessly, where one and one added up to three,
or to ten. Cadderly's emotions similarly fluctuated. He was
angry, furious at . . . what? He did not know, knew only that
he was filled with despair. Then suddenly he felt invulnerable, as if he could walk past his magical barriers and snap
his fingers under puny Fyrentennimar's dragon nostrils.

Still he croaked against the harmonious flow of the beautiful song, still he denied the universal truths the song had
shown to him. Suddenly, Cadderly realized that he had
unleashed something terrible within his own mind, that he
could not stop the flashing images and the shivering pains.

His mind darted randomly, a gamesman's wheel, flitting
through the accessed magical energy with no basis. He was
falling, falling, dropping into an endless pit from which
there could be no escape. He would eat the dragon, or the
dragon would eat him, but either way, Cadderly felt that it
did not matter. He had broken himself—the only logical
thought he could hold onto for more than a fleeting moment
was that he had overstepped his bounds, had rushed in his
desperation into ultimate, unending chaos.

Still he croaked the discordant notes, played the random
rantings of half-truths and untruths in his mind. One and
one equaled seventeen this time.

One and one.

Whatever else assaulted Cadderly's mind, he continued
to call upon the simple mathematics of adding one and one.

A hundred different answers came to him in rapid succession, were generated randomly in this place, his mind, wherein no rules held true.

A thousand different answers, generated without pattern, without guidance, shot past him. And Cadderly let them go away with the rest of his fleeting thoughts, knowing them to be lies.

One and one equaled two.

Cadderly grabbed onto that thought, that hope. The simple equation, the simple, logical truth ringing as a single note of harmony in the discord.

One and one equaled two!

A thin line of Deneir's song played in Cadderly's mind simultaneously, but separately, from the discord. It came as a lifeline to the young priest, and he clutched it eagerly, not intending it to pull him from the discord, but to help him hold his mental footing within this sphere's slippery chaos.

Now Cadderly searched the dangerous sphere, found a region of emotional tumult, of inverted ethics, and hurled it with all his mental strength at Fyrentennimar.

The dragon's rage continued to play, and Cadderly understood that he had not penetrated the innate magical resistance of the beast. Cadderly realized that he was sitting then, that sometime during his mental journey, the earthquake of Fyrentennimar's thrashing had knocked him from his feet.

Again Cadderly searched out the particular region of chaos that he needed—it was in a different place this time—and again he hurled it at the wyrm. And then a third time, and a fourth. His head ached as he continued to demand the enchantment, continued to assault the stubborn dragon with false emotions and false beliefs.

The chamber was deathly quiet, except for some scrambling that Cadderly heard emanating from somewhere down the tunnel behind him, back in the toad room, perhaps. He slowly opened his eyes, to see old Fyren sitting quietly, regarding him.

"My welcome, humble priest," the dragon said in calm, controlled tones. "Do forgive my outburst. I do not know what brought about such a tirade." The dragon blinked its reptilian eyes and glanced all about curiously. "Now, about this small task that you wished me to perform."

Cadderly, too, blinked many times in disbelief. "One and one equals two," he muttered under his breath. "I hope."

Nine

Residual Energy

Danica was the first to come to the end of the tunnel leading to the dragon's chamber. On her hands and knees, the monk quietly crept up to the lighted area and peeked in. She felt the strength drain from her as she gazed upon the magnificent wyrm, a hundred times more dreadful than the legends could begin to describe. But then Danica's delicate features twisted in confusion at the unexpected sight.

Cadderly stood right beside the dragon, talking with it easily and pointing to the *Ghearufu*, the gloves, one black, one white, and the gold-edged mirror that he had placed on the floor some distance away.

Danica nearly cried out aloud when she felt a hand on her leg. She realized that it was only Shayleigh, creeping in behind her as they had planned. The elf maiden, too, seemed stunned by the spectacle in the chamber.

"Should we go in?" she whispered to Danica.

Danica considered the question for a long moment,

honestly unsure of what role they should play. Cadderly
seemed to have things in hand; would their unexpected
presence startle the dragon, bring old Fyren into a fit of terrifying rage?

Just as Danica started to shake her head, there came an
impatient call from back down the tunnel.

"What do ye see?" Ivan demanded, slime-covered from
toad innards and not too happy at all.

The dragon's beaconlike gaze immediately flashed
toward the tunnel, and Danica and Shayleigh again felt
their limbs go weak under the awful glare.

"Who comes uninvited to the lair of . . ." the great wyrm
began, but it stopped in midsentence, cocking its massive
head so that it could better hear Cadderly, whispering
calmly at its side.

"Do come in," the dragon bade the two in the tunnel a
moment later. "Welcome, friends of the humble priest!"

It took Danica and Shayleigh some time to muster the
courage to actually enter the dragon's chamber. They went
straight for Cadderly, Danica hooking his arm with her own
and admiring him incredulously.

Cadderly felt the weight of that trusting gaze. Again, he
had been put into the forefront, had become the leader to
his friends. He alone understood how tentative his hold on
the dragon might be, and now that Danica and the others
had arrived, their fates rested solely in his hands. They
admired him, they trusted him, but Cadderly was not so
sure that he trusted himself. Would he ever shed the guilt if
he failed at the expense of a friend's life? He wanted to be
home at the library, sitting on a sun-drenched roof, feeding
cacasa nuts to Percival, the one friend who placed no
demands upon him (other than the cacasa nuts!).

"The dragon likes me," the young priest explained,
straining to put his smile from ear to ear. "And Fyrentennimar—the great Fyrentennimar—has agreed to help me
with my problem," he added, nodding toward the *Ghearufu*.

Danica looked to the still-glowing floor near the entryway

of the chamber and could guess easily enough that the dragon had utilized its deadly breath at least once already.

But Cadderly appeared unhurt—and unafraid. Danica started to ask him about the strange turn of events, but he quieted her immediately with a concerned look, and she understood that the discussion was better left until later, when they were safely away from the dragon.

Ivan and Pikel skidded into the chamber, Vander coming right behind, nearly tripping over them.

"Uh-oh!" Pikel squeaked at the sight of the wyrm, and Ivan's face went pale.

"*Dwarves!*" Fyrentennimar bellowed, the force of his roar driving the three beards—yellow, red, and green—out behind the friends, the heat of Fyren's breath making the three squint their eyes.

"Friends again!" Cadderly called to the dragon, and, reasoning that treasure-coveting dragons were not overly fond of treasure-coveting dwarves, the young priest motioned for the three to stay back near the tunnel.

Fyrentennimar issued a long, low growl and didn't seem convinced. The dragon could not sustain its ire, though. It blinked curiously, turned an almost plaintive look upon Cadderly, and then looked to the *Ghearufu*.

"Friends again," Fyrentennimar agreed.

Cadderly looked to the *Ghearufu*, thinking it prudent to just get things done and get out of there.

"Remain behind me," old Fyren warned Cadderly and the two women, and then came the sharp intake as the dragon's lungs expanded.

This time when Fyrentennimar breathed, there was no magical protection in place to divert his fire. The flames drove against the *Ghearufu* and against the floor. Stone bubbled, and the *Ghearufu* sizzled, angrily it seemed, as though its potent magic was fighting back against the incredible assault.

"Oooo," Ivan muttered in disbelief. Pikel put his hands on hips and growled at his brother for stealing his line.

Their fight did not continue, though, as the searing heat of the dragon breath assaulted them. Vander grabbed the brothers and fell back against the wall, one huge arm up defensively in front of his eyes.

The dragon's fiery exhalation did not relent. There came a series of snapping explosions from within the flame, and a thick gray smoke arose, encircling the fiery pillar, dimming its blinding yellow light.

Cadderly nodded to Danica and Shayleigh, confident that the dragon fire was doing its work.

The flaming column disappeared, and Fyrentennimar sat back, reptilian eyes scrutinizing the area and the magical item. The smoke continued to swirl, funnel-like above the *Ghearufu*. Small fires burned on both the item's gloves; the gold edges around the mirror had turned liquid and spread out in a wide flat glob. The mirror itself pulsed, bulging weirdly but remaining, it appeared, intact.

"Is it done, humble priest?" Fyrentennimar asked.

Cadderly wasn't sure. The thick smoke seemed to gain momentum in its swirl, the mirror continued to bulge and flatten.

Then it cracked apart.

Cadderly's blue hat flew away, his cape flapped up over his head and shoulders, standing out straight, snapping repeatedly, rapidly, in the sudden suction. Now the smoke whipped in circular fury, and the swirling wind became a thunderous roar.

Shayleigh's arrows left her quiver, smacked against Cadderly's back, and ricocheted past. The young priest could hardly hold his footing, leaning back at a huge angle against the vicious pull. All the small items in the area piled atop the broken mirror. The still pliable molten floor rolled up, wavelike, around the center of that tremendous pull.

Something banged hard against the back of Cadderly's legs, costing him his tentative hold. He looked down to see Shayleigh, blinded by her wild-flying golden hair, scraping her hands against the stone in a futile effort. Cadderly fell over her, and she slid away, toward the fury.

Danica stood very still a few feet back, her eyes closed in meditation, and her legs wide and firmly planted. Over by the tunnel, Vander and the dwarves had formed a chain, the firbolg holding Pikel, Pikel holding Ivan. Pikel's grip slipped suddenly, and Ivan screamed out. He resisted the pull for just a second, long enough for Pikel to dive down and grab him about the ankles.

"Humble priest!" the confused Fyrentennimar roared, and even the dragon's thunder seemed a distant thing against the tumult of the mighty wind.

Cadderly cried out for Shayleigh, found himself going along behind her as the sucking wind increased. Behind him, Danica opened her eyes, and her concern for her friends stole her meditation. She jumped forward a long stride, catching hold of Cadderly, but when she tried to stop, found her momentum too great and wound up going right over the young priest, and right over Shayleigh, and suddenly it was she who was closest to the furious vortex.

Ivan and Pikel were up in the air now, Pikel holding tight to Ivan's ankles, and Vander, behind him, had one hand tight about Pikel's ankle, the other grasping a jut in the tunnel wall.

Danica's horrified scream as she went over the vortex stole the blood from Cadderly's face. Shayleigh went in right behind her, pressed tight against her, and then Cadderly was atop the pile.

"What do I do, humble priest?" the confused dragon called, but Fyrentennimar was distracted as his own piles of treasure whipped to the call of the vortex, smacked hard against the dragon's back and widespread wings. What worth is such treasure? the dragon wondered, and in his magically confused state, Fyrentennimar decided right then that he would soon clear his cave of the worthless debris.

"Ooooooo!" Pikel wailed, blinded by his beard (as was Ivan), his muscled arms aching from the strain and his leg throbbing from Vander's giant-strong grip. Pikel feared that he would be torn right in half, but for the sake of his dear brother, he would not let go.

* * * * *

Cadderly felt an intense burning, felt as if his insides had been torn right through his skin. He was falling, spinning in a gray fog, spiraling down, out of control.

He splashed into muck, stood in the knee-deep sludge, and regarded himself and his surroundings incredulously. He was naked and filthy, apparently unhurt but standing in a vast plain of unremarkable grayness, the lake of oozing sludge stretching out in every direction as far as he could see.

Danica and Shayleigh stood near him, but they, for some reason the young priest could not understand, were still wearing their clothes.

Cadderly modestly crossed his arms in front of him, took note of the fact that both of his companions did likewise.

Danica's lips moved as though she meant to ask, "Where are we?" but there seemed no point in uttering the unanswerable question.

* * * * *

Far down Nightglow's snow-blanketed side, Druzil scratched his ugly face and watched the undead creature's shivering movements.

Ghost had not taken a step in many seconds, the first time Druzil had seen the tireless thing pause in several days. The gruesome creature made no moves at all, except for the obvious trembling.

"Why are you doing that?" the invisible imp asked under his rasping breath, hoping that the creature had not somehow detected him and was not calling upon some innate magics to locate him, or to destroy him.

The trembling intensified to a violent shaking. Druzil

whined and wrapped his leathery wings defensively about him, though since they were invisible, they could not block out the terrifying sight.

Crackling noises came from the undead monster, tiny cracks appeared along its blackened skin, wisps of smoke filtered out into the brightly shining air.

"Hey?" the imp asked a moment later, when the undead thing fell into a pile of charred and shattered flakes.

* * * * *

Cadderly continued his scan of the area, of himself, and of his friends. Danica, too, seemed intent on covering up, but Cadderly didn't see the point since she was fully clothed.

Or was she?

A wail from somewhere in the unseen distance brought them all on the alert. Shayleigh went into a low crouch, slowly turning and scanning, balled fists defensively in front of her.

If she feared an attack, then why didn't she take her bow off her shoulder? Cadderly wondered. And then he understood. With a knowing nod, the young priest let go of his pointless modesty and stood straight.

Another cry, a cry of pain, sounded from somewhere distant, followed by a loud splash.

"Where are we?" Danica demanded. "And why am I the only one who has no clothes?"

Shayleigh looked at her incredulously, then looked down to her own body.

A wave rolled in at them, bringing the uncomfortable brown sludge to their waists. Cadderly grimaced at the feel of the wretched stuff, noticed for the first time the reeking stench.

"What caused so large a wave?" Shayleigh whispered, and her perceptive remark reminded Cadderly that the discomfort might be the least of his troubles.

The apparition, a puny, androgenous form with one arm bent crooked, rose from the sludge twenty feet away from them, its dangerous eyes narrowing as it regarded them.

"The assassin," Danica breathed. "But he is dead, and we . . . " She looked at Cadderly, her brown eyes wide.

"Caught by the *Ghearufu*," Cadderly replied, unwilling to offer the possibility that they, too, had died.

"Caught!" the puny form roared in a mighty, giantlike voice. "Caught that you might be properly punished!"

"Use your bow!" Danica, more afraid than she had ever been, yelled at Shayleigh. Again, the elf gave Danica an incredulous look, then turned helplessly to her bare, as she saw it, shoulder.

Danica sneered and rushed between Shayleigh and Cadderly, taking a blocking stance between them and the approaching apparition.

Cadderly looked down, looked to the unremarkable muck to clear his head and register all that he had seen and heard. Why was he the only one who was naked? Or at least, why did he see himself that way? As did Danica, he knew, by her own words. And if Shayleigh thought that she had her bow, didn't perceive that she, too, had no clothes and no equipment, then why hadn't she taken the weapon from her back?

Danica's hands began an intricate, balancing weave in front of her. The apparition of Ghost showed no fear at all, continued to steadily glide through the muck. Danica noticed that Ghost seemed larger suddenly, and noticed that the apparition continued to grow.

"Cadderly," she breathed quietly, for now their opponent was fully ten feet tall, nearly as large as Vander. It took another step, doubling its size as it did.

"Cadderly!"

They all perceived that they were naked, but each saw the others as they had last seen the others, Cadderly mused, knowing that there must be something pertinent in that fact. He felt along his body, wondering if his equipment only appeared invisible to him, if his potent hand-crossbow might be on his hip, waiting for him to grab it. But he felt only his skin and the slimy splotches of brown, disgusting sludge.

The apparition loomed thirty feet high; its laughter mocked Danica's feeble defensive stance. With a sucking sound, one foot came up from the muck, hovered high in the air menacingly.

"Punishment!" the evil Ghost growled, stamping down.

Danica dove to the side, splashed through the muck and reappeared, her strawberry-blond locks matted to her head by the thick brown sludge.

The splash awakened Cadderly from his contemplations. His gray eyes widened as he glanced about for Danica, fearing that she had been squashed.

Shayleigh was over with the monk by then, pulling her away from the gigantic monster.

Ghost showed no more interest in Danica, though, not with Cadderly, the perpetrator of the disaster, the destroyer of his own form and of the precious *Ghearufu*, standing before him.

"Are you at peace with your god?" the giant voice teased.

Where are we? The question rifled through Cadderly's thoughts, now that the monster had threatened him, had apparently just confirmed that they were not dead. Yet this place somewhat resembled the spirit world, Cadderly knew, for he had made several ventures into that noncorporeal state.

Danica and Shayleigh rushed in front of the young priest, Danica leaping onto the leg of the giant, clawing and biting at the back of its knee. It kicked out, trying to shake her free, but if her savage thrashing was doing any real damage, the smiling Ghost did not show it.

"Perceived vulnerability," Cadderly muttered, trying to jog his thought process. His self-image, the images of his friends, and the image of their nemesis, had to be a matter of perception, since he and both his companions thought themselves naked and the other two clothed.

Shayleigh slipped free of the monster's other leg as Ghost brought it up high above Cadderly's head.

"Cadderly!" both Danica and the elf maiden cried out to their apparently distracted companion.

The huge foot slammed down; Danica nearly fainted at the thought of her lover being squashed.

Cadderly caught the foot in one hand, and absently held it steady above his head.

He, too, began to grow.

"What is happening?" the frustrated, terrified monk cried out, falling from the giant's knee and splashing away. Shayleigh caught her and held her, needing, as much as giving, the support.

Cadderly was half the creature's size, and now it was Ghost who seemed confused. The young priest heaved against the foot, hurling Ghost backward to land crashing into the muck. By the time the creature regained its stance, Cadderly was the larger.

Ghost came on anyway, snarling, wrapping his hated enemy in a tight hug.

Danica and Shayleigh moved away from the titans, not understanding, not able to help.

Cadderly's massive arms flexed and twisted. Ghost's did, too, and for a long while, neither titan seemed to gain any advantage.

Ghost bit down hard on Cadderly's neck, whipping his head about in a frenzy. It was he, not Cadderly, who then cried out in pain, though, for he was biting not vulnerable skin, but steel armor!

The wild monster lifted his arm; his fingers grew into spikes, and he smashed down at Cadderly's shoulder.

The young priest yelped in agony. Cadderly's arm became a spear, and he plunged it through Ghost's belly.

Ghost's skin parted around it, opening a hole through which the arm/spear passed without making a cut. The evil entity's skin then tightened around Cadderly's appendage, holding him fast.

Ghost's mouth opened impossibly wide, seeming the maw of a snake, complete with venom-tipped fangs.

"Cadderly," Danica breathed, thinking her love doomed, thinking that she and Shayleigh would also fall victim to this horrid apparition. She had no words to describe what ensued, could hardly remember to breathe.

Cadderly did not flinch. His head thickened, his face flattened, like the face of a hammer, and he butted straight out. This time his attack apparently caught Ghost by surprise, for the assassin's snake jaws broke apart, blood washing away the venom.

Ghost's eyes widened in shock and agony as Cadderly's impaled arm shifted shape again, angled spikes tearing out the sides of Ghost's torso.

Cadderly understood that the game was one of mental quickness, matching defense to attack, keeping perspective (yes, that word was the key!) against fearsome sights and impossible realities. He had Ghost dazed, confused, and so the momentum was his to play out.

His free arm became an axe, his razor-edged hand slicing in at the side of Ghost's neck. The evil titan reacted quickly enough for its shoulder to grow a shield, but Cadderly had simultaneously sprouted a tail like that of the manticore he had battled on the mountain trail. Even as the axe hand resounded against Ghost's shield, the tail whirled about and snapped like a whip, driving several iron spikes into Ghost's chest.

Cadderly whipped his impaled arm about viciously; Ghost somehow melded and molded his skin to match the movements, preventing Cadderly from literally tearing him in half. The tail came about again, but Ghost's chest thickened with conjured armor, somewhat deflecting the heavy blows.

Cadderly had brought Ghost to his mental limit, had taxed Ghost's formidable mind to the extreme of his thought-processing abilities. It was a game of chess, Cadderly knew, a game of simultaneous movements and anticipating defenses.

Ghost's snake maw reformed in the blink of an eye—
Cadderly was actually surprised that the evil man, still holding his defenses strong, was able to enact the shift. At the
same time, though, Cadderly's head became the head of a
dragon, became the head of Fyrentennimar.

Ghost's snake eyes widened. He tried to shift his head
into something that could deflect the attack, something that
could defeat dragon breath.

He didn't think quickly enough. Cadderly breathed forth
a line of fire that stole Ghost's features, sizzled his skin
away to leave a skull, half human, half snake, atop the
titan's skinny neck.

In the throes of agony, Ghost could not maintain his control, his mental defenses. Cadderly's manticore tail heaved
a half-dozen spikes into Ghost's chest. Cadderly's axe hand
drove deep into Ghost's collarbone.

With a dragon's roar of victory, Cadderly snapped his
impaled arm back and forth, cutting Ghost apart at the
waist. The defeated titan's top half plummeted into the
muck, showering Danica and Shayleigh. Almost immediately, the slain Ghost's torso reverted to its normal size, disappearing under the brown lake. Ghost's quivering legs
toppled as they shrank, slipping into the muck with hardly
a splash.

Cadderly's head became human again as he turned to
regard his overwhelmed companions. He caught only a
fleeting image of them, though, before a wall of blackness
rushed up to smash him into unconsciousness.

Ten

Soaring

"Oof!" Ivan and Pikel groaned in unison when the
balancing force of the tempest abruptly ended
and they dropped, flat-out, to the stone floor.
Vander, too, groaned, and fell back against the
wall, the huge muscles in both his arms quivering
from exhaustion. The wind had simply ceased, and the
smoke now dissipated, revealing Danica, Cadderly, and
Shayleigh lying one on top of the other in a pile.

"Are you all right, humble priest?" Fyrentennimar asked
with sincere concern.

Cadderly looked up to the great beast and nodded, very
glad that the ethics reversal he had enacted upon old Fyren
had not been dispelled by his spiritual absence. Danica
forced herself to her feet, and Cadderly, in turn, climbed off
Shayleigh, his joints aching with every step. He knew
rationally that his fight with Ghost had been a mental combat, not a physical one, a belief only reinforced by the fact
that neither he nor Danica and Shayleigh had any of the

disgusting muck on them, and in fact appeared exactly the same as they had before the journey. Still, the young priest felt as though his body had been through a severe beating.

"What was that monster?" Danica asked. "I thought you said the assassin was already dead and gone."

"That was not Ghost," Cadderly replied. "Not really. What we found was the embodiment of the *Ghearufu*, perhaps a joined spirit, magic item and owner."

"Where?" Shayleigh wanted to know.

Now Cadderly had no definite response. "Some area of limbo between the planes of existence," he answered, shrugging his shoulders to indicate that it was only a guess. "The *Ghearufu* has been in existence for many millennia, was created by powerful denizens of chaos. That is why I had to come here, even before our vital mission to Castle Trinity."

"Ye couldn't've just left the damned thing with the priests?" Ivan grumbled, kicking stones and debris as he searched about for his windblown helmet.

Cadderly started to reiterate the importance of the quest, wanting to explain how the destruction of the *Ghearufu* was more important to the overall scheme of universal harmony than anything which might directly affect their relatively unimportant lives. He gave up, however, realizing that such profound philosophical points had no chance of getting through the pragmatic dwarf's thick head.

Danica put her hand on his shoulder, though, and nodded to him when he looked back to her. She trusted in him again—her eyes showed that clearly. He was glad for that trust, and afraid of it, all at once.

He motioned for Danica and Shayleigh to go over by the door with the other three.

"Mighty Fyrentennimar," he cried to the dragon, dipping a low, appreciative bow. "The words of the gods are proven true." Cadderly took a step to the side and lifted one of the ruined, still smoking gloves. "Nothing in all the Realms but the breath of mighty Fyrentennimar could have destroyed the *Ghearufu*; no power in all the Realms could match the fury of your fires!" The statement wasn't exactly true, but even though the dragon was apparently still thick in the hold of Cadderly's chaotic enchantment, the young priest thought it wise to be generous with the praise.

Fyrentennimar seemed to like it. The dragon puffed out his already enormous chest, honed head held proudly high.

"And now, my friends and I must leave you to your sleep," Cadderly explained. "Fear not, for we'll not again disturb your slumber."

"Must you go, humble priest?" the dragon asked, seeming sad, which prompted a curious and sympathetic "Oo," from Pikel and an assortment of incredulous curses from Ivan.

Cadderly answered with a simple "Yes," bade the dragon lay down and rest, and turned to leave, pausing at the tunnel entrance to consider his friends.

"What of the toads?" he asked, remembering them for the first time since he had gazed upon the awesome dragon.

"Splat," Pikel assured him.

"You should be more concerned for the weather," Vander remarked gravely. "You do not understand the strength of storms in the high mountains, nor the price your private venture may exact from us all."

Cadderly accepted the scolding as the firbolg continued, and Ivan, even Shayleigh, joined in. The young priest wanted to defend himself, to convince them all, as he had convinced Danica, that destroying the *Ghearufu* was the more important quest, and even if they wound up stranded until the spring, even if the delay cost them their lives against Fyrentennimar, and cost the region dearly in its battle with Castle Trinity, the destruction of the malignant magical item had been worth the price. A younger Cadderly would have lashed out at his accusers.

Now Cadderly said nothing, offered no defense against his friends' justifiable anger. He had made his choice in good conscience, had made the only choice his faith and heart could accept, and now he would accept the consequences, for himself, for his friends, and for all the region. Loyal and trusting Danica, holding tightly to his arm, showed him that he would not suffer those consequences alone.

"We will get through the high passes," Danica said when Vander had played out his anger. "And we will prevail against the wizard Aballister and his minions in our enemies' fortress."

"Perhaps alone I could get through them," the firbolg agreed. "For I am of the cold mountains. My blood runs thick with warmth, and my legs are long and strong, able to push through towering drifts of snow."

"Me own legs ain't so long," Ivan put in sarcastically. "What do ye got for me?" he asked Cadderly sharply. "What spells, and how many? Durned fool priest. If ye meant to come here, couldn't ye have waited until the summer?"

"Yeah." Pikel's unexpected agreement stung Cadderly more than gruff Ivan's ranting ever could. But then Cadderly looked back to Danica for support and saw a mischievous look in her sparkling eyes.

"How friendly is that dragon?" she asked, leading all their gazes back to serene Fyrentennimar.

Cadderly smiled at once, though it took Ivan longer to catch on.

"Oh, no ye don't!" the yellow-bearded dwarf bellowed, but by the eager intrigue splayed on the faces of Cadderly and Danica, and by the sudden smiles of Shayleigh and the firbolg, Ivan knew he was blubbering a losing argument.

* * * * *

Shattered! Druzil imparted telepathically, emphatically, for perhaps the tenth time. *Shattered! Gone!* From the other end of the mental connection there was no immediate response, as though Aballister could not comprehend what the imp was talking about. Twice already Aballister had ordered Druzil to find the undead monster, to discover what had transpired to destroy the evil creature's corporeal form. Both times Druzil had replied that the task was quite impossible, that he had no idea of where to start looking.

Wherever the spirit had flown, Druzil knew that it was nowhere connected to the Material Plane. The imp pointedly reminded the wizard that he had been given only one red and one blue pouch of enchanting powder, that Aballister's lack of foresight had stranded him nearly a hundred miles from Castle Trinity with no way to get through any magical gates.

A wave of anger, imparted by Aballister, washed over Druzil. The imp's mind flared with pain; he feared that the wizard's mounting rage alone might destroy him. A dozen commands filtered through, each accompanied by a vicious threat. Druzil was at a loss. He had never witnessed Aballister so enraged, had never seen such a display of sheer power from him, or even from the mighty denizens of the lower planes that he had often dealt with in his centuries there.

Druzil tried to break the connection—he had often done that in the past—but Aballister's telepathic connection remained with him, held him fast.

When Aballister finally finished and released the suddenly exhausted imp, Druzil sat back against a tree stump with his dog-faced head resting forlornly in his clawed hands. He stared at the shattered flakes of the malignant monster, let his gaze meander up the imposing side of Nightglow, to the fog and clouds wherein Cadderly and his friends had disappeared. Aballister wanted Druzil to find the young priest and dog his steps, even to try to kill Cadderly if the opportunity presented itself.

No threat Aballister could possibly impose, no display of power, would prod Druzil to make that desperate attempt. The imp knew that he was no match for Cadderly, and knew, too, that Aballister might be the only one in the region who was.

But it was obvious to Druzil that Aballister didn't want it to come to that. Whatever satisfaction the old wizard might gain in personally crushing Cadderly would not make up for the inconvenience—not at a time when larger issues loomed in the wizard's designs. Aballister had labeled the undead monster as a possible ally. Now it was gone, and Druzil sensed that Cadderly had played some part in its destruction. The imp believed, too, that his own part in this drama had come to an end. The creature had been his guide to Cadderly. Without it, Druzil doubted that he could even locate the young priest. And with the weather fast shifting to the full wintry blasts, Druzil realized that it would take him weeks to get back to Castle Trinity—probably long after Cadderly was no more than a crimson stain on a stone floor.

"Bene tellemara," the imp said repeatedly, cursing foolish Aballister for not giving him more of the enchanting, gate-opening powder, cursing the foul, chill weather, cursing the undead monster for its failure, and ultimately cursing Cadderly.

Thoroughly miserable, Druzil made no move toward Nightglow, made no move at all. For many hours, the snow settling on his doggish snout and folded wings, the stubborn imp sat perfectly still on the tree stump, muttering, *"Bene tellemara."*

* * * * *

"I do not know how long the enchantment will hold the dragon," Cadderly admitted some time later, after Fyrentennimar had eagerly led them to the lair's main entrance, a gigantic cavern on the mountain's north slope with an opening wide enough for the dragon to swoop in and out with its huge wings extended.

"It'd be a real party for old Fyren to remember old Fyren when we're a thousand feet up on the damned thing's back!" Ivan snorted loudly, drawing angry looks from four of his companions and a slap on the back of the head from Pikel.

"Ye just said . . . " the yellow-bearded dwarf started to protest to Cadderly.

"What I just admitted is not information to be given freely to Fyrentennimar!" Cadderly whispered harshly. The dragon was some distance away, peering out into the howling wind and considering their intended course, but Cadderly had read many tales describing the extraordinary senses of dragonkind, many tales where an offhand whisper had cost a parleying party dearly against an easily flattered wyrm.

"The flight will be swift," Shayleigh reasoned. "You will not have to hold Fyrentennimar for long."

Cadderly could see that the fearless elf maiden was looking forward to the ride, could see that Danica, too, held no reservations against the potential gains. Hopping up and down, clapping his chubby hands and smiling all the while, Pikel's mood likewise was not hard to discern.

"What do you say?" Cadderly asked Vander, the one member who had not made clear his feelings.

"I say that you are desperate indeed to even consider this course," the firbolg replied bluntly. "But I am indebted to you for all my life, and if you choose to ride, I will go along." He cast a sidelong glance at grumbling Ivan. "As will the dwarf, do not doubt."

"Who're ye speaking for?" Ivan growled back.

"Would you stay alone in this cave, then, and wait for the dragon's return?" the firbolg casually asked.

Ivan mulled it over for a few minutes, then huffed defiantly, "Good point."

They rushed out the front entrance soon after, into the teeth of the now raging storm. The wind did little to hinder the massive dragon's progress, though, and the heat from Fyrentennimar's inner furnace, heat that lent the power to the dragon's dreadful breath, kept the six companions warm enough.

Bent low, eyes closed, Cadderly sat closest to old Fyren's head, right at the base of the red dragon's serpentine neck. The young priest reached again into the sphere of chaotic magics, focusing all his energies into extending his vital enchantment. To his relief, the dragon seemed pleased enough to carry the riders, seemed pleased just to be out in the wide world again. That thought inspired more than a few fears in Cadderly—what had Ivan said about letting a sleeping wyrm lie?—concerning the potential implications to the people of the region, particularly the implications to Carradoon, not so far away by a flying dragon's reckoning. Cadderly had made his choice, though, and now had to trust in the wisdom of that decision and hope for the best.

Danica sat right behind her love, arms wrapped about his waist, though she took great care not to disturb the young priest's concentration.

They climbed up above the storm, into sparkling sunlight, soaring through the crisp air. When they had passed the region of clouds, Fyrentennimar dove down into a crevice between two mountains, turning sidelong within the narrow pass. His leathery wings caught the updrafts, rode them fully as he came out of his steep bank, gaining speeds beyond the imagination of his thrilled riders.

Reveling in the sensation, which was many times more exciting than air-walking, Danica let go of Cadderly, threw her arms up high and wide and let the wind whip her unkempt hair about.

The world became a blur below them; Ivan complained that he was going to be sick, but no one cared or listened.

They came up fast on a ridge, and all of them, except for the concentrating Cadderly, screamed aloud in fear that they would slam against it. But Fyrentennimar was no novice to dragonflight, and the ridge was suddenly gone, left behind in the blink of an eye.

"Son of a smart goblin!" Ivan yelled, too amazed to remember that he meant to throw up. "Do it again!" he cried in glee, and the dragon apparently heard, for another ridge, and then another, and a jutting peak after that passed below or beside them in a wild rush, to a chorus of exhilarated screams that were outdone by the applauding roars of one yellow-bearded dwarf.

None of them could begin to guess at how fast they were traveling, could even comprehend the rush of dragonflight. They crossed the bulk of the Snowflakes in mere minutes, all of them, Vander and Ivan included, now in wholehearted agreement that the choice to ride the tamed wyrm had been a good one.

But then, suddenly and unexpectedly, mighty Fyrentennimar reared, seemed to hover in the air, as his massive horned head, his great fanged maw turned back to regard Cadderly.

"Uh-oh," Pikel muttered, thinking the fun at its end.

Cadderly sat upright, fearful that he had gone past the limits of control. He could not predict the chaotic magic, for its essence was founded in illogic and was in no way described in the harmonious song of Deneir.

Cadderly looked back to Danica and Shayleigh, no longer wearing expressions of freedom and excitement, and to grim Vander, nodding as though he had expected this disaster all along. Cadderly wanted to call out to the dragon, to ask Fyrentennimar what was wrong, but, sitting atop the volatile beast, suspended a thousand feet above the ground, he couldn't find the courage.

* * * * *

Dorigen watched in amazement as her wooden door bulged and groaned. Great bubbles of wood extended into her room and then retreated. She prudently moved to the side of the small chamber, out of harm's way.

A huge bubble rolled in from the door's center, holding the wood out to its extreme for a long moment. Then the door burst apart into a thousand flying splinters, each of them glowing silver with residual energy. Silver sparks became blue almost instantly, and not a single splinter struck the floor or opposite wall, was simply consumed to nothingness in midflight.

Aballister stormed in through the open portal.

"The ghost has failed," Dorigen remarked before the fuming wizard had even said a word.

Aballister stopped in the doorway and eyed the younger wizard suspiciously. "You viewed it through your crystal ball," he hissed, considering the device on the table before Dorigen.

"I view it in your expression," Dorigen quickly replied, fearing that the wizard would handle her as he had handled the door. She tossed her long salt-and-pepper hair back from her face, ran her crooked fingers through it, and went through a myriad of other movements, all designed to deflect Aballister's mounting rage.

Truly, the older wizard seemed on the verge of an explosion. His deep-set dark eyes narrowed dangerously, bony fingers clenching and unclenching at his sides.

"Your worries are plain to see," Dorigen said bluntly, knowing that it was precisely that fact that was bothering the wizard. Aballister, Dorigen knew, was a man who prided himself on being able to sublimate his emotions, on remaining cryptic at all times so that his enemies and rivals could not find any emotional advantage to use against him. "To remain calm and distant is the secret of a wizard's strength," the coldhearted Aballister had often said in the past, but such was not the case now, not with pesty Cadderly apparently making some headway in his try for Castle Trinity.

"You viewed it with your crystal ball," Aballister accused again, his voice a low growl, and Dorigen understood that it would not be wise for her to disagree a second time.

"The chimera and manticore have been defeated?" Dorigen stated as much as asked, something she had suspected since Aballister's last visit to her room, when he had grown outraged that their scrying would no longer work.

Aballister admitted the loss with a nod.

"And now the undead monster," Dorigen went on.

"I do not know that Cadderly played a part in that one's downfall," Aballister snapped. "I have Druzil looking into the matter even as we speak."

Dorigen nodded, but privately didn't agree at all. If the ghost had been destroyed, then the formidable Cadderly was surely behind it. Whether he would openly admit it or not, Aballister knew it, too.

"Have we anything else with which we might strike out at him?" Dorigen asked.

"Have you located him with your precious crystal ball?" Aballister growled back angrily.

Dorigen looked away, not wanting her superior to see the rage in her amber eyes. If he considered her scrying attempts pitiful, then why didn't Aballister take on the task himself? Aballister was no novice to scrying, after all. He had watched Barjin's movements when the priest had entered Castle Trinity, had even destroyed his valuable enchanted mirror by forcing his magic through it. Since that time, Aballister had not attempted any scrying at all, except one failed attempt earlier in Dorigen's room.

"Well, have you?" Aballister demanded.

Dorigen snapped an angry glare over him. "Simple spells can counteract scrying," she replied. "And I assure you, your son has little trouble with simple spells!"

Aballister's eyes widened, the old wizard seeming shocked that Dorigen had spoken so bluntly to him, had emphasized once more that this danger to Castle Trinity was being perpetrated by Aballister's own son. The wizard virtually trembled with anger and briefly considered lashing out with his power to punish Dorigen.

"Prepare your defenses," Dorigen said to him.

Again, her bluntness stunned the older wizard. "Cadderly will never get close to Castle Trinity," Aballister promised, an evil grin spreading over his face and calming him visibly. "The time has come for me to personally see to that troublesome child."

"You will go out?" Dorigen's tone was incredulous.

"My magic will go out," Aballister corrected. "The mountains themselves will shudder, and the sky will cry for the death of that foolish boy Cadderly! Let us see how a priest measures up against a wizard!" He cackled gleefully and turned away, sweeping determinedly out of the room.

Dorigen rested back in her chair and stared at the blasted portal, its jamb still smoldering long after Aballister had departed. She would keep trying with the crystal ball, more out of curiosity for this young priest and his exceptional friends than for Aballister's sake. In truth, Dorigen believed that she might have made some contact just a few minutes before Aballister had disturbed her, but she couldn't be sure so she didn't mention it to the pestering wizard. It had been just a fleeting sensation of rushing air, a sensation of freedom, of flying.

She hadn't seen the dragon, couldn't even be sure that she had actually made contact with Cadderly. But if it was the young priest, then Dorigen suspected that he would beat the expected timetable and would soon be knocking on Castle Trinity's door.

Aballister didn't need to know that.

Eleven

Strafing

*E*nemies?" Fyrentennimar's thunderous question made the six terribly vulnerable companions hold their breath in dread.

"We are friends," Cadderly replied weakly as the dragon went into a series of short stoops and quick rises, as close to a hovering maneuver as the bulky creature could accomplish.

Fyrentennimar's serpentine neck twisted, putting his head at a half-cocked position, almost like some curious dog.

"Are *they* enemies?" the dragon roared again.

They? Cadderly noted curiously, hopefully. "Who?"

Fyrentennimar bobbed his head and erupted with laughter. "Of course, of course!" he cried, his voice no longer carrying the edge of dragon hysteria. "Your eyes are not so keen as dragon eyes! I must remember that."

"What potential enemies do you speak of?" Cadderly asked impatiently, realizing that Fyrentennimar's aimless banter might continue for some time, and aware that his enchantment might not have much time remaining.

"Back on the trail," the dragon explained. "A procession of goblins and giants."

Cadderly turned to Danica and Shayleigh. "We should continue on our way," he offered. "I can bid Fyrentennimar to let us down far from the monstrous caravan."

"How many?" Shayleigh asked grimly, one hand tightly grasping her bow and an eager sparkle in her violet eyes. Both Cadderly and Danica knew from that look that the elf maiden did not wish to simply pass the monsters by.

Cadderly looked to Danica for support. When it was not immediately forthcoming, he continued, "I do not know how long the dragon will remain calm. The risk . . . "

"All the flight is a risk," Danica replied evenly, and Shayleigh seemed to approve.

"If Shilmista was your home, you would not be so quick to allow giants and goblins to return to their holes," the elf maiden said to Cadderly. "We of the wood know well what the spring will bring upon us."

"If we destroy Castle Trinity, the monsters might not return," Cadderly reasoned.

"If you were of Shilmista, would you take that chance?"

Danica nodded at Shayleigh's logic, but her smile disappeared when she regarded Cadderly's grim expression. "Let us allow our friends to decide," the monk offered.

Not realizing how much the surly Ivan had come to enjoy dragonflight, Cadderly readily agreed.

To this point, Ivan, Pikel, and Vander, enjoying the short, fluttering air-hops of the great red, had remained oblivious to the discussion.

"Ivan!" Danica called back to the dwarf. "Would you care for the chance to smash a few goblin heads?"

The yellow-bearded dwarf roared, Pikel squeaked in glee, and Danica turned a smug smile back Cadderly's way. The young priest scowled, thinking Danica's method of asking Ivan was terribly unfair—what dwarf would say no to that question?

"Let us use our new ally to our best advantage," Shayleigh said to the defeated young priest.

Cadderly relaxed against the scaly dragon neck, trying to sort out this whole situation. He knew that they should go straight on to Castle Trinity, that any fighting now could jeopardize their chance for success later, especially if the dragon escaped his enchantment.

But was he ready for Castle Trinity? After his fight to destroy the *Ghearufu* and his titanic struggle with Ghost, Cadderly wasn't so sure. Up to now, he had been primarily concerned with the *Ghearufu*, but with that task out of the way, he had begun to look ahead—to powerful wizards and a well-trained army, entrenched in a secluded mountain fortress.

Cadderly needed time to catch his breath and to better consider those dangers at the end of his intended road. He decided that an attack on the goblin band, with a dragon on his side, might actually come as a reprieve.

And he couldn't, in good conscience, deny Shayleigh's fears for Shilmista or the plaintive, determined expression on her fair elven face. The young priest had to admit, to himself at least, that there was something alluring about the idea of experiencing unleashed dragon power from this secure vantage point.

"I believe that they are enemies, mighty Fyrentennimar," Cadderly called back to the unusually patient dragon. "Is there anything we might do against them?"

In answer, the dragon dipped one wing and dropped into a stoop, plummeting at breakneck speed, then leveling out and using his momentum to begin a great rush around the mountain. From this lower point, the friends had no trouble spotting the monstrous caravan, several hundred strong and with a fair number of giants among the shuffling, hunched goblinoid ranks, trudging along a trail in a narrow valley bordered by steep, rocky walls.

Fyrentennimar kept close to the ridges, circling away

from the monsters. In mere seconds, the valley and the caravan seemed far removed.

"Do tell me, humble priest," the obviously eager dragon implored Cadderly. Cadderly looked to his friends once more, to confirm the decision, and found five bobbing heads staring back at him.

"They are enemies," Cadderly confirmed. "What is our role in the battle?"

"*Your* role?" the great beast echoed incredulously. "Hang on to my spiked spine with all your pitiful strength!"

The dragon banked, its wings going nearly perpendicular to the ground (drawing another cry of glee from Ivan and Pikel), and then shot off around the targeted peak. The friends felt the warmth growing within the wyrm, the flaring fires of old Fyren's ire. Reptilian eyes narrowed evilly, and in realizing the wyrm's mounting intensity, Cadderly wasn't so certain that he liked this whole scenario.

They came around the base of the mountain into the entrance to the narrow valley, still in a tight bank, the rock walls rushing by the six astonished friends in a dizzying blur. The dragon leveled and dipped even lower, the tips of his wide wings only a dozen feet or so from the sheer walls. The goblins and giants at the rear of the caravan turned and let out terrified shrieks, but so swift was the dragon's flight that they had no time to even break ranks before Fyrentennimar was upon them.

A searing line of fire strafed the trailing monsters. Goblins curled up into charred balls; mighty giants toppled, slapping futilely at the deadly flames as their bodies were consumed.

Acrid smoke rose in the dragon's wake. His flames were exhausted before he had gotten very far into the long line, but Fyrentennimar proudly stayed low in his flight, let his enemies see him and fear him.

All about the valley, the monsters went into an uncontrolled frenzy. Giants squashed goblins and slammed into other giants; goblins clawed and battled with their own kin, even coming to sword blows in their desperation to get away.

"Oh, my dear Deneir," Cadderly muttered, awestruck once again by the bared power of the dragon, by the utter terror Fyrentennimar had evoked in those pitiful creatures on the ground.

No, Cadderly told himself, not pitiful. These were Shilmista's invaders, the plague that had scarred the elven wood and slaughtered many of elf prince Elbereth's people. The plague that would undoubtedly return once more in the spring to complete what had been begun.

Shayleigh, her violet eyes narrow and grim, let fly a few well-aimed bowshots. She saw one goblin aiming a crude bow the dragon's way, but the dim-witted creature could not calculate the incredible speed, and its shot flew far behind. Shayleigh was the better archer, putting an arrow into the cursing goblin's filthy mouth.

Another bowshot followed immediately, this one knifing into a goblin's back and dropping the wretched thing dead to the ground.

Cadderly winced at that one, caught by the realization that this creature was only trying to flee and posed no threat to them. That notion assaulted the young priest's sheltered sensibilities.

Until he again remembered the elven forest, remembered the scars in Shilmista. These were enemies, he decided finally, the taste of vengeance rising in his throat. The young priest fell into the song of Deneir and suddenly wore as grim an expression as that of his elvish companion. He heard the notes loud and strong in his head, as though Deneir approved of his decision, and he readily fell into its flow.

Fyrentennimar banked upward as the valley narrowed. As soon as he had cleared the steep walls the dragon banked again, steeply, swerving around for another run at the creatures.

Those monsters at the front of the caravan might have

gotten away then, slipped out the narrow end of the valley into the wide expanses where they could have broken ranks altogether.

Cadderly stopped them.

He called to the rock walls at the valley's end, concentrated his magic on one high archway. The closest monster, a fat-bellied giant, rushed through that archway, and the rocks came to life, snapping repeatedly like an enormous maw, chomping the surprised giant into a pile of bloody mush.

The second giant in line skidded to a stop, eyeing the rocks with blank amazement. Wanting to test the unbelievable trap, the behemoth plucked up a helpless goblin at its side and tossed the creature forward.

Smacking, munching sounds accompanied the goblin's screams and continued long after the cries had died away, bits and pieces of the goblin flopping through the barrier on the other side.

The grisly scene was gone from Cadderly's sight in a moment as the dragon came about. For the wyrm, the turn was tight, but still huge Fyrentennimar had to travel a great distance from the valley to manage it.

"Have him put me down," Danica implored Cadderly.

"And me!" declared Vander from farther back. The firbolg and Danica exchanged excited looks, eager to fight beside each other.

Cadderly shook his head at the outrageous idea and closed his eyes, falling back into his chanting.

"Put me down, old Fyren!" Danica called out. Cadderly's eyes popped wide, but the obedient dragon pulled up short beside a ridge, and both Danica and Vander hopped from their perches, running off before Cadderly could react.

"Hey, we're missing all the fun!" Ivan realized as the wyrm set off once more, quickly gaining altitude. The dwarf started to call out to the dragon, but Pikel grabbed him by the beard and pulled him close, whispering something into his ear.

Ivan roared happily, and both dwarves scrambled from the dragon's back, one going for each wing.

"What are you doing?" Cadderly demanded.

"Just tell the damned wyrm to hold on tight!" Ivan cried back, and then he disappeared from view, crawling hand over hand down the scaly side. His head popped back up a moment later. "But not too tight!" he added, and then he was gone.

"What?" Cadderly replied incredulously, and it took him a few moments to catch on. "Fyrentennimar!" he cried desperately.

* * * * *

Danica and Vander sped off for the back and wider end of the valley, looking for any monsters that might have found their way through the stench and smoke. Only a few minutes after Fyrentennimar had put them down, with the dragon still flying wide, though now angled for his second pass, the two spotted several goblins and a single, lumbering giant coming down a barren, rocky slope, heading directly for them.

The firbolg and the monk nodded and split up, each seeking the cover of some of the many boulders in the region.

The goblins and the giant were looking back more than forward, too afraid of the dragon to even think that there might be other danger lurking ahead.

Danica came out in a rush from the side, hurling one dagger after another, dropping a pair of goblins, and then charged forward, diving into a roll before her surprised adversaries and coming up with a flurry of ferocious blows.

Facial bones were smashed apart, and knifing fingers crushed a windpipe. Before Danica had even played out her momentum, four of the nine goblins lay dead at her feet.

The evil giant, on the far side of the band, turned to meet her charge, but noticed a movement back the other way and spun about, huge club at the ready. A goblin rushed by, eyeing Danica and shrieking in fear.

Vander cleaved it in half.

"Giant-kin," the club-wielding monster said to Vander in the rolling, thunderous language of the hill giants.

Vander snarled and rushed ahead, his great sword coming across in a blurring arc. The hill giant fell back, throwing its club up in a frantic defense. By sheer luck, the club fell in line with the rushing sword, Vander's blade diving many inches into the wood.

Vander tried to pull back on the sword, to retract it and slash again, but the club's hard wood held it fast.

The hill giant, much larger and several times heavier than Vander's eight hundred pounds, rushed forward, letting go of its club and spreading its huge arms out wide to engulf its foe.

Vander twisted and punched out, connecting solidly but doing little to impede his enemy's momentum. The firbolg went down heavily, under two tons of hill giant flesh.

The four remaining goblins looked as much at each other as at Danica, each waiting for one of its companions to make the first move. They circled the apparently unarmed monk, one lifting a spear.

Now that the initial surprise was gone, Danica stayed down in a defensive crouch, preferring to let her enemies come to her. The goblins wisely spread out around her, but she remained confident, turning slowly so that no creature could remain behind her.

The spear wielder pumped its arm, and Danica started to dive to the right. She stopped almost immediately, though, recognizing the goblin's move as a feint, and used the break to her advantage, coming back hard to the left, spinning low and straight-kicking one of the other goblins in the knee.

The creature jerked straight, then fell back, clutching its broken limb.

Danica was already back to circling, now eyeing the

spear wielder directly, taking its measure, using its body language to discern its every thought.

* * * * *

Cadderly saw the fight off to the side, noticed Vander buried beneath the flabby folds of the monstrous hill giant. He tried to think of a way to help, but suddenly the valley walls were up around him again as Fyrentennimar began another breath-stealing approach.

Shayleigh nimbly moved about on the dragon's back, determined to play a role and firing her bow repeatedly. At first, her shots were random, nearly every one scoring a hit, but then she concentrated her fire on one hill giant. By the time Fyrentennimar's flight took her beyond range of the beast, its wide chest sported a half-dozen arrows.

"Get lower, ye damned fun-stealing wyrm!" came a cry from below, a cry informing Cadderly that Ivan and Pikel were in position. The young priest fell flat to his belly and peered over the front edge of the dragon's wing.

Hanging below him were the Bouldershoulder brothers, one in each of Fyrentennimar's clutching talons. The dragon did fly lower, and Pikel howled in glee as he put his tree-trunk club in line and used the dragon's momentum to splatter the head of a giant that was too slow in ducking.

Ivan took an axe swipe on the other side as they passed, but he mistimed the blow badly and caught nothing but air.

"Sandstone!" the frustrated dwarf bellowed.

Cadderly's orderly sensibilities could not accept the craziness about him. Helplessly shaking his head, he managed to sit back up and dropped a hand into a berry-filled pouch. He uttered the last words of the enchantment in resigned tones, then took out a handful of the berries and tossed them randomly into the air. The seeds exploded into tiny bursts of flame as they hit, startling and stinging giants, wounding and even killing a few goblins.

Fyrentennimar swerved up again, slightly, as the valley

started to narrow, but the friends knew that he would not soar away, knew that he had not finished the run.

A swarm of creatures huddled about the back end of the valley, hemmed in by the sheer walls and Cadderly's biting enchantment. Their frenzy multiplied many times over as the dragon reared near them. Giants stuffed goblins through the archway (one actually passed through without being hit, to run screaming down the rocky slope on the other side), and then many giants, in sheer terror of the great dragon, jumped in themselves.

The dragon's serpentine neck shot forward, and then came the flames. Fyrentennimar's maw waved from side to side, changing the fire's angle, immolating the whole mass of creatures.

On and on it went, interminably long for the stunned Cadderly.

Agonized cries came from creatures who were soon no more than crackling bones; all the monstrous swarm seemed to flow together in a singular bubbling mass.

"Oo," Pikel muttered admiringly, the dwarf having a fine view of the catastrophe from his low perch. Ivan, shaking his head in disbelief, couldn't find the words to reply.

* * * * *

Danica saw the panic welling in the goblin, knew that it wanted to throw the spear and run off. She locked her gaze upon it fully, forced it to stare into her eyes, almost hypnotizing in their intensity.

She had to hold the goblin's shot a bit longer, until the anxious club wielder to her right made the first move.

Danica straightened and seemed to relax, though she kept her intimidating gaze steady. She dipped and turned suddenly, caught the club in both hands as it predictably came across, and slid down, hooking the surprised goblin's knees with her feet and pulling the creature around her.

The goblin jerked suddenly, its eyes popping wide, and

Danica, though she couldn't see the spear sticking from the goblin's back, knew that her timing, and her understanding of her enemies, had been perfect.

She came up in a spin, tearing the club from the dying creature's grasp and hurling it straight back, into the chest of the next charging goblin. The creature fumbled with the unexpected missile for a moment, getting it tangled with its sword, then finally tossing it aside. It managed to focus its attention on Danica just as her foot snapped into its throat.

Again Danica was spinning, leaping over the dead club wielder and tearing the spear from its back. Three running strides later, she let fly the crude weapon. The spear didn't hit the mark exactly, but it did get tangled up in its original owner's legs enough to drop the goblin hard to its face.

It lay on its belly for a moment, trying to shake away its dizziness.

Then Danica was upon it, and it was dead. The monk looked back to the one remaining goblin, the first of the four she had hit. It was floundering about, half-hopping, half-crawling, as it continued to grasp at its shattered kneecap. It struggled past two of its companions, two goblins that had died grasping at daggers. Thinking to arm itself, the struggling creature ambled for the daggers, but stopped and looked up, dismayed, for Danica had gotten there first.

* * * * *

Vander slapped futilely against the giant's bulk, thrashing about with all his strength, even biting the monster on the neck. But all the savagery the powerful firbolg could muster seemed puny beneath the sheer size of the hill giant.

Vander found his breathing hard to come by and wondered how long he could hold out beneath the two-ton behemoth. His estimate lessened considerably when the hill giant began to bounce, pushing off the ground with its huge hands and free-falling back on top of poor Vander.

Vander's initial thoughts were to curl up in a ball. He realized, though, that his body could not take the pounding for long, whatever he might do—the first bounce had blasted out his breath, and he could only draw small amounts of air between each subsequent slam. Every time the hill giant came crushing back down, Vander expected his rib cage to collapse.

Without even thinking of the movement, Vander used one moment of freedom to tuck his legs up near his belly. Fortune was with the firbolg, for when the hill giant came back down, its own weight drove Vander's knees hard into its abdomen. Back up went the hill giant, higher this time, fully extending its arms that it might come back with one final slam.

Up came Vander's feet, straight out in pursuit of the monster's belly, locking the giant up high before its fall could build momentum. The desperate firbolg strained with all his might; leg muscles flexed and ripped and stood out like iron cords. The giant, its girth hanging several feet off the ground, freed up one hand and punched Vander across the face, nearly knocking him senseless.

Vander accepted the blow, but kept his focus on his legs and groaned against the strain, compelling his massive legs to straighten.

The giant rose up a few more inches; Vander knew that he could not hold the weight. He kicked out a final time, trying to buy himself precious seconds and space, then curled his legs and rolled, securing the butt of his sword against the ground and angling the blade straight up.

The giant's eyes widened in horror as it flailed its arms and thrashed about for the instant of its descent, but it could not get to the side, could not get out of line. The sword entered it at the juncture between its belly and its chest, driving upward through the monster's diaphragm. The hill giant planted its quivering arms firmly, broke its fall so that it would not further impale itself.

Vander was free, now, but he did not immediately roll out

from under the giant. He grasped his blade in both arms and heaved it straight up, driving it deeper into the giant's flesh.

The quivering arms buckled altogether, and the giant slid down the blade, issuing a long, low groan as the tip of the sword came against its backbone and stopped its descent for a moment. Then the sword broke clear, and the behemoth lay very still, feeling no pain, feeling nothing at all.

Vander, pressed again under the enormous weight, jerked the sword a few times to make sure the monster was dead, then began the task of crawling out. Danica, finished with her own work, was soon crouched beside him.

* * * * *

Eventually the dragon's fire ceased, leaving the entire horde of creatures at the narrow end of the valley lying together in a bulbous, smoldering mass.

Those monsters behind the dragon could have rushed in to strike at the low-flying beast's back, but they did not, for they were too terrified to even approach the deadly wyrm.

Ivan and Pikel waved weapons at them and taunted them, trying to draw them in.

"Aw, run off then, ye cowardly bunch!" a frustrated Ivan yelled.

A moment later, when the dragon's talons let go of the dwarves, Ivan yelled a singular note of surprise. He and Pikel dropped fifteen feet to the ground, bounced right back to their feet, and hopped about, dazed.

Fifty feet behind them, the fleeing giants and goblins turned and stared curiously, not knowing which way to run.

"Humble priest, get you down!" Fyrentennimar roared, shaking Cadderly from his daze. The young priest turned back to old Fyren, wondering if the ethics enchantment had ceased, wondering if he was about to die.

"*Get you down!*" Fyrentennimar cried again, and the force of his stone-splitting voice nearly knocked Cadderly from his perch. He and Shayleigh were moving in an instant, crawling down the spiked back and tail and dropping the last few feet to the ground to stand beside Ivan and Pikel.

"Playing with dragons," Ivan remarked sarcastically under his breath.

Shayleigh lifted her bow but had to close her eyes and look away as Fyrentennimar, wings beating fiercely, pivoted in the air, whipping the smoke and dust about. The dragon dipped into a short stoop, reared again, and then fell over the remaining group of monsters, tail thrashing, spiked foreclaws slashing, great hind legs kicking, and wings beating a hurricane of wind. A swoop of the dragon's tail sent four goblins soaring, splattering them against the valley wall with force enough to shatter most of the bones in their bodies, and then the tail itself connected on the wall, opening a huge crack in the stone and leaving crimson marks where the goblins had been. A giant, horrified beyond reason, lifted its club and charged.

Fyrentennimar's maw clamped over it, hoisting it easily into the air. Squealing like some barnyard animal at the slaughterhouse, the giant freed one arm from the side of the wyrm's maw and slapped its pitiful club against the armored head.

Fyrentennimar bit the giant in half, its legs dropping free to the stone.

Even sturdy Ivan was shaken by the spectacle of the dragon's wholehearted slaughter, by the mass of bubbling corpses and the flying and broken bodies of those enemies caught in close to the enraged wyrm.

"Glad he's on our side," Ivan said, his breathless voice barely a whisper.

Cadderly grimaced at the words, remembering again the tone Fyrentennimar had used when ordering him down. He studied the dragon's lusty, hungry movements as old Fyren reveled in the blood and carnage.

"Is he?" the young priest muttered under his breath.

Chaos

A giant's broken form came flying up over the wall of the valley, landing hard and bouncing down the rocky slope past Vander and Danica.

They heard the chaos within the valley, heard the dragon's primal roars and the horrified screams of the doomed monsters. Neither Danica nor Vander held much pity for the evil goblins and giants, but they looked to each other with honest fear, simply overwhelmed by the awakening storm within those entrapping walls. Danica motioned for Vander to move around to the valley entrance, while she took a more direct course up the slope.

Before she even got to the top, she saw monsters, and pieces of monsters, flipping into the air, tumbling about and dropping back into the frenzy. Her nerves on end, Danica could not hold back a chuckle, thinking that the scene reminded her of Pikel's work in the Edificant Library's kitchen, the druidic-minded dwarf stubbornly (and clumsily) tossing a salad of woodland flora despite

135

Ivan's roaring protests.

The dragon's tail must have hit the stone wall then, for Danica, though she was separated from the blow by forty feet of solid stone, suddenly found herself sitting down.

* * * * *

Cadderly slipped into the dreamstate, into the song of Deneir, and reached his mental perceptions out to Fyrentennimar.

A wall of red blocked his entry.

"What do you know?" Shayleigh asked, recognizing the concern, even dread, in the young priest's expression.

Cadderly did not answer. Again he fell into the song, reached out to the dragon. But Fyrentennimar's savage rage blocked him and held any real communication far away.

Cadderly knew in his heart that old Fyren would no longer consider him an ally, that in the bloodlust, the dragon had reverted to its true, wicked nature. He moved the notes of the song toward the sphere of chaos, thinking to delve there again and attempt to tame the wyrm once more.

He opened his eyes for just a minute, regarded the complete slaughter of the few remaining monsters, and sensed that no such spell could get through the outraged dragon's instinctual mental defenses.

"Get back to the far end of the valley," he said as calmly as he could to Shayleigh. "Ready your bow."

The elf maiden eyed him gravely, considering the implications of his grim tone. "The enchantment is no more?" she asked.

"Ready your bow," Cadderly repeated.

There wasn't much left of the monstrous column; Fyrentennimar would be finished in mere minutes. Cadderly called up his protective magics, drew a line of dragonbane across the valley floor, and brought a magical fire shield around him and the two confused dwarves at his side.

"What are ye doing?" Ivan demanded, always suspicious of magic and especially on edge with an enraged dragon barely a hundred yards away.

"It is a spell of the elements," Cadderly tried to quickly explain. "On me, it will stop the dragon fire."

"Uh-oh," Pikel mumbled, figuring out the implications of Cadderly's precautions.

"On you it will diminish the fire, but not completely," the young priest finished. "Get to the wall and find a rock to hide behind."

The dwarves didn't have to be asked twice. Normally, they would have remained boldly at their ally's side, ready for battle. But this was a dragon, after all.

So Cadderly stood alone in the center of the valley, surrounded by carnage, by torn reminders of the dragon's wrath. He stooped low and grabbed a handful of dirt from one of Fyrentennimar's footprints, then stood straight and resolute, reminding himself that he had done as the tenets of Deneir demanded. He had destroyed the *Ghearufu*.

Still, he thought of Danica, his love, and the new life they had begun in Carradoon, and he did not want to die.

Fyrentennimar swallowed whole the last cowering goblin and turned about. Reptilian eyes narrowed, shooting glaring beams even under the light of day. Almost immediately, those beams focused directly on Cadderly.

"Well done, mighty wyrm!" Cadderly cried out, hoping that his guess might be wrong, that the dragon might still be caught within a goodly moral code.

"*Humble priest . . .*" Fyrentennimar replied, and Cadderly thought the booming voice would surely destroy his hearing. Since he had leveled the enchantment at the dragon, Cadderly had only heard that voice twice, both times when the dragon had suspected that enemies were about. Crouched low like a hunting dog, walking on all fours with his leathery wings tucked in tight to his back, the dragon quickly halved the hundred-yard distance to Cadderly.

"You have done us a great service," Cadderly began.

"*Humble priest!*" Fyrentennimar interrupted.

The song of Deneir played in Cadderly's thoughts. He knew that he would need a diversion, something physical and powerful to gain time as he sorted through the notes of a spell he had not yet fully come to understand.

"A service both in your cave and in taking us across the mountains," Cadderly went on, hoping that he might steal some time with flattery. He remained conscious of the song as he spoke, the notes of the needed spell coming clearer with each playing. "But now, it is time for you . . . "

"*Humble priest!*"

Cadderly found no answer to the thunderous roar, the absolute indication that Fyrentennimar did not yet consider the killing to be at its end. With low growls shivering the stone beneath Cadderly's feet, the dragon stalked in.

Those eyes! Cadderly lost his concentration, caught in their hypnotizing intensity. He felt helpless, hopeless, surely doomed against this godlike creature, this terror beyond imagination. He fought for breath, fought against the welling panic that told him to run for his life.

Fyrentennimar was close. How had Fyrentennimar gotten so damned close?

The dragon's head slowly moved back, serpentine neck coiling. A foreclaw tucked up tight against the massive beast's chest, while its hind legs tamped down securely on the stone.

"Get outa there!" Ivan roared from the side, recognizing that the beast was about to spring. Cadderly heard the words and agreed wholeheartedly, but could not get his legs to move.

An arrow zipped above Cadderly's head, splintering harmlessly as it struck the dragon's impenetrable natural armor.

Intent on Cadderly the deceiver, Fyrentennimar did not seem to even notice.

Of all the things Cadderly of Carradoon would see in his

life, nothing would come close to the sheer terror of seeing Fyrentennimar's ensuing spring. The dragon, so huge, shot forward with the speed of a viper, came at Cadderly with a maw opened wide enough to swallow him whole, showing rows of gleaming teeth, each as long as the young priest's forearm.

In that split second, Cadderly's vision failed him, as though his mind simply could not accept the image.

Just a dozen feet in front of him, Fyrentennimar's expression changed suddenly. His head snapped to the side and contorted weirdly, as if he was pushing against some resilient bubble.

"Dragonbane," Cadderly muttered, the success of his ward bringing him some small measure of hope.

Old Fyren twisted and struggled, bending the blocking line, refusing to relent. The great hind legs dug deep scratches into the stone, and the hungry maw snapped repeatedly, looking for something tangible to tear.

Cadderly began his chant. Another arrow whipped past him, this one grazing Fyrentennimar's eye.

The dragon's wings spread wide, lifting old Fyren upright. The dragon roared and hissed and sucked in air.

Cadderly closed his eyes and continued to chant, locking his thoughts on the notes of Deneir's song.

The flames engulfed him, scorched and melted the stone at his feet. His friends cried out, thinking him consumed, but he did not hear them. His protective globe sizzled green about him, thinning dangerously as though it would not endure, but Cadderly did not see.

All he heard was the song of Deneir; all he saw was the music of the heavenly spheres.

* * * * *

When Danica came to lip of the valley wall and saw her love apparently immolated below her, her legs buckled and her heart fluttered—she thought it would stop altogether.

Her warrior instincts told her to go to the aid of her love, but what could she do against the likes of Fyrentennimar? Her hands and feet could be deadly against orcs and goblins, even giants, but they would do little damage slamming the iron-hard scales of the wyrm. Danica could hurl her crystal-bladed daggers into the heart of an ogre ten yards away, but those blades were tiny things when measured against the sheer bulk of Fyrentennimar.

The dragon fires ended, and, looking at Cadderly, so boldly facing the wyrm in the open valley, Danica knew that she had to do something.

"Fyrentennimar the awesome?" she cried incredulously. "A puny and weak thing is he, by my own eyes. A pretender of strength who cowers when danger is near!"

The dragon's head snapped around to face her, high above on the lip of the valley wall.

"Ugly *worm*," Danica chided, emphasizing her use of "worm" instead of "wyrm," perhaps the most insulting thing one could say to a dragon. "Ugly and weak worm!"

The dragon's tail twitched dangerously, reptilian eyes narrowed to mere slits, and old Fyren's low growl reverberated through the valley stone.

Standing before the distracted dragon, Cadderly picked up the pace of his chanting. He was truly glad for the distraction, but terribly afraid that Danica was pushing the explosive dragon beyond reason.

Danica laughed at old Fyren, just crossed her hands over her belly and shook with laughter. Her thoughts were quite serious, though. She recalled the ancient writings of Penpahg D'Ahn, the Grandmaster of her sect.

You anticipate the attacks of your enemy, the Grandmaster had promised. *You do not react, you move before your enemy moves. As the bowman fires, his target is gone. As the swordsman thrusts ahead, his enemy, you, are behind him.*

And as the dragon breathes, Penpahg had said, *so its flames shall touch only empty stone.*

Danica needed those words now, with Fyrentennimar's

head waving only a hundred feet below her. Penpahg D'Ahn's writings were the source of her strength, the inspiration for her life, and she had to trust them now, even in the face of an outraged red dragon.

"Ugly, ugly Fyrentennimar, who thinks he is so good," she sang. "His talons cannot tear cotton, his breath cannot light wood!" Not an impressive rhyme perhaps, but the words assaulted the overly proud Fyrentennimar more profoundly than any weapon ever could.

The dragon's wings beat suddenly, ferociously, lifting the dragon into the air—almost.

Cadderly completed his spell at that moment, and the stone beneath Fyrentennimar reshaped, animated, and grabbed at the dragon's rear claws. Old Fyren stretched to his limit, seemed almost springlike as he came crashing back down, falling tight against his haunches, but all of his subsequent thrashing could not break the valley floor's hold.

Fyrentennimar knew at once the source of his entrapment, and his great head whipped around, slamming hard against the blocking line of the dragonbane spell.

Cadderly paled—could his protective globe defeat a second searing blast of dragon breath?

"His wings cannot lift his blubber," Danica cried out. "His tail cannot swat a gnat."

The dragon's ensuing roar echoed off mountain walls a dozen miles away, sent animals and monsters rushing for the cover of their holes throughout the Snowflake Mountains. The serpentine neck stretched forward, and a gout of flames fell over Danica.

Stone melted and poured from the ledge in a red-glowing river. Pikel, hiding in an alcove beneath the region, let out a frightened squeak and rushed away.

Cadderly verged on panic, thought for sure that he had just seen his love die, and knew in his heart, despite the logical claims of his conscience, that nothing, not the destruction of the *Ghearufu* or the downfall of Castle Trinity, could be worth such a loss.

He calmed, though, when he remembered who he was thinking of, remembered the wisdom and almost magical talents of his dear Danica. He had to trust in her, as she so often trusted in him, had to believe that her decisions would be the correct decisions.

"His horns get caught in archways," Danica continued the rhyme, laughing over the words as she came back up to the ledge at a point thirty feet to the side. "And his muscles are no more than fat!"

Fyrentennimar's eyes widened with outrage and incredulity. He thrashed his tail and legs, slammed his horned head repeatedly against the magical dragonbane barrier, and beat his wings so fiercely that goblin corpses shifted and slid, caught up in the wind.

Like Danica, Cadderly was grinning widely, though he knew that the fight was far from won. One of Fyrentenni-mar's claws had torn free of the stone, and the other would soon break through. The young priest completed his next enchantment, pulled from the sphere of time, and hurled waves of magical energy at the distracted dragon.

Old Fyren felt the stone loosen about his one trapped leg, though it retightened immediately. The dragon, wise with years though he was, did not understand the significance, did not understand why the valley suddenly seemed much larger to him.

Again the wyrm sensed that Cadderly was somehow involved, and he calmed his tirade and steeled an angry glare over the supposedly "humble" priest. "What have you done?" Fyrentennimar demanded.

The dragon jerked suddenly, slammed from behind by Vander, the firbolg's huge sword smashing in hard at Fyrentennimar's trapped haunch.

"Time to go!" Ivan yelled to his brother, and the two dwarves appeared from behind their rocks, heads down in a wild charge.

To the still huge Fyrentennimar, the firbolg's hit did no

real damage. A tail slap sent Vander flying away, crashing down against the base of the valley wall. Resilient, Vander came right back up, understanding that none of the band could give in to the pain and the terror, that there could be no retreat and no quarter against such a merciless and terrible foe.

The new distractions could not have come at a better moment for Cadderly. Again came the waves of his insidious magic, and to old Fyren, the valley seemed larger still.

Then the dragon understood—the "humble" priest was stealing his age! And to a dragon, age was the measure of size and strength. "Old Fyren" was more than a match for the pitiful companions, but suddenly "young Fyren" found himself in dire straits.

"Bat-winged newt with a bumpy head, run away, run away before you're dead!" Danica cried out.

The immediate threats were the charging dwarves and the humble priest with his wicked magic. Fyrentennimar knew this rationally, knew that he should put his mouth in line with the charging dwarves and incinerate them before they got near him. But no respectable red dragon could ignore the taunt of "bat-winged newt," and Fyrentennimar's head went back up toward the ledge, his fire bursting forth in Danica's direction.

Or at least, bursting forth to where Danica had been.

By the time the fires ended with more molten stone slipping down from the ledge, Ivan and Pikel were hacking and smashing away, and while their weapons would have skipped harmlessly off the scale plating of "old Fyren," they now cracked and smashed apart the thinned and smaller scales. After only three furious swings, Ivan's axe dug deep into dragon flesh.

Similarly, Shayleigh's line of arrows chipped away at the dragon's scales. So perfect was the elf maiden's aim that the next six arrows that left her quiver hit the dragon in a concentrated pattern no larger than the brim of Cadderly's blue hat.

Cadderly was truly exhausted. His eyelids drooped heavily; his heart pounded in his chest. He went back into the song again, though, stubbornly steeled his gaze, and loosed the energies.

This time, Fyrentennimar was ready for the magical assault, and the spell was turned aside.

Cadderly came at him again, and then a third time. The young priest could barely focus his vision, could hardly remember what he was doing and why he was doing it. His head throbbed; he felt as if every ounce of magical energy he let loose was an ounce of energy stolen from his own life-force.

Yet he sang on.

Then he was lying on the stone, his head bleeding from the unexpected impact on the valley floor. He looked up and was glad to see that his enchantment had gotten through once more, that Fyrentennimar seemed not so large to him, barely taller than a hill giant. But Cadderly knew that the spells were not lasting, that Fyrentennimar's stolen centuries would soon return. They had to hit at the dragon hard right now; Cadderly had to find some offensive magic that would smash the monster while the dragon was caught in his lessened state.

But the song of Deneir would not play in the young priest's head. He could not bring to mind the name of his holy book, could not even recall his own name. The pain in his head throbbed, blocking all avenues of thought. He could hardly draw breath past the sheer physical exertion of his beating chest. He brought a hand to his pounding heart and felt his bandolier, then, following that singular focused thought, drew out his hand-crossbow.

Ivan and Pikel went into a flurry of activity under the dragon's slashing foreclaws. Ivan got buffeted by a wing, but hooked his axe over the limb's top and would not be thrown away.

Vander's next hit on the dragon's haunch shattered several scales and drove a deep gash. Fyrentennimar roared in agony, swooped his serpentine neck about, launching his opened maw for the dangerous giant.

Vander tugged his sword free, knew that he had to be quick, or be snapped in half.

It took Cadderly several moments to load and cock his weapon, and when he looked back to the fight, he found Fyrentennimar, on the stone and level with him, staring him in the eye from just a few feet away!

Cadderly cried out and fired, the quarrel blasting into the dragon's nostril and blowing pieces from his face. Cadderly, scrambling on all fours with the little strength he had left, didn't even see the hit. He calmed considerably when he at last looked back, though, when he realized that Fyrentenni-mar's head had only been near him, had only crossed the line of dragonbane, because Vander had lopped it off, halfway up the neck.

Pikel stood by the fallen torso, mumbling, "Oooo," over and over. Cadderly, his senses slowly returning, did not understand the green-bearded dwarf's apparent concern, until he saw the top of Ivan's head wriggle out from under the chest of the dead wyrm. With a stream of curses to make a barkeep of Waterdeep's dock ward blush, Ivan pulled himself out, slapping Pikel's offered helping hand away. The yellow-bearded dwarf hopped to his feet, hands planted squarely on his hips, eyeing Vander dangerously.

"Riding stupid dragons!" he huffed, glancing menacingly Cadderly's way.

"Well?" the dwarf roared at the confused firbolg. Vander looked to Pikel for some explanation, but the green-bearded Bouldershoulder only shrugged and put his hands behind his back.

"Move the damned thing so I can get back me axe!" Ivan howled in explanation. He shook his head in disgust, stomped over to Cadderly, and roughly pulled the man to his feet.

"And don't ye ever think o' bringing a stupid dragon along again!" Ivan roared, poking Cadderly hard in the chest. The dwarf shoved by and stormed away, looking for a quiet spot where he could brood.

Pikel followed, after patting Cadderly comfortingly on the shoulder.

Cadderly smiled, despite his pain and exhaustion, when he looked upon Pikel. As long as everything turned out all right, the easygoing dwarf cared little for any troublesome details—as was evidenced by the dwarf's not-too-well hidden "Hee hee hee" as he skipped along behind his surly brother.

Cadderly would have shaken his head in disbelief, but he feared that the effort would cost him his tentative balance.

"She is all right," Shayleigh remarked to him, coming up and following his worried gaze toward the melted ledge.

True to the elf maiden's words, Danica came running in through the valley entrance a moment later, flying with all speed for her love.

She grabbed Cadderly tightly and held him close, and he needed her support, for the weariness, more complete than Cadderly had ever experienced, had come rushing back in full.

To Trust

She viewed the dragon, full-sized once more, dead in the rocky vale, focused on its severed head lying a few feet from the scaly torso. All about the grisly scene, Dorigen saw the smoldering, torn remains of goblins and giants, scores of the beasts. And walking out of the valley, weary perhaps, but not one of them showing any serious wounds, went Cadderly and Danica, flanked by the two dwarves, the elf maiden, and the traitorous firbolg.

Dorigen slipped back into her chair and allowed the image to disappear from her crystal ball. At first she had been surprised to so easily get through Cadderly's magical defenses and locate the young priest, but when she gazed upon the scene, upon the carnage and the fury of Fyrentennimar, she had understood the priest's excusable defensive lapse.

Dorigen thought that she was witnessing Cadderly's end, and the end of the threat to Castle Trinity. She had almost called in Aballister, almost advised the older wizard to go out and recruit Fyrentennimar as an ally for their unhindered attack against Carradoon.

Her surprise as Cadderly literally shrank the great wyrm—by stealing its age, Dorigen presumed—could not have been more complete, and complete, too, was Dorigen's surprise as she sat back and honestly considered her own feelings during the viewing.

She had felt saddened when she thought Cadderly was surely doomed. Logically, ambitious Dorigen could tell herself that Cadderly's death would be a good thing for the designs of Castle Trinity, that the interference of the young priest could no longer be tolerated, and that in killing the young priest Fyrentennimar would have only saved Aballister the trouble. Logically, Dorigen should not have felt sympathy for Cadderly as he stood, apparently helpless, before the dreaded wyrm.

But she had, and she had silently cheered for Cadderly and his brave friends in their titanic struggle, had actually leaped up in joy when the firbolg came up from behind and lopped the dragon's head off.

Why had she done that?

"Have you sighted anything this day?" The voice startled Dorigen so badly that she nearly fell out of her chair. She quickly threw the wrap over the crystal ball, though its interior was a cloud of nothingness once more, and fumbled to straighten and compose herself as Aballister threw open the curtain now serving as her front door and whisked in beside her.

"Druzil has lost contact with the young priest," Aballister continued angrily. "It would seem that he is making fine progress through the mountains."

If only you knew, Dorigen thought, but she remained silent. Aballister could not begin to guess that the young priest was now no more than a day's march from Castle Trinity. Nor could the old wizard imagine that Cadderly and his friends would be resourceful and powerful enough to overcome the likes of old Fyren.

"What do you know?" the suspicious Aballister demanded, drawing Dorigen from her private contemplations.

"I?" Dorigen replied innocently, poking a finger against her own chest, her amber eyes wide with feigned surprise.

If Aballister had not been so self-absorbed at that moment, he would have caught Dorigen's defensive and obvious overreaction.

"Yes, you," the wizard snarled. "Have you been able to make contact with Cadderly this day?"

Dorigen looked back to the crystal ball, mulled the question over for a short moment, and then replied, "No."

When she looked back, she saw that Aballister continued to eye her suspiciously.

"Why did you hesitate before answering?" he asked.

"I thought that I had made contact," Dorigen lied. "But in considering it, I have come to believe that it was only a goblin."

Aballister's scowl showed that he was not convinced.

"I fear that your son purposely misdirected my scrying attempt," Dorigen quickly added, putting the older wizard on the defensive.

"The last time Druzil saw Cadderly, he was near the mountain called Nightglow," Aballister said, and Dorigen nodded her agreement. "There is a storm brewing in that area, so it is unlikely that he will have gone very far."

"That would seem logical," Dorigen agreed, though she knew better.

The old wizard grinned evilly. "A storm brewing," he mused. "But unlike any storm my foolish son has ever encountered!"

Now it was Dorigen's turn to eye him suspiciously. "What have you done?"

"Done?" Aballister laughed. "Better to ask what I will do!" Aballister spun about in a circle, as animated as Dorigen had seen him since this whole business had begun, nearly a year before when Barjin had entered the Edificant Library.

"I grow weary of the game!" Aballister said suddenly, fiercely, stopping his spin so that his hollowed face was barely inches from Dorigen's crooked nose. "And so now, I will end it!"

With a snap of his fingers, he left the room, left Dorigen to wonder what he had in mind. The curtain now serving as her door seemed a poignant reminder of Aballister's wrath, and she couldn't contain a shudder when she thought of the magics that Aballister might soon be launching Cadderly's way.

Or at where he believed Cadderly to be.

Why hadn't she told her mentor the truth? Dorigen wondered. Aballister was planning something big, perhaps even going out personally to deal with his son, and Dorigen hadn't told him what she knew about Cadderly's position, that the young priest was many miles beyond Nightglow. Rationally, it seemed to the woman that letting Aballister go out and deal with Cadderly would be her safest course, for if Cadderly's attempt at Castle Trinity proved successful, Dorigen, no ally of the young priest, would likely find herself in serious trouble.

Dorigen ran a finger along the length of her crooked nose, shook her long hair back from her face, and eyed the cloth covering the crystal ball. Cadderly might arrive in a day, and she had not told Aballister!

Dorigen felt strangely removed from the cascading events about her, like some distant spectator. Cadderly could have killed her in Shilmista Forest, had her unconscious at his feet. He had broken her hands and taken her magical items, putting her out of the fight.

But he had spared her life.

Perhaps it was honor that guided Dorigen now, an unspoken agreement between her and the young priest. A sense of obligation told her to let it all play out, to stand aside while they learned who was the stronger, the father or the son.

* * * * *

Back in his private chambers, Aballister held a smoking beaker aloft in trembling hands. He focused his thoughts on Nightglow, the target area, and focused his magical energies on the contents of the beaker, an elixir of great strength.

He uttered the enchanting words, spoke the arcane syllables from a nearly meditative state, losing himself in the swirling, growing energies. He continued for nearly an hour, until the vibrating power within the beaker threatened to blow apart and take Castle Trinity down with it.

The wizard hurled the beaker across the room, where it shattered at the base of the wall. A gray puff of smoke arose above it, growling, rumbling.

"*Mykos, mykos makom deignin,*" Aballister whispered. "Go out, go out, my pet."

As though it had heard the wizard's request, the gray cloud filtered through a crack in the stone wall, worked its way through all the walls and out of Castle Trinity. It rose up high on the winds, sometimes following, sometimes moving of its own accord, and all the while the wizard's magical storm cloud began to grow and darken.

Contained bursts of lightning rumbled as it soared across the mountains. Still the ominous thing thickened and darkened, and seemed as if it would explode with building energy.

It raced across the high peaks of the Snowflakes, unerringly aimed for the region around Nightglow.

* * * * *

Cadderly and his friends noticed the strange cloud, so much darker than the general overcast of the snowy day. Cadderly noticed, too, that while the more common clouds seemed to be drifting west to east, as was usual for the area's weather patterns, this strange cloud was racing almost due south.

They heard the first rumble of thunder soon after, a tremendous, though distant blast that shook the ground under their feet.

"Thunder?" Ivan balked. "Who ever heared o' thunder in the middle o' the damned winter?"

Cadderly bade Vander to lead them up higher, where they might see what was happening behind them. When they reached a higher plateau, affording them a view between several other peaks all the way back to Nightglow, the young priest wasn't so sure that he wanted to watch.

Bolt after searing bolt of lightning, crystalline clear across the miles as the already dim daylight began to wane, slammed the mountainside, splintering rocks, splitting trees, and sizzling into the snow. Huge winds bent the pines on the mountain's lower slopes nearly horizontal and pelting ice quickly accumulated in the thick branches, bending the trees lower.

"We were wise in riding the dragon," Shayleigh remarked, quite overwhelmed, as were her companions, by the ferocity of the storm. Vander grunted, as though he had told them all, but in truth, even the firbolg, who had grown to adulthood in the harsh climate of the northern Spine of the World range, was at a loss to explain the sheer power of this distant storm.

Another tremendous bolt slammed the mountainside, brightening the deepening gloom, its rumbling wake dislodging tons of snow into a cascading avalanche down Nightglow's northern face.

"Who ever heared of it?" Ivan asked incredulously.

The worst had not yet come. More lightning, more pelting ice assaulted the region about the mountain. Other avalanches soon began, tons and tons of snow plummeting down the mountainside to resettle far below. Then came the tornado, blacker than the impending night, a twister as wide, it seemed, as the foundation of the Edificant Library. It circled Nightglow, tearing trees, burrowing huge chasms in the high-piled snow.

"We must go," the firbolg reminded them all, for he—and, he correctly guessed, his friends—had seen more than enough. Shayleigh mentioned again that they were fortunate in riding out on the dragon, and Vander put in a word that winter storms so high up were unpredictably and ultimately deadly.

Everyone readily agreed with the firbolg, but they all understood that what had happened back at Nightglow was more than a "winter storm."

Vander soon found them an uninhabited cave not too far from the valley of carnage, and truly, they were all glad to be sheltered from the suddenly frightening elements. The place was three-chambered, but snug, with a low ceiling and a lower doorway that blocked most of the wintry wind.

Vander and the dwarves set up their bedrolls in the entry cavern, the largest of the chambers. Cadderly took the smallest chamber—to the left—as his own, with Danica and Shayleigh going to the right, the monk glancing back at Cadderly with concern every step of the way.

Dusk came soon after, and then a quiet and star-filled night, so different from the storm. Soon the usual grumble-and-whistle snoring of Ivan and Pikel echoed throughout the chambers.

Danica crept back into the entry cavern, saw Vander's huge form propped in the doorway. Though he had volunteered once more to take the watch, the firbolg was asleep, and Danica didn't blame him. It seemed safe enough to her, seemed as if all the world had taken a break from the chaos, and so she slipped through to Cadderly's chamber quietly, without disturbing the others.

The young priest was sitting in the middle of the floor, hunched over a tiny candle. Deep in meditation, he did not hear Danica's approach.

"You should sleep," the monk offered, putting a hand gently on her lover's shoulder. Cadderly opened his sleepy eyes and nodded.

He reached over his shoulder to grab Danica's hand, pulled her around to sit next to him, close to him.

"I have rested," he assured her. Danica had taught Cadderly several rejuvenating meditation techniques, and she did not dispute the claim.

"The road has been more difficult than you expected," Danica said quietly, a trace of trepidation evident in her normally solid voice. "And with perhaps the most difficult obstacle yet ahead of us."

The young priest understood her reasoning. He, too, believed that the fury they had witnessed battering the slopes of Nightglow had been a calling card from Aballister. And he, too, was afraid. They had survived many brutal ordeals in the last year and over the last few days on the trail, but if that storm was any indication, their greatest trials were yet ahead of them, waiting for them in Castle Trinity. Since the manticore and chimera attack, Cadderly had known that Aballister was on to them, but he had not imagined the great strength of the wizard.

An image of the landslide and the tornado assaulted his thoughts. Cadderly had enacted great magics of his own recently, but that display was far beyond his powers, he believed, far beyond his imagination!

The young priest, trying to hold fast to his resolve, closed his eyes and sighed. "I did not expect so many troubles," he admitted.

"Even a dragon," Danica remarked. "I still cannot believe . . . " Her voice trailed off into an incredulous sigh.

"I knew that dealing with old Fyren would not be an easy task," Cadderly agreed.

"Did we have to go there?" There remained no trace of anger in Danica's soft tones.

Cadderly nodded. "The world is a better place with the *Ghearufu* destroyed—and with Fyrentennimar destroyed, though I did not foresee that as a probability, even as a possibility. Of all that I have accomplished in my life, the destruction of the *Ghearufu* might be the most important."

A wistful smile crossed Danica's face as she caught the glimmer in Cadderly's barely open, but surely smiling, gray eyes.

"But not the most important of all you mean to do," the monk said coyly.

Cadderly's eyes widened, and he regarded Danica with sincere admiration. How well she knew him! He had just been thinking of the many deeds that were sorting themselves out before him, of the many demands his special relationship with his god Deneir would make on him. Danica had seen it, had looked into his eyes, and had known exactly the tone of his thoughts, if not the specifics.

"I see a course before me," he admitted to her, his voice subdued, but firm with resolve. "A dangerous and difficult course, I do not doubt." Cadderly chuckled at the irony, and Danica looked at him quizzically, not understanding.

"Even after what we witnessed before setting our camp, I fear that the most difficult of my future obstacles will be the ones brought on by friends," he explained.

Danica stiffened and shifted away.

"Not from you," Cadderly quickly assured her. "I foresee changes at the Edificant Library, drastic changes that will not be met with approval from those who have the most to lose."

"Dean Thobicus?"

Cadderly nodded, his expression grim. "And the head-masters," he added. "The hierarchy has evolved away from the spirit of Deneir, has become something perpetuated by false traditions and piles of worthless paper." He chuckled again, but there was something sad in his voice. "Do you understand what I did to Thobicus for him to allow us to come out here?" he asked.

"You tricked him," Danica replied.

"I dominated him," Cadderly corrected. "I entered his mind and bent his will. I might well have killed him in the attempt, and the effects of the assault could remain with him for the rest of his years."

An expression of confusion came over Danica, confusion fast turning to horror. "Hypnosis?"

"Far beyond hypnosis," Cadderly replied gravely. "In hypnosis, I might have convinced Thobicus to change his thoughts." Cadderly looked away, seeming ashamed. "I did not convince Thobicus. I evoked the change against his will, and then I entered his mind once more and modified his memory so that there would be no repercussions when . . . if, we return to the library."

Danica's almond eyes were wide with shock. She had known that Cadderly was uncomfortable with what he had done to Thobicus, but she had assumed that her love had exacted some charm spell over the dean. What Cadderly was talking about now, though the results had been similar to a charm, seemed somehow more sinister.

"I grabbed his will in my hand, and I crushed it," Cadderly admitted. "I stole from him the very essence of his ego. If Thobicus recalls the incident, then his pride will never, ever recover from the shock."

"Then why did you do it?" Danica demanded softly.

"Because my course was determined by powers greater than me," Cadderly said. "And greater than Thobicus."

"How many tyrants have made such a claim?" Danica asked, trying hard not to sound sarcastic.

Cadderly smiled helplessly and nodded. "That is my fear.

"Yet I knew what I must do," he continued. "The *Ghearufu* had to be destroyed—to study such a sentient, evil artifact would bring only disaster—and the war with Castle Trinity, if it comes to pass, will prove a travesty that cannot be tolerated, whatever side is victorious.

"I went after Thobicus in a way that left a foul taste in my mouth," Cadderly admitted. "But I would do it again, and I may have to if my fears prove true." He quieted for a moment and considered the many wrongs he had witnessed, the many things within the Edificant Library that had long ago veered from the path of Deneir, searching for some solid example he might offer to Danica. "If a young cleric in the library has an inspiration," he said at last, "divine though he believes it to be, he cannot act upon it without first receiving the approval of the dean and the permission to take time away from meaningless duties."

"Thobicus must oversee . . . " Danica began to argue, playing the pragmatic point of view.

"That process often takes as long as a year," Cadderly interrupted, no longer interested in hearing logical arguments for a course he knew in his heart to be wrong. Cadderly had heard those arguments from Headmaster Avery for all of his life, and they had fostered in him an indifference that swelled to so great a level that he had nearly deserted the order of Deneir. "You have seen how Thobicus works," he said firmly. "A wasted year will pass, and though the thoughts of the story the young cleric wished to pen, or the painting he wished to frame, might remain, the sense, the aura, that something divine might be guiding his hand will have long since flown."

"You speak from personal experience," Danica reasoned.

"Many times," Cadderly replied without hesitation. "And I know that many of the things I have become comfortable with in my life, many of the things I now know I must change, I do not want to change, for I am afraid."

He brought his finger up to Danica's lips to stem her forthcoming response. "You are not among those things," he assured her, and then he grew very quiet, and all the world, even the dwarven snoring, seemed to hush in anticipation.

"I do believe that our relationship must change, though," Cadderly went on. "What began in Carradoon must grow, or it must die."

Danica grabbed his wrist and pulled his hand away from her face, eyeing him unblinkingly, not sure of what would come next from this surprising young man.

"Marry me," Cadderly said suddenly. "Formally."

Now Danica did blink, and she closed her eyes, hearing the echoes from those words a thousand times in the next second. She had waited so long for this moment, had longed for it and feared it all at the same time. For while she loved Cadderly with all her heart, being a wife in Faerun carried expectations of servitude. And Danica, proud and capable, served no one.

"You agree with the changes," Cadderly said. "You agree with the course my life will take. I cannot do it alone, my love." He paused and nearly faltered. "I do not want to do it alone! When I have completed what Deneir has asked, when I look upon the work, there will be no satisfaction unless you are there beside me."

"When *I* have completed?" Danica echoed and asked, emphasizing Cadderly's use of the personal pronoun and trying to get some sense of what role Cadderly meant for her to play in it all.

Cadderly thought about the emphasis of her response and then nodded. "I am a disciple of Deneir," he explained. "Many of the battles he guides me to, I must fight alone. I think of it as you think of your studies. I know that, as each goal is attained, richer by far will be my satisfaction if . . . "

"What of my studies?" Danica interrupted.

Cadderly was ready for the question and understood Danica's concern. "When you broke the stone and achieved Gigel Nugel," he began, referring to an ancient test of achievement that Danica had recently completed, "what were your thoughts?"

Danica remembered the incident, and a smile spread wide across her face. "I felt your arm around me," she replied.

Cadderly nodded and pulled her close, kissing her gently on the cheek. "We have so much to show each other," he said.

"My studies might take me away," Danica said, pulling back.

Cadderly laughed aloud. "If they do, then you shall go," he said. "But you will come back to me, or I will go to you. I have faith, Danica, that our chosen paths will not take us apart. I have faith in you, and in myself."

The somber cloud seemed to fly from Danica's fair features. Her grin widened to a dimpled smile, and her brown eyes sparkled with the moisture of joyful tears. She pulled Cadderly back to her, kissing him hard and long.

"Cadderly," she said coyly, as her wistful, mischievous smile sent a stream of thoughts careening through him. A shiver rippled up his spine and then back down again as Danica added, "We are alone."

Much later that night, with the sleeping Danica cradled in his arms and the dwarven snoring continuing its relentless pace, Cadderly rested back against the wall and replayed the conversation.

"How many tyrants have made such a claim?" he whispered to the empty darkness. His considered his course once more, thought of the profound impact his intended actions would have on all the region surrounding Impresk Lake. He believed in his heart that the changes would better everyone, that the library would once again take on the true course of Deneir. He believed that he was right, that his course was inspired by a trusted god. But how many tyrants had made such a claim?

"All of them," Cadderly answered grimly after a long pause, and he hugged Danica close.

The Fortress

Aballister rested back in his chair, exhausted from his magical assault. He had thrown his full weight against Cadderly, had pounded the mountain region mercilessly. The wizard's smile held firm for a long while as he pondered what Cadderly, in the unlikely event that the boy was still alive, might be thinking now.

Aballister felt a tug within his mind, a gentle prodding. It was Druzil, he knew, for he had expected the imp's call. The wizard's smile became an open laugh—what might the imp, who had been so close to Nightglow, think now of him? Anxious to know, he let the imp into his mind.

Greetings, dear Druzil, Aballister said.

Bene tellemara!

Aballister cackled with glee. *My dear, dear Druzil*, he thought after a moment, *what could be the trouble?*

The imp ripped off a series of outcries, curses, and sputterings against Aballister and against wizards in general.

160

Druzil had been caught in the edges of Aballister's storm, had been pelted by hail and nearly sizzled by a lightning blast.

Now the imp, cold and miserable, only wanted to get back to Castle Trinity. *You could come out for me*, Druzil telepathically asked.

I have not the energy, came Aballister's expected reply. *Since you allowed Cadderly to get away, I was forced to take matters into my own hands. And still I have preparations before me, for the unlikely event that Cadderly or any of his foolish friends survived.*

"*Bene tellemara*," the frustrated imp whispered under his breath. Now that Druzil believed he needed Aballister, he was careful to put up a blocking wall of innocuous thoughts so that the wizard would not hear the insult.

Better that I am with you if Cadderly arrives, Druzil replied, trying to find some argument to change the stubborn wizard's mind. With his magic, powerful Aballister could teleport to Druzil's side, scoop the imp up, and put them both safely back in Castle Trinity in a matter of two minutes.

I told you that I was too weary, Aballister's casual thoughts came back—and Druzil understood that Aballister was simply punishing him. *Better that you are with me?* the wizard scoffed. *I sent you on a most important mission, and you failed! Better to face Cadderly alone, I say, than with an unreliable and troublesome imp at my side. I do not yet know what happened to facilitate the destruction of the evil spirit, Druzil, but if I find that you were in any way involved, your punishment will not be pleasant.*

More likely it was your own son, Druzil's mind growled back.

The imp felt a wave of unfocused mental energy, an anger so profound that Aballister had not taken the moment to give it a clear flow of words. Druzil knew that his reference once again to Cadderly as Aballister's son had struck a sensitive nerve, even though Aballister had apparently taken care of the problem.

You will seek out the bodies of Cadderly and his friends, Aballister answered. *Then you will walk back to me, or flap those weak wings of yours when the wind permits! I'll tolerate little more from you, Druzil. 'Ware the next storm I send out to the mountains!*

With that, Aballister promptly broke off the connection, leaving Druzil cold in the snow, pondering the wizard's last words.

Truly, the imp was disgusted by the ridiculous accusation and by Aballister's continual threats. He had to admit, though, that they carried some weight. Druzil could not believe the devastation Aballister had rained on Nightglow and the surrounding region. But Druzil was cold and miserable now, deep in the wintry mountains, and constantly had to shake the fast accumulating snow off his leathery wings.

He certainly didn't like where he was, but in a way, Druzil was relieved that Aballister had refused his request to bring him home. If indeed the young priest had somehow escaped Aballister's fury—and Druzil did not think that such an impossibility—then Druzil preferred to be far away when Aballister at last faced his son. Druzil had once battled Cadderly in mental combat and had been overwhelmed. The imp had also fought against the woman, Danica, and had been defeated—even his poison had been ineffective against that one. Druzil's repertoire of tricks was fast emptying where the young priest was concerned.

The stakes were simply too high.

But these mountains! Druzil was a creature of the lower planes, a dark region mostly of black fires and thick smoke. He did not like the cold, did not like the wet feel of the wretched snow, and the glare of sunlight on the angled whitened surface of the mountain slopes pained his sensitive eyes. He had to go on, though, and would, eventually, have to return and face his wizard master.

Eventually.

Druzil liked the ring of that thought. He brushed the

snow from his wings and gave a lazy flap to get him up into the air. He decided immediately that searching for Cadderly and his friends would be a foolhardy thing, and so he veered away from the settling mass of misplaced snow around Nightglow. Neither was his direction north, toward Castle Trinity. Druzil went east, the shortest route out of the Snowflakes, a course that would take him down to the farmlands surrounding Carradoon.

* * * * *

"Prepare your defenses," Dorigen said as soon as she entered Aballister's room, unexpectedly and unannounced.

"What do you know?" growled the weary wizard.

"Cadderly lives!"

"You have seen him?" Aballister snapped, coming fast out of his chair, his dark eyes coming to life with an angry sparkle.

"No," Dorigen lied. "But there are still wards blocking my scrying. The young priest is very much alive."

Reacting in quite the opposite way Dorigen had expected, Aballister erupted in laughter. He slapped a hand on the arm of his chair and seemed almost giddy. Then he looked to his associate, and her incredulous expression asked many questions.

"The boy makes it enjoyable!" the old wizard said to her. "I have not faced such a challenge in decades!"

Dorigen thought that he had gone quite insane. You have never faced such a challenge, she wanted to scream at the man, but she kept that dangerous thought private. "We must prepare," she said again, calmly. "Cadderly is alive, and it might be that he escaped your fury because he was much closer than we anticipated."

Aballister seemed to sober at once, and turned his back at Dorigen, his skinny fingertips tapping together in front of him. "It was your scrying that led me to assail Nightglow," he pointedly reminded her.

"It was Druzil's guidance, more than my own," she quickly corrected, sincerely afraid to accept blame for anything, given Aballister's unpredictable, and incredibly dangerous, mood.

She sighed, noticing Aballister subtly nod his head in agreement.

"Prepare . . . " she started to say a third time, but the wizard spun about suddenly, his scowl stealing the words from her mouth.

"Oh, we shall prepare!" Aballister hissed though gritted teeth. "Better for Cadderly if he had fallen to the storm!"

"I will instruct the soldiers," Dorigen said, and she turned for the door.

"No!" The word stopped the woman short. She slowly turned her head, to look back over her shoulder at Aballister.

"This is personal," Aballister explained, and he led Dorigen's quizzical gaze across the room, to the swirling ball of mist hanging on the far wall, the entrance to Aballister's extradimensional mansion. "The soldiers will not be needed."

* * * * *

They looked down from a high perch to new battlements and a singular tower. From the outside, Castle Trinity did not seem so remarkable, or so formidable, even with the new construction that had been done. Vander, who had seen the tunnel networks beneath the rocky spur, assured them otherwise. Work on the new walls was slow now, with winter blowing thick, but guards were in abundance— humans mostly—pacing predetermined routes and continually rubbing their hands together to ward away the icy breeze.

"That is the main entrance," Vander explained, pointing to the central area of the closest wall. A huge door, oaken and ironbound, was set deep into the stone, enveloped by walkways and parapets and many soldiers. "Beyond that door is a cave entrance, barred by a portcullis, and a second, similar door. We will find guards, well-armed and well-trained, positioned every step of the way."

"Bah, we're not for going straight in the front door!" Ivan protested, and this time, the yellow-bearded dwarf found some allies for his grumbling. Danica readily agreed by reminding everyone that their only chance lay in stealth, and Shayleigh even suggested that perhaps they should have come out with Carradoon's army at their heels.

Cadderly hardly listened to the talk, trying to think of some magic that might get them in, but that would not overly tax his still-limited energies. His friends had remained optimistic, believing that he could handle the situation. Cadderly liked their confidence in him; he only wished that he shared it. That morning, leaving the cave, with the sky shining blue, Ivan had scoffed at the storm that had hit Nightglow, had called it a simple wizard's trick, and berated Aballister for not being able to aim straight.

"First rule in shootin' magics!" the dwarf had bellowed. "Ye got to hit the damned target!"

"Oo oi!" Pikel had heartily agreed, and then the green-bearded dwarf, too, had made light of it all with a quiet, "Hee hee hee."

Cadderly knew better, understood the strength of the wizard's incredible display. The young priest still believed that he walked along the true path of Deneir, but images of Aballister's fury, slamming the mountain itself into surrender, stayed with him all morning.

He shook the unpleasant thoughts away and tried to focus on the situation at hand. "Is there another way in?" he heard Danica ask.

"At the base of the tower," Vander answered. "Aballister brought us. . . . brought the Night Masks in that way, through a smaller, less guarded door. The wizard did not want the commoners of his force to know that he had hired the assassins."

"Too much open ground," Danica remarked. The tower was set some distance behind the two nearly finished perpendicular walls, and though the tower, too, had apparently not been completed, it stood an imposing thirty feet high, with temporary battlements ringing its top. Even if the friends managed to get past the guards on the closest walls, just a couple of archers up in that tower could make life miserable for them.

"What tricks ye got to keep them off our backs while we make the run?" Ivan asked Cadderly, gruffly slapping the young priest on the shoulder to force him from his private contemplations.

"The shortest route would be from the right, from below the spur," he reasoned. "But that would leave us running uphill, vulnerable to many defensive measures. I say that we come in from the left, down the slope of the rocky spur and around the shorter wall."

"That wall's guarded," Ivan argued.

Cadderly's wry smile ended the debate.

The friends spent the better part of the next hour in a roundabout hike to a point on the rocky spur far above Castle Trinity. With this new angle, around the side of the largest, frontal wall, they could see scores of soldiers, including large, hairy bugbears, ten-foot-tall ogres, and even a giant. Cadderly knew that this would be quite a test—for his friends' trust in him, and for his abilities. If that formidable force intercepted them before they got inside the back door, all would be lost.

The tower was fully thirty yards back from the front wall and fully forty yards away from the outermost tip of the perpendicular wall, the wall they had to run around. Ivan shook his hairy head; Pikel added an occasional "Oo," showing that even the dwarves, the most battle-hardened members of the troupe, did not think the idea feasible.

But Cadderly remained undaunted; his smile had not ebbed an inch. "The first volley will alert them—the second should get them into positions where we might get near the wall," he explained.

The others looked around to each other in confusion, their expressions incredulous. Most eyes centered on Shayleigh's quiver and the hand-crossbow at Cadderly's side.

"On my cue, when the third volley of flaming pitch soars out for the front wall, we go for the tower," Cadderly went on. "You lead the charge," he said to Danica.

Danica, though she still had no idea of what "volleys" the young priest was talking about, smiled wryly, pleased that Cadderly would not patronize her, would not try to protect her when the situation obviously called for each of them to perform specific, and dangerous, tasks. Danica knew that not many men of Faerun would allow their beloved women to rush out into danger ahead of them, and it was Cadderly's implicit trust and respect of her which made her love him so very much.

"If the archers up above catch sight of us," Cadderly continued, aiming this remark at Shayleigh, "we will need you to cut them down."

"What volley?" Shayleigh demanded, tired of the cryptic game. "What flaming pitch?"

Cadderly, already falling away, deep into his spellcasting concentration, didn't reply. In a moment, he was chanting, singing softly, and his friends hunched down and waited for the clerical magic to take effect.

"Wow," muttered Pikel at the same moment that one of the guards along the front gate cried out in surprise. Balls of flaming pitch and large spears were appearing in midair, thundering down near the wall. Soldiers scrambled and dove from the gate; the giant hoisted a slab of stone and put it in front of him defensively.

It was over in just a few instants, with no fires left burning and no apparent damage to the stonework. The soldiers remained under cover, though, calling frantic orders and pointing out many potential artillery hiding places in the ridges beyond the gates.

Cadderly nodded to Danica, and she and Shayleigh began

the procession from the side, slipping from stone to stone. The diversion had apparently worked thus far, for few guards seemed concerned with the high ground to the side of the walls.

The second illusory "volley" roared in farther down the front wall, well beyond the main gates, luring the enemy's attention to the vulnerable corner where the third wall would be built. As Cadderly had predicted, those soldiers along the side wall rushed into defensive positions behind the shielding, and thicker, front wall.

Again the explosions lasted only a few seconds, but the guards were in a near-panic now, huddled tight against the battlements and the base of the wall. Not a single eye turned to the southwest, to the higher ground from which the companions approached.

Danica and Shayleigh led them up to the now-abandoned perpendicular wall without incident, light-stepped along its base away from the front wall, and peered around to the empty courtyard.

Cadderly moved in front of the group and held his hand up to keep his friends back. He concentrated on the front wall and reached out to the particles of air about him, seeing their nature revealed in the notes of Deneir's song. Slowly and subtly, using triggering words and the energy of clerical magic, the young priest altered the composition of those particles, brought them together, thickened them.

A heavy mist swelled up around the front wall, and around the front half of the uncompleted courtyard.

"Go," Cadderly whispered to Danica, and he motioned for the dwarves to follow, and for Shayleigh to come into position where she could view the tower. Without hesitation, the brave monk ran off, zigzagging across the rough, frozen ground.

On impulse, Cadderly took Shayleigh's arrow from her hand. "Get it up on top of the tower," he instructed, casting an enchantment over it and handing it back.

Danica was twenty yards out, halfway to the tower, before

anyone there noticed her. Three archers took up their bows and started to call out, when Shayleigh's arrow smacked solidly into the shoulder of one. The man went down in a heap; the other two went into a frenzy, their mouths wagging wide as they tried to cry out for their companions manning the front gate.

Not a sound came from the top of the tower, the area magically silenced by the enchanted arrow.

The remaining two enemy archers opened up on Danica, but her course was too erratic and her agility too great. Arrows skipped off the frozen ground, or snapped apart as they struck, but Danica, rolling and diving, cutting sharper angles than the soldiers could anticipate, never came close to being hit.

"Hee hee hee," chuckled Pikel, running with Ivan far behind the monk and thoroughly enjoying the spectacle.

Shayleigh returned the fire with vicious accuracy, skipping arrows in between the parapet stones and forcing the guards to concentrate more on keeping their heads down than on firing at Danica. Still the men tried futilely to cry out, to warn their associates of the peril.

Vander scooped up Shayleigh, settled her atop his broad shoulders, and ran after the dwarves.

Cadderly focused once more on the front wall, loosing another illusory volley to ensure that the soldiers would remain tight in their holes. Smiling at his own cleverness, the young priest raced off after his friends.

As Danica reached the base of the tower, the door burst open and a swordsman rushed out to face her. Always alert, she rolled headlong and came up within his weapon's descending arc, the ball of her fist connecting under his chin and driving him away.

Above Danica, one of the archers leaned out, angling for a killing shot. Shayleigh's arrow, loosed before he had even drawn his bow, sank deep into his collarbone.

The other archer, tight against the corner of a squared stone, responded with a shot that caught Vander in the chest, but the arrow did little to slow the giant. Howling and growling, Vander yanked out the puny bolt and hurled it away.

Her angle improved by the fact that she was ten feet above the ground, Shayleigh smiled grimly and loosed another arrow. It skipped off the squared stone and ricocheted into the enemy archer's eye. The man fell back in agony, obviously screaming—but again, not a sound came from the enchanted area.

Ivan and Pikel disappeared into the tower behind Danica; Cadderly could see that there was some fighting within. The young priest ran with all speed, slipping in on Vander's heels, but by the time he, the firbolg, and the elf maiden got there, the five goblin guards of the tower's first floor were already dead.

Danica kneeled before another doorway across the small chamber, studying its lock. She pulled the clasp off of her belt and straightened it with her teeth, then gently slipped it in and began working it, side to side.

"Hurry," bade Shayleigh, standing by the outer door. Across the courtyard, cries of "Enemies in the tower!" could be heard. The elf maiden shrugged—the deception was no more—and leaned out the door, shooting off an arrow or two to keep the enemy forces back. One quiver empty, her second growing lighter, she regretted now her decision to join in the battle in the valley.

Cadderly pulled her in by the elbow and closed the door. It was an easy thing for the priest to magically reach into the essence of the wood, to swell it and warp it so that the portal was sealed tight. Vander piled the dead goblins against the door as added security, and again all eyes focused on Danica.

"Hurry," Shayleigh reiterated, her words taking on more weight as something heavy slammed against the tower door.

With a grin to her companions, Danica slipped her makeshift lockpick behind one ear and pushed open the door, revealing a descending stairway.

Cadderly looked at the passage curiously. "Not heavily guarded and not trapped?" he mused aloud.

"It was trapped," Danica corrected. She pointed to a wire along the side of the jamb, secured in place with the other part of her belt. None of them had the time to admire the skilled monk's handiwork, though, for another, louder crash sounded on the outer door, and the tip of an axe blade poked through the wood.

Ivan and Pikel pushed ahead of Danica and rambled side by side down the stairs. Vander and Shayleigh went next, the firbolg using his innate magics to reduce himself to the size of a large man. Next came Cadderly, and then Danica, who turned back and, with a subtle twist of her pick, locked the door and rearmed the trap.

Another door blocked the way at the bottom of the stairs, but the dwarven brothers lowered their heads, locked arms, and picked up their pace.

"It may be warded!" Cadderly called out to them, understanding their intent.

The Bouldershoulders blew through the door, a series of fiery explosions erupting on their heels as they tumbled down in the midst of shattered and smoking wood. The two had been fortunate indeed to get through the portal so quickly, for tiny darts protruded from both doorjambs, dripping poison. In the underground tunnels beyond the door, the blare of horns sounded—probably magical alarms, Cadderly thought.

"What'd ye say?" Ivan yelled above the clamor, as the others came into the lower passage.

"Never mind," was all that Cadderly replied. His voice was grim, despite the sight of Pikel hopping all about, trying to put out wisps of smoke trailing from his heels and backside. The whole objective in coming to Castle Trinity with so small a force was to strike at the leaders of the enemy conspiracy, but that goal seemed unlikely now, with horns blaring and enemies beating at the closed doors behind them.

"Aw, come on and find a bit of fun!" Ivan bellowed at the obviously worried young priest. "Hold on to me cloak, boy! I'll get ye where ye want to go!"

"Oo oi!" Pikel piped in, and the brothers thundered away. They hit resistance before they even turned the first corner, and plowed through the surprised band of goblins with abandon, slaughtering and scattering the creatures.

"Which way?" Ivan called back, his words coming out at the end of a grunt as he drove his mighty axe through the backbone of one goblin that had turned to flee a split second too late. The torchlit corridor beyond the dead goblin showed several doors and at least two branching tunnels.

The friends looked to Cadderly, but the young priest shrugged helplessly, having no immediate answers amidst the sudden confusion. A series of explosions far behind them told Cadderly that their enemies had breached the second door—and had not been successful in disarming the trap.

Ivan kicked open the nearest door, revealing a huge room holding a battery of human archers and a group of giants at work leveling a ballista. "Not that way!" the gruff dwarf explained, quickly closing the door and rushing on.

In the wild run that followed, Cadderly lost all sense of direction. They passed through many portals, turned many corners, and clobbered many very surprised enemies. Soon they came to an area of better worked tunnels, with runes and bas reliefs of the teardrop symbols of Talona carved into their stone walls.

Cadderly looked to Vander, hoping that the firbolg might recognize some landmark, but Vander could not be sure.

A jolt of electricity threw Pikel back from the next door. Ivan growled and hit the portal shoulder-first, bursting through into yet another long and narrow corridor, this one lined by tapestries depicting the Lady of Poison, smiling evilly as though she clearly saw the intruders. Resilient Pikel, the hairs of his green beard dancing free of the tight braid, joined his brother in an instant.

Twenty steps in, the group was enveloped by a ball of absolute darkness.

"Keep moving!" Shayleigh bade the dwarves, for with her keen elven hearing, she had heard the approach of enemies from behind.

Cadderly felt the air beside his face move as the elf put an arrow into the air. He did not take serious note of Shayleigh's movements, though, for he was fumbling with the straps of his backpack, searching for his light tube, or for the wand, to battle the conjured darkness.

Apparently sensing that he had stopped moving, Danica grabbed the young priest's arm and pulled him along—gently, so that she would not disturb his efforts.

There came a loud click and a scrape of stone against stone, followed by a diminishing, "Ooooooo . . . "

"*Domin illu!*" Cadderly cried, holding up the wand, and the darkness fled. Cadderly stood ready with his wand, Shayleigh with her bow, and Danica and Vander were into similarly defensive crouches, feeling their way along the walls.

But Ivan and Pikel were gone.

"Trapdoors!" Danica cried, spotting tiny lines in the floor ahead. "Ivan!"

There came no response, and Danica found no apparent way to open the neatly fit portals, no cranks or handles anywhere in sight.

"Go on!" Shayleigh yelled suddenly, pulling Cadderly past her and drawing back her bowstring. Enemy soldiers were at the door behind them, barely fifty feet away.

Danica leaped the trapped region; Vander reverted to his full size and stepped across, hoisting Cadderly behind him.

"Close your eyes," the young priest whispered to his friends, and he thrust the wand back toward the door and uttered, "*Mas illu!*" A burst of brilliant lights shot forth, green and orange and popping in all colors of the spectrum in a myriad of blinding flashes.

It was over in an instant, leaving the soldiers rubbing their eyes and stumbling about the end of the corridor.

"Go on!" Shayleigh said again, firing off two more arrows into the confused throng. The other three started for the door at the corridor's other end, calling for Shayleigh to catch up.

When the elf maiden turned back around to follow her friends, they realized that she, too, had been caught in Cadderly's magical flash. Her once-clear violet eyes showed as dots of bloodshot red, and she inched down the corridor, trying to discern when to jump.

"We'll come for you!" Danica called out, but Shayleigh had already begun her leap. She landed with her heels on the edge of the trapdoor, which clicked open, and she balanced on the edge of the fall for what seemed an eternity.

Vander dove headlong, spread out wide on the floor, grabbing desperately.

He caught only air as Shayleigh fell backward into the pit, the devilish door swinging tight behind her.

Danica was beside the firbolg, pulling at his sleeve, and Cadderly was beside her, his wand extended once more.

"*Mas illu,*" he said again, his voice subdued, and the brilliant burst hit the recovering soldiers once more. Many of them thought to close their eyes this time, and the charge, though slowed, would not be halted.

Vander led the rush to the far door and almost got there, but a ten-foot section of the corridor shifted suddenly, its entire perimeter turning diagonal to its original position. The surprised firbolg fell to the side, into the suddenly angled wall/floor, and disappeared from sight as that corner of the trapped area rotated on a central pivot.

Danica leaped past the angled section of corridor and snapped a kick into the door, breaking apart the locking mechanism. The door creaked open, back toward Danica, just an inch, and the monk grabbed it and pulled it fiercely, as if she were daring another trap to go off.

Cadderly, overwhelmed, came up to her, still looking back to the floor where three of his friends had disappeared, and to the wall that had taken the firbolg.

Danica grabbed his hand and pulled him in—a short passage this time, its walls bare of tapestries, that ended in another door just a dozen feet away. As soon as they crossed the threshold, a solid slab of stone dropped behind them, sealing off any possible retreat, and a portcullis fell in front of the door before them, blocking the way. They knew instantly, of course, that they were trapped, but did not appreciate the depth of their predicament until a moment later, when Danica noticed that the small passage's sidewalls had begun to close together.

The Holy Word

Danica threw her back against the wall, pushing with all her strength while trying to plant her feet firmly on the smooth floor. She only slid forward, and the corridor narrowed relentlessly.

Cadderly's frantic gaze darted all about, from the stone slab to the portcullis, to the closing sidewalls. He tried to summon the song of Deneir, but remembered nothing immediately within its lyrical notes that might aid them now.

The walls were barely eight feet apart.

Seven feet.

Cadderly fought back his panic, closed his eyes, and told himself to concentrate and to trust in the harmonious music.

He felt Danica grab his arms roughly, but tried to ignore the disturbance. She pulled again, harder, forcing Cadderly to look at her.

"Hold your hands stiffly in front of you," she instructed, turning Cadderly's palms upward. He watched curiously as Danica turned horizontally across his palms, planting her feet against one wall and holding her arms out past her head to "catch" the other, approaching wall.

"You cannot," Cadderly started to protest, but even as he spoke, the walls closed within Danica's reach, closed and then were stopped by the meditating monk's stiffened form as surely as if a beam of metal had been placed between them.

Cadderly moved his hands away from Danica's belly— her stiffened position supported her fully—and forced himself to turn his attention away from the amazing Danica and consider the larger predicament. If the enemy detected that the walls had stopped moving, then he and Danica might soon expect some unwelcome company. Cadderly drew out his hand-crossbow and loaded an explosive dart.

He heard some mumbling from beyond the portcullis and the far door, and moved closer, straining to hear.

"Buga yarg grrr mukadig," came a deep guttural sound, and Cadderly, with his exceptional training in the various languages of Faerun, understood that an ogre outside the door had just insisted that the walls must be finished with their business by then.

Cadderly ran back, slipped under and around Danica, and placed his crossbow arm across her back for support. He also put his spindle-disks atop Danica, within easy reach, and clutched his enchanted walking stick in his free hand.

There came a cranking sound as the portcullis began to rise, and Cadderly heard a key slip into the door's lock. He steadied his crossbow and his nerves, realizing that he had to fend off the enemy long enough for Danica to dislodge herself and rush out behind him.

The door swung in, and with it came the face of an eager ogre, stupidly grinning as it looked for the squished remains of the intruders.

Cadderly's dart hit it right between the gap in its two front teeth. The young priest charged boldly, scooping up his spindle-disks.

The ogre's cheeks bulged weirdly, its eyes nearly popped free of their sockets, and then its lips flapped, spewing a stream of blood and broken teeth.

"Duh, Mogie?" its stunned companion asked as the splattered monster slid down to the floor. The second ogre bent low, trying to figure out what had happened, then looked back toward the trap-room just in time to catch Cadderly's flying adamantite spindle-disks on the side of its nose.

Cadderly flicked his wrist hard, sending the disks spinning back to him, stinging his palm, then hurled them again fiercely. The ogre's hand started up, but didn't get high enough for a block, and the beast caught the missile in the eye.

The ogre's arm, continuing its upward motion, hooked the wire, though, and Cadderly could not properly retract the disks for a third throw. Always ready to improvise, the quick-thinking young priest took up his walking stick in both hands and bashed it hard against the dazed ogre's thick forearm.

He came lower with his next strike, slamming exposed ribs, and the ogre, as Cadderly had expected, reflexively brought its arm swinging down. Cadderly's next cut came in high again, smashing the ogre on its already splattered nose. He followed through, reversed his grip, and came back around the other way, the ram's head of his walking stick connecting solidly on the base of the ogre's skull.

The monster was kneeling suddenly, its weakened arms down at its side.

Back and forth slammed Cadderly's walking stick, three times, five times, and then Danica raced past, driving a knee under the kneeling monster's chin. The ogre's head snapped back viciously, and finally, the huge thing toppled to the floor beside its dead companion.

"Load it!" Danica instructed Cadderly, handing him back

his crossbow. Behind them, they heard the crunch of wood as the closing walls bit against the opened door.

Neither one of them cared to look back.

* * * * *

The chute was slick and steep, and Shayleigh, for all her frantic efforts, could hardly slow her descent. Finally, she got her back tight against the sloping floor and pushed up into the air with her longbow, searching for some hold.

There were none. The chute's ceiling, like the floor, was perfectly smooth.

A dozen unpleasant images rushed through the elf maiden's head, mostly ones of her being impaled against a wall of poison-tipped spikes beside Ivan and Pikel. Or behind Ivan and Pikel, slamming against her already stuck friends to drive them deeper onto the imagined spikes.

Still holding fast to her bow, Shayleigh angled herself to put her feet against one wall and her shoulder diagonally across the narrow chute against the other. She lifted her head and peered down into the darkness across the length of her body, hoping for some warning before she hit. With her heat-sensing eyes, she could make out traces of the dwarves' passing, residual body heat from Ivan and Pikel still showing in spots along the floor and against the curving walls.

And then there was just a blank wall, the end of the chute, and Shayleigh understood, in the split second before she collided, that since the dwarves were nowhere in sight, it must be some type of swinging trapdoor.

She hit and pushed through, but grabbed both sides of the door with widespread arms. Her bow fell below her, and she heard a dwarf grunt, followed by a small splash.

The trapdoor swung back, pinning Shayleigh's forearms between it and the stone wall. She held on stubbornly, guessing that this might be their only way out of the devious pit.

"Glad ye could make it, elf," Ivan said from below. "But ye might think of getting away from that door if any more are on their way down."

Shayleigh managed to look straight below her, to see the blurry, heated forms of Ivan and Pikel, standing waist-deep in some murky pool. She couldn't tell the exact dimensions of the room, but it was not large, and there was no other apparent door.

"Are you all right?" she asked.

"Just wet," Ivan grumbled. "And I got a bump on me head where me brother fell on me."

Pikel began to whistle and turned away. A moment later, the green-bearded dwarf spun back, frantically, and leaped onto his brother, nearly knocking Ivan under the water.

"What are ye about?" the surly dwarf demanded.

Pikel squeaked and worked hard to get his feet out of the water.

Ivan gave a sudden yell and heaved Pikel into the air. As the green-bearded dwarf hit the water, Ivan, axe in hand, began chopping wildly, his splashes even reaching Shayleigh, high on the wall.

"What is it?" Shayleigh cried. Both dwarves scrambled about, slapping at the water with their weapons.

"Something long and slimy!" Ivan bellowed back. He rushed to the wall directly below the hanging elf and began jumping up, trying futilely to reach her boots. Pikel was at his back in an instant, clambering over him, but Ivan ducked low, sending Pikel facedown into the murk, and then he leaped atop Pikel's back.

All the while, Shayleigh begged for them both to calm down. And finally they did, exhausted, without coming close to reaching the elf.

"Use my longbow," Shayleigh reasoned.

"Eh?" Pikel squeaked confusedly, but Ivan understood. He splashed about, finally retrieving the dropped bow, then came to the wall and reached up with it, hooking Shayleigh's foot.

"Ye sure ye got a good enough hold?" the dwarf politely asked.

"Hurry," Shayleigh replied, and Ivan jumped and grabbed, pulled himself along the bow to get high enough to catch a handhold on the elf's boot.

"Come up over me," Shayleigh instructed. "You will have to get into the corridor first and find some way to brace yourself."

Sturdy Ivan felt guilty climbing over a slender elf maiden like that, but he understood the practicality of it, especially when his brother, still below, gave a worried, "Uh-oh."

Ivan looked down to see Pikel standing very still; a serpentine head lifted clear of the water and swayed slowly, back and forth, only a foot out from Pikel and nearly eye-level with the dwarf.

"Me brother," Ivan whispered, hardly able to find his voice. He thought of leaping back to the water and jumping between Pikel and the serpent.

"Climb," Shayleigh said to him.

Pikel began to sway with the snake, whistling as he went from side to side. They seemed somehow in harmony, dancing almost, and the snake gave no indication that it meant to strike out at the dwarf.

"Climb," Shayleigh said again to Ivan. "Pikel cannot get up until you are out of the way."

Ivan had always been protective of his brother, and a big part of him wanted to leap back atop that snake, to rush wildly to Pikel's defense. He managed to fight back the impulse, both because of his agreement with Shayleigh's logic, and because he was terribly afraid of snakes. He carefully picked handholds along Shayleigh's clothing and got up even with her, taking solace in Pikel's continued whistling, a calm song that took much of the tension from the nasty situation.

Ivan worked his way around to Shayleigh's back and squeezed through the narrow gap between her and the heavy door. When he got fully into the sloping chute, he turned sideways, bracing with his hands and feet on opposite walls.

"Pikel?" Shayleigh asked breathlessly, for the whistling had stopped.

"Oo oi!" came the hearty reply from below, and Shayleigh felt the weight on her foot as the second brother began his climb up the longbow. Pikel thoughtfully took the bow with him as he scaled Shayleigh, then slipped into the corridor and crossed over Ivan, planting his wet sandals firmly against the stretched-out Ivan's side and reaching back over his brother to help Shayleigh. This was the trickiest part of the maneuver, for Pikel and Ivan had to somehow open the doorway wide enough and long enough for Shayleigh to get through, and at the same time give the elf something solid to hold on to.

Pikel braced his club against the door, between Shayleigh's outstretched and aching arms.

"When me brother pushes, ye gotta let go with one hand and get it up to me," Ivan instructed. "Ye ready?"

"Open it," Shayleigh begged, and slowly, Pikel began to push.

As soon as the pressure lessened, Shayleigh reached back for Ivan.

She missed, and her grip with her other arm was not solid enough to support her. With a cry, the elf maiden began to fall.

Ivan caught her wrist, his stubby fingers wrapping her tightly and holding her fast against the slimy wall.

"Oooo," Pikel wailed as the whole group began to slide back dangerously toward the end of the chute.

But Ivan growled and straightened his powerful back, locking himself firmly into place. And Pikel, though his arms ached with the strain of the awkward angle, kept the pressure on the heavy door, kept it open enough for Shayleigh to scramble through. She came over Ivan, up beside Pikel, and he let the door slam shut. Then he straightened perpendicularly to his braced brother, and Shayleigh climbed above him and turned as Ivan had turned.

Ivan climbed up Pikel next, as Pikel held fast to the braced elf maiden. Ivan went across Shayleigh, standing straight up the chute. Pikel clambered up to the top, turned sidelong to Ivan, and set the next brace, and so it went, the three working as a living ladder.

"Eh?" Pikel squeaked as he set another stretching brace, around a bend and far out of sight of the chute's end.

"What ye got?" Ivan asked, climbing even with him. Then Ivan, too, saw the lines in the chute's wall—even, parallel lines, like those of a door.

The dwarf planted himself across Pikel's back, his hands fumbling about the wall. He felt a slight depression—only a dwarf would have been able to detect so minute an inconsistency in the unremarkable wall—and pushed hard. The secret door slid aside, revealing a second passageway, angling up as was this one, but with an easier grade.

Ivan looked back to Shayleigh and to Pikel.

"We know what is above us," Shayleigh reasoned.

"But can we get through the trapdoor?" Ivan replied.

"Sssh," Pikel begged them both, motioning with his chin toward the new passage. When the others quieted, they heard some scuffling from within, far away, as though some battle had been joined.

"Might be friends and might be needing us!" Ivan roared, and he went into the new passage, pulling Shayleigh, and then Pikel, in behind him. Fumbling again for the depression in the stonework, Ivan managed to close the secret door behind them, and with the lesser slope, the three made better time.

They came to a fork a short time later, the passage continuing up one way, but angling down in a narrower chute to the side. Their instincts told them to keep climbing—they had left their friends on a higher level—but the sounds of battle emanated from the lower tunnel.

"It could be Cadderly," Shayleigh reasoned.

"Giant dog!" came a familiar voice from down below.

"Traitor!" roared another powerful, and even deeper-toned, voice.

Pikel was into the chute, sliding headlong, before Ivan even cried out "Vander!"

* * * * *

Which door? Cadderly wondered, looking around at the many possible exits from the large circular room as he crossed over the bodies of the two dead ogres. He noticed, too, the many symbols carved into the walls, tridents with small vials above each point interspersed with triangular fields holding three teardrops, the more conventional design for the evil goddess, Talona.

"We must be near the chapel," Cadderly whispered to Danica. As if in confirmation, the door across the way opened and a horribly scarred man, dressed in the ragged gray and green robes of a Talonan priest, hopped into the circular room.

Danica went into a crouch; Cadderly brought his crossbow level with the man's face.

The priest only smiled, though, and a moment later all the doors of the circular room burst open. Cadderly and Danica found themselves facing a horde of orcs and goblins and evilly grinning men, including several more wearing the robes of Talonan priests. Both friends looked back to the trapped corridor, the only possible escape, but the walls were tight against each other by this point and showed no signs of opening.

For some reason, the enemy force did not immediately attack. Rather, they all stood looking from Cadderly and Danica to the first priest who had entered, apparently the leader.

"Did you think it would be so easy?" the scarred man shrieked hysterically. "Did you think to simply walk through our fortress unopposed?"

Cadderly put a hand on Danica's arm to stop her from

leaping out at the foul man. She might get to him, might well kill him, but they had no chance of defeating this mob. Unless . . .

Cadderly heard the song playing in his thoughts, had a strange feeling that some powerful minion of his god was calling to him, instructing him, compelling him to hear the harmony of the music.

The evil priest cackled and clapped his hands and the floor in front of him heaved suddenly, rose up and took a gigantic, humanoid shape.

"Elementals," Danica breathed, drawing Cadderly's attention. Indeed, two creatures from the plane of earth had arisen to the evil priest's beckoning, and Cadderly realized that this man must be formidable indeed to command such powerful allies.

But Cadderly shook the dark thought away, fell back into the song, heard the music rising to a glorious crescendo.

"He is spellcasting!" one of the other priests cried out, and the warning sent the whole of the enemy force into wild action. The foot soldiers charged, weapons waving, lips wetted with eager drool. An archer took up his bow and fired, and the clerics went into their own spellcasting, some creating defensive energy, others calling out for magical spells to assault the intruders.

Danica yelled for her love and reflexively kicked out, barely deflecting an arrow that was soaring for Cadderly's chest. She wanted to protect Cadderly, knew that they were both surely doomed, for they had no time. . . .

A single word, if it was a word, escaped the young priest's lips. A trumpet note, it seemed, so clear and so perfect that it sent shivers of sheer joy rushing along Danica's spine, invited her into its perfect resonance and held her, trancelike, in its lingering beauty.

The note created a much different effect over Cadderly's enemies, over the evil men and monsters who could not tolerate the holy harmony of Deneir's song. Goblins and orcs, and some of the men, grabbed at their bloodied ears and fell dead or unconscious to the floor, their eardrums shattered by the word. Other men swooned, their strength stolen by the bared glory of Deneirian truth, and the elementals fell back into the stone of the floor, fled back to their own plane of existence.

For many moments Danica stood trembling, her eyes closed, and then, when the last lingering echoes of the perfect note died away, she realized the folly of hesitation and expected that the horde would be upon her. But when she opened her eyes, she found only three enemies standing: the first priest who had entered the room and an associate along a side wall, both holding their ears, and a third man, a soldier not a priest, standing not so far away and glancing about in absolute confusion.

Danica leaped forward and kicked the man's sword from his hand. He looked up at her, still too perplexed to react, and the monk grabbed him by the front of his tunic and threw herself backward in a roll, planting her feet into his belly as he came over her and heaving him hard against the wall beside Cadderly, where he crumbled down in pain. Danica was upon him in a moment, fingers coiled for a deadly strike.

"Do not kill him," Cadderly said to her, for the young priest realized that if this man had escaped the pains of his most holy spell, if the man could withstand the purely harmonious note, then he was probably not of an evil nature. Cadderly glanced at him only briefly, but he noticed revealing shadows atop the man's shoulder, the man's aura personified. These were not huddled, evil things, like the ones the young priest had often witnessed when viewing wicked men in similar fashion.

Danica, trusting in Cadderly's judgment, put the man in a defensive lock, and Cadderly turned his attention back to the still-standing priests.

"Damn you!" the horribly scarred leader growled in a loud voice—and the awkward volume of that response revealed to Cadderly that his holy utterance had probably deafened the man.

"Where is Aballister?" Cadderly called out, and the man regarded him curiously, then tapped his ears, confirming Cadderly's suspicions.

Both evil priests began chanting frantically, beginning new spells, and Danica slammed the soldier to the floor and started forward.

"Get back!" Cadderly warned, and the monk was truly torn. She knew the importance of getting at the spellcasters before they could complete their enchantments, but knew, too, to trust in Cadderly's warnings.

With supreme confidence, feeling invulnerable against the priests of an evil god, Cadderly fell back into the flowing music and began his song. He felt waves of numbing energy as the priest to the side hurled a paralyzing spell at him, but within the protective river of Deneir's music, such a spell had no hold over Cadderly.

The scarred leader lifted his arm and hurled a gemstone, glowing with the mighty energies it contained. Danica leaped in front to block it, as she had blocked the arrow, while Cadderly pointed to it and cried out.

The glow in the gemstone disappeared, and on a sudden inspiration (a silent telepathic message from Cadderly), Danica caught the stone.

Cadderly grabbed the back of Danica's tunic and pulled her behind him, singing all the while. Equations and numbers flashed through his thoughts with every note. He saw the very fabric of the area about him, the relationships and densities of the different materials. Energy flowed from the torches set into sconces on the walls, and a more static energy, the very binding force which held everything in place, was clearly revealed.

The evil priests began chanting again, stubbornly, but now it was Cadderly's turn. The young priest focused on that binding force, replayed equations and changed their factors, forcing truth into untruth.

No, not untruth, Cadderly realized. Not chaos, as was the

enchantment he had forced over old Fyren. In the revealing equations, Cadderly found an alternate truth, a distortion, not a perversion, of physical law. By sheer willpower and the insights the song of Deneir had offered to him, the young priest bent the binding force, turned it in on the scarred enemy leader, making him the center of gravity.

For every unsecured item near the scarred man, the floor was no longer a resting place.

Dead and downed soldiers "fell" at their leader; they did not slide along the floor, but actually toppled and plunged, as though the floor was now a vertical slope. A desk from the room behind the surprised priest crashed against his back, all its items clinging to him as though he had become a living magnet. Two of the torches within the area of warped reality leaned toward the evil priest and slowly slid along the sides of their sconces, coming to an angled rest in a precarious perch, their flames burning out to the side away from the cursed man.

The priest who had been standing at the side of the room hung straight out, his feet toward his master, his hands clutching desperately at the doorjamb.

Danica couldn't prevent a chuckle at the ridiculous sight. A ball of bodies and items had converged on the scarred leader, smashing him from every angle. The priest to the side fell last, slamming hard against a dead orc. And then everything had settled once more, everything unattached or unsupported within fifty feet of the evil priest had come to rest atop him, had pounded him and buried him.

Several groans came from within that confused pile, mostly those of the battered leader, buried somewhere far beneath the jumble.

The man's associate, lying on the outside layer of the confused pile, looked at Cadderly with sheer hatred and began again his stubborn chant.

"Do not!" Cadderly warned him. The priest did stop, but not because of Cadderly's warning. Out of the same room that had held the desk now fell an incredibly fat giant, hitting the pile with such tremendous force that those bodies on the opposite side of the pile, near Cadderly and Danica, bounced out to the side, then fell back and settled on the pile once more. The scarred leader went quiet then for the first time, and Cadderly winced, realizing that the giant had probably crushed the man.

The giant was far from dead, though. It roared and thrashed, launching bodies far to the side, then smashing them apart as they inevitably fell back into the pile.

"How long will it last?" Danica asked. Her darting eyes revealed her fear, for their was no apparent way for her and Cadderly to get out of the area. Many of the men stricken unconscious by the holy word were awakening, and that ferocious giant had not been badly wounded.

Trepidation welled up within Cadderly, dark fears for what he must do to complete this battle. He searched his spells, listened carefully to the song, seeking something that would allow him and Danica to get through without further bloodshed. But what of his friends? he wondered. If they came out behind him, and the spell was no more, they would face a formidable force.

Again the raging priest atop the pile chanted; a soldier to the side of him hurled a dagger Cadderly's way, but it was as if he were throwing up the side of a cliff, and the knife dropped back to the jumble, sticking into the back of a dead goblin. The giant climbed through next, a look of sheer hatred on its huge face.

Cadderly looked to Danica, to the gemstone, a hunk of amber, that she held. Of all the trials the young priest would ever face, none would be so agonizing as this trial of conscience. He could not fail now, though, could not allow his own weakness to threaten his mission, to threaten all the goodly peoples of the region. He waved his hand over the gemstone, uttered a few words, and it began to glow again, teeming with magical energy.

"Toss it," he instructed.

"At them?"

Cadderly thought about it and shrugged as though it did not matter. "To the side," he said, pointing to the doorjamb where the priest had been hanging.

Danica still seemed not to understand, but she tossed the enchanted stone. It followed a normal, expected course for a few feet, then crossed into the area warped by Cadderly's spell and fell in an arcing, unerring curve to strike at the pile.

With a blinding flash, all the jumble was aflame. Men cried out for a moment, then fell silent. The giant thrashed wildly, but had nowhere to run, could find nothing to roll in that was not also burning. It went on for what seemed a long and agonizing time, but was in reality merely minutes, then the only sound was the crackle of hungry flames.

* * * * *

Pikel plowed through another angled doorway and fell fifteen feet to hit the corridor floor with a resounding "Oof!"

Dazed, and unable to find his balance, the dwarf turned his gaze to the side and saw Vander—Vander's furred boots, at least—stumbling about the bodies of several dead ogres. Even larger boots moved to keep up with the dancing firbolg, a hill giant, probably, along with the dirty, naked feet of yet another ogre.

Pikel knew that Vander needed him, so he gave a determined grunt and started to pull himself off the floor.

The plummeting Ivan hit him squarely in the back. The yellow-bearded dwarf bounced up from his cushioned landing and rushed ahead, recognizing Vander's desperate situation. The hill giant had Vander wrapped in its huge arms, and the ogre, wielding a huge spiked club, was circling about them, looking for an opening.

"Traitor!" the hill giant bellowed once more.

Vander butted with his forehead, splattering the giant's nose. With a roar, the giant swung about and launched Vander into the wall with such force that it shook the whole corridor. Vander bounced back a step, trying to get his sword up, but the ogre rushed in at his side and hit him with a roundhouse that drove a spike right into the side of his head.

Down on his knees, the dying firbolg noticed Ivan rushing in and with heroic effort heaved his sword forward as though it were a spear. The blade slashed into the hill giant's shoulder, knocking the monster back, slumping, against the opposite wall, its huge hands trying to find some hold that it might pull the thing out.

The ogre's great club smashed in again, and Vander saw no more.

Tears welled in Ivan's dark eyes as he pounded down the corridor. He leaped atop the wounded giant and crunched his axe into the monster's thick skull. The ogre roared at the sight of the dwarf and rushed back across the corridor, swinging wildly.

Ivan hopped away, and the ogre's spiked club drew bloody creases down the giant's face and sent the behemoth sprawling to the floor.

"Duh," the ogre groaned stupidly, and then it jerked to the side as Ivan's axe chopped it on the leg. Like a lumberjack, the sturdy dwarf went to work, hacking with abandon, and four blows later, the ogre toppled to the floor.

Behind Ivan, the giant groaned and tried to rise. The cry of "Ooooooo!" followed by the resounding smack of a treetrunk club against flesh brought a grim smile to the yellowbearded dwarf.

Pikel hit the stunned giant again and moved for a third strike. But the stubborn behemoth, far from finished, caught the club and pulled it aside.

Pikel let go with one hand and pointed it straight out at the giant, who seemed not to understand—not until something snapped out of Pikel's loose-fitting sleeve, snapped out with venom-dripping fangs into the surprised giant's face.

The giant let go of the club and fell back, clawing at the

stinging wound, horrified.

It heard Pikel's "Ooooooo!" as the dwarf, club in hand, wound up, but it never saw the killing blow coming.

Without its weapon, the ogre across the hall raised its arms defensively and called out a surrender.

But those arms, however thick, were no match for Ivan's blind fury. Vander lay dead behind him, and the dwarf was hardly in the mood to listen to anything the desperate monster might have to say. The dwarf's axe chopped down repeatedly, smashing through flesh and bone, and by the time Shayleigh joined Ivan and put a hand on his shoulder to calm him, the ogre's cries were forever silenced.

Sixteen

A Call on the Wind

The man at the base of the wall groaned, and Danica was on him in an instant, roughly pulling his arms behind his back and pushing him facedown against the hard stone. "How long will your enchantment block our way?" she snapped at Cadderly.

"Not long," the young priest replied, surprised by Danica's harsh tone.

"And what are we to do with him?" Danica gave a rough tug on the captured soldier's arms as she asked the question, drawing another groan from the battered man.

"Be easy with him," Cadderly said.

"As you were with them?" Danica asked sarcastically, waving a hand out to the smoldering pile.

Now Cadderly understood Danica's ire. The battle had been rough, as the rising stench of burning flesh reminded them.

"Why didn't you tell me what that orb would do?"

Danica's question sounded as a desperate plea.

Cadderly had a hard time sorting through this seeming reversal of roles. Usually he was the one who was too soft-hearted, who got them into trouble by not fighting hard enough against the declared enemies. He had spared Dorigen in Shilmista Forest, had let her live when he had her helpless on the ground before him, though Danica had instructed him to finish her. And now, Cadderly had been merciless, had done as the situation demanded against his own peaceful instincts. Cadderly held little remorse—he knew that all those humans in the fiery jumble were evil-hearted men—but he was more than a little surprised by Danica's cold reaction.

She gave another tug on the prisoner's arms, as if she was using the man's pain to torment Cadderly, lashing out at the young priest by going against what he obviously desired.

"He is not an evil man," Cadderly said calmly.

Danica hesitated, her exotic eyes searching out the sincerity within Cadderly's gray orbs. She had always been able to read the young priest's thoughts and believed now that he was speaking truthfully (though where he had garnered that piece of information, Danica had no idea).

"And they were?" Danica asked somewhat sharply, again indicating the pile.

"Yes," Cadderly answered. "When I uttered the holy word, how did you feel?"

The simple memory of that wondrous moment eased much of the tension from Danica's fair face. How did she feel? She felt in love, at ease with all the world, as if nothing ugly could come near her.

"You saw how it affected them," Cadderly went on, finding his answers in Danica's serene expression.

Following the logic, Danica lessened her grip. "But it did not adversely affect this one," she said.

"He is not an evil man," Cadderly reiterated.

Danica nodded and lessened her grip. She looked back

at Cadderly, though, and her expression was cold once more, a look more of disappointment than of anger.

Cadderly understood, but had no answers for his love. There had been human beings among the evil monsters in this group, men among the goblins. Danica was disappointed because Cadderly had done what was necessary, had given in to the fighting fully. She had been angry with Cadderly when he had spared Dorigen, but it was an anger founded in her fear of the wizard. In truth, Danica had loved Cadderly all the more because of his conscience, because he had tried to avoid the horrors of battle at all costs.

Cadderly looked back to the pile of corpses. He had given in, joined the fighting with all his heart.

It had to be that way, Cadderly knew. He was as horrified as Danica over what he had just done, but he would not take back the action even if he could. The friends were in desperate straights—all the region was in desperate straights—and that danger was being precipitated by the minions of this fortress. Castle Trinity, and not Cadderly, would have to take responsibility for the lives that would be lost this day.

But while that argument held solid on a logical basis, Cadderly could not deny the pain in his chest when he looked upon the pile of dead men, or the sting in his heart when he viewed Danica's disappointment.

* * * * *

"We must go!" Shayleigh said to Ivan, tugging on the dwarf's arm and looking back to the corridor behind them, where the steps of many boots could be heard.

Ivan sighed as he regarded Vander, the firbolg's head crushed and misshapen. A similar sigh behind him turned Ivan about to regard Pikel. He eyed his brother curiously, for something seemed out of place along the length of Pikel's tunic and undershirt.

"How'd ye get away from the snake?" Ivan asked, suddenly remembering their past predicament.

Pikel gave a short whistle, and on cue, the serpent's head streamed up from his collar and hovered in the air right beside his green-bearded cheek.

Shayleigh and Ivan fell back in shock, Ivan's axe coming up defensively between himself and his surprising brother.

"Doo-dad!" Pikel announced happily, petting the snake, which seemed to enjoy the treatment. Pikel nodded to the side, then, indicating that they should be on their way.

"Doo-dad?" Shayleigh inquired of Ivan as Pikel hopped off.

"Wants to be a druid," Ivan explained, moving to follow his brother. "He don't know that dwarves can't be druids."

Shayleigh considered the words for a long moment. "Neither does the snake," she decided, and with a final, helpless look at the dead Vander, she rushed off after her companions.

* * * * *

"My thanks to you," the soldier whispered to Cadderly, all the while eyeing the charred mass of his dead allies. The pile fell apart then, resetting upon the floor, as Cadderly's strange enchantment dissipated.

"Where is Aballister?" the young priest demanded. The man's lips seemed to tighten into thin lines.

Cadderly leaped past Danica, grabbed the man by the collar, and slammed him hard against the wall. "You are still a prisoner!" he growled in the surprised man's face. "You can be an asset to us, and we will repay you accordingly.

"Or you can be a detriment," Cadderly went on grimly. He looked back to the pile as he spoke, and the unvoiced threat drained the blood from the captured man's face.

"Lead on to the wizard," Cadderly instructed. "Along the most direct route."

The man glanced at Danica, as if pleading for some support, but the monk looked away impassively.

That gesture did not reveal the turmoil in Danica's heart. Cadderly's move and threat against the prisoner, a person he had just declared was not an evil man, had surprised her. She had never seen Cadderly so calculatingly cold, and while she could understand his determined actions, she could not deny her fears.

The prisoner took them through a door to the side, halfway around the circular room. They had only gone a dozen steps when Cadderly grabbed the man again, pushed him up against the wall and began roughly stripping off every piece of his noisy armor, even to the point of removing the man's hard-soled boots.

"Quietly," he whispered to the man. "I have but one battle left to fight, a battle against Aballister."

The man growled and pushed Cadderly away, and found Danica's silver-hilted dagger at his throat in the blink of an eye.

"The wizard is powerful," the prisoner warned, wisely keeping his voice soft.

Cadderly nodded. "And you fear the consequences of your actions should Aballister win out against us," he reasoned.

The man's lips went tight again, and he made no move to respond. Cadderly eased Danica away and again put his face close to the man's, his jaw firm and unrelenting. "Then choose," the young priest said, his voice low and threatening. "Do you take the chance that Aballister will not win out?"

The man glanced about nervously, but again said nothing.

"Aballister is not here," Cadderly reminded him. "None of your allies are here. It is just you and I, and you know what *I* can do."

The man started off again immediately, his bare feet making little noise as he padded along the corridor with appropriate caution. They crossed several side corridors, often hearing the sounds of other soldiers rushing about, probably in search of them. Each time some group was about, Danica looked nervously to Cadderly, as if to say that this man, who could betray them with a simple call, was his responsibility.

But the man held true to the terms of his capture, moving with all stealth as they worked their way past one guard position or patrol group after another.

When they entered one long corridor, though, a group of goblins entered it simultaneously from the other end, and they found that they had nowhere to run. The goblins, six of the beasts, advanced cautiously, weapons drawn.

The prisoner addressed them in their own croaking language, and Cadderly understood well enough to know that the man had concocted some lie about being on a mission for the priests, going to Aballister with some important information.

Still, the goblins eyed Cadderly and Danica dangerously, exchanging a few quiet remarks—doubts, Cadderly knew—amongst themselves.

Even the cooperative prisoner looked back, his expression showing sincere worry.

Danica didn't wait for events to take their obvious course. She leaped out suddenly, punching the nearest goblin in the throat, circling about, her leg flying high to connect on the next one's chest, and whipped a dagger into the face of yet another. She ducked low under a sword swipe and sprang up high from her crouch, double-kicking the sword wielder in the face and chest.

Two goblins rushed by her, more concerned with escape than with tangling against Cadderly and the soldier, but Cadderly got one with his walking stick, shattering its knee, and the soldier tackled the other.

Danica spun about and again kicked, sending one goblin flying into the wall. The creature smacked hard against the stone and bounced back, and Danica, timing her spin perfectly, promptly kicked it again. Again it bounced out; again it was launched backward by a perfectly timed kick.

The fourth time, the goblin was allowed to fall to the floor, for Danica sprang away, leaping over the prone prisoner at the back of the goblin that had slipped his grasp. One hand reached around to cup the goblin's chin while the other grabbed the hair on the back of its head.

The goblin squealed and tried to stop and turn, but Danica rushed right beside it, twisting her arms viciously, snapping the wretched thing's neck.

"Down!" Danica called, coming around behind Cadderly. The young priest fell to the floor and the goblin facing him was caught fully by surprise as Danica rushed by, connecting with a heavy punch into its ugly face. It flew backward several feet, hit the stone with a groan, and Danica ran past.

The goblin she had hit in the throat was up to its knees again, trying to find its footing. Danica leaped high into the air, coming down with her knees driving against the skinny creature's back, slamming it down fiercely. She pulled her second dagger from her boot, grabbed a clump of hair with her free hand and pulled the goblin's head back, cutting a neat line across its throat.

She did likewise to the helpless goblin that had her other dagger sticking from its face, ending its misery. And then she turned back, to see Cadderly and the prisoner staring at her incredulously.

"I do not parley with goblins," Danica said grimly, wiping her blades on the nearest monster's dirty tunic.

"You could not outrun her," Cadderly remarked to the prisoner, and the man, in turn, gave the young priest an incredulous look.

"I just thought I would mention that," Cadderly said.

They set out at once, Cadderly and Danica anxious to put some distance between themselves and the scene of the slaughter. The prisoner said nothing, just continued to lead them at a swift pace, and soon the tunnels became quieter and less filled with rushing soldiers.

Cadderly sensed that the walls in this region were not

natural, though they were lined by uncut stone. The young
priest could feel the residual energies of the magics that
had been used to make this place, as though some powerful dweomer had pulled the natural stone from between
these walls.

The sensations sent a mix of emotions through the
young priest. He was glad that the captured soldier was
apparently not leading them astray, glad that their search
might soon come to its end. But Cadderly was worried, too,
for if Aballister had created these tunnels, had magically
torn the stone from these halls, then the storm at Nightglow only hinted at his powers.

Something else assaulted Cadderly's thoughts then, a
fleeting, distant call, as if someone was summoning him. He
paused and closed his eyes.

Cadderly.

He heard it clearly, though distantly. He felt for the
amulet in his pocket which he'd acquired some time ago
and with which he could communicate with the imp, Druzil.
Now it was cool, indicating that Druzil was nowhere about.

Cadderly.

It was not Druzil, and Cadderly did not believe that it was
Dorigen, either. Who then? the young priest wondered.
Who was so attuned to him that they might make telepathic
contact without his knowledge or consent?

He opened his eyes, determined not to get sidetracked.
"Keep going," he instructed his comrades, taking his place
beside them.

But the call remained, fleeting and distant, and what
bothered Cadderly more than anything else was that it
somehow sounded so very familiar.

Seventeen

Dwarven Stealth

"We must move quietly," Shayleigh pointedly instructed her dwarven companions, what seemed to her an obvious precaution. Still, Shayleigh soon came to understand that her definition of "moving quietly" was apparently very different from Ivan and Pikel's. The clomp of Ivan's boots echoed loudly off the stone walls, and Pikel's sandals double-slapped—once against the floor and once against his foot—with every pumping stride.

They rambled along several long, dark corridors, the only light coming from widely spaced torches hanging in iron sconces. Around a bend and through an archway, the three companions found the walls lined by fonts, filled with a clear, watery substance.

Ivan, needing a refreshing drink, paused and moved to scoop up some, but Pikel quickly slapped his hand away, waggling a finger in his startled brother's face.

"Uh-uhhh," the green-bearded dwarf implored, and he

hopped up high and pulled a torch from its sconce. Still waggling the finger tucked under his arm, Pikel touched the fire to the liquid. The stuff hissed and sputtered, and a noxious gray cloud arose, making Ivan pinch his nose. Pikel hung his tongue out of his mouth and muttered, "Yuch."

"How did he know?" Shayleigh asked Ivan when they had cleared the stinky area.

Ivan shrugged. "Must be something to this druid stuff."

"Doo-dad!" Pikel agreed.

"Yeah, doo-dad," muttered Ivan. "Or ye just knowed that this place is for Talona, and Talona's the goddess of poison."

Sly Pikel wasn't letting on. He just followed the other two, every so often chuckling, "Hee hee hee."

Around a sharp bend in the corridor, the friends found a group of enemies waiting for them.

Shayleigh fired her bow between the bobbing dwarven heads, catching the leading orc in the chest and dropping it dead.

"Frog!" Ivan called, a reference to a game he and his brother used to play. Pikel rushed in front and braced himself, squared to the next leading orc, and Ivan leaped up from behind and straddled Pikel's shoulders. Pikel fell forward, hooking Ivan's feet and his propelling his forward-flying brother into a downward arc.

The orc froze with surprise, stood there with no practical defenses, and Ivan's axe cleaved its skull, drove right down through the stupid creature's head so that it seemed as if it would literally be split in half.

The move left both dwarves sprawled on the floor, with several enemies still standing, unharmed (though after witnessing a comrade practically split down the middle, none of them seemed overly anxious to rush in). With the line of fire clear between them and Shayleigh, their hesitation was not a wise thing.

The elf maiden set her bow to furious work, hardly aiming, just firing for the mass of enemy bodies.

A few seconds, and a few arrows, later, what was left of the enemy band was in full flight.

"Now move *quietly*," Shayleigh instructed through gritted teeth.

"Quietly!" Ivan balked incredulously. "Bring the whole damned bunch of them on, I say!"

"Oo oi!" Pikel cried. The agreeing brothers turned together toward Shayleigh, to find the elf maiden back against the inner wall of the last corner, her bow up as she looked behind them.

"You may get your wish," she explained. "Goblins, led by an ogre."

Ivan and Pikel rushed up to the corner beside her and nodded to each other, as if they already had come to a silent agreement on how to approach this next fight. Ivan stooped, and this time Pikel went up on his shoulders, leaning against the wall and putting one hand up high, fingers conspicuously wrapped around the edge of the wall, in plain sight of the approaching force.

Ivan nodded for Shayleigh to fall back a few steps.

The ogre came around the corner expecting, from Pikel's high-placed hand, to find a tall foe. Pikel fell away as the monster spun around the bend, its flying club smacking harmlessly off the empty stone wall.

Ivan's axe chop gashed into the thigh of its lead leg, severing muscles and tendons.

Unable to stop its momentum, the wounded ogre continued its turn, squaring its back to Shayleigh. Still backpedaling, it jerked twice in rapid succession as arrows drove through its shoulder blades, and then it tripped altogether, falling backward. One arrow shattered under the tremendous weight, but the other, angled perfectly so that it hit the ground straight up, plunged through the massive beast, through its heart, with the arrow tip bursting out the front of the ogre's chest.

By the time the goblins, just two steps behind the ogre, came around the corner, they found their leader dead.

Not that the lead goblins even had time to register the scene. Pikel, crouched back in the corner, swiped his club across, smacking shins and sending two of the monsters sprawling—right at Ivan's feet. The yellow-bearded dwarf, his axe chopping viciously, made quick work of them.

The rest of the force, with typical goblin loyalty, turned and fled.

"They will be returning from the front," Shayleigh said grimly.

"Yeah, and the stupid goblins will hear the fighting and come back the other way, probably with a hunnerd kin!" Ivan agreed.

"You may indeed get your wish, Ivan," the elf answered grimly. "The whole force of Castle Trinity might soon squeeze us between them." Shayleigh moved to the corner and looked back, then ran up ahead and peered as far along as she could, hoping for a side tunnel, for something that could get them free of this tight area.

Pikel, already understanding their dire predicament, tuned out of the conversation. Down on his knees, he crawled along the worked wall, butting his forehead against any promising stones.

"What is he doing?" Shayleigh demanded, obviously dismayed by the dwarf's apparently ridiculous actions.

Even as she spoke, Pikel pressed his forehead back against one of the rocks. He turned to Ivan, smiling from ear to ear, and squeaked.

"There's the way!" Ivan bellowed, falling to his knees beside his brother, both of them digging with their fingers at the edges of the cut stone.

"They always put secret tunnels beside the corridor," Ivan explained to Shayleigh's doubting expression. "Drains the water in case of a flood."

Shayleigh's keen ears caught the sounds of footsteps approaching from both directions. "Hurry," she implored the dwarves, and she ran to the wall and grabbed a torch. Shayleigh rushed back around the corner, as far down as she could go, then reversed direction and ran back, dipping the torch in every font she passed, and pulling out all the other torches. All the corridor behind her was soon filled with a noxious gray cloud, leaving the passage in smoky darkness. Through it, Shayleigh could see the red dots of goblin eyes, using their heat-sensing infravision.

"Stubborn," she muttered, and she ran around the corner, down the hallway the other way, repeating the procedure. By the time she got back to the dwarves, enemies were closing from both directions. A goblin peeked around the corner, then fell back with an arrow in its eye.

"Hurry!" Shayleigh whispered harshly, coughing as the evil smoke descended over her.

"Hurry, yerself," Ivan growled back. He pulled the elf maiden down to the floor and practically stuffed her through the opening, dropping her down a muddy, descending chute. Pikel came in behind, chuckling and placing both his club and Ivan's axe in the slope behind him.

"What is he doing?" Shayleigh asked, but Pikel only put a stubby finger over his lips and whispered, "Ssssh!"

Ivan rushed across and put his back to the corner, closing his eyes so that the red glow of infravision would not give him away. Goblins shuffled around behind him.

The enemy host came moving down from the other direction.

"More than we thinks!" Ivan roared in the goblin language, a squeaking and croaking tongue. Those goblins beside the dwarf, peering ahead through the confusing veil, took up their weapons.

"Charges them! Killses them!" Ivan bellowed, and the call was repeated by many goblins as the horde rushed the approaching force. In a confusing instant, the two groups were together, hacking away, each thinking the other to be the intruders that had come to Castle Trinity.

Ivan calmly walked over to stand in front of the secret tunnel. Pikel reached out to him, but Ivan hesitated, thoroughly enjoying the battle. Finally, Pikel's patience evaporated, and he reached out with both hands, grabbed Ivan by the ankles, and jerked him from his feet, dragging him into the tunnel.

Pikel clambered over his facedown brother, out of the tunnel far enough to retrieve the block and tug it somewhat back in place. Now it was the green-bearded dwarf who hesitated, enthralled by the raging action, chuckling as one severed goblin head came bouncing by. Never one to miss an opportunity for payback, Ivan grabbed Pikel by the ankles and yanked him through the mud.

Soon after, the three friends found a way out of that crawl tunnel, into another stone-worked corridor some distance from the fighting. Ivan and Pikel led the way, their muddy faces set in a determined grimace.

Shayleigh shook her head in disbelief many times over the next few minutes as the dwarves rambled through the complex, overturning everything in their path, including a few startled goblins. Shayleigh didn't tell them to be quiet, though. She knew that their escape had been a temporary reprieve, that no matter how stealthily they might now travel, sooner or later they would meet an organized defense.

The elf smiled then, glad that she was beside the rugged Bouldershoulders. She had seen the brothers like this before, in the battles of Shilmista. Let the enemy come on, she decided. Let them face the battle-lust of the hearty dwarves!

Ivan and Pikel did slow down and become somewhat quieter when they neared a staircase, rising up out of sight just beyond a four-way intersection of wide corridors. A perfect place for an ambush. They heard singing coming from the stairs, a booming, giant voice. The corridor behind them and the two to the sides seemed empty, so they crept across.

The stairs went up, which was the way they all figured they had to go, but they could see the boots of a giant not so far up the stairs. The huge monster continued its off-key singing, apparently unaware of the intruders that had come to Castle Trinity.

"Get ye up fast," was the only explanation Ivan offered to Shayleigh, and with a wink to his brother, the two dwarves set off, using the giant's booming voice to cover their heavy steps on the wooden stairs.

Shayleigh glanced all about nervously, thinking this a bad situation. She heard the dwarves roar out in glee, though, heard the smacks as Ivan's axe and Pikel's club connected on the giant's legs. Then the whole ground shook as the behemoth tumbled down the stairs.

Shayleigh considered putting an arrow into the tumbling thing, but heard the three corridors behind her fast filling with enemy soldiers. Instead, she turned about and launched the arrow into the thickening mass behind her, not waiting to see if she had scored a hit.

The giant, though very much alive and very much enraged, lay on its back, its head toward Shayleigh and its feet still far up the staircase. It struggled to right itself, but its bulk filled the not-too-wide stairs, and in that awkward position, with both legs injured, it floundered miserably.

Shayleigh drew out her short sword and leaped ahead, skipping off the monster's face, nearly tripping on its huge nose. The giant grabbed at her with its hands, but she dodged them and stuck one when it got too near. The giant lifted a huge leg and curled it in at the knee, forming a barrier of flesh, but Shayleigh drove her sword deeply into the thick thigh and the barrier flew away. As she cleared the huge torso, the elf saw Pikel coming the other way, rushing under the one upraised leg.

Shayleigh called out, thinking that Pikel would surely be crushed, but the dwarf was already wedged tightly between the stairs and the giant's huge buttocks.

A swarm of enemies came to the bottom of the stairs, some clambering to get atop the giant, others drawing out bows and taking a bead on Shayleigh and on Ivan as the yellow-bearded dwarf rushed down to grab the elf maiden.

Pikel's pet snake bit the giant on the fleshy backside, and the monster's predictable hop gave the dwarf all the momentum he needed. Bracing his shoulder, the powerful little dwarf heaved and groaned, turning the behemoth up onto its shoulders, lifting a wall of flesh between his friends and the enemies. The giant grunted several times as it intercepted arrows, and then, with Pikel's stubby legs driving relentlessly, it went right over, wedging tightly into the low, narrow stairway entrance.

Pikel gave his snake a pat on the head and tucked it back into his sleeve, then rushed to join his friends, taking his club back from Ivan as he hopped past.

Shayleigh stood shaking her head once more.

"Stronger than ye thought, ain't he?" Ivan asked, tugging her along.

They met no foes at the top of the stairs, and Ivan and Pikel immediately lined up side by side and resumed their battle charge. Shayleigh heard no sounds about them other than the echoes of dwarven sandals and boots, and while that fact gave her some comfort, she realized that this blind rush through the complex would likely get them nowhere.

Finally Shayleigh was able to stop the brothers' wild run, reminding them that they had to sort out the maze of tunnels and try to find Cadderly and Danica.

When the dwarves had quieted, they did hear some noise, a general murmur, down a corridor to the left. Shayleigh was about to whisper that she should go ahead and stealthily check out the place, but her words were buried under Pikel's hearty "Oo oi!" and the resounding clamor of the renewed charge.

Eighteen

The Fifth Corner

There," the prisoner said to Cadderly and Danica, pointing across a last intersection to an unremarkable door. "That is the entrance to the wizard's chambers."

Cadderly.

The call came again in the young priest's mind, from somewhere not so far away. Cadderly closed his eyes and concentrated, coming to understand that the call came from somewhere beyond the unremarkable door. When he opened his eyes once more, he found Danica eyeing him curiously.

"The man does not lie," Cadderly said to her.

The prisoner seemed to relax at that.

"Then why are there no guards?" Danica asked, more to the prisoner than to Cadderly.

The man had no answer for her.

"This is a wizard," Cadderly reminded them both. "A powerful wizard by all that we have heard. There may indeed be a guardian or some protective magic."

Danica roughly pushed the prisoner forward. "You shall lead," she said coldly.

Cadderly immediately moved up beside the man, catching his arm to hold him back, and looked across him to regard Danica.

"We go together?" he asked as much as stated.

Danica looked to the door, to Cadderly and the other man. She understood her love's sympathy and protectiveness toward the helpless prisoner, understood that Cadderly, convinced that this was not an evil man, would not use the prisoner as fodder.

"He and I lead," Danica decided, pulling the man from Cadderly's light grasp. "You follow."

The monk soft-stepped up to the intersection, bent low and peered both ways. She turned back to Cadderly and offered a shrug, then motioned for the prisoner to keep pace and skittered across to the door—almost.

The creature seemed to unfold from the air itself, becoming first a black line, then expanding left and right, two dimensional, then three dimensional. Five serpentine heads waved in front of the startled companions.

A hydra.

Danica skidded to a stop and hurled herself to the left, rolling from the lunging reach of three great heads. The prisoner, not as quick as the monk, managed only a single step before a monstrous maw clamped down across his waist.

He screamed and batted futilely at the scaly head as the needle-sharp teeth ripped him. A second maw descended over the man's unprotected head, stifling his scream fully. Both heads working in unison, the hydra tore the man in half.

Cadderly nearly swooned at the sight. He got his loaded crossbow up in front of him, shifting it this way and that, trying to follow the almost hypnotic motion of the weaving heads.

Where to fire?

He shot for the center of the great body, and the hydra roared in rage as the dart hit and exploded. Two heads still snapped at the dodging Danica, two continued their feast on the slaughtered man, and the fifth shot forward, far short of Cadderly, but compelling the hydra's bulky body into a short rush at the young priest.

Danica started for Cadderly, but reversed direction abruptly as the hydra shuffled by, and chose instead to work her way behind the beast. She cried out for Cadderly to run, though she could not see him around the bulk of the monster.

The lead maw came, straight as an arrow, for the young priest, testing his nerve as he struggled to get his weapon readied a second time. The serpentine maw was barely two feet away when Cadderly's arm at last came up, and he fired, the quarrel skipping off six-inch fangs, diving into the monster's mouth and blasting in a muffled explosion.

The head and neck dropped in a line on the floor, slowing the charge.

The two heads that had been after Danica, and the one finished with the dead prisoner, came swooping in, though, and the young priest wisely fell back, desperately bringing up his walking stick to fend off the nearest attack.

He knew that he had to get far enough away to reload the crossbow, had to fall into the song of Dencir and pull something, anything, from the notes. But with the maze of darting heads, the creature pacing his every retreat, Cadderly couldn't begin to hear the song, had to concentrate simply on whipping his walking stick back and forth in front of him. He did connect once, luckily, the enchanted ram's head knocking a tooth from the closest maw. That head went up to issue a roar, and Cadderly, purely on instinct, rushed under it, used the serpentine neck as a shield against the other two pursuing heads.

The fourth head, the other one to the right, spit aside the dead man's torso and would have had the young priest then, except that Danica came around from behind and snapped a kick under its jaw.

The monster's maw smacked shut; its flickering tongue fell severed to the floor.

Cadderly continued toward the door, concentrating on readying the crossbow. Danica came, too, by his side, looking back as the hydra lumbered about, dragging its one dead head along the floor as it turned.

"Get in!" she called, but Cadderly, for all his desperation, kept his wits enough to keep clear of the door. It was warded, he knew, sensing the magics upon it. Shoulder to shoulder with Danica, he brought his crossbow up again as if to shoot at the hydra. But then he turned, firing instead at the lock on the door, blowing a wide hole in the wood.

Danica hit Cadderly on the shoulder, throwing him aside. He came up against the wall, dazed, to see his love engulfed by four eagerly snapping hydra heads.

She rushed straight for the beast, ran inside its initial bites, twisting and turning, swatting blindly at anything that came near. A head turned enough to get at her, and she grabbed it by the horn, twisting with a jerk that angled the maw so that it could not wrap around her, so that the snout butted her in the ribs. Danica's other hand shot out the other way, her stiffened fingers driving through the eye of still another snapping head.

All the hydra's heads were turned completely about, facing its bulky torso. Danica grabbed the half-blinded head, threw her back against the thick serpentine neck, then dodged away as another head rushed in, its wide-opened maw biting hard into its own companion's neck. Before the hydra even realized its error, the other head fell dead.

Danica was still pinned in that hellish spot, but a quarrel skipped off the side of one turned neck—off the side of one to solidly strike a second. The first head that had been struck wheeled about to view the newest attacker, while the force of the ensuing explosion drove the second head aside, opening a hole for Danica to rush out.

"The door is warded!" Cadderly cried at Danica as she darted straight for the loose-hanging portal.

It was a moot point, for Danica had no intentions of going through. She stopped and, sensing a maw rushing at her back, leaped up high, catching the top of the jamb and pulling herself straight up. The hydra's head burst through the door.

Lightning flashed several times; fire roared out from every side of the magically trapped doorjamb.

Only two heads remaining, the blasted hydra backed away. Serpentine necks crossed; reptilian eyes regarded the two companions with sudden respect.

Cadderly tried to line one up for a shot, but he hesitated, not wanting to risk a miss.

"Damn," he hissed, frustrated, after a long and unproductive moment had slipped past. He fired the bolt into the hydra's bulk, apparently doing no real damage, but driving it back another step. The hydra's living heads roared in unison. It hopped to the side, three dead necks bouncing along.

"Shoot for my back," Danica instructed and before Cadderly could ask her what she was talking about, she rushed forward, charged right between the swaying heads, drawing them in to her. "Now!" Danica ordered.

Cadderly had to trust in her. His crossbow clicked, and Danica dropped suddenly to her back, the quarrel crossing above her and splattering a very surprised serpentine face.

That wounded head did not die, though, and Danica, on her back, now had two snapping maws above her.

"No!" Cadderly cried out, and he charged ahead boldly, both hands tight on his ram's-head walking stick.

Danica kicked up, one foot and then the other, keeping the heads at bay. Cadderly saw that the head he had shot appeared fully blind, and he leaped right across Danica's prone form, smashing the head with a two-handed overhead chop.

The head recoiled, and Cadderly pursued, smacking it

repeatedly.

The second head rushed in at Cadderly's back, but Danica threw her legs up and then down, snapping her back in a quick arch and hurling herself to her feet. A single stride brought her alongside the chasing head and she dipped low, drawing a dagger from her boot, then shot back up, driving the knife up to its silver dragon-sculpted hilt into the bottom jaw.

Cadderly's arms pumped relentlessly, beating the already disfigured head into a bloody pulp.

The remaining head soared up high, but Danica locked her arm over the neck and went along for the ride, holding fast to her stuck dagger. She curled up around the neck, bringing her boot to her free hand and managing to extract her second dagger.

Then she held on, stubbornly, as the monster bucked and whipped. When its frenzy finally abated, Danica plunged her second knife into its eye, pulled it back, and drove it home a second time.

Again came the monstrous frenzy. Cadderly, trying to get to Danica, got clipped on one rushing pass and was hurled ten feet down the corridor.

But Danica held on, kept both her daggers buried, working them back and forth, turning their handles around in her palms. She fell hard to her back, smacking against the stone, the monstrous neck dropping over her.

Stunned, the monk could not find her breath, could not focus her gaze, and was hardly conscious of her grip on her knives. Her instincts screamed out at her to react, to wriggle away. Her instincts screamed out at her that she was vulnerable, that the hydra head could easily shake free and snap her in half.

But the hydra was no longer moving, and a moment later, Cadderly was standing above Danica, pulling her arms free, shifting the bulky serpentine neck off her.

* * * * *

Shayleigh heard a murmuring up ahead, the drone of many muffled voices. She started to call out a warning to the Bouldershoulder brothers, but the dwarves had apparently heard the sound as well, for they lowered their heads and picked up the pace, Pikel's sandals slapping and Ivan's boots thumping.

Shayleigh slipped along silently right behind them, her bow ready. Around a bend in the corridor they saw a straight run past two intersections and ending at a set of double doors.

"Too many!" the elf maiden whispered harshly, slowing her pace. "Too many!"

Double doors blocked their way, then double doors hung awkwardly on broken hinges. Ivan and Pikel burst in, weapons high.

"Uh-oh," muttered the green-bearded dwarf, echoing his brother's sentiments exactly, for they had come into a huge hall, a dining area, now apparently doubling as a command post, lined with dozens of tables and more than a few enemies. Shayleigh sighed helplessly and rushed to catch up with the furious dwarves, who, in their momentum, had already charged past the first empty tables.

A group of orcs sitting closest to the door barely had the time to look up from their bowls before the dwarves fell over them, hacking and kicking, Ivan butting with his deer-antlered helmet, and Pikel a flurry of flying knees and elbows, butting forehead, and tree-trunk club.

Only one of the six orcs even managed to get out of its chair, but before the startled creature took two steps away, an arrow sliced through the side of its head, dropping it dead to the floor.

On ran the dwarves and on chased Shayleigh. Their only hope was in movement, the elf maiden knew, in rushing through too quickly for the multitude of enemies in this hall to organize against them. In full flight, she put an arrow to the side, catching a man in the shoulder as he tried to raise a bow of his own.

Tables overturned, chairs skidded aside, as the men and monsters scrambled to get out of harm's way. One unfortunate goblin got tangled up in its companion's chair. When the dwarves had passed, both the goblin and that chair lay flattened on the floor. One ogre did not run, but crossed its huge arms over its chest and stood with legs firmly planted, thinking itself an imposing barrier.

It got wounded in more than its pride when Ivan rushed right through those widespread legs, the dwarf's axe up high over his head. The ogre lurched, grabbing at its torn loins, and Pikel ran beside it, caving in the side of its knee. The ogre hadn't even hit the floor yet when Shayleigh sprang up, planting one foot on the cheek of its turned face, another on its ribs as she ran right down the falling creature's side.

There seemed to be no method to the dwarven rush, no aim above the general chaos. Then Pikel spotted the serving area, a long counter running along the back wall.

"Oooo!" the green-bearded dwarf squeaked, his stubby finger pointing the way.

One of the three servers lifted a crossbow, but Shayleigh's arrow took him down. A second lifted a wooden tray before him like a shield, but Ivan's axe cleaved it in two and cleaved the man's face in two as well. The third man's shield, an iron pot, seemed more formidable, but Pikel's club hit it head on, and the pot snapped back to hit the man head-on.

The three friends were over the counter in a flash, Shayleigh spinning about and setting her bow into frantic motion, for many enemies were now in pursuit. She scored hit after hit, but there seemed no way that she could possibly stop the closing horde.

Ivan and Pikel leaped atop the counter to either side of her, armed with stacks of metal plates. The dwarves opened up a barrage of flying metal. Dishes whizzed through the air, spinning and swerving, battering the approaching enemies.

Battering them and holding them up long enough for Shayleigh to methodically cut them down.

"Hee hee hee," chuckled Pikel, and he hopped down from the counter and grabbed up a pot of thick green soup. Over it went, splashing and spilling, setting up the obstacle of a slippery floor for those enemies that came too near.

The dwarf also scooped up a huge ladle of boiling water before he climbed back atop the counter.

An arrow skipped right past Ivan's ear, knocking into the wall behind the dwarf. Shayleigh, intent on the largest approaching monster, another ogre, noted the archer to the side, crouched beside an overturned table.

"Yerself takes the bowmen!" Ivan cried. "Me and me brother'll take on them fools that come close!"

The reasoning seemed sound, and the elf maiden forced herself to hold her nerve, forced herself to ignore the closest threats and trust in her companions. She swerved her bow to the side, saw the bowman's hip foolishly hanging out from the barrier while he reloaded, and promptly stuck an arrow into him.

The approaching ogre carried four arrows in its chest but still stubbornly came on, right for Pikel and the helpless Shayleigh.

The dwarf's eyes widened in feigned fear, and Pikel seemed to cower, causing Shayleigh to cry out. Pikel came up straight at the last moment, though, whipping out the ladle, splashing the surprised ogre's eyes and face with boiling water.

Predictably, the ogre lurched, throwing its arms up over its burned eyes. The shift cost the beast its already tentative balance in the green soup, and it skidded in to slam its knees against the sturdy stone counter. Down low, trying to recover its balance and its sight, the ogre felt a burning flash, a club-inspired explosion that caved in the top of its head.

Pikel laid his brain-stained club aside and took up more plates, sent them spinning off at enemies who were suddenly more interested in getting out of harm's way than in getting to the intruders.

"None better at kitchen fighting than a Bouldershoulder," Ivan remarked, and, looking at the chaos and carnage, Shayleigh wasn't about to disagree.

But the elf knew that more than the initial fury would be needed to win this battle. Dozens of enemies remained, for more had come into the room, overturning tables before them, getting down under cover. She saw another archer peek up over the top rim of a table to the side, saw his bow come up.

Shayleigh was the quicker on the draw, and the better shot. While the man's arrow flew harmlessly high and wide, Shayleigh's got him between the eyes. The elf's satisfaction was short-lived as she realized that she had only five arrows remaining, and exhausted, too, was Ivan and Pikel's supply of metal plates.

* * * * *

Cadderly kneeled above what was left of his prisoner, the man's torn head and shoulders. Black shadows of guilt assaulted the young priest's sensibilities, hovering images judging him, telling him that this helpless man's death was his fault.

Danica was beside the young priest, urging him to his feet.

Cadderly pulled his arm free and stared hard at the gruesome sight. He thought of going into the realm of spirits, to find the dead man and . . .

And what? Cadderly realized. Might he bring the spirit back? He looked behind him, to the man's chewed lower torso. Bring the spirit back to where? Did he possess the magics to mend the torn body?

"It is not your fault," Danica whispered, his thoughts obvious to her. "You gave the man a chance. That is more than most would have offered in our situation."

Cadderly swallowed hard, swallowed Danica's wise words and let them push away his dark thoughts, his guilt.

"It could have been any one of us," Danica reminded him.

Cadderly nodded and rose from the corpse. The hydra had come at all three of them, could have snapped Danica in half, and would have if she had not been so quick. Even if Cadderly had allowed the prisoner to keep his weapon, he could have offered no defense against the hydra's brutal initial charge.

"We have to be gone from here," Danica said, and again Cadderly nodded, turning to face the loose-hanging, scorched, and blasted door. He and Danica walked through it together, side by side, coming into a small anteroom. No living enemies presented themselves immediately, but that fact did little to calm the nervous companions, for leering gargoyles stared down at them from a ledge running around the top of the room, holding needle-sharp daggers, Talona's favored weapon. Demonic bas reliefs covered the stone of supporting pillars, hordes of ghastly things dancing about the deceptively beautiful Lady of Poison. Tapestries surrounded the room, all depicting gory scenes of battle wherein evil hordes of goblins and orcs, their weapons dripping blood and poison, overran hosts of fleeing humans and elves.

A single chair dominated the floor; it sat atop a raised dais and was flanked by tall, iron statues of fierce warriors holding gigantic swords before them—while their other hands inconspicuously clasped tiny daggers. No other doors were apparent, though a curtain covered the section of wall immediately behind the chair.

With Danica hovering protectively about him, Cadderly called up the song of Deneir, searched for clues its notes could give to him about the nature of the many things around him. He stood easier when he detected no magical influences on the gargoyle sculptures, but nearly retreated when he turned to the iron statues. Parts of them—mouth and arms, mostly—tingled with residual magical energy.

"Golems?" Danica whispered, seeing the young priest's eyes open wide.

Cadderly honestly did not know. Golems were wholly magical creatures, animated bodies of iron, stone, or other inanimate materials. They would have seemed appropriate here, for such monsters were usually created by powerful wizards or priests to serve as guardians. Certainly with everything Cadderly had heard about Aballister, the thought of the wizard possessing iron golems, the most powerful of golemkind, was not out of the question. But Cadderly would have expected to detect more magic upon such a creature.

"Where to go?" Danica asked, her tone revealing that she was growing increasingly uneasy standing vulnerable in a wizard's anteroom.

Cadderly paused for a long moment. He felt that they should go to the curtain, but if these were iron golems, and he and Danica walked up between them. . . .

Cadderly shook the unpleasant image from his mind. "The curtain," he said resolutely. Danica started forward, but Cadderly caught her by the arm. If she was to trust him, when he could not be sure that he should trust himself, then he would walk beside her, not behind her.

With his walking stick, Cadderly gingerly pushed the curtain aside, revealing a door. He started to turn to Danica, to smile, but suddenly, before either of the companions could react, the iron statues swung about, swords stopping barely an inch from them, one in front and one in back.

"Speak the word," the iron statues demanded in unison.

Cadderly saw Danica tense, expected her to go in a rush at her metallic adversary. A few flickering notes slipped past his consciousness, and he saw, too, the building magical energy in the iron statues' arms, particularly in the less obvious arms holding the daggers. Cadderly did not have to use magic to guess that the tips of those sneaky weapons would likely be poisoned.

"Speak the word," the statues demanded again. Cadderly focused his senses on the magical energy, saw it rising to a dangerous crescendo.

"Do not move," he whispered to Danica, sensing that if she struck out, the two daggers would do their work with deadly efficiency. Danica's hands eased down to her sides, though she hardly seemed to relax. She trusted his judgment, but Cadderly honestly wondered if that was a good thing. The magical energy appeared as if it would soon boil over, and Cadderly still had not figured out how he might begin to counter or dispel it.

It seemed to the young priest as if the golems were growing impatient.

"Speak the word!" Their unified chant rang out as a final warning. Cadderly wanted to tell Danica to dive away, hoping that she, at least, might get free before the nasty daggers struck, or those swords chopped in.

"The word is Bonaduce," came a call from beyond the door, a female voice that the two companions recognized.

"Dorigen," Danica breathed, her face scrunched with sudden anger.

Cadderly agreed, and knew that trusting in Dorigen would surely be a move wrought of desperation. But something about the word, "Bonaduce," struck a note of truth, a note of familiarity, within the young priest.

"Bonaduce!" Cadderly yelled. "The word is Bonaduce!"

Danica's incredulous stare turned even more disbelieving as the golems shifted back to their frozen, impassive stances.

Cadderly, too, did not understand any of it. Why would Dorigen aid them, especially when they were in such dire trouble? He started forward for the door and pulled the curtain fully aside.

"It must be trapped," Danica reasoned softly, taking hold of Cadderly's arm to prevent him from reaching for the pull ring.

Cadderly shook his head and grabbed the ring. Before

Danica could argue, he yanked the door open.

They came into a comfortably furnished room. Soft, padded chairs were generously placed, quiet tapestries of solid color lined every wall, and a bearskin rug carpeted the floor. The only hard-edged furnishing was a wooden desk, angled in a corner opposite the door. There sat Dorigen, tapping a slender wand against the side of her crooked, oft-broken nose.

Danica was down in a defensive crouch in an instant, one hand going down to her boot to draw a dagger.

"Have I mentioned before how much you both amaze me?" the woman calmly asked them.

Cadderly sent a silent, magical message into Danica's thoughts, bidding her to hold easy and see how this might play out.

"Are we any less amazed?" the young priest replied. "You gave us the password."

"So she might kill us herself," Danica added grimly. She flipped the dagger over in her hand, grasping it by the point so that she could flick it out at Dorigen in an instant.

"That is a possibility," the wizard admitted. "I have many powers"—she tapped the wand against her cheek—"that I might use against you, and perhaps this time, our battle would have ended differently."

"Would have?" Cadderly noted.

"Would have ended differently if I held any intention of renewing our battle," Dorigen explained.

Danica was shaking her head, obviously not convinced. Cadderly, too, had trouble believing in the woman's sudden change of heart. He fell into the notes of his song, sought out the *aurora*, the aura sight.

Shadows flickered atop Dorigen's delicate shoulders, reflections of what was in her heart and thoughts. These were not huddled, evil things, as Cadderly expected, but quiet shadows, sitting in wait.

Cadderly came back from his spell, stared at Dorigen with heightened curiosity. He noticed Danica slide a step to the side and realized that she was trying to put some ground between them, giving the wizard only a single target.

"She speaks the truth," the young priest announced.

"Why?" Danica replied sharply.

Cadderly had no answer.

"Because I grow tired of this war," Dorigen responded. "And I grow tired of playing Aballister's lackey."

"You believe the horrors of Shilmista will be so easily forgotten?" Danica asked.

"I do not wish to repeat those horrors," Dorigen replied immediately. "I am tired." She held up her hands, fingers still bent from the beating Cadderly had given them. "And broken." The words stung Cadderly, but Dorigen's soft, benign tone did not.

"You could have killed me, young priest," the wizard went on. "You could now, probably, with my own ring, which you wear, if with nothing else."

Cadderly unconsciously clenched his hand, and felt the onyx-stoned ring with his thumb.

"And I could have let the golems kill you," Dorigen went on. "Or I could have assailed you with an assortment of deadly spells as you walked through the door."

"Is this repayment?" Cadderly asked.

Dorigen shrugged. "Weariness, more than that," she said, and the woman did indeed sound tired. "I have stood beside Aballister for many years, watched him assemble a mighty force with promises of glory and rulership of the region." Dorigen laughed at the thought. "Look at us now," she lamented. "A handful of elves, a pair of silly dwarves, and two children"—she indicated Cadderly and Danica with a wave of her hand, her expression incredulous—"have brought us to our knees."

Danica moved again to the side, and Dorigen snapped the wand down in front of her, her face suddenly twisted with a scowl.

"Do we continue?" she demanded, poking the wand

ahead. "Or do we let this play out as the gods always intended?"

Another silent message came into Danica's thoughts, compelling her to relax.

"What do you mean?" Cadderly asked.

"Is it not obvious?" Dorigen replied, and then she chuckled, remembering that Cadderly still had no idea that Aballister was his father. "You against Aballister, that is what this war is all about."

Cadderly and Danica looked to each other, both wondering if Dorigen had gone insane.

"That was not Aballister's intent," Dorigen went on, chuckling still between every word. "He did not even know that you were alive when Barjin began the whole affair."

The name of the dead priest caused Cadderly to unconsciously flinch.

"And certainly it was not your intent," Dorigen continued. "You did not, do not, understand the significance, did not even know that Aballister existed."

"You babble," Cadderly said.

Dorigen's laughter heightened. "Perhaps," she admitted. "And yet I must believe that it was more than coincidence that has brought us all to this point. Aballister himself played a part in it, a part that he will possibly regret."

"By starting the war," Cadderly reasoned.

"By saving your life," Dorigen corrected. Cadderly's face screwed up even tighter.

"Inadvertently," the woman quickly added. "His hatred for Barjin, his rival, outweighed his understanding of the poisonous thorn you would become."

"She lies," Danica decided, inching a step closer to the desk, apparently preparing to spring out and throttle the cryptic wizard.

"Do you remember your final encounter with Barjin?" Dorigen asked.

Cadderly nodded grimly; he would never forget that fateful day, the day he had first killed a man.

"The dwarf, the one with the yellow beard, was held fast by Barjin's magic," Dorigen prompted, and the image came clearly to the young priest. Ivan had stopped his advance toward the evil priest, had simply frozen in place, leaving Cadderly practically helpless. Cadderly was no powerful cleric back then, could barely win against a simple goblin, and the evil priest would surely have finished him. But Ivan came out from the enchantment at the last moment, allowing Cadderly to slip from Barjin's deadly clutches.

"Aballister countered the priest's magic," Dorigen announced. "The wizard is not your friend," she quickly added. "He holds no love for you at all, young priest, as is evidenced by the assassin band he sent to kill you in Carradoon."

"Then why did he aid me?" Cadderly asked.

"Because Aballister feared Barjin more than he feared you," Dorigen answered. "He did not anticipate what the gods had in store for him where young Cadderly was concerned."

"How, then, does it play out, wise Dorigen?" Cadderly asked sarcastically, tiring of the woman's private amusement and her cryptic references to the gods.

Dorigen motioned to the far wall, spoke a word of enchantment to reveal a swirling door of misty fog. "I was instructed to strike out at you with all my powers, and then retreat. I was to try to separate you from your friends and lead you through that door," she explained. "Therein lies Aballister's private mansion, the place where he planned to finish off the young priest who has become such a problem."

Cadderly studied Dorigen closely through every word, using his aura sight to determine any traps the woman might have in store. Danica looked to him for answers, and he shrugged, convinced, against his own reason, that Dorigen had again spoken truthfully.

"And so I surrender to you," Dorigen said, and Cadderly and Danica's surprise could not have been more absolute.

The woman laid her wand on the desk and sat back comfortably. "Go and play this out to the end, young priest," she bade Cadderly, again motioning to the swirling door. "Let the destiny of the region be determined by the private battle, as fate intended it all along."

"I do not believe in fate," Cadderly replied firmly.

"Do you believe in war?" Dorigen asked.

"Do not do it," Danica whispered over her shoulder.

Dorigen's smile was wide once more. " 'Bonaduce' will get you through this portal as well."

"Do not," Danica said again, this time loudly.

Cadderly walked away from her, walked toward the wall.

"Cadderly!" Danica called after him.

The young priest wasn't listening. He had come here to defeat Aballister, to decapitate the force of Castle Trinity, so that thousands needn't die in a war. This might be a trap, might be a portal that would take him to one of the lower planes and leave him there for eternity. But Cadderly could not ignore the possibilities presented to him by Dorigen's claims, by that swirling door, and he could not ignore the truths his magic had shown to him.

He heard Danica moving behind him. "Bonaduce!" he cried, and he jumped into the swirl, and was gone.

Nineteen

Friends Lost,
Friends Found

The four-foot-high counter surrounded the three trapped companions on two sides, with a thick column, floor to ceiling, supporting it on either end of the eight foot front section. The wall blocked their backs, leaving only a small gap to get behind the counter on one side, wide enough for two goblins or one large man. So far, only a single enemy had opted to try that route—and he was summarily blasted away by the elf maiden with her deadly bow.

Ivan and Pikel stood atop the counter as the throng advanced, throwing taunts and throwing fists, though no enemies had yet come close enough to hit. At Ivan's proclamation that orcs were "born only to clean the gooey-greens outa ogre noses," three of the pig-faced humanoids took up a wild charge. The first skidded in the spilled soup as it was about to leap for Pikel, its back leg flying out from under it and its front leg straight out and up high. It slammed hard against the counter, its ankle and lead foot up above the ledge, and Pikel promptly brought his heel around the orc's toe and bent it down flat atop the counter, bringing his full weight atop it.

The trailing orcs stumbled about, but using their fallen friend as support, managed to hold a tentative balance as they banged against the side of the counter. Ivan's axe cleaved one in the side of the head, but the other managed to deflect Pikel's first clubbing attack.

That orc was soon crushed against the side, though, as many of its companions, seeing the intruders suddenly pressed, rushed in.

"We cannot hold!" Shayleigh cried out.

"Just get yerself the archers," Ivan replied, huffing and puffing with each word as he worked his axe furiously to keep the sudden mob at bay. "Me and me brother'll handle this crew!"

Shayleigh looked helplessly to her nearly empty quiver. Her hand started for her short sword as a soldier came around to the open side, but the elf realized that she did not have the time to spare for melee combat. She lamented the waste of an arrow but shot the man down anyway, hoping that his sudden death might give other enemies pause before they tried a similar route.

The counter bucked suddenly as an ogre slammed against the back of the crowd, and Shayleigh thought it would break apart, thought that she would be crushed against the wall as the irrepressible monsters pushed on.

Her actions purely wrought of terror, she turned to face the counter and put an arrow in the ogre's face. It fell back and the counter appeared to resettle on its braces. Still unsure of its solidity, the elf maiden scrambled up on a shelf against the back wall, a position that afforded her a better view of the area beyond the immediate battle.

A man braced both his hands and one foot on the counter and started to leap up, thinking the dwarves too engaged to stop him.

Ivan's axe promptly broke his spine, though the dwarf took a vicious hit on the hip for the distraction. Ivan grimaced in pain, growled the wound away, and chopped furiously at the goblin attacker, the dwarf's mighty axe smashing through the creature's upraised spear, and through the creature's upturned face.

Ivan couldn't revel in the kill, though, for the press of swords and spears, cruelly tipped pole arms and slashing daggers did not relent. The dwarf skipped and hopped, dodged and parried, and every now and then managed an offensive strike.

An arrow appeared suddenly, stuck halfway through Ivan's yellow beard, and the waves of pain that assaulted the dwarf told him that it had gashed his chin as well.

"I told ye to get yerself the archers!" he cried angrily at Shayleigh, but his bluster was lost when he looked in the direction from which the arrow had come, looked to the enemy archer lying dead on the floor, and the elven-crafted arrow sticking from his forehead.

"Never mind," the humbled dwarf finished. He hopped as a sword sliced low across and came down with one boot trapping the weapon against the counter. Ivan kicked out, shattering the man's jaw, knocking him back into the mob. Two others took his place, though, and Ivan was sorely pressed once more.

Pikel fared little better. The dwarf scored three quick kills, but was bleeding in several places, with one of the wounds fairly serious. He worked his club back and forth, tried to forget the weariness in his muscled arms, tried to forget the obvious hopelessness of it all.

He swooped left, batting aside one lunging spear, but a sword sliced in behind his club, striking against something under his sleeve and then driving through to nick at Pikel's forearm.

"Ow!" the green-bearded dwarf squeaked, bringing his arm defensively in tight to his side. Pikel's pain flew away in a moment, though, replaced by shock when the upper half of his pet snake fell out of his sleeve onto the counter.

"Ooooooo!" Pikel wailed, his little legs pumping suddenly. "Ooooooo!"

The sword wielder came in a straight thrust, but Pikel caught the blade in a free hand and flung it aside, oblivious to the lines of blood growing on his unarmored hand. The dwarf's other arm pumped straight ahead, the end of his club slamming into the attacker's face. Pikel grabbed up the club in both hands and chopped three times in rapid succession, driving the man to the floor.

Then the furious dwarf whipped a backhand cut that flung a goblin, trying to use the moment to climb atop the counter, several feet away. Back and forth came the heavy club, swatting weapons, breaking bones. Back and forth with undeniable fury; no defenses withstood the roaring dwarf's assault.

"Ooooooo!"

An ogre threw men and orcs aside to charge the counter, leaped up bravely, stupidly.

Pikel smashed its knee out, spun a complete circuit and hit it again as it fell, squarely in the chest, sending it tumbling into the crowd. With the enemies directly before him knocked away by the sprawling ogre, the outraged dwarf hopped sidelong.

"Ooooooo!" A swordsman lunged for Ivan, but Pikel smashed the man's elbow against the lip of the counter before his sword ever got close.

"Hey, he's mine!" Ivan started to protest, but Pikel, not even hearing him, continued to wail and to batter. His next swipe snapped the man's neck, but the dwarf followed through too far on his backhand, clipping Ivan and sending him flying backward from the counter.

Pikel was not even aware that he now stood alone. All that he saw was his dead snake, the serpent that had befriended him. He ran back and forth along the counter, showing no weariness in his furiously pumping limbs, feeling no pain from his many, and mounting, wounds, tasting only sweet vengeance as he continued to beat back, to overwhelm, the suddenly hesitant mob.

"We need more support up in front!" Ivan bellowed angrily as Shayleigh helped him back to his feet.

"Arrows?" Shayleigh explained, indicating her empty quiver and the single arrow she held to her bowstring.

Ivan reached up and yanked the arrow out of his face. "Here's another one for ye," the dwarf explained grimly. He jerked suddenly, weirdly, then reached over his shoulder and produced yet another long bolt.

Shayleigh's eyes widened as she looked past the dwarf, looked to a table the enemy had rolled into position so that some archers might get shots through the opening at the side of the counter. She put up her bow immediately and fired, hitting only the wood of the blocking table, but forcing the enemy bowmen to duck down behind.

"I'll get ye some arrows!" Ivan bellowed as he turned to regard the scene. Out ran the dwarf, full speed. An archer popped his head up, taking a bead. But he lost his nerve as the roaring dwarf drew near, and his shot flew harmlessly high.

Ivan narrowed his focus straight ahead, ignored the many enemies shouting and pointing his way from the side. He lowered his head and hit the heavy table full force, knocking it back over onto its legs and winding up atop it.

The three stunned archers underneath looked up in surprise. They didn't realize how vulnerable they had suddenly become with their barrier now above them until an arrow whistled in, killing one.

Two sets of eyes looked back to Shayleigh; both men were relieved to see a goblin rush across, inadvertently intercepting the elf's next shot at the cost of its own life.

Ivan came over the back side of the uprighted table, rolled in at the men headfirst, the flat side of his axe smacking one of the remaining archers on the side of the head. The other man scrambled to get a dagger out and readied before the dwarf could right himself and bring his axe to bear again. But Ivan had let go of his weapon, scrambled in and clamped his strong hands against the sides of the remaining enemy's head.

A dagger cut into the dwarf's shoulder, but with a growl, Ivan heaved straight upward, the man's head going flat against the bottom of the table. The dwarf continued to press, planted his feet under him and his shoulders against the table and heaved up with all his strength. Ivan ducked low as the table flew up a foot and then started to descend, but he kept his arms, and the enemy's head, up high.

"Bet that hurt," the dwarf muttered as the table slammed back down, and the man's face scrunched up.

The man was sitting awkwardly, his legs twisted beneath him, his eyes still closed tightly. Ivan punched him in the face anyway, to get him out of the way, then the dwarf scooped up his axe and the nearest quivers and charged out from under the table, back for the counter area. A crossbow quarrel drove through his calf, and he pitched headlong, but he was up in a moment, running again, gnawing his thick lips against waves of searing pain.

Shayleigh had to spin about and put her third, and last, shot into the face of an orc that had slipped over the far side of the counter, around Pikel's continuing frenzy. When the elf maiden turned back Ivan's way, she found herself faced off against another goblin. Desperate, with no time to go for her sword, Shayleigh whipped her bow across, trying to drive the creature back.

"Yous is dead," the goblin promised, but Shayleigh shook her head, even smiled, seeing a large, double-bladed axe come up high behind the creature's head.

Ivan stumbled across the goblin's back as it fell. "Here're yer arrows!" he cried, tossing Shayleigh three nearly full quivers. He had no time to hear her reply, for he spun about, axe flying wildly before him, to knock aside a thrusting spear.

Shayleigh, too, spun about, fitting an arrow as she turned and firing above the counter opposite Ivan, firing once, and then again as the press became general on all three sides.

"Dead snake!" Ivan cried repeatedly, prodding his frenzied brother on. "Dead snake!"

"Ooooooo!" Pikel wailed, and another enemy was swatted away.

But Shayleigh knew that they would need more than Pikel's frenzy to hold out, and more than the two-score arrows Ivan had just given to her. Her arms pumped repeatedly, firing to the side and out in front beside Pikel, every shot scoring a direct hit, every shot blasting an opening for yet another enemy to step in.

* * * * *

"Bonaduce!" Danica called, and she headed for the wall, leaping up into the swirling fog. She hit the stone hard, and fell back, dazed, into the room.

She rolled in a defensive somersault, feeling betrayed and vulnerable. Dorigen had gotten rid of Cadderly, and the dangerous woman still held that wand. Danica turned another somersault, coming back to her feet more than halfway across the room from the still-sitting wizard.

"The password was Bonaduce," Danica accused.

"Only those so designated by Aballister may enter his private chambers, even with the word," Dorigen explained calmly. "He wanted to see Cadderly. Apparently, you were not included."

Danica's arm jerked suddenly, and one of her daggers flew at Dorigen. It sparked as it connected with a magical shield and bounced to the floor beside the woman, who promptly put her wand in line with Danica and held her free hand up, warning the monk to stay back.

"Treachery," Danica breathed, and Dorigen was shaking her head in denial through every syllable of the word.

"Do you believe that you will kill me with that wand?" Danica asked, beginning to circle, her balance perfect, her legs ready to launch her away, with every measured step.

"I do not wish to try," Dorigen replied sincerely.

"One spell, Dorigen," Danica growled. "Or a single try with your wand. That is all you will get."

"I do not wish to try," the older woman said again, more firmly, and to accentuate her point, Dorigen dropped the wand to the desktop.

Danica stood a bit straighter, her perplexed look genuine.

"I did not lie to you," Dorigen explained. "Nor did I trick Cadderly into going somewhere he does not truly belong."

Again, the indication was that Dorigen believed a larger fate to be guiding this encounter. Danica was not so convinced as her counterpart. She believed in the power of the individual, in the choice of the individual, and not in some predestined path.

"Aballister will likely punish me for letting the young priest through," Dorigen went on, against Danica's doubting expression. "He hoped I would kill Cadderly, or at least exhaust Cadderly's magical powers." She chuckled and looked away, and Danica realized that she could spring atop that desk and throttle Dorigen before the wizard ever reacted. But Danica did not move, held by the continued note of sincerity in the wizard's voice.

"Aballister thought the malignant spirit, the evil personification of the *Ghearufu*, would end the threat to Castle Trinity," Dorigen went on.

"The ghost that you sent after us," Danica accused.

"Not so," Dorigen replied calmly. "Originally, Aballister did send the Night Masks to Carradoon to kill Cadderly, but the return of the spirit was purely coincidence—purely a fortunate coincidence as far as Aballister was concerned.

"He did not know that Cadderly could defeat that spirit," Dorigen continued, and again came that curious chuckle. "He thought that his storm would surely destroy you all, and so it would have, except that Aballister did not know that you were far from Nightglow by that point. Fearful would he have been indeed, if he learned that Cadderly could defeat even old Fyren after he was finished manipulating the wyrm."

Danica nearly fell over backward, her almond-shaped eyes opened wide.

"Yes, I watched that battle," Dorigen explained, "but I did not tell Aballister about it. I wanted his surprise to be complete when Cadderly arrived so soon at Castle Trinity."

"Is this penitence?" Danica asked.

Dorigen looked down at her desk and slowly shook her head, running her crooked fingers through her long black-and-silver hair. "More pragmatism, I would guess," she said, looking back to Danica. "Aballister has made many mistakes. I do not know that he will defeat Cadderly, or you and your other friends. And even if we win this day, how can we hope to conquer the region with our army shattered?"

Danica found that she honestly believed the woman's words, and that made her more defensive, fearing that Dorigen had cast some charm enchantment over her. "Your reversal now does not excuse your actions over the past months," she noted grimly.

"No," Dorigen agreed without hesitation. "Nor would I call it a 'reversal.' Let us see who wins in there." She indicated the swirling mist on the wall. "Let us see where fate guides us."

Danica shook her head doubtfully.

"You still do not understand, do you?" Dorigen asked sharply, and with the change in tone, the agile monk was down immediately into her threatening crouch.

"What are you talking about?" Danica demanded.

Dorigen's answering shout stole the strength from Danica's knees, hit her so unexpectedly that she could not even babble a retort. "They are father and son!"

* * * * *

Ivan fared the best of the three trapped friends as the fighting in the dining hall raged on. In the tight opening along the side of the cubby, the stout dwarf and his mighty axe formed an impenetrable barrier. Men and monsters came against him two at a time, but they couldn't hope to get by his furious defense. And though Ivan was sorely wounded, he took up a dwarven battle chant, narrowed his focus so greatly that it did not allow him to feel the pain, did not allow his wounded limbs to weaken.

Still, the relentless press of enemies prevented Ivan from going to his brother, or to Shayleigh, both of whom needed support. The best that the yellow-bearded dwarf could do was yell out, "Dead snake!" every now and again to heighten Pikel's fury.

Shayleigh blew away the first man who tried to come over the counter, hit the next adversary, a bugbear, with four arrows in rapid succession, the hairy creature slumping dead before it ever got atop the narrow area. Shayleigh then fired one to her side, between Pikel's legs, catching an orc in the face, then turned back as another enemy, a goblin, leaped up on the counter.

She shot it in the chest, dropping it to a sitting position, then shot it again, putting out the light in its eyes.

The goblins behind this victim proved smarter than usual, though, for the dead goblin did not fall away. Using its bleeding body as a shield, the next goblin in line came up atop the counter. Shayleigh got it anyway, in the eye as it peeked over its dead comrade's shoulder, but the rush as both creatures pitched in behind the counter gave the following goblin a clear path to the elf maiden.

With no time to notch another arrow, Shayleigh instinctively grabbed for her sword. She whipped her bow across with one hand, deflecting the straight-ahead spear attack, and just managed to angle her short sword in front of her as the goblin barreled in, its own momentum impaling it.

Shayleigh jerked the dead thing to the side, throwing it down, and tore free her blade, its fine edge glowing fiercely with its elven enchantments. She had no time to take up her bow, though, and knew that she wouldn't likely get a chance to put it to use in this fight again. She dropped it to the floor and rushed ahead, meeting the next adversary before it fully cleared the counter.

The goblin was off-balance, just beginning its leap to the floor, when Shayleigh got there, her sword snapping one way, knocking the goblin's defenses aside, and then the other. Quicker than the goblin could recover, Shayleigh poked her sword straight ahead, popping a clean hole in the creature's throat. She used its shoulders as a springboard as it slumped and got up to the counter at the same time as the next enemy soldier. The man hadn't expected the rush and was pushed back, sprawling into the pressing throng, leaving Shayleigh free to smash down at the orc that was next in line.

She killed it cleanly, but a spear arced over its shoulder as she bent for the strike.

Shayleigh stood very straight, tried to keep her focus through the sudden jolt and blur of agony. She saw the spear hanging low from her hip, saw a man grab at its other end. If he managed to twist the shaft about . . .

Shayleigh hit the spear just under its embedded tip with her sword. The fine-edged elven weapon slashed through the wood, but the shocking jolt nearly sent Shayleigh falling into blackness. She held on through sheer stubbornness, forcing her sword through her most familiar attack routines to keep the pressing foes at bay until the waves of dizziness swept by.

"Ooooooo!" Pikel's club did a rotating-end dance before the stupefied expression of an ogre. The giant monster swiped across with its hand, trying to catch the curious weapon, but by then, the club was gone, brought up high above the dwarf's head.

"Duh?" the ogre stupidly asked.

The club slammed down on its skull.

The ogre shook its head, its thick lips flapping noisily. It looked up to see what had hit it, looked up and up some more, its gaze continuing for the ceiling until it overbalanced and fell backward, taking down three smaller comrades under it.

Pikel, already down at the other end of the counter, didn't even see the ogre fall. A man had come up, and the dwarf slid down low, club swiping across to blow the man's feet out from under him.

A sword gashed Pikel's hip, but down low, he saw even more clearly his poor dead snake. His club came flashing across, snapping the sword wielder's head to the side, breaking the man's neck.

"Ooooooo!" Pikel was up in an instant, fury renewed. He skidded back the other way, defeating a potential breach, then came flying back again, tripping up a climbing goblin. The creature stumbled back, its chin slamming, and hooking, against the counter's lip.

That was not a good position with Pikel's club fast descending.

But how long could Pikel last? The dwarf, for all his rage, could not deny that his movements were beginning to slow, could not deny that the press of enemies had not relented, that two soldiers had come into the back of the dining hall for every one that the companions had killed. And the friends were all hurt, all bleeding, and all weary.

Across the hall, near the door, a man flew up into the air suddenly, over the ogre that was standing before him, his arms and legs flailing helplessly. Pikel glanced back curiously that way whenever he got the chance, glanced back just in time to see a huge sword explode through the front of the ogre's chest. With power beyond anything the dwarf had ever seen, the ogre's attacker tore the impaling sword straight up, tore it through the ogre's chest and collarbone to exit at the side of the dead creature's neck. A giant arm swung around, connecting on the ogre's shoulder with enough force to send the dead thing flying head over heels away.

And Vander—Vander!—waded ahead, his fierce swipes taking down enemies two at a time.

"Oo oi!" Pikel cried, pointing his stubby finger toward the door. Shayleigh, too, noticed the firbolg, and the sight renewed her hopes and her fury. Tangled with an orc atop the counter, she punched out with her free left hand, slamming the creature's jaw. She feigned a jerk with her sword, then punched again, and a third time.

The orc swayed, balanced precariously on the counter's edge. It somehow blocked Shayleigh's darting sword, but her flying foot got it squarely on the chest, knocking it backward.

"Vander is come!" she cried, so that Ivan, too, might know, and she rushed to the forward edge, crouching low and slicing down to drive back the next would-be attacker.

"That damned ring!" Ivan bellowed into the face of the man standing before him, referring to the magical, regenerative ring that Vander wore, a ring that had once before (and now, apparently again) brought the firbolg back from the dead.

Ivan's wild laughter gave his opponent pause. The dwarf brought his axe up over one shoulder, and the startled man reacted by throwing his sword up high.

Ivan loosened his grip with his bottom hand and drove his top hand down, the butt end of the axe shooting straight out to pop the man in the face. He fell back, dazed, and Ivan tossed his axe up into the air, and in a single, fluid motion, caught it low in both hands at the bottom of its handle and whipped it diagonally across, slashing the man's shoulder.

Near the middle of the room, a spearman jabbed at the firbolg's hip, scoring a minor hit. Vander twisted about and kicked, his heavy boot connecting with the man's belly, driving up under his ribs and launching him fifteen feet into the air.

Vander spun back the other way, all his weight behind an overhead chop that cleaved a goblin in half.

The sight proved too much for the goblin's closest companions. Howling with terror, they rushed from the room.

Too many other enemies presented themselves for Vander to consider pursuing the goblins. An ogre rushed in at him, its club coming across to score a direct hit on Vander's breast. Vander didn't flinch, but smiled wickedly to show his attacker that he was not hurt.

"Duh?"

"Why do they keep saying that?" the firbolg wondered, and his sword took the surprised ogre's head from its shoulders.

To the companions still at the counter, Vander's walk resembled a ship rushing through choppy seas, throwing a spray of goblins and orcs and men high into the air at his sides as he passed, leaving a wake of blood and broken bodies. Vander was at the counter in a mere minute, cutting the enemy force in half. Pikel came down beside him and together they blasted an opening around to the side so that Ivan, too, might link up.

By the time the three got to Shayleigh, she was sitting atop the counter, leaning heavily on the pillar support, for her remaining enemies had gone screaming away into the halls.

Vander picked up the wounded maiden, cradling her in one arm. "We must flee this place," he said.

"They'll be back," Ivan agreed. They looked to Pikel, who was reverently extracting the bottom half of his sliced snake from his torn sleeve, muttering a quiet, "Oooo," as each inch slipped free.

Twenty

Bolt for Bolt,
Fire for Fire

Cadderly did not understand where he might be; this plush, carpeted room in no way resembled the harsh stone of the underground Castle Trinity. Gold leaf ornamentation and beautifully woven tapestries hung thick on the walls, all depicting images of Talona or her symbol. The ceiling was sculpted and decorated with some exotic wood that Cadderly did not recognize. Any one of the ten chairs in the huge room, their backs and seats carved to resemble teardrops, seemed worth a dragon's hoard of treasure, with sparkling gemstones running up their legs and armrests and silk upholstering covering them from top to bottom. The whole of the image reminded Cadderly of some pasha's palace in far off-Calimport, or the private chambers of one of Waterdeep's lords.

Until he looked deeper. The song of Deneir came into Cadderly's thoughts without his conscious bidding, as though his god was reminding him that this was no ordinary room, with no ordinary host. The place was extradimensional, Cadderly realized, created by magic, woven, to the last detail, of magical energy.

Looking more closely at the nearest chair, the song playing strong in his thoughts now, Cadderly recognized the gems as variations of magical energy, saw the smooth silk as a uniform field of magic and nothing more. Cadderly remembered an experience in the tower of the wizard Belisarius, when he had battled an illusory minotaur in an illusory dungeon. On that occasion, the young priest had perverted Belisarius's handiwork, had reached down the minotaur's throat and extracted an illusory heart of his own design.

Now, in this unfamiliar and obviously dangerous setting, Cadderly needed a boost to his confidence. He focused again on the chair, grabbed at the backing's magical field, and transmuted it, elongated it, and turned it flat.

"A table would look better here," he announced, figuring that his host, Aballister, could hear his every word. And so the chair became a table of polished wood with thick, curving supports carved with eyes and candles and rolled scrolls, the symbols of Cadderly's god and the brother god, Oghma.

Cadderly looked to the only apparent exit from the grand room, a wide hallway supported by sculpted arches running directly opposite the wall he had somehow walked through. He shifted the song of Deneir slightly, searching for invisible objects or other extradimensional pockets within this pocket, but saw no sign of Aballister.

The young priest moved to the table he had created, felt its smooth polish beneath its hands. He smiled as an inspiration—a divine inspiration, he mused—swept over him, then called upon his magic and reached out to the nearest tapestry, reweaving its design. He recalled the marvelous tapestry in the great hall of the Edificant Library, pictured its every detail in his mind, and made this one a nearly exact replica.

A chair beside him became a writing desk, complete with an inkwell lined with Deneirian runes. A second tapestry became the scroll of Oghma, the words of the most holy prayer of that god replacing the former image, one of evil Talona and her poisoned dagger.

Cadderly felt his strength swell from the images of his own creations, felt as if his work was moving him closer to his god, his source of power. The more he altered the room, the more this place came to resemble a shrine at the Edificant Library, and the more the young priest's confidence soared. With every image of Deneirian worship he created, more loudly did the holy song play in Cadderly's thoughts and in his heart.

Suddenly, Aballister—it had to be Aballister—stood at the opening of the ornate hall.

"I have made some . . . improvements," Cadderly announced to the cross wizard, sweeping his arms out wide. His bravado might have hid his nervousness from his enemy, but Cadderly couldn't deny the moisture that covered his palms.

In a sudden motion, Aballister smacked his hands together and cried out a word of power that Cadderly did not recognize. Immediately, the new clerical dressings disappeared, leaving the room in its former state.

Something about the wizard's motion, about the sudden flash of anger from the obviously controlled man, struck a familiar chord in Cadderly, tugged at the edges of his consciousness from a distant place.

"I do not approve of the icons of false gods decorating my private chambers," the wizard said, his voice steady.

Cadderly nodded and brought an easy smile to his face; there really was no point in arguing.

The wizard walked to the side of the entrance, his dark robes trailing out mysteriously behind him, his hollowed gaze locked fully on the young priest.

Cadderly turned to keep himself squared to the man, studied every move the dangerous wizard made, and kept the song of Deneir flowing through his thoughts. Already several defensive spells were sorted out and in line, ready for Cadderly to release them.

"You have proven a great discomfort to me," Aballister said, his voice a wheeze, his throat injured from years of compelling forth mighty magics. "But also, a great benefit."

Cadderly concentrated on the tone of the voice, not on the specific words. Something about it haunted him, again from a distant place; something about it conjured images of Carradoon, of long ago.

"I might have missed all the fun, you see," Aballister went on. "I might have sat back here in comfort and let my formidable forces bring the peoples of the region under my thumb. I shall enjoy ruling—I do so love intrigue—but the conquest, too, can be . . . delicious. Do you not agree?"

"I have no taste for food gotten at the expense of others," Cadderly said.

"But you do!" the wizard declared immediately.

"No!" the young priest was even quicker to retort.

The wizard laughed at him. "You are so proud of your accomplishments to date, of the conquests that have brought you to my door. You have killed, dear Cadderly. Killed men. Can you deny the delicious tingle of that act, the sense of power?"

The claim was absurd. The thought of killing, the act of killing, had brought nothing more than revulsion to Cadderly. Still, if the wizard had spoken to him thus a few weeks before, when the guilt of having killed Barjin hung thick around Cadderly's shoulders, the words would have been devastating. But not any more. Cadderly had come to accept what fate had placed in his path, had come to accept the role that had been thrust upon him. No longer did his soul mourn for the dead Barjin or for any of the others.

"I did as I was forced to do," he replied with sincere confidence. "This war should never have started, but if it must be played out, then I play to win."

"Good," the wizard purred. "With justice on your side?"

"Yes." Cadderly did not flinch at all with the confident reply.

"Are you proud of yourself?" Aballister asked.

"I will be glad when the region is safe," Cadderly answered. "This is not a question of pride. It is a question of morality, and, as you said, of justice."

"So cocksure," the wizard said with a soft chuckle, more to himself than to Cadderly. Aballister put a skinny finger to his pursed lips and studied the young priest intently, scanning Cadderly, every inch.

It seemed a curious gesture to the young priest, as though this man expected Cadderly, for some reason, to desire his approval, as though the wizard's estimation of Cadderly's measure might be an important thing to the younger man.

"You are a proud young cock in a yard of foxes," the wizard announced at length. "A flash of confidence and brilliance that is quickly lost in a pool of blood."

"The issue is bigger than my pride," Cadderly said grimly.

"The issue *is* your pride!" Aballister snapped back. "And my own. What is there in this misery that we call life beyond our accomplishments, beyond the legacy we shall leave behind?"

Cadderly winced at the words, at the thought that any man, particularly one intelligent enough to practice the art of wizardry, could be so singularly driven and self-absorbed.

"Can you ignore the suffering you have caused?" the young priest asked incredulously. "Do you not hear the cries of the dying and of those the dead have left behind?"

"They do not matter!" Aballister growled, but the intensity of the denial led Cadderly to believe that he had struck a sensitive chord, that perhaps there was some flicker of conscience under this man's selfish hide. "*I* am all that matters!" Aballister fumed. "*My* life, *my* goals."

Cadderly nearly swooned. He had heard those exact words before, spoken in exactly the same way. Again he pictured Carradoon, but the image was a foggy one, lost in the swirl of . . . of what? Cadderly wondered. Of distance?

He looked up again to see the wizard chanting and waggling the fingers of one hand in the air before him, his other hand extended and holding a small metallic rod.

Cadderly silently berated himself for being so foolish as to let down his guard. He sang out the song with all his voice, frantic to get up his defenses before the wizard fried him.

The words stuck in Cadderly's throat as a lightning bolt thundered in, blinding him.

"Excellent!" the wizard applauded, seeing his blast absorbed into blue hues around the young priest.

Cadderly, his vision returned, took measure of his protective shield, saw that the single attack had thinned it dangerously.

A second blast roared in, grounding out at Cadderly's feet, scorching the rug about him.

"How many can you stop?" the wizard cried, suddenly enraged. He took up his chant for a third time, and Cadderly knew that his protection spell would not deflect the full force of this one.

Cadderly reached into his pouch and pulled forth a handful of enchanted seeds. He had to strike fast, to interrupt the wizard's spell. He cried out a rune of enchantment and hurled the seeds across the room, triggering a series of popping, fiery explosions.

All images were stolen in the burst of swirling flames, but Cadderly was wise enough to doubt that his simple spell had defeated his foe. As soon as the seeds left his hand, he took up a new chant.

Aballister stood trembling with rage. All the room about the wizard smoldered, several small fires sizzled and sparked along the folds of a magical tapestry behind him. He seemed uninjured, though, and the area immediately around him was unscathed.

"How *dare* you?" the wizard asked. "Do you not know who I am?"

The wild look in the wizard's eyes, purely incredulous, frightened Cadderly, brought back distant memories and distant images, and made the young priest feel small indeed. Cadderly didn't understand any of it—what unknown hold might this wizard have over him?

"Your magics fended the lightning," Aballister cackled. "How do you fare against fire?"

A small glowing globe arced through the air, and Cadderly, distracted, could not dispel its magic in time. The fireball engulfed the room, except for Aballister's protected area, and Cadderly glowed green, as the same defensive spell he had used against old Fyren's breath successfully defeated the attack.

But more insidious were the aftershocks of the wizard's spell. Smoke poured from the tapestries; sparks flew from all directions at the continuing release of magical energies. Each one ignited a new green or blue spot on Cadderly's defensive shields, further wearing at them. And the young priest had no defense against the thick smoke stinging his eyes, stealing his breath.

Cadderly could hear that Aballister was casting again. Purely on reflex, the young priest threw up his clenched fist and cried out, "*Fete!*" A line of fire shot out from his ring at the same time Aballister's next lightning bolt thundered in.

This one blew away the blue globe, snaked through to slam Cadderly in the chest and hurl him backward into the burning wall. His hair danced wildly, his blue cape and the back rim of his wide hat smoldering from the hot contact.

The air cleared enough for him to see Aballister once more, standing unhurt, his hollowed face contorted in an expression of rage. What magics did he possess to get through the wizard's seemingly impenetrable globe? the young priest wondered. Cadderly had known all along that wizardry was a more potent offensive force than clerical magics, but he hadn't expected Aballister's defenses to be so formidable.

Panic welled in the young priest, but he focused on the sweet harmonies of the song and forced his fears away. He worked fast to create the same reflective field he had used against the manticore; his only chance was to turn the wizard's magic back against him.

Aballister worked faster, waggling his skinny fingers again and uttering some quick runes. Bursts of greenish energy erupted from his fingertips and hurtled across the room. The first burned painfully into Cadderly's shoulder. The young priest stubbornly held his concentration, though, enacting the shimmering field, and the second missile, and the three flying behind that, seemed to disappear for an instant and then appear again, heading back the way they had come.

Aballister's eyes widened with surprise, and he instinctively started to dodge aside. As it had with Cadderly's spells, though, the wizard's globe absorbed the energy.

"Damn you!" the frustrated Aballister cried. Out shot the metallic rod, in thundered another lightning bolt, and Cadderly, still dazed and pained from the previous hits, still trying to find his breath in the thick smoke, ducked away.

The lightning blasted into the reflective field and shot back out the other way, smashing against Aballister's globe, throwing multicolored sparks in every direction.

"Damn you!" Aballister growled again.

Cadderly noted the frustration, wondered if the wizard might be running out of attack spells or if his globe neared the end of its duration. The battered young priest tried to hold on to that hope, to use Aballister's obvious distress as a litany against the pain and the hopelessness. He tried to tell himself that Deneir was with him, that he was not overmatched.

Another lightning bolt sizzled in, this one low, cutting a wake in the carpet and slipping under Cadderly's shield. The young priest felt the burst under his feet, felt himself flying suddenly, spinning in the air.

"Not so large a shield!" Aballister cried out, his tone

brimming with confidence once more. "And pray tell, how does it handle angles?"

Lying on the floor, trying to shake away the stunning effects, Cadderly realized that he was about to die. He focused his thoughts on the wizard's last question, saw the wizard chanting again, holding that metal rod, but looking to the side, to the wall.

Desperation grabbed hold of the young priest, an instinctual urge to survive that momentarily numbed him from the pain. He heard the song of Deneir, remembered the bridge he had dropped in Carradoon and the walls he had caused to bite in the mountain valley. Frantically, he searched out the elemental makeup of the bare wall behind him.

Aballister's lightning bolt hit the wall to the side and deflected at a right angle. Cadderly, reaching for the wall behind him, grabbed its stone with his magical energy and pulled a section of the slab out, reshaping it.

The lightning bolt hit the back wall, would have deflected again at the perfect angle to destroy Cadderly, except that the wall's surface had changed, was now angled differently. The bouncing blast shot out straight across the room, again slamming the wizard's globe to shower harmlessly in multicolored sparks.

Still on the floor, Cadderly closed his eyes and fell more deeply into the song. More magical missiles came in, leaping around the reflective field, diving in to scorch and slam at the young priest. The divine song compelled Cadderly to fall into its sweetest notes, the notes of healing magic, but Cadderly understood that the delay created by attending to his wounds would only invite more attacks from the wizard.

He pushed the song in a different direction, heard the croak of his pained voice, and thought he would surely suffocate from the acrid smoke. Another missile slammed his face, scorching his cheek, feeling as if it had burned right to the bone.

Cadderly sang out with all his strength, followed the

song into the elemental plane of fire, and pulled from there
a hovering ball of flame that shot a line of fire down on the
wizard.

Cadderly couldn't see any of it, but he heard Aballister's
agonized cry, heard retreating footsteps clicking on the
stone of the hallway beyond the room. The smoke continued to thicken, to choke him.

He had to get out!

Cadderly tried to hold his breath, but found no breath to
hold. He tried to grab at the song, but his mind was too
numb, too filled with confused images of his own impending death. He kicked and crawled, grabbing at torn carpet
edges and pulling himself along blindly, hoping that he
could remember the exact course out of the room.

Twenty-One

Truce?

Danica spent a long while staring blankly at Dorigen. Unsure of her feelings and stunned by the news that Dorigen had just given her, the monk had no idea of where to turn or where to go. And what was Danica to do with this dangerous adversary, this woman she had battled before, this woman she had told Cadderly to kill when he had Dorigen down and helpless in Shilmista Forest?

"I have no intention of interfering with this," Dorigen said, trying to answer some of the questions etched plainly on Danica's delicate features. "Against Cadderly or against you and your other friends."

Other friends! In all the craziness of the last few minutes—the fight with the hydra, the desperate attempt to get at the wizard Aballister—Danica had almost forgotten them.

"Where are they?" the monk demanded.

Dorigen held her hands out, her expression curious.

"We were separated in a corridor," Danica explained, realizing that Dorigen probably did not know the course that had gotten her to this room. "A corridor lined with many traps. Darkness engulfed us, and the end of the corridor tilted as one tried to pass through."

"The clerical halls area," Dorigen interrupted. "They are quite adept at defending their territory."

The woman's obviously derisive tone as she mentioned the clerics gave Danica hope that the apparent rivalries within Castle Trinity might reveal a weakness.

"The dwarves and the elf fell through trapdoors," Danica went on, though she wondered if she might be giving her enemy information that could be used to the detriment of her lost friends. Danica sensed that she could trust Dorigen, had to trust Dorigen, and that realization put her doubly on her guard, again bringing fears that the wizard had used some enchantment on her. Danica reached within herself, sought out her discipline and her strong will. Few charms could affect one of her rigid mental training, especially if she was aware that one might be in place.

When she focused again on Dorigen, the wizard was slowly shaking her head, her expression grim.

"The giant went through a side chute," Danica went on, wanting to finish her thought before the woman cast some evil tidings over her.

"Then the giant has probably fared better than the others," Dorigen said. "The chute would place him in a lower passage, but the trapdoors . . . " She let the thought hang ominously, slowly shaking her head.

"If they are dead . . . " Danica warned, similarly letting the words hang unfinished. She dropped into a defensive position as Dorigen stood up behind the desk.

"Let us discover their fate," the wizard replied, taking no apparent heed of the threat. "Then we might better decide our next actions."

Danica had just begun to stand straight when the room's door flew open and a contingent of several armed guardsmen, a mix of men and orcs, rushed in. Danica leaped straight for Dorigen, but the wizard uttered a quick spell and vanished, leaving the monk to grab at empty air.

Danica spun about to face the approaching soldiers, six of them, fanning out with weapons drawn.

"Hold!" came a cry as Dorigen reappeared, standing along the wall behind the soldiers. The soldiers skidded to a stop and glanced back incredulously at Dorigen.

"I have declared a truce," Dorigen explained. She looked directly at Danica as she continued, "The fighting is ended, at least until greater issues can be resolved."

None of the fighters put up their swords. They glanced from the monk to the wizard, then looked to cach other for some explanation, as though they feared that they were being deceived.

"What is you about?" one burly orc demanded of the wizard. "I gots fifty dead in the dinner hall."

Danica's eyes sparkled at the news; perhaps her friends were indeed still alive.

"Fifty dead, and where are the enemies?" Danica had to ask.

"Shut up!" the orc roared at her, and Danica smiled at its unbridled anger. An orc rarely cared for the deaths of companions as long as the threat to its own worthless hide had been eradicated.

"The truce stands," Dorigen declared.

The burly orc looked to the soldier standing beside it, another orc, its filthy hands wringing its sword hilt anxiously. Danica knew that they were silently deciding whether or not to attack, and it seemed as if the wizard believed the same thing, for Dorigen was chanting softly.

Dorigen blinked out of sight once more; the orcs turned to Danica, roared, and came on.

Dorigen reappeared right in front of the burly orc, her hands out before her, thumbs touching and fingers wide spread. The orc threw its arms up defensively, but the sheets of flame that suddenly erupted from the wizard's fingertips rolled around the meager fleshy barriers, licked at the creature's face and chest.

The other orc came in hard at Danica. She started for the desk, hopping as though she meant to go over it. The orc swerved, heading for the side, but Danica dropped back to her feet, and kicked its sword out wide. It tried to bring the weapon back in to bear, but Danica caught its wrist, then caught its chin with her free hand. She whipped the monster's head back and forth fiercely, then snapped a quick punch to its throat that dropped it in a gasping heap.

Danica's foot was upon the side of the orc's face in an instant, ready to snap its neck if any of its companions were advancing.

They were not, and all but one of them had replaced their weapons on their belts. The single enemy still holding his sword looked at Dorigen and the smoking corpse before her, looked at the fierce Danica, and quickly decided that his remaining friends were wise in putting up their weapons.

"I declare a truce," Dorigen growled at the soldiers, and none of them made any moves to indicate that they did not agree. Dorigen turned to Danica and nodded. "To the dining hall."

* * * * *

Cadderly lay on the stone floor, sucking air into his parched throat as the fires in the room behind him died away, having consumed the magical manifestations of curtains, tapestries, carpet, and wood.

Cadderly understood that this grand hallway was purely the image of stone, magical fields too dense to be sparked apart by mere flames. The young priest felt safe from any advancing flames, and he thought it a curious thing that the properties of such extradimensional pockets followed the same physical laws that governed true materials. What might be the potential, then, if he could create something in an extradimension, through the use of magic, and bring it back to his own plane? he wondered.

Cadderly filed the notion far away in his mind, reminding himself that his present business was more pressing than any hypothetical possibilities flashing around in his always questioning thoughts. He forced himself to his knees and noted the wizard's sooty footsteps on the floor, noted by their long stride and small imprint that Aballister had left the room in full flight.

A dozen yards down, with several doors lining either side of the corridor, the wizard had apparently realized his obvious tracks, for they simply disappeared, leaving Cadderly to figure out which way Aballister had gone.

Still kneeling, Cadderly took out his crossbow and loaded an explosive dart. He laid the weapon on the floor beside him and realized, with a quiet nod of his head, that he held one advantage over Aballister, the greatest advantage of a cleric over a wizard. By Cadderly's estimation, Aballister had not been wise to break off the combat, no matter how badly Cadderly's pillar of flame had hurt him, for now the young priest fell back into the song of Deneir, let it take him where it had compelled him previously, into the sphere of healing.

He brushed a hand over his scorched cheek, closing the wound and perfectly mending the skin. He placed his hand firmly against the mark on his chest, where the lightning bolt had thundered home. When he took up his crossbow and stood, just a few minutes later, his wounds did not seem so serious.

But where to go? the young priest wondered. And what traps and wards had the clever Aballister set for him?

He moved to the nearest door, a simple, unremarkable one to his left. He scanned for any obvious traps, then called upon his magic to scrutinize it more fully. Unremarkable, it seemed, and from what Cadderly could tell, unlocked.

He took a deep breath to steady himself, held his

crossbow out in front of him, grabbed the knob in one hand, and slowly turned it. He heard a distinctive click, a hissing sound as the door's edge slipped past the jamb.

The door flew from his hand, snapped open in the blink of an eye. A fierce, sucking wind grabbed at Cadderly, pulling him to the open portal. His eyes widened in fear as he came to realize that this was a gate to yet another plane—one of the lower, evil planes judging from the growling shadows and acrid smoke filling the unbordered region in front of him. He grabbed at the doorjamb and held on with all his strength, and held on, too, to his precious crossbow.

He was stretched out fully into the new plane, feet leading the way. Fearful tingles caressed his body, a sensation that evil things were near him, touching him! The pull was too great; Cadderly knew that he could not hold on for long.

Cadderly locked his hands in place and forced himself into a state of calmness. As he had done in the previous room, he used his magic to study the magic of this area, of the door and the threshold.

All of the portal area was magical, of course, but a single spot stood out to Cadderly, its emanations of magic different and more intense than the fields about it. The young priest let go with one hand, straightened his crossbow, and drew a bead.

He couldn't be sure if this was the place of the actual gate, the specific key to the interplanar barrier, but his actions were wrought of desperation. He put the crossbow in line and let fly. His shot did not hit the mark, but struck close enough so that the resulting explosion encompassed the target spot.

The wind stopped. Cadderly's instincts and mounting knowledge of magic screamed at him to roll for the threshold, to tuck his legs in and get his hands clear of the doorjamb. He was wise enough not to question those instincts, and he dove headlong for the threshold, just ahead of the suddenly swinging door.

The door snapped shut, slamming Cadderly and pushing him on his way. He stopped rolling when he hit the corridor's opposite wall, his legs and lower back bruised and sore. He glanced back and was amazed as the door swelled and shifted shape, twisting tightly into place, seeming to meld with the surrounding jamb.

Aballister's extradimensional mansion apparently protected itself from such torn planar rifts. Cadderly managed a smile, glad that Aballister's work had been so complete and so farsighted, glad that he was not hanging in some nonspace, some formless region between the known planes.

Ten steps down the stone corridor two more doors loomed. One was unremarkable, like the one Cadderly had just encountered, but the other was ironbound with heavy straps and showed a keyhole below the handle. Cadderly searched for traps, checked around the edges for any areas that might reveal this, too, to be a portal to another plane. Nothing dangerous became apparent, so he reached down and slowly turned the handle.

The door was locked.

It crossed Cadderly's mind more than once in the next few seconds that Aballister might be harboring yet another of his pet monsters behind this door, that blowing it open might put him into a fight with another hydra, or perhaps even something worse.

The flip side to that argument, of course, was that Aballister might be behind this door, recuperating, preparing some devilish magics.

Cadderly leveled the crossbow at the lock and fired, shielding his eyes from the expected flash. He used the moment to put another dart in place, and when he looked back, he found a scorch mark where both the lock and the handle had been, and the door hanging loose on its hinges.

Cadderly ducked to the side and pushed the door in, crossbow ready. His bow slipped down, his smile widened once more when he realized the contents of this room—an alchemy shop.

"What might bring you out of hiding, wizard?" the young priest muttered under his breath. He pushed the door closed behind him and crossed to the beaker-covered tables. Cadderly had read many texts on potions and magical ingredients, and though he was no alchemist, he knew which ingredients he could safely mix.

And, more importantly for what the young priest now had in mind, which ingredients he could not.

* * * * *

Ivan and Pikel led the charge down one corridor, cut through a room to the side, and headed out a back door into another corridor. Vander came roaring right behind them, still cradling Shayleigh, though the elf maiden was conscious and demanding to be put down. No enemies stood against the friends for this first scrambling rush. The enemy soldiers they encountered, even two ogres, fell all over themselves trying to run away. Ivan, more wounded than he cared to admit, let them go. The dwarf wanted only to find Cadderly and Danica, or to find some place where he and his three companions might hide and recover.

Through the back door of another room, the two dwarves surprised a man trying to come through the other way. He had just grabbed the door's handle when Pikel's club hit the thing, launching him across the corridor to slam against the wall. Both dwarves swarmed across the corridor and fell over him, Ivan connecting with a left hook, Pikel with a right, at the same time, on opposite sides of the unfortunate man's face.

Ivan considered finishing the unconscious soldier as his friends ambled past, but he put up his axe and ran after them. "Damned young colt," he muttered, referring to Cadderly, whose constant demands for compassion had apparently worn at the tough-skinned dwarf.

"To the side!" Shayleigh cried as Vander and Pikel dashed across the entrance to a side passage.

"Oo!" Pikel squeaked, and he and the firbolg sprinted on, a group of enemy soldiers wheeling around the corner behind them.

Ivan barreled into the midst of the force, his great axe chopping wildly.

Twenty feet ahead, Vander put down Shayleigh, who went right to work stringing an arrow. The firbolg spun about beside Pikel, determined to crash through to Ivan's rescue. The two had only taken a step or two when Shayleigh cried out, "The other way!"

Sure enough, enemies poured into the corridor from another side passage farther down, a large force led by a contingent of ogres. Shayleigh put three arrows into immediate flight, felling one of the leading ogres, but another took its place, running right over the monster's back as it fell.

Shayleigh fired again, scored another hit, and put her next arrow to her bowstring. She couldn't hold them back, though. Even if every shot were perfect, if every shot killed an enemy, she would surely be buried where she stood.

She fired again, and then the ogre was upon her, its club up high, a victorious scream erupting from its huge head.

Vander's forearm slammed it in the chin and knocked it flying into its comrades. The firbolg's great sword swiped across, disemboweling the next ogre, driving the enemies farther back.

Ivan chopped and spun, every swipe connecting. He saw an arm go flying free of one orcan torso and smiled grimly, but that smile was smacked away as he continued to turn and a goblin's club slammed him squarely in the face, taking out a tooth.

Dazed, but still swinging, the dwarf backpedaled and sidestepped, trying to keep his balance, knowing that to fall was to be overwhelmed. He heard his brother calling from not far away, heard an enemy grunt and groan as Pikel's club smacked hard against bare skin. Something slashed Ivan's forehead. Blinded by his own blood, he chopped out, connecting solidly. He heard Pikel again, to the side, and took a stumbling step in that direction.

An ogre's club caught the yellow-bearded dwarf in the lower back, launched him tumbling through the air. He crashed through several bodies, the last being Pikel's, and went down atop his brother.

Pikel heaved Ivan over behind him and hopped back to his feet, clubbing wildly at the tangled mass in front. He squeaked frantically for his brother to join him, and Ivan tried, but found that his legs would not move to his mind's call.

Ivan struggled to stand, to get beside his brother. He realized only then that he had somehow lost his axe, realized that he could not see and could not stand. Darkness engulfed his thoughts as it had his eyes, and the last thing he felt was slender but strong hands grabbing his shoulders and hauling him backward along the floor.

* * * * *

They were greeted at the dining room entrance by the groans and shrieks of the wounded. Danica started forward, her first instincts telling her to run through the carnage and seek out her friends. She stopped immediately, though, and spun about, hands crossing before her.

The sight of their dead comrades had put the soldiers who had accompanied Danica and Dorigen into a rage, and two of them stood right before the monk, their spears leveled, their faces firmly set for battle.

"The truce holds," Dorigen said calmly, acting not at all surprised by the piles of dead and mutilated Trinity soldiers.

One of the spearmen backed away, but the other stood unblinking, unmoving, trying to decide if the consequences of disobedience would outweigh the satisfaction of impaling this intruder.

Danica read his thoughts perfectly, saw the boiling

hatred in his eyes. "Do it," she prodded, as eager to strike at him as he was to hit her.

Dorigen put her hand on the man's back. Flickers of electricity arced up the wizard's body, slipped down her arm and through her fingers, blowing the man to the floor several feet away. He rolled to a sitting position, the shoulder of his leather tunic smoking, metal speartip split in half, and hair dancing on end.

"The next time, you will die," Dorigen promised grimly, to him and to the other soldiers milling nervously nearby. "The truce holds."

The wizard nodded to Danica, who sped off around the room. She quickly discerned that her friends had made their valiant stand behind the small counter at the back of the hall. Finding their trail as they left the place was not difficult, since it was dotted with blood.

"M'lady Dorigen!" cried a man, rushing in behind the wizard and her soldiers. "We have them!"

Danica's almond eyes flickered at the painful news, and she ran back across the hall.

"Where?" Dorigen demanded.

"Two passages over," the man was happy to report, though his smile lessened when he noticed Danica running free. He gripped his weapon tightly, but, thoroughly confused, made no immediate moves to threaten the dangerous monk.

"Are they dead?" Danica asked, demanded.

The man looked to Dorigen plaintively, and she nodded that he should answer.

"They were alive by last reports," he replied, "but fully surrounded and sorely pressed."

Danica was again surprised by the sincerity in Dorigen's alarmed expression.

"Quickly," the wizard said to her, and Dorigen took Danica's hand and ran off, the shrugging, confused soldiers of Castle Trinity falling into ranks behind them.

* * * * *

Pikel dodged back and forth along the corridor, his club holding back the enemy line while Shayleigh picked her deadly shots around him. Pikel's club rarely came close to hitting anything other than an enemy weapon, but the corridor was fast filling with dead and wounded.

Shayleigh emptied one quiver, began working furiously on another.

"Ogre!" she heard Vander yell, and she had to spin about. An ogre had slipped past the furious firbolg and was bearing down on the elf. She put her bow up quickly and fired point-blank, her arrow disappearing into the fleshy bulk. But the ogre was not stopped, and the clubbing it gave Shayleigh sent her flying back against the wall, tumbling over Ivan. On the very edge of consciousness, she tried again to load her bow as the monster advanced.

Pikel glanced back over his shoulder—and a sword slipped over his lowered club to slash his upper arm.

"Ow," he groaned, and he turned back just in time to see another sword slip in the other way, gashing his other arm.

"Ow."

The dwarf darted forward in a feigned charge, and his enemies fell back, then he swung around, transferring the momentum of his spin into his wide-flying club. The ogre roared as its hip bone cracked loudly, and it lurched to the side.

Shayleigh's next arrow dove into its chest; Vander's heavy sword gashed into its side.

It fell headlong over Pikel as he muttered, "Uh-oh," and dove forward, trying desperately to get away. A man behind Pikel, fully intent on the dwarf, did not react quickly enough and was squashed under six hundred pounds of ogre flesh.

Pikel, laid out straight, scrambled and clawed his way from under the prostrate torso, past the ogre's hips and right out between its legs.

Other enemies had run over the creature's back and were waiting for, and stabbing at, the dwarf as he reappeared. He squeaked, "Ow! Ow!" repeatedly, taking stinging hit after stinging hit, trying to get his balance and turn about, that he might fend off the wave of weapons.

An arrow cut the air above him, and he used the distraction and the shield of a falling body to roll all the way out from under the fallen ogre. Three scrambling steps put him beside Shayleigh, the elf now holding her sword low before her, standing unsteadily.

"Together," she mumbled to Pikel, but as she spoke, a club twirled through the air and smashed her in the face, and she fell heavily to the stone.

More clubs and daggers came flying the dwarf's way. Pikel's waving club blocked a few; he looked down curiously to regard a dagger's hilt quivering from his shoulder, looked curiously to his arm that had suddenly fallen limp to his side.

Pikel tried to backtrack, stumbled and fell over Shayleigh, and had not the strength to get back up.

The side of her face against the stone, only one eye opened, Shayleigh noted the measured approach of the enemy horde, though her fleeting consciousness could not comprehend the grim consequences. The elf saw only blackness as a heavy boot slammed to the stone right before her face, its heel only an inch away from her bleeding nose.

Twenty-Two

Trump Card

Cadderly ran from the alchemy shop, pulling the ruined door closed behind him. A moment later the young priest was sprawled out on the floor, and that ironbound door was no more than a pile of burning kindling against the corridor's opposite wall. Cadderly hadn't expected the mixture to react so quickly! He put his feet under him and started running, managing to hold his balance as a second blast rocked the area, this one blowing apart the door opposite the alchemy shop and cracking the walls along the corridor.

Cadderly rounded a corner, glancing back as a fireball engulfed the area. He could only hope that the second door he had ruined was not another portal to the lower planes, could only hope that some evil, horrid denizens would not come leaping through into the corridor behind him.

He ran past another door, then skidded as he crossed by yet another, this one made of iron, not wood, and hanging open.

264

"What have you done?" came an angry cry from inside.

I have forced you to face me, Cadderly answered silently, a satisfied look stealing the trepidation from his face. He moved slowly to the iron door, pushing it all the way open.

Cages and glass cases of various sizes lined the huge room's walls, and a tumult of growls and squawks greeted the young priest. The wizard stood across the way, in front of another door and between the four largest cages. Three of these were empty—for the manticore, the chimera, and the hydra? Cadderly wondered—but the fourth held a creature that would grow into a fearsome beast indeed. A young dragon, its scales glossy black, narrowed its reptilian eyes evilly as it regarded Cadderly.

Cadderly noted the slight trembling of the wizard's shoulders, could tell that the exhausted man's magical energies had been greatly taxed. And the young priest's pillar of flame had hurt Aballister, for the side of the wizard's neck was red and blistered, and his fine blue robe hung in tatters.

Another explosion rocked the extradimensional complex.

Aballister gnashed his teeth and shook his head. He tried to speak, but his words came out as a singular growl.

Cadderly did not know how to respond. Should he demand the man's surrender? He, too, was weary, perhaps as weary as the older wizard. Perhaps this fight was far from over.

"Your war against Shilmista Forest was unjustified," the young priest said, as calmly as he could manage. "As was Barjin's attack on the Edificant Library."

The wizard chuckled. "And what of the attack in Carradoon?" he brazenly asked. "When I sent the Night Masks to kill you."

Cadderly believed that the man was daring him to act, was baiting him to make the first move. He looked again to that young black dragon, staring at him hungrily.

"There is still the option of surrender," Cadderly

remarked, trying to equal the wizard's confidence.

"I might accept your surrender," Aballister replied sarcastically, "or I might not!" The wizard's dark eyes flashed suddenly, and his hands began a circling motion.

Cadderly had his readied crossbow up in an instant and launched the dart at Aballister without the slightest hesitation. His shot was true, but the dart skipped off the wizard's newest magical shield and struck up high on the back wall, blowing a clean hole. Sparks flared at the scorched edges, the force of the explosion threatening to unravel the binding magical energies—magical energies that were already being assaulted from the continuing bursts from the alchemy shop.

As soon as the dart skipped wide, Cadderly knew that he was vulnerable. His choice of a conventional attack prevented him from throwing up a defensive shield. Fortunately, the wizard's attack came in the form of fire, with Aballister hurling a small ball of flame across the room. The fire hit Cadderly squarely, would have burned his face and hair except that enough of his protective globe remained so that the flames were dispersed into a green glow.

The young priest recovered from the shock quickly, reaching into his pouch for some seeds to hurl back. Cadderly dropped them right back into the pouch, though, and nearly swooned, for it was neither his turn to attack, nor the wizard's.

The black dragon spit a line of acid from between the bars of its cage.

Cadderly cried out and spun, falling away to the side. He did not throw his arms up in front of him (and if he had, they surely would have been charred) as his instincts demanded. He used the training Danica had given to him, threw as much of his body as he could out of harm's way.

The acid slashed across his chest, burning and biting at his skin. Rolling on the floor, Cadderly saw that his tunic was burning, that his bandolier was burning.

His bandolier was burning!

Screaming in terror and in pain, the young priest twirled up to his knees and pulled the bandolier over his head. Apparently thinking that the battle had turned his way, Aballister paid Cadderly's frantic movements no heed, was deep in the throes of casting another spell.

Cadderly put the flaming bandolier into a few quick spins over his head like a lasso and hurled it across the room, diving for cover as he threw, curling up in a fetal position with his hands tucked behind his head.

Aballister screamed in shock and fear, and the dragon roared as the first of the magical darts exploded.

One after another, the tiny bombs went off, each blast seeming louder than the one before. Metal tips and ends of the darts whipped about the room, pinging off metal bars, ricocheting off stone walls, and smashing glass.

Cadderly could not count the explosions, but he knew that he still had well over thirty darts in his bandolier. He tightened his arms instinctively about his head, continued to scream if for no better reason than to block out the terrible tumult in the room.

And then it was over, and Cadderly dared to look out. Residual sparking fires had been lit all about the huge room. The dragon lay dead, its torso shredded by many flying darts, but the wizard was nowhere to be seen.

Cadderly had started to stand when out of the corner of his eye he noticed a giant snake slipping out of the broken side of a glass container. He put his walking stick in the constrictor's face, held it back until he could quick-step past.

A metal pole to the other side disintegrated in a flash of light. Another followed suit, and Cadderly began to understand that he had inadvertently unlocked the bindings of this entire magical pocket.

The young priest rushed across the room, through the far door, and into another, narrower corridor. The wizard stood forty feet away, one arm limp at his side, blood oozing from his shoulder, and his face blackened with soot.

"Fool!" Aballister yelled at him. "You have broken my house, but have damned yourself in its collapse!"

It was true, Cadderly realized. The magical bindings were unraveling. He started to reply, but Aballister wasn't listening. The wizard scurried through a nearby door and was gone.

Cadderly ran up and tried to follow, but the heavy wooden door would not budge. There came another explosion, and the floor bucked violently, knocking him to one knee. He glanced frantically up and down the corridor, looking for some escape; he grabbed up his crossbow, only to remember that he had no more explosive darts.

Glaring light flickered through the open door he had left behind—the light of disintegrating material, Cadderly knew. He tried to fall into his magic, to search the song for a way out.

A flash ran along the ceiling above him, leaving a wide crack in its wake, and Cadderly realized that he did not have time.

He took up his adamantite spindle-disks and looped the cord over his finger. He sent them into a few fast movements, running them down to the end of the cord, then snapping them back into his palm, to tighten the cord.

"I hope you made these good," he mumbled, speaking as if Ivan Bouldershoulder were standing next to him. With a determined grunt, the young priest hurled the spindle-disks at the door, and they cracked off the wood, knocking a deep dent in its surface. A flick of Cadderly's wrist sent them spinning back to his hand, and he hurled them again, at the same spot.

The third throw popped a hole in the wood and a fierce wind filled with red stinging dust assaulted Cadderly. He kept his balance and his composure and whacked the door again, his spindle-disks widening the hole.

The flickering light to his side became continuous, and Cadderly glanced that way to see the very corridor dissolving, arcing fingers of electricity leading the way toward him, breaking apart the magically created stone so that it might be consumed.

Barely twenty feet away loomed nothingness.

Cadderly's weapon hit the door with all his strength behind it. He couldn't even see through the stinging dust, just flailed away desperately.

Ten feet away, the corridor was gone.

Cadderly sensed it, hurled the disks one final time, and threw all his weight against the weakened door.

* * * * *

Danica and Dorigen worked their way past scores of swarming Trinity soldiers, men and monsters alike. Many stopped to regard the fierce monk curiously, but seeing Dorigen beside Danica, they only shrugged and went on their way.

Danica knew that Dorigen could have had her overwhelmed with a single word at any time, and she spent more time looking at the wizard than at the scrambling soldiers, trying to figure out exactly what was motivating Dorigen.

They heard the firbolg's roar from beyond as they came up on one corner, heard the wind-cutting sweep of Vander's great sword and the frantic cries of dodging enemies. A goblin rushed around the bend, skidding to a stop right before Dorigen.

"Three of 'ems is down!" it shrieked, holding four crooked fingers up before it. "Three of 'ems is down!" A sickly feeling washed over Danica. "Three of 'ems is down!"

The goblin's smile disappeared under the weight of Danica's fast-flying fist.

"We have a truce," Dorigen calmly reminded the volatile monk, but it seemed to Danica that Dorigen was not overly concerned, was even amused, by the wounded goblin squirming about on the floor.

Danica was up to the corner in an instant, peering around

at the sight she feared to view. Ivan, Pikel, and Shayleigh lay helpless on the floor, with Vander, showing a dozen grievous wounds, straddling them, the firbolg's huge sword working back and forth furiously to keep the multitude of pressing enemies back.

An orc cried out something Danica did not understand, and the enemy troops broke ranks, rushing away from the firbolg, rushing past Danica and turning, diving, into the corridor behind her. She understood the retreat when the scene cleared, revealing a battery of crossbowmen down the hall beyond the firbolg, weapons leveled and ready.

Vander cried out in protest, apparently realizing his doom. Then a glowing apparition of a hand appeared behind him, touched him, and he swung about, his sword cutting nothing but the empty air.

Danica's first reaction was to spin and clobber the wizard, guessing that Dorigen must have been the one who had brought forth the spectral hand, and fearing what the wizard might have done to Vander. Before the monk moved, though, the crossbow battery opened up, launching a score of heavy bolts Vander's way.

They skipped and deflected harmlessly off the firbolg. Some stopped in midair, quivering before Vander, then fell, their momentum expended, to the ground.

"I am true to my word," Dorigen said dryly, walking past Danica and into the open corridor. She called for Vander to be at ease, called for her own troops to cease the fighting. Some soldiers, orcs mostly, near Danica eyed the monk dangerously, clutching their weapons as though they did not understand and did not trust the strange events.

The soldiers who had accompanied the monk and Dorigen from the wizard's area, who had witnessed Dorigen's fury against the orc that had gone against her commands, sent a line of whispers spreading throughout the ranks, and Danica soon relaxed, the threat apparently ended. She rushed around the corner, found Vander, too, slumping against the wall, thoroughly exhausted and gravely wounded.

"It is over?" the firbolg asked breathlessly.

"No more fighting," Danica answered. Vander closed his eyes and slid slowly down to the floor, and it seemed to Danica that he would die.

Danica found the dwarves and Shayleigh alive, at least, and Shayleigh actually managed to sit up and raise one hand in greeting. Ivan was by far the worst off of the three. He had lost a lot of blood and was losing more even as Danica tried futilely to stem the flow. Even worse, his legs had gone perfectly limp and were without feeling.

"Have you any healers?" Danica asked of Dorigen, who was standing over her.

"The clerics are all dead," a nearby soldier answered for the wizard, his words sharp-edged as he, too, tended to a wounded man, a Trinity soldier fast slipping into the realm of death.

Danica winced, remembering Cadderly's brutal work against that group, thinking it terribly ironic that his necessary actions against Trinity's priests might now cost his friends their lives.

Cadderly! The word assaulted Danica as surely as would an enemy spear. Where was he? she wondered. The potentially disastrous consequences of his showdown against Aballister, his father, rang clearer to the monk now, with Ivan cradled helplessly in her arms. Shayleigh seemed stronger with every passing moment; Vander's cuts had already clotted and were somehow mysteriously on the mend; and Pikel groaned and grumbled, finally rolling over with a curious, "Huh?"

But Ivan . . . Danica knew that only his dwarven toughness was keeping him alive, doubted that even that considerable strength would support him for much longer. Ivan needed a priest who could access powerful spells of healing—Ivan needed Cadderly.

Dorigen ordered several men to assist Danica in her efforts, sent several others to the priests' private quarters to search for bandages and healing potions and salves. None of the men, standing in the blood of their own allies, seemed overly eager to aid the brutal intruders, but none dared to disobey the wizard.

Danica, pressing hard against a pumping wound in Ivan's chest, her armed soaked with blood, could only wait and pray.

* * * * *

The small sun shone red. The air was hazy with swirling dust, and the rocky, barren landscape ranged from orange hues to deep crimson. All was quiet, save for the endless, mournful call of the gusting, stinging wind.

Cadderly saw no life about him, no plants or animals, no sign even of water, and he couldn't imagine anything surviving in this desolate place. He wondered where he was and knew only that this barren region was nowhere on the surface of Toril.

"No place that has any name," Aballister answered the young priest's unspoken question. The wizard walked out from a nearby tumble of boulders and stood facing Cadderly. "At least none that I have ever heard."

Cadderly took some comfort in the fact that he could still hear Deneir's song playing in his mind. He began to sing along, quietly, his hand with the magical ring clenched at his side.

"I would be very careful before attempting any spells," Aballister warned, guessing his intent. "The properties of magic are not the same here as they are on our own world. A simple line of fire"—the wizard looked to the ring as he spoke—"might well engulf this entire planet in a ball of flame.

"It is the dust, you see," the wizard continued, holding his hand up into the wind, then folding his long, skinny fingers to rub against the red powder in his palm. "So volatile."

Aballister's sincere calm bothered the young priest.

"Your extradimensional home is no more," Cadderly said, trying to steal the wizard's bluster.

Aballister frowned. "Yes, dear Cadderly, you have become such a bother. It will take me many months to reconstruct that magnificent work. It was magnificent, don't you agree?"

"We are stranded." It was spoken as a statement, but Cadderly, fearful that his words might be true, privately intended it as a question.

Aballister's face screwed up incredulously, as though he thought the claim absurd. Cadderly took comfort in that, for if the wizard possessed some magic that would get them home, the young priest believed that Deneir would show him the way, as well.

"You are not a traveler," Aballister remarked, and he shook his head, seeming almost disappointed. "I never would have guessed that you would become so paralyzed by the comforts of that miserable library."

Now it was Cadderly who screwed up his face. What was the man saying? He never would have guessed? What revelations lay in the wizard's choice of words, his choice of tense?

"Who are you?" Cadderly asked suddenly, without thinking, without even meaning to speak the thought aloud.

Aballister's burst of laughter mocked him. "I am one who has lived many more years than you, who knows more about you than you believe, and who has defeated men and monsters much greater than you," the wizard boasted, and again his tone reflected sincere serenity.

"You may have done me a favor with your stubborn determination and your surprising resourcefulness," Aballister went on. "Both Barjin and Ragnor, my principle rivals, are dead because of you, and Dorigen as well, I would guess, since you came into my home alone."

"Dorigen showed me the way in," Cadderly corrected, more interested in deflating Aballister than in protecting the woman. "She is very much alive."

For the first time, Aballister seemed truly bothered, or at least perplexed. "She would not appreciate your telling me of her treachery," he reasoned. He started to elaborate, but stopped suddenly, feeling an intrusion in his thoughts, a presence that did not belong.

Cadderly pressed the domination spell, the same one he had used to "convince" Dean Thobicus to allow him to head out for Castle Trinity. He focused on the area of blackness he knew to be Aballister's identity, sent forth a glowing ball of energy to assault the wizard's mind.

Aballister stopped the glowing ball and pushed it back toward the young priest. *How easily you work around the limitations of our physical surroundings*, the wizard congratulated telepathically. *Though you prove yourself a fool to challenge me so!*

Cadderly ignored the message, pressed on with all his mental strength. The glowing ball of mental energy seemed to distort and flatten, moving not at all, as Aballister stubbornly pushed back.

You are strong, the wizard remarked.

Cadderly held similar feelings for his adversary. He knew his focus on the ball was absolute, and yet Aballister held him at bay. The young priest understood the synaptic movements of Aballister's thoughts, the clear flow of reasoning, the desperation of curiosity, and it seemed to Cadderly almost as if he was looking into some sort of mental mirror. They were so similar, the two opponents, and yet so different!

Cadderly's mind began to wander, began to wonder how many people of Faerûn might possess similar mental powers, a similar synaptic flow. Very few, he believed, and that led him to begin calculating the probabilities of this meeting. . . .

The glowing ball, the mental manifestation of pure pain, leaped his way, and Cadderly dismissed the tangent thoughts, quickly regaining his focus. The struggle continued for many moments, with neither man gaining any advantage, neither man willing to relinquish an inch to the other.

It is of no avail, came Aballister's thoughts.

Only one will leave this place, Cadderly replied.

He pressed on, again making no headway. But then Cadderly began to hear the melody of the song of Deneir, flowing along beside him, falling into place near him and then within him. These were the notes of perfect harmony, sharpening Cadderly's focus to a point where the unbelieving wizard could not follow. Aballister's mind might have been Cadderly's equal, but the wizard lacked the harmony of spirit, lacked the company of a god figure. Aballister had no answers for the greatest questions of human existence, and therein lay his weakness, his self-doubts.

The glowing ball began to move toward the wizard, slowly, but inevitably.

Cadderly felt Aballister's welling panic, and that only scattered the wizard's focus even more.

Do you not know who I am? the wizard telepathically asked. The desperation in his thoughts made Cadderly believe the words to be another pointless boast, a fervent denial that anyone could hope to defeat him in mental combat. The young priest was not distracted, maintained his focus and the pressure—until Aballister played his trump.

"I am your father!" the wizard screamed.

The words slammed into Cadderly more profoundly than any lightning bolt. The glowing ball was no more, the mental contact shattered by the overwhelming surprise. It all made sense to the young priest. Awful, undeniable sense, and after viewing the wizard's thought processes, so similar, even identical, to his own, Cadderly could not find the strength to doubt the claim.

I am your father! The words rang out in Cadderly's mind, a damning cry, a pang of loneliness and regret for those things that might have been.

"Do you not remember?" the wizard asked, and his voice sounded so very sweet to the stunned young priest.

Cadderly blinked his eyes open, regarded the man and his unthreatening, resigned pose.

Aballister crooked his arms as though he were cradling a baby. "I remember holding you close," he cooed. "I would sing to you—how much more precious you were to me since your mother had died in childbirth!"

Cadderly felt the strength draining from his legs.

"Do you remember that?" the wizard asked gently. "Of course you do. There are some things ingrained deeply within our thoughts, within our hearts. You cannot forget those moments we had together, you and I, father and son."

Aballister's words wove a myriad of images in Cadderly's mind, images of his earliest days, the serenity and security he had felt in his father's arms. How wonderful things had been for him then! How filled with love and perfect harmony!

"I remember the day I was forced to give you up," Aballister purred on. His voice cracked; a tear streamed down his weary old face. "So vividly, I remember. Time has not dulled the edge of that pain."

"Why?" Cadderly managed to stammer.

Aballister shook his head. "I was afraid," he replied. "Afraid that I alone could not give you the life you deserved."

Cadderly felt only compassion for the man, had forgiven Aballister before the wizard had even asked for forgiveness.

"All of them were against me," Aballister went on, his voice taking on an unmistakable edge—and to Cadderly, the sharpness of the wizard's rising anger only seemed to validate all that Aballister had claimed. "The priests, the officials of Carradoon. 'It will be better for the boy,' they all said, and now I understand their reasoning."

Cadderly looked up and shrugged, not following the logic.

"I would have become the mayor of Carradoon," Aballister explained. "It was inevitable. And you, my legacy, my heart and soul, would have followed suit. My political rivals could not bear to see that come to pass, could not bear to see the family of Bonaduce attain such dominance. Jealousy drove them, drove them all!"

It all made perfect sense to the stunned young priest. He found himself hating the Edificant Library, hating Dean Thobicus, the old liar, and hating even Headmaster Avery Schell, the man who had served as his surrogate father for so many years. Pertelope, too! What a phony she had been! What a hypocrite!

"And so I have risen against them," Aballister proclaimed. "And I have searched you out. We are together again, my son."

Cadderly closed his eyes, put his head down, and absorbed those precious words, words he had wanted to hear from his earliest recollections. Aballister continued talking, but Cadderly's mind remained locked on those six sweet words. *We are together again, my son.*

His mother had not died in childbirth.

Cadderly did not really remember her, just in images, flashes of her smiling face. But those images certainly did not come from Cadderly's moment of childbirth.

And I have searched you out.

But what of the Night Masks? Cadderly's reasoning screamed at him. Aballister had indeed searched him out, had sent killers to search him out, to murder him and to murder Danica.

It was only then that Cadderly suspected that the wizard had placed an enchantment over him, had sweetened his words with subtle magical energies. The young priest's heart fought back against the reasoning, against the logical protests, for he did not want to believe that he was being deceived, wanted desperately to believe in his father's sincerity.

But his mother had not died in childbirth!

Aballister's charming tapestry began to unwind. Cadderly focused on the wizard's continuing words once more—and found that the man was no longer coaxing sweet images, but was chanting.

Cadderly had let his guard down, had no practical defense against the impending spell. He looked up to see Aballister loose a sheet of sizzling blue lightning that wobbled and zigzagged through the popping red dust. The wizard apparently understood the properties of this landscape, for the blast deflected unerringly toward Cadderly. The young priest threw his arms up, felt the jolting, burning explosion jerk his muscles every which way, felt it grab at his heart and squeeze viciously.

He sensed that he was flying, but felt nothing. He sensed that he had slammed hard against some rock, but was beyond the sensation of pain.

"Now you are dead," he heard Aballister say, distantly, as though he and the wizard were no longer facing each other, were no longer on the same plane of existence.

Cadderly understood the truth of that claim, felt his lifeforce slipping from his mortal coil, slipping into the world of the spirit, the realm of the dead. Looking down, he saw himself lying on the red ground, broken and smoldering. Then his spirit was bathed in the divine light, the same washing sensation he had felt weeks ago at the Dragon's Codpiece when he had gone in search of Headmaster Avery's spirit.

One, two, played the notes of Deneir's song.

He knew only peace and serenity, felt more at home than he had ever felt, and knew that he had come to a place where he might find some rest.

One, two.

All thoughts of the material world began to fade. Even images of Danica, his dearest love, were not tainted with regret, for Cadderly held faith that he and she would one day be rejoined. His heart lifted; he felt his spirit soar.

One, two, came the song. Like a heartbeat.

Cadderly saw his body again, far below him, saw one finger twitch slightly.

No! he protested.

One, two, compelled the song. Cadderly was not being asked, he was being told. He looked to Aballister, spell-casting once more, creating a shimmering doorway in the red air. Aballister would return to Castle Trinity, the young priest suddenly realized, and all the region would be plunged into darkness.

Cadderly understood the plea of Deneir, and no longer did his spirit protest. *One, two,* beat his heart.

When he opened his material eyes and looked upon Aballister, he was again flooded with the warm sensation of the images of childhood the wizard had conjured. Rationally, Cadderly understood that he had been under an enchantment, understood that simple logic proved Aballister's lies. But the lure of what Aballister had shown him could not be easily overcome.

Then another image came to the young priest, a memory he had blocked out, packed away in a remote corner of his mind long, long ago. He stood before the doors of the Edificant Library, a young and not so fat Headmaster Avery facing his father before him. Avery's face was blotched red from rage. He screamed at Aballister, even cursed the man, and reiterated that Aballister had been banned from ever again entering the Edificant Library.

Aballister showed no sign of remorse, even laughed at the burly priest. "Then take the brat," he cackled, and he roughly shoved Cadderly forward, tearing a handful of hair from Cadderly's head as he pulled his hand away.

The pain was intense, physically and emotionally, but Cadderly did not cry out, not then and not now. In looking back on that awful moment, Cadderly realized that he did not cry out because he was so accustomed to Aballister's commonplace abuse. He had been the outlet for the wizard's frustrations. He was the outlet as his mother had been the outlet.

His mother!

Cadderly was somehow standing, growling, and Aballister turned about, his eyes popping wide with surprise when he saw that his son still lived. Behind the wizard, the portal glowed and shimmered, sometimes showing an image of the anteroom to the wizard's mansion within its magical borders. Aballister would abandon him now, as he had abandoned him then, would go about his business and leave his son, "the brat," to fate.

More memories assaulted the young priest, as though he had opened a box that he could not close. He saw Aballister's face, twisted demonically with rage, heard his mother's pitiful cries and his own quiet sobs.

The manifestation of a huge sword appeared in the red air before him, waving menacingly. "Lie down and die," he heard the wizard say.

That sword! Aballister had used it against Cadderly's mother, had used this very same spell to kill Cadderly's mother!

"Oh, my dear Deneir," the lost young priest heard himself whimper. The song thrummed in his head of its own accord; Cadderly did not compel it to play and hardly heard the harmony of its sweet notes. He thought he heard Headmaster Avery's voice at that moment, but the notion was lost when he saw the magical sword arcing his way, slicing for his unprotected neck, too close for him to dodge.

The sword struck him and then dissolved with a sharp sizzle.

"Damn you!" the wizard, his father, cried.

Cadderly saw nothing but his mother's face, felt nothing but a primal rage focused on this murderer, this imposter. He heard a sound escaping his lips, a burst of anger and magical energy too great for him to contain. It came forth as the most discordant note of the Deneirian song Cadderly had ever heard, a purely destructive twist of the precious notes.

The very ground heaved before him, and he continued to scream. Like an ocean wave, the red soil rolled toward Aballister, a crack widening in its mighty wake.

"What are you doing?" the wizard protested, and so weak and minuscule did his voice sound beneath the roar of Cadderly's primal scream!

Aballister lurched into the air, thrown by the wave. He flailed his arms as he descended, flapping futilely, and fell into the torn crack. The wave diminished as it rolled on, the ground becoming quiet once more.

"I am your father!" came Aballister's pleading, pained cry from somewhere not too far below the rim of the crack.

Another cry erupted from Cadderly's aching lungs, and he threw his hands up before him and clapped them together.

And following his lead, the crack in the ground, too, snapped shut. Aballister's cries were no more.

Twenty-Three

War's End

An exhausted Cadderly stepped through the door Aballister had conveniently created, stepped through the wall, which was no longer covered with a swirling mist, and into the room where he had left Danica. A dozen enemy soldiers were there, milling about and grumbling to each other, but, oh, how they scrambled when the young priest suddenly appeared in their midst! They screamed and punched each other, fighting to get away from the dangerous man. In but a few moments, only six remained in the room, and these kept their wits enough to draw their weapons and face the young priest squarely.

"Go to Dorigen!" one of them barked at another, and the man ran off.

"Stay back, I warn you!" another man growled at Cadderly, prodding forward threateningly with his spear.

Cadderly's head throbbed; he wanted no fight with this crew, or with anyone for that matter, but he could hardly ignore his precarious situation. He accessed the song of Deneir, though the effort pained him, and the next time the man prodded ahead, he found that he was holding not a spear, but a writhing, obviously unhappy serpent. The man shrieked and dropped the thing to the floor, scrambling back away from it, though it made no move to attack.

"We have your friends!" another man, the soldier who had ordered a companion to go for Dorigen, cried. "If you kill us, they, too, will be killed!"

Cadderly didn't even hear the second sentence. The proclamation that his friends were prisoners, and not dead, sent his hopes soaring. He rested back against the wall and tried hard not to think of the fact that he had just destroyed his own father.

Danica raced into the room a moment later, slammed hard into Cadderly, and threw her arms around him, crushing him in a hug.

"Aballister is dead," the young priest said to Dorigen over Danica's shoulder.

Dorigen gave him an inquisitive look, and Danica, too, backed away to arm's length and stared hard at her love.

"I know," Cadderly said quietly.

"He was your father?" Danica asked, her expression as pained as that of Cadderly.

Cadderly nodded, and his lips went thin as he tried to firm up his jaw.

"Ivan needs you," Danica said to him. She regarded the young priest carefully, then shook her head doubtfully, seeing his obvious exhaustion.

Dorigen led Cadderly and Danica back to the room they had set up for the care of the wounded. Cadderly's four friends were there—though Vander hardly seemed wounded anymore—along with a handful of Castle Trinity's human soldiers. The orcs and other goblinoid creatures had followed their own custom of slaughtering their seriously wounded companions.

Pikel and Shayleigh were both sitting up, though neither

looked very steady. Their expressions brightened at Cadderly's approach, and they motioned for him to go to Ivan, lying, pale as death, on a nearby cot.

Cadderly knelt beside the yellow-bearded dwarf, amazed that Ivan still drew breath, given the sheer number of garish wounds he had suffered. The young priest realized that Ivan, for all his toughness, didn't have much time, and knew that he had to somehow find the strength to follow the song to the sphere of healing and bring forth powerful magics.

Quietly, Cadderly began to chant, and he heard the music, but it was distant, so distant. Cadderly mentally reached for it, felt the pressure in his temples, and closed his eyes as he fell into its flow, guiding it along. He swam past the notes of the minor spells of healing, knowing they would be of little use in tending the dwarf's most serious wounds. The song built to a thrumming crescendo in his thoughts, moved at Cadderly's demand into the realm of the greatest spells of healing.

The next thing the young priest knew, he was lying on the floor, looking up into Danica's concerned expression. She helped him back to a sitting position and he looked upon Ivan hopelessly.

"Cadderly?" Danica asked, and the young priest could think of several questions reflected in that one word.

"He is too tired," Dorigen answered, coming to kneel beside them both. The wizard looked into Cadderly's hollowed gray eyes and nodded, and understood.

"I must access the magic," the young priest said determinedly, and he fell right back into the song, fought hard, for now it seemed to him even more distant.

Twenty minutes passed before he woke up the next time, and Cadderly knew then that he would need several more hours of rest before he could even attempt to get into the greatest levels of healing magic again. He knew, too, in looking at the dwarf, that Ivan would not live that long.

"Why do you do this to me?" Cadderly asked aloud, asked

his god, and all those about him regarded him curiously.

"Deneir," he explained privately to Danica. "He has abandoned me in my time of desperation. I cannot believe that he will let Ivan die."

"Your god does not control the minor fates of minor players," Dorigen said, again moving close to the two.

Cadderly shot her a derisive glance that plainly asked what the wizard might know of it.

"I understand the properties of magic," Dorigen replied squarely against that arrogant expression. "The magic remains to be accessed, but you have not the strength. The failing is not Deneir's."

Danica moved as if to strike out at the woman, but Cadderly grabbed the monk immediately and held her back, nodding his head in agreement with Dorigen.

"And so your magic is held," Dorigen remarked. "Is that all that you have to offer the dying dwarf?"

At first, Cadderly took her unexpected words to mean that he should bid Ivan farewell, as a friend would do, but after a moment's thinking, the young priest came to interpret the words in a different way. He motioned Danica away, spent a long minute in contemplation, searching for some possible answers.

"Your ring," he remarked to Vander suddenly.

The firbolg glanced quickly at his hand, but the initial excitement of the group died away immediately. "It will not work," Vander explained. "The ring must be worn while the wounds are received."

"Give it to me, I beg," Cadderly said, not letting down a bit in light of the grim explanation. He took the ring from the willing firbolg and slipped it over his own finger.

"There are two types of healing magic," Cadderly explained to Vander and the others. "Two types, though I have called only upon the method that begs the blessing of the gods to mend torn skin and broken bones."

Danica started to inquire further, but Cadderly had closed his eyes and was already beginning to sing once more. It took him some time to catch up to the flow of the song. Again he felt the pressure in his temples as he followed its tiring current, but he kept heart, knowing that this time, he would not have to go so far.

The four friends and Dorigen gathered around the cot, and gasped in unison as Ivan's severe throat wound simply disappeared, then gasped again as it reappeared on Cadderly's neck!

Blood bubbled from the young priest's opened throat as he continued to force the words from his mouth. Another of Ivan's wounds was erased from the dwarf's body, to appear in a similar position on Cadderly.

Danica cried out for her love and started forward, but Dorigen and Shayleigh held her back, reasoning with her to trust in the young priest.

Soon Ivan was resting peacefully, and Cadderly, showing every brutal wound the dwarf had suffered, fell to the floor.

"Oooo," groaned an unhappy Pikel.

"Cadderly!" Danica cried again, and she tore free of Shayleigh and Dorigen and ran to him. She put her head to his chest to hear his heartbeat, brushed his curly brown locks from his face, and put her face close to his, whispering for him to live.

Vander's laughter turned her angrily about.

"He wears the ring!" the firbolg roared. "Oh, clever young priest!"

"Oo oi!" Pikel squealed with glee.

When Danica turned back, Cadderly, his head uplifted, gave her a peck of a kiss. "This really hurts," he groaned, but he managed to smile as he spoke the words, his head drifting slowly back to the floor, his eyes slowly closing.

"What's wrong with *him*?" Ivan grumbled, sitting up and looking about the room with a confused expression.

By the time his friends had pushed Ivan aside and lifted Cadderly into place on the cot, the young priest was breathing much easier, and many of his wounds were unmistakably on the mend.

Later that night, the still weary priest rose from his bed and moved about the makeshift infirmary, singing softly once more, tending the wounds of his other friends, and those of Castle Trinity's soldiers.

* * * * *

"He was my father," Cadderly said bluntly. The young priest rubbed a hand across his wet eyes, trying to come to terms with the sudden explosion of memories that assaulted him, memories he had buried away many years before.

Danica shifted closer to him, locking his arm with her own. "Dorigen told me," she explained.

They sat together in the quiet darkness for many minutes.

"He killed my mother," Cadderly said suddenly.

Danica looked up at him, a horrified expression on her fair face.

"It was an accident," Cadderly continued, looking straight ahead. "But not without blame. My fath . . . Aballister was always experimenting with new magics, always pressing the energies to their very limits, and to his very limits of control. He conjured a sword one day, a magnificent glowing sword that sliced back and forth through the air, floating of its own accord."

Cadderly could not help a slight, ironic chuckle. "He was so proud," the young priest said, shaking his head, his unkempt sandy-brown locks flopping from side to side. "So proud. But he could not control the dweomer. He had overstepped his magical discipline, and before he could dispel the sword, my mother was dead."

Danica mumbled her love's name under her breath, pulled him tighter, and put her head on his shoulder. The young priest moved away, though, so that he could look Danica in the eye.

"I do not even remember her name," he said, voice trembling. "Her face is clear to me again, the first face I ever saw in this world, but I do not even remember her name!"

They sat quietly again, Danica thinking of her own dead parents, and Cadderly playing with the multitude of rushing images, trying to find some logical recollection of his earliest years. He remembered, too, one of Headmaster Avery's scoldings, when the portly man had called Cadderly a "Gondsman," referring to a particular sect of priests known for creating ingenious, and often destructive, tools and weapons without regard for the consequences of their creations. Now, knowing Aballister, remembering what had happened to his own mother, Cadderly could better understand dear Avery's fears.

But he was not like his father, he silently reminded himself. He had found Deneir, found the truth, and found the call of his conscience. And he had brought the war—the war Aballister had precipitated—to the only possible conclusion.

Cadderly sat there assaulted by a tumult of long-buried and confusing memories, assaulted by empty wishes of what might have been and by a host of more recent memories which he could now look at with a new perspective. A profound sadness that he could not deny washed over him, a sense of grief that he had never felt before, for Avery, for Pertelope, for his mother, and for Aballister.

His sadness for his father was not for the man's death, though, but for the man's life.

Cadderly repeatedly saw the red ground of that distant world closing over the fallen wizard, ending a sad chapter of wasted, misused potential.

"You had to do it," Danica said unexpectedly. Cadderly blinked at her in disbelief that soon turned to amusement. How well she knew him!

His reply was a nod and a sincere, if resigned, smile. Cadderly felt no guilt for what he had done; he had found the truth as his father never had. Aballister, not Cadderly, had forced the conclusion.

The small room lit up as Dorigen entered, bearing a

candelabra. "Castle Trinity's soldiers are scattering to the four winds," she said. "All of their leaders are dead—except for myself, and I have no desire to continue what Aballister has started."

Danica nodded her approval, but Cadderly scowled.

"What is it?" the surprised monk asked him.

"Are we to let them run free, perhaps to cause more mischief?" he asked.

"There remain nearly three thousand of them," Dorigen reminded him. "You really have little choice in the matter. But take heart, young priest, for the threat to Carradoon, to the library, to all the region is surely ended. And I will return with you to your library, to face the judgment of your superiors."

My superiors? Cadderly thought incredulously. Dean Thobicus? The notion reminded him that he had many things yet to accomplish if he was to follow the course Deneir had laid out before him. One battle was ended, but another was yet to be fought.

"Their judgment will be harsh," Danica replied, and from her tone it was obvious that she did not wish any serious harm to come to the repentant wizard. "They may execute . . . " Danica's grim voice trailed off as Dorigen nodded her acceptance of that fact.

"No, they will not," Cadderly said quietly. "You will come back, Dorigen, and you will serve a penance. But with your powers and sincere desire, you have much that you can contribute. You, Dorigen, will help heal the scars of this war, and help better the region. That is the proper course, and the course the library will follow."

Danica turned a doubting look Cadderly's way, but it fell away as she considered the determination etched on the young priest's face. She knew what Cadderly had done to Dean Thobicus to get them out here in the first place; she suspected then what Cadderly meant to do to the man once they got back to the Edificant Library.

Again, Dorigen nodded, and she smiled warmly at

Cadderly, the man who had spared her in Shilmista Forest, the man who apparently meant to spare her once more.

"Tell me of mercy, wise Cadderly," Dorigen remarked. "Is it strength, or weakness?"

"Strength," the young priest answered without hesitation.

* * * * *

Cadderly stood on the rocky slope above Castle Trinity, flanked by his five friends. "You have ordered them to abandon this place?" he asked Dorigen, coming up the rise to join them.

"I have told the men that they will be welcomed in Carradoon," the wizard replied. "Though I doubt that many will head that way. I have told the ogres, the orcs, and the goblins to go and find holes in the mountains, to run away and cause no more mischief."

"But many remain within the fortress?" Cadderly stated as much as asked.

Dorigen looked back to Trinity's uncompleted walls and shrugged. "Ogres, orcs, and goblins are stubborn beasts."

Cadderly eyed the fortress contemptuously. He remembered the other plane, the earthquake he had brought about to bury Aballister, and thought of doing the same thing now, of destroying Castle Trinity and cleansing the mountainside. Grinning wickedly, the young priest fell into the song of Denier, searching for the powerful magic.

He found nothing to replicate the earthquake. Confused, Cadderly pressed the notes, mentally called for guidance.

Then he understood. His release of power on the other plane had been a reaction to primal emotions, not consciously conjured, but forced by events around him.

Cadderly laughed aloud, and opened his eyes to see all six of his companions standing around him, eyeing him curiously.

"What is it?" Danica asked.

"You were thinking of destroying the fortress," Dorigen reasoned.

"Aw, do it!" bellowed Ivan. "Split the ground and drop it in!"

"Oo oi!"

Cadderly glanced around at his companions, those friends who believed him invincible, godlike. When his gaze fell over Shayleigh, though, he found the elf maiden slowly shaking her head. She understood.

As did Danica. "Split the ground and drop it in?" the monk asked Ivan incredulously. "If Cadderly can do such a feat, then why did we run about inside that cursed place?"

"We have come to expect too much," Shayleigh added.

"Oo." Pikel said it, but it aptly reflected Ivan's thoughts.

"Well, come on, then," Ivan remarked after a long pause. He put his hand on Cadderly's back and pushed the young priest along with him. "We've got a month's hiking ahead, but don't ye worry, me and me brother'll get ye all through!"

It was a good start, Cadderly decided. Ivan was taking the lead, was assuming some of the responsibility.

A good start on a long road.

Epilogue

Waves of agony rolled over Druzil when
Aballister died, pains that only a familiar
who had lost his wizard master could ever
know. Unlike many familiars, Druzil managed to survive the assault, and when the
agony had at last subsided, the imp limped his way down
the trails of the eastern Snowflakes.

"*Bene tellemara*, Aballister," he grumbled under his
breath, his litany against his mounting fears. It was easy
enough for the intelligent imp to figure out who had
brought Aballister down, and easy enough for him to figure
that without the wizard, even if Castle Trinity had survived,
his role in the plans of conquest had come to a sudden end.
He thought briefly of going to the castle, to see if Dorigen
had survived. He quickly dismissed the thought, reminding
himself that Dorigen wasn't overly fond of him.

But where to go? Druzil wondered. Wizard masters were
not so easy for renegade imps to find, nor were planar gates

that might return Druzil to the smoky and dark lands where he truly belonged. Also, Druzil figured that his business on this plane was not quite finished, not with the precious chaos curse he'd concocted bottled up in the catacombs of the Edificant Library. Druzil wanted the bottle back, had to figure out a way to get it before that wretched Cadderly, if Cadderly was still alive, returned.

For now, though, the imp's needs were more immediate. He wanted to get out of the Snowflakes, wanted to get indoors and out of winter's chilly bite, and so he continued his course down from the high ground, down toward the town of Carradoon.

After several days, and several close calls with the wary farmers living on the edges of the wild mountains, Druzil, perched in the rafters of a barn, overheard what sounded like a promising situation. A hermit had taken up habitation in a remote shack not too far from the outer farmhouses, a solitary recluse with no friends and no family.

"No witnesses," the imp rasped, his poison-tipped tail flicking eagerly. As soon as the sun went down, Druzil flapped off for the shack, figuring to kill the hermit and take his home, and spend the cold winter feasting off the dead man's flesh.

How his plans changed when he looked upon the hermit, looked at the mark branded clearly on his forehead! Suddenly Druzil was more concerned with the possibilities of keeping this man alive. He thought again of the Edificant Library, and the powerful bottle of the chaos curse locked away in its catacombs. He thought again that he must possess it, and now, by some chance of fate, it seemed to Druzil as if his wish might come true.

Bent low under the burden of an armful of firewood, Kierkan Rufo plodded slowly, dejectedly, back to his ramshackle hut.

FANTASY ADVENTURE

STARLESS NIGHT

An Excerpt

by R. A. SALVATORE

PROLOGUE

Drizzt ran his fingers over the intricate carvings of the panther statuette, its black onyx perfectly smooth and unmarred even in the ridged areas of the muscled neck. So much like Guenhwyvar, it looked, a perfect representation. How could Drizzt bear to part with it now, fully convinced that he would never see the great panther again?

"Farewell, Guenhwyvar," the dark elf ranger whispered, his expression sorrowful, almost pitiful, as he stared at the figurine. "I cannot in good conscience take you with me on this journey, for I would fear your fate more than my own." His sigh was one of sincere resignation. He and his friends had fought long and hard, and at great sacrifice, to get to this point of peace, and yet Drizzt had come to know that it was a hollow victory. He wanted to deny that, to put Guenhwyvar back in his pouch and go on, blindly hoping for the best.

Drizzt sighed away the momentary weakness and handed the figurine over to Regis, the halfling.

Regis stared up at Drizzt in disbelief for a long silent while, shocked by what the drow had told him and had demanded of him.

"Three weeks," Drizzt said again.

The halfling's cherubic, boyish features crinkled. If Drizzt did not return in three weeks, Regis was to give Guenhwyvar over to Catti-brie and tell both her and King Bruenor the truth of Drizzt's departure. Regis could tell from the drow's dark tones that Drizzt did not expect to return.

On sudden inspiration, the halfling dropped the figurine to his bed and fumbled with a chain about his neck, its clasp caught in the long and curly locks of his brown hair. He finally got the thing undone and produced a pendant, dangling a large and magical ruby.

Now Drizzt wore the shocked expression. He knew the value of Regis's gemstone and the halfling's craven love of the thing. To say that Regis was acting out of character would be an incredible understatement.

"I cannot," Drizzt argued, pushing the stone away. "I may not return and it would be lost . . ."

"Take it!" Regis demanded sharply. "For all that you have done for me, for all of us, you surely deserve it. It's one thing to leave Guenhwyvar behind—it would be a tragedy indeed if the panther fell into the hands of your evil kin. But this is merely a magical token, no living being, and it may aid you on your journey. Take it as you take your scimitars." The halfling paused, his soft eyes locking with Drizzt's violet orbs. "My friend."

The dark elf received the pendant with humility.

Regis snapped his fingers suddenly, stealing the quiet moment. He rambled across the floor, his bare feet slapping on the cold stone and his nightshirt swishing about him. From a drawer he produced yet another item, a rather unremarkable mask.

"I recovered it," he said, not wanting to reveal the whole story of how he had acquired the familiar item. In truth, Regis had gone out from Mithril Hall and had found the assassin Artemis Entreri hanging helplessly from a jutting stone far up the side of a sheer ravine. Regis had promptly looted the man, and had then cut the seam of Entreri's cloak, listening with some measure of satisfaction as the cloak, the only thing holding the battered, barely conscious man aloft, began to rip.

Drizzt eyed the magical mask for a long time. He had taken it from the lair of a banshee more than a year before. With it, its user could change his entire appearance, could hide his identity.

"This should help you get in and out," Regis said hopefully. Still, Drizzt made no move.

"I want you to have it," Regis insisted, jerking it out toward Drizzt, misunderstanding the drow's hesitation. Regis did not realize the significance the mask held for Drizzt Do'Urden. Drizzt had once worn it to hide his identity, because a drow walking the surface world was at a great disadvantage. But Drizzt had come to see the mask as a lie, however useful it might be, and he could not bring himself to don it again, whatever the potential gain.

He held out his upraised hand, denying the gift, and Regis, after one more unsuccessful pump Drizzt's way, shrugged his little shoulders and put the mask away.

Drizzt left without another word. Many hours remained before dawn; the torches burned low in the upper levels of Mithril Hall, and few dwarves stirred. It seemed so perfectly quiet, so perfectly peaceful.

The dark elf's slender fingers traced down the grain of a wooden door far down the hall, lightly touching, making not a sound. He had no desire to disturb the person within, though he doubted that her sleep was very restful. Every night, Drizzt wanted to go to her and comfort her, and yet he had not, for he knew that his words would do little to soothe Catti-brie's grief. Like so many other nights when he had stood by this door, a watchful, helpless guardian, the ranger ended up padding down the stone corridor, filtering through the shadows of low-dancing torches, his toe-heel step making not a whisper.

Drizzt soon crossed out of the living areas, with only a short pause at another door, the door of his dearest dwarven friend. He came into the formal gathering places, where the king of Mithril Hall entertained visiting emissaries. A couple of dwarves were about in here—Dagna's troops probably—but they heard and saw nothing of the drow's silent passing.

Drizzt paused again as he came to the entrance of the Hall of Dumathoin, wherein the dwarves of Clan Battlehammer kept their most precious items. He knew that he should continue, get out of the place before the clan began to stir, but he could not ignore the emotions pulling at his heartstrings. He hadn't come to this hallowed hall in the two weeks since his drow kin had been driven away, but he knew that he would never forgive himself if he didn't take at least one look.

The mighty warhammer Aegis-fang rested on a pillar at the center of the adorned hall, the place of highest honor. It seemed fitting, for to Drizzt's violet eyes Aegis-fang far outshone all the other artifacts: the shining suits of mail; the great axes and helms of heroes long dead; the anvil of a legendary smith. Drizzt smiled at the notion that this warhammer hadn't even been wielded by a dwarf. It had been the weapon of Wulfgar, Drizzt's friend, who had willingly given his life so that the others of the tight band might survive.

Drizzt stared long and hard at the mighty weapon, at the gleaming mithril head, unscratched and showing the perfectly etched sigils of the dwarven god Dumathoin despite the many vicious battles the hammer had seen. The drow's gaze drifted down the item, settling on the dried blood on its dark adamantite handle. Bruenor, so stubborn, wouldn't allow the blood to be cleaned away.

Memories of Wulfgar, of fighting beside the tall and strong, golden-haired and golden-skinned man flooded through the drow, weakening his knees and his resolve. In his mind Drizzt looked again into Wulfgar's clear eyes, the icy blue of the northern sky and always filled with an excited sparkle. He had been just a boy, his spirit undaunted by the harsh realities of a brutal world.

Just a boy, but one who had sacrificed everything, a song

on his lips, for those he had called his friends.

"Farewell," Drizzt whispered, and he was gone, running this time, though no more loudly than he had walked before. In a few seconds, he crossed onto a balcony and down a flight of stairs, into a wide and high chamber, under the watchful eyes of Mithril Hall's eight kings, their likenesses cut into the stone wall. The last of the busts, that of King Bruenor Battlehammer, was the most striking. Bruenor's visage was stern, a grim look intensified by a deep scar running from his forehead to his jawbone, and with his right eye gone.

More than Bruenor's eye had been wounded, Drizzt knew. More than that dwarvish body, rock tough and resilient, had been scarred. Bruenor's soul was the part most pained, slashed by the loss of a boy he had called his son. Was the dwarf as resilient in spirit as in body? Drizzt knew not the answer. At that moment, staring at Bruenor's scarred face, Drizzt felt that he should stay, should sit beside his friend's likeness and help heal the wounds.

It was a passing thought. What wounds might still come to the dwarf? Drizzt reminded himself. To the dwarf and to all his remaining friends?

* * * * *

Catti-brie tossed and squirmed, reliving that fateful moment, as she did every night—at least, every night that exhaustion allowed her to find any sleep. She heard Wulfgar's song to Tempus, his god of battle, saw the serene look in the mighty barbarian's eyes, the look that denied the obvious agony, the look that allowed him to chop up at the loose stone ceiling, though blocks of heavy granite had begun to tumble all about him.

Catti-brie saw Wulfgar's garish wounds, the white of bone, the skin ripped away from his ribs by the sharklike teeth of the Yochlol, an evil, extradimensional beast that resembled a half-melted candle.

The roar as the ceiling dropped over her love brought Catti-brie up in her bed, sitting in the darkness, her thick auburn hair matted to her face by her cold sweat. She took a long moment to get control of her breathing, told herself repeatedly that it was a dream, a terrible memory, but, ultimately, an event that had passed. The torchlight outlining her door comforted her and calmed her down.

She wore only a light slip of clothing, and her thrashing had knocked her blankets away. Goosebumps rose on her arms, and she shivered, cold and damp and miserable. She roughly retrieved the thickest of her covers and pulled them tightly up to her neck, then lay flat on her back, staring up into the nearly complete blackness.

Something was wrong. She sensed that something was out of place.

Rationally, the young woman told herself that she was imagining things, that her dreams had unnerved her. The world was not right for Catti-brie, far from right, but she told herself forcefully that she was in Mithril Hall, surrounded by an army of friends.

She told herself that she was imagining things.

* * * * *

Drizzt was a long way from Mithril Hall when the sun came up. He didn't sit and enjoy the dawn this day, as was his custom. He hardly looked at the rising sun, for it seemed to him now a false hope of things that could not be. When the glare had diminished, the drow looked to the south and east, far across the mountains, and remembered.

His hand went to his neck, to the hypnotic ruby pendant Regis had given him. He knew how much Regis relied upon this gem, loved this gem, and considered again the halfling's sacrifice, the sacrifice of a true friend. Drizzt had known true friendship; his life had been rich since he had walked into a forlorn land called Icewind Dale and met Bruenor Battlehammer and his adopted daughter, Catti-brie. It pained Drizzt to think again that he might never see any of them again.

The drow was glad that he had the magical pendant, though, an item that might allow him to get his answers and return to his friends, but he held more than a little guilt for his decision to tell Regis of his departure. That choice seemed a weakness to Drizzt, a need to rely on friends who, at this dark time, had little to give. He could rationalize it, though, as a necessary safeguard for the companions he would leave behind. He had instructed Regis to tell Bruenor the truth in three weeks, so that, in case Drizzt's journey proved unsuccessful, Clan Battlehammer would at least have the time to prepare for the darkness that might come.

It was a logical act, but Drizzt had to admit to himself that he had told Regis because of his need, because he had to tell someone.

And what of the magical mask? he wondered. Had he been weak in refusing that, too? The powerful item might well have aided Drizzt, and thus aided his friends, and yet, he had not the strength to wear it, to even touch it.

Doubts floated all about the drow, hovered in the air before his eyes, mocking him. Drizzt sighed and rubbed the ruby between his dark, slender hands. For all his prowess with the blade, for all his dedication to principles, for all his ranger stoicism, Drizzt Do'Urden needed his friends. He glanced back toward Mithril Hall and wondered, for his own sake, if he was choosing right in undertaking this quest privately and secretly.

More weakness, stubborn Drizzt decided, and he let go of the ruby, mentally slapped away the lingering doubts, and slid his hand inside his forest-green traveling cloak. From one of its pockets he produced a parchment, a map of the lands between the Spine of the World Mountains and the Great Desert of Anauroch. In the lower right-hand corner Drizzt had marked a spot, the location of a cave from which he had once emerged.

A cave that would take him home.

PART 1

Duty Bound

Vengeance. No race in all the Realms better understands that word than the drow. Vengeance is the dessert of their daily table, the sweetness they taste upon their smirking lips as though it was the ultimate delicious pleasure. And so, hungering, did the drow come for me.

I cannot escape the anger and guilt I feel for the loss of Wulfgar, for the pains the enemies of my dark past have brought upon those friends I hold so dear. Whenever I look into Catti-brie's fair face, I see a profound and everlasting sadness that should not be there, a burden that has no place in the sparkling eyes of a child.

Similarly wounded, I have no words to comfort her and doubt that there are any words that might bring comfort. It is my course, then, that I must continue to protect my friends. I have come to realize that I must look beyond my own sense of loss for Wulfgar, beyond the immediate sadness that has taken hold of the dwarves of Mithril Hall and the hardy men of Settlestone. By Catti-brie's account of that fateful fight, the creature Wulfgar battled was a Yochlol, a handmaiden of Lloth.

With that grim information, I must look beyond the immediate sadness and consider the sorrow I fear is to come.

I do not understand all the chaotic games of the Spider Queen—I doubt that even the evil high priestesses know the true designs of that foul creature—but there is a significance to the presence of a Yochlol that even I, the worst of the drow religious students, cannot miss. The handmaiden's presence revealed that the hunt was sanctified by the Spider Queen. And the fact that the Yochlol intervened in the fighting does not bode well for Mithril Hall.

It is all supposition, of course. I know not that my sister Vierna acted in concert with any other of Menzoberranzan's dark powers, or that, with Vierna's death, the death of my last relative, my link to the city of drow would ever again be explored.

When I look into Catti-brie's eyes and Bruenor's horrid scars, I am reminded that hopeful supposition is a feeble and dangerous thing. My evil kin have taken one friend from me.

They will take no more.

I can find no answers in Mithril Hall, will never know for certain if the dark elves hunger still for vengeance—unless another force from Menzoberranzan comes to the surface to claim the bounty on my head. With this truth borne on my shoulders, how could I ever travel to Silverymoon, or to any other nearby town, resuming my normal lifestyle? How could I ever sleep in peace while holding within my heart the fear that the dark elves might soon return and once more imperil my friends?

The apparent serenity of Mithril Hall, the brooding quiet, will show me nothing of drow future designs. Yet, for the sake of my friends, I must know those dark intentions. And so I fear that there remains only one place for me to look. Wulfgar gave his life so that his friends might live. In good conscience, I can do no less.

—Drizzt Do'Urden

CHAPTER 1

The Adventurous Baenre

Jarlaxle leaned against the pillar anchoring the wide stairway of Tier Breche, on the northern side of the great cavern that housed Menzoberranzan, the city of drow. The mercenary removed his wide-brimmed hat and ran a hand over the smooth skin of his bald head, muttering a few curses under his breath.

Many lights were on in the city, flickering torches sparkling from the high windows of houses carved from natural stalagmite formations. Lights in the drow city! Many of the elaborate structures were decorated by the soft glow of faerie fire, mostly purple and blue hues, but this was different.

Jarlaxle shifted to the side and winced as his weight came upon his recently wounded leg. Matron Baenre herself, the highest ranking priestess in the city, had tended the wound, but Jarlaxle suspected that the wicked old priestess had purposely left the job unfinished, had left a bit of the pain to remind the mercenary of his failure in recapturing the renegade Drizzt Do'Urden.

"The glow wounds my eyes," came a remark from behind

him. Jarlaxle turned to see Triel Baenre, Matron Baenre's oldest daughter and Matron Mistress of Arach-Tinilith, the drow school of Lloth. Triel was shorter than most drow, nearly a foot shorter than Jarlaxle, but she carried herself with undeniable dignity and poise. Jarlaxle understood her powers (and her volatile temperament) better than most, and he treated the diminutive female with the highest caution.

She moved beside him, staring, glaring, out over the city with squinting eyes. "Curse the glow," she muttered.

"It is by your own mother's command," Jarlaxle reminded her. He did not look at her but replaced his great hat, pulling it low in front as he tried to hide his smirk at her resulting snarl.

Triel was not happy with her mother. Jarlaxle had known that since Matron Baenre had begun to hint at her plans. But Triel was possibly the most fanatical of the Spider Queen's priestesses and would not go against Matron Baenre, the First Matron Mother of the city—not unless Lloth instructed her to.

"Come along," the priestess growled, turning and making her way across Tier Breche, to the largest and most ornate of the drow Academy's three buildings, a huge structure shaped to resemble a gigantic spider. As soon as he entered the temple, the mercenary was assaulted by myriad aromas, everything from incense to the drying blood of the latest sacrifices, and chants rolled out of every side portal. Triel took no note of these at all. She merely shrugged past those few disciples who bowed to her as they saw her walking the corridors.

The single-minded Baenre daughter moved into the higher levels, the private quarters of the school's mistresses, and came down one small hallway, its floor verily alive with crawling spiders (including a few that stood as tall as Jarlaxle's knee).

Triel stopped between two doors, equally decorated, and motioned for Jarlaxle to enter the one on the right. The mercenary paused, did well to hide his confusion, but Triel was expecting it and looking for it.

She grabbed Jarlaxle by the shoulder and roughly spun him about. "You have been here before!" she accused.

"Only upon my graduation from the school of fighters," Jarlaxle said, shrugging away from the female, "as are all of Melee-Magthere's graduates."

"You have been in the upper levels," Triel snarled, eyeing Jarlaxle squarely. The mercenary chuckled.

"You hesitated when I motioned for you to enter the chamber," Triel went on, "because you know that the other is my private place. That is where you expected to go."

"I did not expect to be summoned here at all," Jarlaxle retorted, trying to subtly shift the subject. He was indeed a bit off his guard that Triel had watched him so closely. Had he underestimated her trepidation at her mother's latest plans?

Triel stared at him long and hard, her eyes unblinking and jaw firm.

"I have my sources," Jarlaxle admitted at length.

Another long moment passed, and still Triel did not blink.

"You asked that I come," Jarlaxle reminded her.

"I demanded," Triel corrected.

Jarlaxle swept into a low, exaggerated bow, sweeping off his hat and brushing it out at arm's length. The Baenre daughter's eyes flashed with anger.

"Enough of your impunity!" she growled.

"And enough of your games!" Jarlaxle spat back. "You asked that I come to the Academy, a place in which I am not comfortable, and so I have come. You have questions, and I, perhaps, have answers."

His qualification made Triel narrow her eyes. Jarlaxle was ever a cagey opponent, she knew—knew as well as anyone in the drow city. She had dealt with the cunning mercenary many times and still wasn't sure if she had broken even against him. She turned about and motioned for him to enter the left-hand door instead, and with another graceful bow, he did so, stepping into a thickly carpeted and decorated room lit in a soft magical glow.

"Remove your boots," Triel instructed, and she slipped out of her own shoes before she stepped onto the plush rug.

Jarlaxle stood against the tapestry-adorned wall just inside the door, looking doubtfully to his own boots. Everyone who knew the mercenary knew that they were magical.

"Very well," Triel conceded, closing the door and sweeping past him to take a seat on a huge, overstuffed chair. A rolltop desk stood behind her, in front of yet another tapestry, this one depicting the sacrifice of a gigantic surface elf by a horde of dancing drow. Above the surface elf loomed the nearly translucent specter of a half-drow, half-spider creature, its face beautiful and serene.

"You do not like your mother's lights?" Jarlaxle asked. "But you keep your own room aglow."

Triel bit her lower lip and narrowed her eyes once more. Most priestesses kept their private chambers dimly lit, that they might read their tomes. Heat-sensing infravision was little use against the runes on a page. There were some inks that would hold distinctive heat for many years, but these were expensive and hard to come by, even for one as powerful as Triel.

Jarlaxle stared back at the Baenre daughter's grim expression. Triel was always mad about something, the mercenary mused. "The lights seem appropriate for what your mother has planned," he went on.

"Indeed," Triel remarked, her tone biting. "And are you so arrogant as to believe that you understand my mother's motives?"

"She will go back to Mithril Hall," Jarlaxle said openly, knowing that Triel had long ago drawn the same conclusion.

"Will she?" Triel asked coyly.

The cryptic response set the mercenary back on his heels. He took a step toward a second, less cushiony chair in the room, and his heel clicked hard, even though he was walking across the incredibly thick and soft carpet.

Triel smirked, not impressed by the magical boots. It was common knowledge that Jarlaxle could walk as quietly or as loudly as he desired on any type of surface. His abundant jewelry, bracelets and trinkets, seemed equally enchanted, for they would ring and tinkle or remain perfectly silent, apparently as the mercenary willed.

"If you have left a hole in my carpet, I will fill it with your heart," Triel promised as Jarlaxle slumped comfortably into the covered stone chair, smoothing a fold in the armrest so that the fabric showed a clear image of a black and yellow *Gee'antu* spider, the Underdark's version of the surface tarantula.

"Why do you suspect that your mother will not go?" Jarlaxle asked, ignoring the threat, though, knowing Triel Baenre, he honestly wondered how many other hearts were entwined in the carpet's fibrous strands.

"Do I?" Triel asked.

Jarlaxle let out a long sigh. He had suspected that this would be a moot meeting, a discussion at which Triel tried to pry out what bits of information the mercenary had attained, while offering little information of her own. Still, when Triel had insisted that Jarlaxle come to her, instead of their usual arrangement, when she went out from Tier Breche to meet with the mercenary, Jarlaxle had hoped for something substantive. It was obvious to Jarlaxle that the only reason Triel wanted to meet in Arach-Tinilith was because, in this secure place, even her mother's considerable ears would not hear.

Now, for all those arrangements, this all-important meeting had become a useless bantering session.

Triel seemed equally perturbed. She came forward in her chair suddenly, her expression fierce. "She desires a legacy!" the female declared.

His bracelets tinkled as Jarlaxle tapped his fingers together, thinking that now they were finally getting somewhere.

"The rulership of Menzoberranzan is no longer sufficient for the likes of Matron Baenre," Triel continued, more calmly, and she moved back in her seat. "She must expand her sphere."

"I had thought your mother's visions Lloth-given," Jarlaxle remarked, and he was sincerely a bit confused by Triel's obvious disdain.

"Perhaps," she admitted. "The Spider Queen will welcome the conquest of Mithril Hall, particularly if it, in turn, leads to the capture of that renegade Do'Urden. But there are other considerations."

"Blingdenstone?" Jarlaxle asked, referring to the city of the svirfnebli, the deep gnomes, traditional enemies of the drow.

"That is one," Triel replied. "Blingdenstone is not so far off the path to the tunnels connecting to Mithril Hall."

"Your mother has mentioned that the svirfnebli might be dealt with properly on the return trip," Jarlaxle offered, figuring that he had to throw some tidbit out if he wanted Triel to continue so openly with him. It seemed to the mercenary that Triel must be deeply upset to be permitting him such an honest view of her most private emotions and fears.

Triel nodded, accepting the news stoically and without surprise. "And there is more," she went on. "The task Matron Baenre is undertaking is enormous and will require allies along the way, perhaps even illithids."

The Baenre daughter's reasoning struck Jarlaxle as sound. Matron Baenre had long kept an illithid consort, an ugly and dangerous beast if Jarlaxle had ever seen one. He was never comfortable around the octopus-headed humanoids. Jarlaxle survived by understanding and outguessing his enemies, but his skills were sorely lacking where illithids were concerned. The mind flayers, as the evil race was called, simply didn't think the same way as other races, and acted in accord with principles and rules that no one other than an illithid seemed to know.

Still, the dark elves had often dealt with the illithid community, and successfully. Menzoberranzan housed twenty thousand skilled warriors, while the illithids in the region numbered barely a hundred. Triel's fears seemed a bit overblown.

Jarlaxle didn't tell her that, though. In the mood she was in, the mercenary preferred to do more listening than speaking.

Triel continued to shake her head, her expression typically sour. She leaped up from the chair, her black and purple, spider-adorned robes swishing as she paced a tight circle.

"It will not be House Baenre alone," Jarlaxle reminded, hoping to comfort her. "Many houses show lights in their windows."

"The Matron Mother has done well in bringing the city together," Triel admitted, and the pace of her nervous stroll lessened.

"But still you fear," the mercenary reasoned. "And you need information so that you might be ready for any consequence." Jarlaxle couldn't help a small, ironic chuckle. He and Triel had been enemies for a long while, neither trusting the other—and with good reason! Now she needed him. She was a priestess in a secluded school, away from much of the city's whispered rumors. Normally her prayers to the Spider Queen would have provided her all the information she needed, but now, if Lloth sanctioned Matron Baenre's actions (and that seemed obvious), Triel would be left, literally, in the dark. She needed a spy, and in Menzoberranzan, Jarlaxle and Bregan D'aerthe, his spying network, had no equal.

"We need each other," Triel pointedly replied, turning to eye the mercenary squarely. "Matron Baenre treds dangerous ground, that much is obvious. If she falters, consider who would assume the seat of the ruling house."

True enough, Jarlaxle conceded. Triel, as the eldest daughter of the house, was indisputably next in line and, as the Matron Mistress of Arach-Tinilith, held the most powerful position in the city, behind the Matron Mothers of the eight ruling houses. Triel already had established an impressive base of power. But, in Menzoberranzan, where pretense of law was no more than a facade against an underlying chaos, power bases tended to shift as readily as lava pools.

"I will learn what I may," Jarlaxle answered as he rose to leave, "and will tell you what I learn."

Triel understood the half-truth in the sly mercenary's words, but she had to accept his offer.

Jarlaxle was walking freely down the wide and curving avenues of Menzoberranzan a short while later, passing by the watchful eyes and readied weapons of house guards posted on nearly every stalagmite mound—and on the ringed balconies of many low-hanging stalactites, as well. The mercenary was not afraid, for his wide-brimmed hat identified him clearly to any in the city, and no house desired conflict with Bregan D'aerthe. His was the most secretive of bands; few in the city could even guess at the numbers of the group, and its bases were tucked away in the many nooks and crannies of the wide cavern. Bregan D'aerthe's reputation was widespread, tolerated by the ruling houses, and most in the city would name Jarlaxle as among the most powerful of Menzoberranzan's males.

So comfortable was he that Jarlaxle hardly noticed the guards' lingering stares. His thoughts were inward, trying to decipher the subtle messages of his meeting with Triel. The assumed plan to conquer Mithril Hall seemed very promising. Jarlaxle had been to the dwarven stronghold, had witnessed its defenses, and, though formidable, they seemed meager against the strength of a drow army. When Menzoberranzan conquered Mithril Hall, with Matron Baenre at the vanguard, Lloth would be supremely pleased and House Baenre would know the pinnacle of glory.

As Triel had put it, Matron Baenre would have her legacy.

Announcing the NEW
2nd Edition of the
FORGOTTEN REALMS®
Campaign Setting

A perfect introduction for newcomers – and a concise update for long-standing players!

Designed for the AD&D® 2nd Edition Game, the new *FORGOTTEN REALMS® Campaign Setting* is a major expansion and complete revision of the original, best-selling boxed set. Not only does the new campaign setting tie together information from all the novels and game accessories released since 1987, it reveals this world and its wondrous cultures in greater detail than ever before. Don't miss the big event!

On Sale in July 1993 at book and hobby stores everywhere!